PETERLOO SHADOWS

PETERLOO SHADOWS

Joyce Bentley

This first world edition published in Great Britain 1995 by
SEVERN HOUSE PUBLISHERS LTD of
9–15 High Street, Sutton, Surrey SM1 1DF.
First published in the USA 1995 by
SEVERN HOUSE PUBLISHERS INC of
595 Madison Avenue, New York, NY 10022.

British Library Cataloguing in Publication Data
Bentley, Joyce
  Peterloo Shadows
  I. Title
  823.914 [F]

  ISBN 0-7278-4818-6

Typeset by Hewer Text Composition Services, Edinburgh.
Printed and bound in Great Britain by
Hartnolls Ltd, Bodmin, Cornwall.

In memory of my father, the teller of tales.

Chapter 1

Jancine Ridley had never heard so rapturous a ringing of bells in all her nine years. If bells could enjoy themselves these were having the time of their life! Something special must have happened, she thought, to set them all ringing together like this.

Struggling to sweep the factory floor with a big, clumsy brush, she remembered looking up into the square of sky between the high walls of the yard this morning, and being surprised that the sky was clear . . . well, at least it wasn't foggy. Most November days in Manchester were foggy . . . perhaps the angels had drawn back the curtains of heaven . . . sweeping the sky clear, for the sound to swell and soar over every chimney and steeple in the township.

Bells of all kinds filled the air, sharp and flat, cracked and clear, fast and slow; some jingled, others jangled. All giving voice, wanting to have their say, eager to make their contribution to the great public rejoicing for Lord Nelson's victory over the French at Trafalgar. The fact that England's greatest hero had been mortally wounded did not appear to affect the Mancunians' exuberance. Jancie was never to forget the sound of those bells, for the night of this great public rejoicing was to change her life and that of her younger sister, Violet, for ever.

21 November 1805 had been declared a half holiday. Excitement was running as fast as the Irwell in full spate; huge bonfires were built, even bigger than those on Guy Fawkes Night; and a firework display was to be assembled

1

on Ardwick Green. The rejoicing went off better than the magistrates expected; and if the Reverend Joshua Brookes failed to put in an appearance at the service of thanksgiving, the wardens of the collegiate church of St Mary were glad no one noticed.

Sir Oswald Mosley, Lord of the Manor, gave a rousing speech which seemed to put Napoleon Bonaparte firmly into place, made light of the length of the war, and gave some justification for the ever increasing taxes.

Even the factory children were not to be left out of the celebration. Jancie and Violet Ridley were part of a consignment of child labour contracted out from the workhouse to Jepson's cotton factory, where they worked for their keep and so relieved the parish rate. As such, they expected little. But when the Manchester Philanthropic Society – known locally as just 'the Philanthropic' – rose splendidly to the occasion by announcing their intention of taking a wagon-load of factory children to see the firework display, all their expectations were raised.

Jancie's curiosity was not yet dulled by the system. She wondered about fireworks . . . what were they? What would they do? Would Ardwick Green be a long way . . . and would the horses that pulled the wagons be black?

She and her sister, although as emaciated as the others, stood out from the rest because of their looks. Jancie was green-eyed and copper-haired. Violet, a year younger, was a beautiful child, with large, deep-set eyes, which changed with mood from amethyst to violet.

Jancie was still wondering about the fireworks, when Mr Dexter, the factory overseer, anxious to lock up and be off for his half holiday roared for the child labourers to assemble. He was a grey man. Hair, face and factory smock were all grey – except when he roared, and then the flaccid folds of skin which hung about his cheeks like a turkeycock became puce. "By God, I'll make 'em run!" he used to say. And they did.

Hearing Dexter's roar, Jancie flung down the brush, and

taking her sister by the hand, hurried toward the others. "Always stick hold of yer sister's hand . . ." her father used to say. One of her best memories was of family picnics, sitting on the grass of St Peter's Field, making daisy-chains. It was then that Jancie first realised there was something wrong with her eyesight. She could not see clearly enough to make her own daisy-chains; but those of her mother's about a yard away were quite visible. They had teased her and laughed, thinking it a capital excuse for ineptitude . . .

Her parents were hand-loom weavers, driven from their trade by the power looms to seek employment in Manchester. Then the river, fed by heavy February rain, overflowed its banks; both parents were among the many drowned.

Four-year-old Jancie was pulled from the icy water holding her sister's hand. How long they had been held by the weir no one knew, but in later life Jancie reckoned it had been a test of constitution – if the icy Irwell hadn't killed her, nothing would.

As orphans, they were taken to Strangeways Work-house where every night they cried bitterly. It was not long before the sisters were transferred to Jepson's cotton-factory, where they lived on the premises, working for their keep. Even in such miserable circumstances, or perhaps because of them, there existed a hierarchy, in which the wage-earning children – and a meagre wage at that – were at the top, and the contract orphans, like Jancie and Violet, at the bottom.

Jancie's eye defect made her very unhappy. Because her eyes looked perfectly normal no one believed her. "She's putting it on," Mrs Dexter declared, "lying to avoid work!" She endured taunts and tricks with indifference, and suffered the many applications of Mr Dexter's cane in silence . . . saving all the frustrated tears and misery up, until Violet was fast asleep, and only the rats and a predatory cat were witnesses.

3

To make matters worse, Jancie had developed the habit of backing away a little until the object of attention came into focus. That's it, thought Dexter, as though divine light had shone, that answers everything – the child's an imbecile!

The overseer and his wife provided a frugal diet of gruel and scraps for the contract children, creaming off part of the subsistence allowance for themselves. The child labourers slept where they dropped, ragged bundles of exhaustion. If they were unfortunate enough to drop in the path of the others they were kicked awake and made to crawl into a more convenient place. The Dexters were not answerable to anyone; if everything ran smoothly and there was no trouble, Messrs Jepson and Co. were satisfied, and if Jepson's were, that was good enough for the guardians of Strangeways.

These shadows of children, undernourished, uncared for, unwanted and uneducated, stood at their looms for twelve to fifteen hours. Violet and those who could cultivated the habit of sleeping on their feet, eyes wide and staring, until the cane of the overseer stung their backs.

Sunday was the only break from labour in the lives of the factory children. Those who lived out were sent home, and those who lived in were marshalled for church attendance; faces were washed and heads dipped into water-butts. But Jancie's passion for washing endorsed the overseer's opinion that she was an imbecile. Who but an idiot would stand in the yard while her sister pumped water over her?

The ablutions finished, workaday rags were exchanged for the grey workhouse smock and all were marched solemnly to St Mary's church, where they sat, tier upon tier, with other white-faced children from Strangeways Workhouse.

Jancie and Violet looked forward to matins, no matter what the weather. The attraction lay not in collect, text or sermon, but in the bow-fronted window of Mrs Clowes'

4

sugar bakery in Half Street. They liked it when there was a crowd waiting to get into the church, and this delay afforded the children mouth-watering glimpses of striped humbugs, treacle toffee and horehound lozenges.

Sometimes exciting things happened, such as when a horse bolted, or a child was brave enough to break out of line and make off down Long Millgate. When it was clear they had escaped, an involuntary ripple of relief gave way to barely suppressed giggles, as the Beadle, huffing and puffing, strode down from the church steps to make Dexter's flaccid folds bright red with accusations of negligence.

Jancie, when crossing the narrow yard, would often look up to the sky beyond the high walls and spikes, and think of daisy-chains and St Peter's Field. Not that she and Violet would ever have the courage to run away . . .

Pulling the threadbare shawl tighter round her thin shoulders, she stood in line next to Violet, heart racing, eyes fixed on the man from 'the Philanthropic'. Rotund and bewhiskered, he stood in front of the ragged workforce, intoning their names rapidly from a list, scarcely giving each child time to stand forward before he was on to the next.

"Ridley, Jancine and Violet . . ."

She stepped forward quickly, pulling Violet with her.

"Get back you two! Get back, I say!" yelled Dexter.

Jancie felt the anguish of the command more than the sting of the long cane which accompanied it. She couldn't believe her ears. Her colour rose. Her lower lip trembled.

"Please, can we go?" she pleaded to the man from 'the Philanthropic'. "Oh, please, sir . . . please?"

The man cast an enquiring look at the overseer, who, indicating Jancie, tapped his forehead significantly. "She'll be trouble," he said darkly, as Violet edged closer to her sister. The man from 'the Philantropic' did not want to interfere with the smooth running of affairs. He

5

nodded agreement and turned to supervise the others; the afternoon was drawing in and the wagons were waiting.

The sky over Manchester on Trafalgar Night had never been so illuminated. It was speckled with crimson sparks, bright with bouts of flame, and fireworks flashed across the heavens like lightning. Those not fortunate enough to be at Ardwick Green witnessed another spectacle.

"Fire! Fire! Jepson's is ablaze! Send for the engine!"

Soon the shouts of "Fire!" turned oddly triumphant as the crowd recognised a deliberate act of arson. Jepson's were following the government's lead to repress the forming of trade unions and lay off those who joined them. Protest was on the march and Manchester was not to be left out.

The sight of the magnificent flames mesmerised the spectators. Long, orange-coloured tongues poked out from the upper storey windows, flicking stone and lintel. The hoist at the loading bay crumbled; timbers fell, and a shaft covered by a skylight suddenly burst open with a great explosive crack, shooting flames high into the air and rendering the Ardwick Green display insignificant. No one noticed two little figures running frantically away from the crashing timbers.

Something had startled Jancie into wakefulness. After they watched the others leave for Ardwick Green, fright had taken the edge off their bitter disappointment. They were alone in the silence and stillness of the gloomy factory, with no candle, no lamp. Alone for the first time, with scurrying rats, and the slinking shadow of a predatory cat. Jancie's heart began to bump uncomfortably against her ribs. The gaunt, spectral outlines of the empty looms took on the appearance of St Mary's graveyard at night. Thoughts of hell and hauntings crowded in. She wanted to sink to the floor, to hide from the demons and goblins which were there . . . waiting . . .

"Jancie—?" Violet crept closer. "I'm frightened . . ."

6

she whispered, and then on a dreadful sigh which lingered in the darkness. "I wish I was dead . . ."

"Don't say that, dear!" The demons and goblins scuttled away as Jancie hugged her sister fiercely. She remembered her father using that term of endearment, and it had become their special word for each other. It linked them, like the daisy-chains, as a family. "Oh, never say that again – you mustn't even think it."

"Will it be dark when we die?"

"No. The Reverend Brookes said in his sermon that it were all bright up there."

"I don't like it in the dark."

"No, I don't either, but I'm not wishing to die! C'mon now, dear, let's try the doors – and see if we can get into the boiler house yard and sleep on the warm ashes."

"Violet?" Jancie called, as they nestled down like a pair of dormice. "We'd better say our prayers."

But Violet was fast asleep.

It was the explosive crack of the flue-like shaft which startled Jancie into wakefulness. She sprang to her feet, dragging her sleeping sister with her, away from the blazing mill. "C'mon!"

They ran as fast as their spindly legs would carry them; as though Constable Nadin himself were on their heels. They stumbled down streets, courts and alleys; away from the main thoroughfares; away from the glare of the fire. Window shutters were closed and the only light came from the opening of tavern doors. Trying to keep away from people on a night like this was difficult. Terrified of stopping lest they were caught, yet needing to stop for breath, Violet slowed to a stand still, panting and coughing.

"Hullo . . . hullo! What's all the row then?" The question came on a lilting, sing-song voice belonging to Aberdaron Dick, the town's odd job man. Due to the celebratory events of the night he thought to earn himself a sixpence or two by lighting people's way with his lantern. "Well . . . well," he smiled. Then, thinking Jancie's backing away was due to fright, added, "Steady, there, lass, you'll come to no harm."

"She only does that because of her eyes," said Violet breathlessly.

Wondering what to make of this strange statement, he stood there considering the two. They were odd little creatures, he thought . . . the younger one would be a stunner given the chance. Violet regarded him softly, with a sweet kind of sadness that brought a lump to his throat. He swallowed hard.

"Running away are we?" he said at length.

"Yes, sir," confessed Jancie, feeling able to trust this tall, strange scarecrow of a figure. She told him about the workhouse, and the fire and why they were running away.

"So – the trouble makers have fired Jepson's," he mumbled. "They'll be cutting bloody heads off next like the French! But you won't know anything about that . . ."

"Oh, but we know about Trafalgar," she was quick to point out. Yes, he thought, she'll soon catch up with everything. Those green eyes, whatever was the matter with 'em, were bright and challenging, her mouth resolute. He was not altogether sure that such resolution in one so young was a good thing. But through it all he observed a hint of mischief, of impertinence. Ay, they'd make out, all right. Poor little things, fancy being caged up. Aberdaron Dick liked freedom; he roamed the town at will and couldn't recall ever having done anything else.

He lowered the lantern. "Shouldn't worry too much about getting caught. Joe Nadin's Runners'll think you was burned to death," he said cheerfully. "C'mon." He set off with a long, loping stride. "I know a stable where you can bed down for the night, but you'll 'ave to make yerself scarce come dawn. An' you'd best find a cap – anyone'd spot that copper crop of yours a mile off."

8

Chapter 2

When Aberdaron Dick peered into the loft of the Swan stables at daybreak, the sisters had gone. Frightened of being caught and taken back to Strangeways they left while it was still dark and, keeping to lonely thoroughfares, found themselves on the old quays looking toward Blackfriars Bridge.

The River Irwell, a main route of commerce for Manchester, wore the yellow fog like a shroud; barges, colliers and river-carriers loomed like giant hearses; packet boats like coffins, and big steamers, ethereal in the fog, like phantoms, their mooring chains clanking and creaking. The slap of sluggish water echoed eerily against the hull of ghostly pleasure craft, laden with flags, and limp with buntings; smaller boats, like lost souls, drifted to and fro on the eddies.

Violet, clutching some cabbage leaves scooped from the gutter, began to cry. "I don't like it, Jancie . . . let's go."

"Where to? Oh, don't be daft. It's only the fog makes it like this. Once the river men start work it'll be different."

Violet peered into the cavernous entrance and, hearing the echo of gurgling water, shrank and pulled on her sister's hand. "I'm not going in there . . ."

"That's why it's such a good hiding place . . ." Jancie's voice trailed. Worms and damp had weakened and rotted the piles on which the warehouses had stood. Some were already pitched into the water, while the rest, leaning and

9

lounging, awaited an opportunity to follow suit. "Find somewhere else." Violet was whimpering with fright.

"Like Strangeways! You heard Aberdaron Dick say it was safe. You heard him. If we stand about much longer someone'll notice us – and you know what happens to runaways when they're caught." She paused for the words to sink in, and added. "Are you comin' with me, or waiting for Mr Dexter?" The reluctant hand became at once compliant.

Stepping warily over spar and plank into the shadowy interior, they were so far removed from civilisation as to feel in another world.

"Look . . .," whispered Violet, pointing to the dull red embers of a small fire. She then indicated a makeshift bridge over a chasm where the floor had once been. "Listen . . ." Even Jancie held her breath; there it was again. Drag . . . clonk . . . drag . . . clonk. The emptiness gave substance to the echo . . . and it was coming nearer.

Jancie wanted to slide into the water, to hide from the approaching demon. Violet wanted to die. But before either of them could do anything, the drag and clonk was before them in the very human form of a one-legged man, whose other leg, being wooden, dragged a little behind, making a 'clonk' as it came to attention beside the other.

The man was as raggedly dressed as themselves, except for his good leg, which was clad in a fine grey stocking and a shiny black half-boot, done up with laces. "They call me the Admiral," he said, slapping the thigh of his absent leg. "Damned scurvy French took it off in a naval engagement. Welcome," he continued with an unsteady bow, "you're welcome to warm yerselves by the fire."

The sisters looked beyond him at a sprinkling of beggar children, peering through the half-light, gathering out of curiosity. Among the other outcasts there was an old man, shrivelled, with long whiskers and bow legs.

Another was blind, and the rest in various states of disintegration.

"Yer finds yer own quarters," the Admiral was saying as the damp steamed off their rags. He indicated the roof. "The higher you climb up the rigging, the drier it is." He pointed to the fire. "It burns all the time, no shortage of fuel. There are no names here, and no questions asked." He tapped the side of his crooked nose significantly. "We fends for ourselves, comes and goes as we please."

When Violet and Jancie were warmed and dry, their natural curiosity, subdued for so long by the factory system, began to surface. They found an old office 'up the rigging' as the Admiral had said, which was fairly dry.

The sisters liked being at the top because none of the others possessed the catlike ability to climb so high. On nights when the wind blew keenly and the frost was white and hard, they slept round the fire with the others, all curled together in an untidy heap of rags; some covered with a tarpaulin salvaged from the river, and others with sacks.

On these nights, shadowy figures slunk in off the streets, risking the rotten spars and icy planks to beg a place by the fire. These were tolerated, but regarded with suspicion by the Admiral.

The quayside community then, ebbed and flowed with the river; vagrants and thieves came and went as so much flotsam, only the maimed and the blind stayed, watched over by the Admiral – to them familiarity was all.

It was here that Violet and Jancie learned by observation and experience the best times to scavenge at the half-dozen markets held in the town; the best pitch to await coaches – and that the passengers from the London coach were more liberal than those from Doncaster. They learned to exploit the gullible, and recognise a 'soft touch' – and if you heard anything good to keep it to yourself. One of the cripples was adept at picking pockets, but Jancie would have none of this for fear of being caught – their freedom was precious.

They sometimes saw Aberdaron Dick, about the coach yards, sweeping the crossings, shovelling snow, or in his capacity as the town's water-man. Indeed he held so many jobs that people swore there were two of him! The girls were always pleased to see his friendly face; pleased to have so busy and popular an acquaintance. Dick could have found them scullery work in exchange for a dinner, but it was all close work, with which Jancie's long-sighted vision could not cope, and Violet was too timid to go anywhere alone.

Winter frosts and February rain gave way at last to spring warmth, Easter and Whitsuntide. "Whit week," explained the Admiral to Jancie and Violet, "giddy week, more like! Most towns have one fair, but Manchester has three – all at Whit! The roads are jammed wi' folk all comin' and goin', buyin' and sellin', drinkin' and brawlin'. There's country gobbins rubbin' shoulders wi' clerks, and dog fights, cock fights, races, an' river trips . . ."

The sisters seized every opportunity to make themselves useful. They discovered that people in a Whitsun mood were so generous that even the smallest service did not go unrewarded. Jancie, ever curious about everything, watched horses being bought and sold; alarmed Violet by spying on apprentice lads swimming naked in the river; and made herself useful at the cockpit in Shudehill, cleaning out the pens and watching the breeders prepare the birds for contest.

The fighting, drunkenness and debauchery which accompanied the fairs did not shock the Ridley girls. The close, oppressive atmosphere at Jepson's had lent itself to brawling – and debauchery was never far away.

The overseer's wife, having a vested interest, warned

growing girls about what she called 'being taken advantage of'. "If any of the fellas have hold of you," she said mysteriously, "yell for all yer worth".

Jancie had not realised what either of these phrases meant, until behind some bales, where Violet was already asleep, she saw the overseer with a woman thrust up against the wall, breeches down and skirts up. She was struggling, and he stifling her cries – which in any case would scarce be heard because of the machinery. As they sank to the floor, the woman beneath him, Jancie had turned away and began to cry very softly.

No, the drunkeness and debauchery of the fair was merely a fact of life, and by far the greatest impression on both girls, was created by the church's answer to 'giddy week'. They had never, ever seen anything like the Sunday School Scholars procession. Started six years before, it had taken its place as one of the town's customs and had as many, if not more spectators lining the route than the Mad Donkey Race.

All Church of England scholars from outlying parishes who had a full attendance certificate, walked behind their clergy, and all converged on St Mary's Collegiate Church, where either the Warden or the Reverend Brookes preached a sermon, and after a refreshment of buns and milk, they once more formed into a procession for the walk home.

Children and adults were obviously and proudly sporting their best clothes. The men wore hedgerow blossom in their hats, the young girls carried flowers, and some were dressed in white. "If our mother and father hadn't drowned," said Jancie importantly. "We would have been in that procession."

"How d'you know?" demanded Violet. "You're always saying what we would or wouldn't have done!"

"I just know they would have entered us as scholars. I know, that's all."

"You just fancy yourself in a white gown."

13

"An' I suppose you don't!"

"No," she giggled in reply. "I fancy meself in the one with a pink sash – an' I'd have pink pumps like she has, and pink ribbons in me hair!" As the fife and drum band, which led the procession this year, passed, her voice became plaintive. "I wish we weren't beggars . . ."

Chapter 3

Jancie and Violet might still have been beggars if Capper's Circus had not come to St Peter's Field a few weeks after Whit. Mr Capper believed in the personal touch, his motto being, 'if you want anything doing well, do it yourself'. Consequently, he strode the streets of Manchester in white buckskin breeches, thigh boots and a tall hat, cracking a long whip to attract attention, and shouting the circus bill until his cheeks were puce.

Jancie was fascinated, not by Mr Capper, but by his colourful clothes. As for his oratory, the only item which grabbed her imagination as she watched him strutting across Piccadilly, was the reference to a 'Japanese Dancing Act'.

"Oriental!" he yelled. "A dance from the mysterious Orient! This is the chance of a lifetime, ladies and gentlemen, which must not be missed!"

The words echoed about Jancie's head long after he had disappeared into the market street crowds. "The Orient . . . the mysterious Orient . . . a Japanese Dancing Act." It sounded exciting, too exciting to miss. She hurried down Mosley Street, where a sight of the big tent beckoned. Her mind was made up; she was going to sneak in and the best way was beneath the flooring.

The day had been one of their 'hungry days' and Violet, being miserable when hungry, had returned to the warehouse to sleep. Jancie envied this ability of her sister to find solace in sleep; sometimes it annoyed her,

15

but on reflection she decided it was better than tears, or wishing to be dead.

When the evening shadows lengthened, she pounced, darting like a mouse beneath the canvas; and on hands and knees moved swiftly under the flooring, until finding a crack wide enough to peep through.

Anticipation made light of the draught, of the cramped position, of the deafening noise created by the appreciative stamping of feet. The dust made her sneeze and the crick in her neck was almost intolerable, but when the Japanese Dancing Act came on all the discomfort disappeared. All the hardness and privations of her young life fell away, and for a few moments she was lost, fascinated by the dancing of the young woman dressed in what the Ringmaster called a kimono. The black material, embroidered with a crimson dragon, glistened in the lamplight as she moved, and Jancie had never seen anything so lovely; the white-gowned Sunday School scholars and the flamboyant Mr Capper paled into insignificance.

The stamping of feet on the flooring above, brought her back to reality. The circus audience were impressed; and as Jancie crawled out her sharp mind recognised at once the novelty value of the act in terms of money. Street entertainment was much more lucrative than straightforward begging, where, more often than not, you got a cuff about the head and were told to clear off. Singers – good ones, that is – were sometimes paid to sing a particular song; the fiddler's tin box at his feet was never empty; people waiting to enter the theatre seemed always to be tossing halfpennies to buskers . . . Nothing could hold Jancie back now, she just had to see the act again to consolidate her daring idea.

Back at the top of the derelict warehouse, with Violet as a critical audience, Jancie practised the Japanese Dancing Act. Violet giggled at the first attempt to imitate the rhythm of the sinuous movements, but Jancie persevered, copying the picture in her mind, cultivating little mincing steps, the attitude of folded hands, the fluttering of the fan; until Violet later conceded that her sister's height and natural body grace made a pleasing performance.

"But, whoever heard of a ragged dancer?" Violet remonstrated. "You've got to look like the Sunday School scholars – no one'll watch you just doing that. Without the pumps and the kimono thing it'll be no use."

"I know that, don't I!" Jancie did not mean to be sharp, but she was in no mood for criticism. The idea was too good to pass up. This, like running away from Jepson's blazing mill, was an opportunity which once missed would be forever regretted. Time was running out and the circus moving on. Kimono and pumps were necessary, and Capper's Circus was well on the way to Bolton before they discovered both were missing.

To Jancie the stolen kimono was even more beautiful than the white gowns of the Sunday School scholars. The colour was black, but it was a rich, shiny black, which took on a dramatic look when teamed with the wide crimson sash. But the back, oh the back! She thought the vividly embroidered dragon the most beautiful creature she had ever set eyes on.

The theft, her only theft, was not on her conscience. It had been necessary. Besides, she justified, the Japanese dancer had many kimonos and pairs of pumps; the disappearance of one outfit was not going to hold up the show.

Apart from Violet, who still preferred the white gowns and pink sashes of the scholars, Jancie wanted the Admiral's opinion.

"Stunning!" he declared, as she twirled about in front of him. "Could've been made for you." With great solemnity he put both hands together and bowed his head over them. "That's an oriental acknowledgement," he told her. "You must always do that before the dance

17

and after. C'mon, take the grin off your face and let's see you do it!"

She stopped in the middle of practising to ask wide-eyed, "Have you really been to the Orient – the mysterious Orient?"

"Wasn't so bloody mysterious when I was there! But, yes, your old friend the Admiral's sailed round the world and seen all the wonders, but never a red-haired Jap . . ." He shook his head. "It don't look right, lass. Best not to spoil the ship for a ha'porth of tar, eh? Now, if you could lay yer hands on a black hat or scarf, and shove your hair underneath . . ."

"I know! I'll ask Aberdaron Dick to see if the man at the dye works'll dip me green cap to black!"

"Eh, yer never stuck for an idea, lass, I'll say that for you!"

A few days later when Dick had produced the dyed cap, she tucked her costume into a sailor's knapsack provided by the Admiral; and set off to make her debut. They avoided prime sites like Piccadilly, St Ann's Square, or the market places, partly because these were jealously guarded, and partly because there still lingered the fear of seeing the grey-faced Mr Dexter, or the Guardian of the workhouse.

They established a pitch at Tinker's Tea Gardens, in Collyhurst on the outside of town. This was a popular evening venue for Manchester folk, and Aberdaron Dick reckoned people out to enjoy themselves were usually in a good humour and more likely to put a coin into the battered tin which Violet, with her smiling eyes raised, pushed in front of them. It was a hard heart which refused either the appealing glance of the pretty beggar child, or the sheer ingenuity of the Japanese Dancing Act.

On arrival at Tinker's, Jancie put on the kimono with as much pride and private ceremony as the Reverend Brookes put on his silken robes for service. She swore it had magical properties, for, after wrapping it around her threadbare rags, she felt transformed and in charge of everything. After tying the broad sash she was no longer a street urchin, but a Japanese lady from the mysterious Orient.

"Ladies and gentlemen," she called, walking up and down like Mr Capper had done. "Roll up, roll up for the one and only Japanese Dancing Act!"

Then, waiting until a small crowd had gathered, she bowed low as the Admiral had advised, and went confidently into the practised routine.

Nothing in the world could have stopped her dancing; every pulse in her thin body beat to make a success of the venture. At the back of her mind she recalled Violet's words as they had watched the scholars. "I wish we weren't beggars". And now, because she felt powerful and strong beyond her years, she resolved that they would not always be beggars.

If she heard titters of amusement in the crowd they were ignored, and the calls of the rowdy went unheard. She was above it all, dancing her way into a fantastic dreamland of dragons, lanterns, where everyone wore kimonos.

Very quickly, imperceptibly, the crowd were all drawn into silence as she fastened her personality on them. They were enchanted by the childish grace; the seriousness; the artful use of the fan; the total absorption with which she danced – and the strangeness of the black garment with a red dragon embroidered on the back.

They applauded, put money in Violet's tin and sauntered off in a happier mood; and with some, it became a ritual start to an evening's entertainment. The success of the venture meant she and Violet could eat every day instead of every other day.

But, as the summer wore on, the pumps wore out, and the kimono, despite – or because of – regular washing in the Irwell, began to look shabby. Jancie watched them fade as a dream fades, and with the same helplessness. A bedraggled kimono, frayed at the hem, the shining lustre of the material dulled with spatters of mud which would not come off, was no attraction. To dance barefoot reduced the illusion still further, and when a dog ran off with the tattered fan, they returned to the warehouse crestfallen, miserable and hungry.

To make matters worse, the weather was turning cold and Jancie, helping the Admiral build the fire, caught her already ragged dress on a nail, tearing it from shoulder to waist.

"If you don't get Violet to sew it together," observed the Admiral, "you'll be mother-naked come Sunday, and no doubt catch yer death."

"It won't mend anymore," came the small-voiced answer.

"What about the kimono, lass?"

"No! I couldn't bear to − it's been, well, different. It made me feel different. Kimonos weren't made for running errands, and helping Dick swill the streets, and cleaning out cock pens . . ."

"Neither were they made to double up as a shroud!" Instead of leaning forward to impress, he had developed the habit with Jancie of leaning back, so she could see the expression on his face. He leaned back. "All the Japanese lasses wear kimonos to do everything you've just said. It's the way they dress. Wrapped tightly round their bodies it keep's 'em warm. You see if it don't." He knew that would get to her; knew it would appeal. Fiercely fastening the sash, Jancie determined this was not the end − she and Violet would not always be beggars.

Throughout the winter, driven from their own quarters by the intense cold, Jancie clung as tenaciously to her resolve as she and others of the quayside community clung to life. Day fused into day. Days of hunger; nights which only conserved life by the collective warmth of huddling round the Admiral's fire.

20

If Aberdaron Dick had been in town he would have found them a stable, but after Christmas he always went away, disappearing without telling anyone. Folk would miss him and say to each other dolefully, "Dick's gone." Speculation broke out afresh as to where he went. No one knew. He had been heard to say in his lilting singsong voice. "Ah . . . but it's the valleys and the mountains . . . they call me, see, and like the migrating bird I 'ave to spread my wings and go." Some thought it inconsiderate of the valleys and mountains to call him in the depth of winter, when travel and weather were hard. But, whatever he did, or wherever he went, he returned in springtime wearing a new coat and breeches. Spring in Manchester without Aberdaron Dick would be no spring at all, his return was looked for as eagerly as the larksong and swallows.

At the beginning of February, the sisters stood on the corner of St Mary's Gate waiting to scavenge when the market closed. As they loitered, shivering, against the wall, Jancie's gaze was attracted toward the barber's shop opposite. The top half of the door was open, like that of a stable, and through it she saw a tall, black stove, its crimson mouth agape, as the barber lifted the shovel of coal to stoke it.

She gazed longingly, imagining the warmth coming off it, wondering if she would ever be warm again and wishing the days would warm into spring. Warmth . . . warmth . . . Her teeth began to chatter, the wet kimono clung uncomfortably to her body. Then, quick as the thought, she seized Violet's hand, and stumbling down the three steps into the shop, pushed the wet hair from her face, and said breathlessly. "Please sir, can we warm ourselves at the stove? Just till the market's shut. We'll be no bother, honest, sir."

"Well, well!" exclaimed Bob Smollett, looking up from trimming a beard. "An' here's me thinking I'd got two

21

more customers. Two little lasses come for a shave, I thought!"

They both giggled nervously, but Bob's joke made them feel easier.

Smollett, a round-faced, brown-eyed young man of twenty-four, was still in mourning for his fiancée, who had been one of those killed in a recent protest in Shude Hill against the price of bread. The militia had been called in and events got out of hand. Always a mild person, he had affectionately indulged his fiancée's militancy without taking part himself. "The only strong feelings I have," he used to tell her, with a mischievous wink, "are for you." But her death had changed him, and his reactionary views had already earned him the title of 'the revolutionary barber'.

"Go on, then." He indicated the stove with his poised razor, and added with a wink, "Don't get too close, it's hot!"

On future scavenging expeditions Jancie and Violet became daily visitors to Bob Smollett's shop, waiting by the stove until the market wagons trundled homeward. If the weather was dry, they peered first into the small paned window, curious and giggly, making guesses at what the various implements were used for. Against a revolutionary-coloured backcloth there was another source of entertainment, for on strings stretching the length of the window hung a selection of wigs, curls, part wigs, short wigs, and moustaches. On stands or the window bottom were jars of bear's grease, pomatums, and a whole unassorted mess of male scents, oils, and soaps.

Once inside the shop Violet curled up in a corner and went to sleep, but Jancie, sitting on the floor, knees to her chin, listened, not merely to the views expressed, but the way they were expressed.

These were tradesmen, shopkeepers, brushmakers, coal-men, farriers, and clerks. She had never been among men like these, where argument was reasoned and opinion either respected or treated with good humoured tolerance.

The only nice men they knew were Aberdaron Dick and the Admiral. Jancie was sure Mr Capper from the circus was nice, but they didn't know him; Mr Tinker from the Tea Gardens had been kind . . . but both girls instinctively knew they had a champion in Bob, especially as he spoke well of Aberdaron Dick. The girls never mentioned the Admiral, they knew he wouldn't have liked it – as he had often told them, "We quayside folk keep to us-selves."

Jancie's mind was like a sponge, soaking up everything she heard as the year drew on, absorbing attitude and tone. She realised by their gravity that what happened in the world in the long run affected their lives in Manchester, and by their levity that outwitting Constable Nadin and the establishment could be great fun.

The victory at Trafalgar had not "put Napoleon firmly in his place," as Sir Oswald Mosley had prophesied at the Ardwick Green celebration. It was now two years gone, Johnson the brushmaker reminded them, "and that scurvy Frenchman's still going strong – controls Europe from Lisbon to Moscow!"

It was here, in Smollett's shop, that Jancie first heard the name that would shadow her life: that of Lord Castlereagh, now Secretary for War. The war, she learned, had apparently turned landward from the sea, and a young general, Sir Arthur Wellesley, was heading for Portugal with an army of thirty thousand, to halt the advance of Napoleon Bonaparte.

Not that the talk was always about war; the subjects changed with the status of the clients. There were those who had nothing good to say about anybody – King, Regent, Parliament, Army – and the working classes! What was it they wanted? Were they never content? Instead of rioting and petitioning about

23

the price of food, why didn't they work harder and earn more?

Others advocated "A reet good clean out – get rid of King and Cabinet, like the French!" As for the Prince Regent – what did he, sitting there in London on his big, fat arse, know or care about conditions in the north?

Sometimes, the more rational would raise a warning. "One o' these days, Bob Smollett, you'll find yerself in the New Bailey – a lot o' this talk's treasonable!"

"That reminds me." Bob wheeled round to Jancie, concern on his round face. "I was talking to Miss Etherington, the other day – Etherington's Smallware Manufactory on Shude Hill – it's right opposite the Seven Stars – an assortment of umbrellas and things in the window. She said you were to call on her." He winked. "Could mean a new kimono if you play yer cards right!"

Jancie was not sure she understood about the cards, and wasn't for stopping to ask. She grabbed Violet's protesting hand, for she would rather have stayed by the stove, and with a quick smile at Bob, was up the steps in a trice, through the half door, and running along Cateaton Street, impervious to the chill of the darkening afternoon.

"What's the use?" panted Violet, dragging free of her sister's hand. "Once she knows you can't see close up—"

"Don't you dare tell her anything about me eyes, Violet Ridley!"

"But, she's bound to—"

"She's not 'bound to' anything! Sometimes, I despair of you. We've scarce a rag to our backs; next to nothing in our stomachs; we're perished with cold, and rather than take a chance you'd stay dozing by the stove all day!"

Violet's retort, as they turned into Withy Grove, was lost in so busy and narrow a street, the overhanging balconies of which acted as a sounding board for all

24

the noise below. Emerging into Shude Hill, which was more of a square than a street, Jancie seized her sister's hand again and pulled her toward the Smallware Manufactory.

It was only after walking up the steps and pulling the bell for attention that she saw the highly polished, brass nameplate. It possessed a gleam and patina that the others nearby lacked, making her realise, with a lurching dismay, just how ragged and dirty they were, for it was now too cold to wash in the river.

But Miss Etherington, tall and distinguished, saw past the rags and grime; she recalled what Smollett had told her and recognised in Jancie, the eagerness, the kind of chirpy confidence he had mentioned. She saw Jancie's protective hand holding that of her younger sister – not missing the mutinous glance which was still smouldering behind the violet-coloured eyes.

But it was the kimono that decided the issue; the faded glory to which Jancie clung, as though to discard it was to cast off her dreams. Miss Etherington, an incurable romantic, was a firm believer in dreams.

Chapter 4

Miss Etherington owed her survival to a dream – a childhood dream of one day inheriting her father's print works out at Smedley Vale. His only child, she was pleased to hear him boast, "Good as a lad wi' trade, knows more about calico printing than me!".

An attractive girl, tall and slender, Charlotte attended the Academy for Young Ladies, and when not there, could be found at the works, in the counting-house or on the printing floor. She could never remember a day passing without being there. While others dreamed of handsome young men, her dream was to see her name on the brass doorplate, alongside that of her father. "When you're of age," he had promised. "We'll have a reet good plate struck – solid brass."

It was on August Bank Holiday Monday, two months away from Charlotte's twenty-first birthday, when her parents fancied a trip in the new launch on the River Irwell, starting at Manchester, which was three miles away. There had been trouble with one of the presses and Mr Etherington, waiting for the engineer, was likely to be delayed.

"Dear, oh dear," he sighed, "and your mother has been so looking forward to the outing. The Moxhams took her boating on the Thames when she was staying with 'em." He smiled and raised an eyebrow, for his wife's London relatives were a subject of kindly amusement. "The Honourable Mirabelle Moxham has a lot to answer for! Still, I don't like disappointing your mother . . ."

"Let me wait, Father. You know I can deal with the engineer."

He hesitated, then shook his head. "Listen, if I'm not there on time, you go with her, there's a good lass."

The memory of that Bank Holiday turned her dream into a nightmare. Until the very last moment Charlotte scanned the crowd, hoping he would come. The last thing she wanted was a boat trip on the Irwell. It had been on her mind to visit the works stables, to have a good look at the new shire-horse and walk him round the yard. She felt press-ganged and wondered why on her earth her mother wanted to go on the Irwell at all.

"C'mon on, now, ladies and gentlemen," chivvied a man in a striped jersey. "Make haste for the maiden voyage of the *Clive of India!*" The new launch was decked out in what passed for eastern trappings; fringed canopies, flags with elephants' heads printed on, and the skipper wearing a turban.

The spectators, craning their necks to watch, grew excited.

"Mind yer don't get sea sick!" they yelled.

"Watch out for pirates the other side o' the bridge!"

"Bring us back a parrot, eh!"

"An' a monkey!"

The man in the striped jersey waited until the last passenger boarded, and untied the mooring rope with great verve and flourish. A merry blast from the boat's claxon, and cheers from the crowds accompanied the vessel gliding from the quay.

Passengers waved, and Mrs Etherington sighed her pleasure. The sun was hot, parasols were opened and everyone marvelled at the speed and ease with which the *Clive of India* cut through the water.

In less than no time they were approaching the New Bailey Bridge. Charlotte frowned. She jumped up from her seat. The boat was not on course. People gasped.

27

The launch was not going under the bridge! Oh, God, dear God!

The turbaned skipper struggled to control the steering and rammed the pillar of the bridge at full speed. The vessel shuddered from stem to stern, and keeled over almost at once. Passengers were flung screaming into the water, clinging to each other, pulling each other down in panic, as the suction and eddy of bridge and boat tugged at their limbs.

Charlotte, who had swum as a child in the works lodge, struggled out of her cumbersome skirts, kicked off her shoes and dived again and again into the tangled mass of holiday hats, fringed canopy, and parasols. She was not aware of how many she brought to the side, where they were landed like so many fish, by horrified spectators.

Some had remained above water, kept buoyant by their clothing, others had sunk like stones. She tried to recall what her mother had been wearing, but could only see the smile of pleasure, the raising of the parasol.

Mother! Mother! The word echoed in her brain like the thrum of an engine. Down she dived, against suction and eddy, down to the mud, coming up for breath and going under again. Mother! Mother!

Exhausted, and not knowing her mother's body had been recovered further downstream, Charlotte was about to dive under again. when she was grabbed by one of Humane Society.

"C'mon, lass, tha's done reet well," he said calmly as she struggled to get free. "There's been enough lost today." Gasping for breath, and suddenly feeling weak, she allowed herself to be wrapped in a blanket and carried to one of the houses thrown open to receive survivors.

Women wept frantically for their dead husbands, parents for children, and, Mr Etherington for his wife.

"If I hadn't have stayed behind . . ." he declared after the funeral. "If I hadn't have been delayed by that damned press, I'd have been with her – and she wouldn't have drowned. No, by God!"

If he blamed himself for his wife's death, he blamed his daughter more. Her continued existence was a constant reminder of his loss. The commendation she received from the Humane Society and the gratitude from those she had saved reinforced his opinion that time lost in saving others had contributed to her mother's death.

No unhappiness had ever undermined their family life; Charlotte and her father had been great friends, whose aim was to build up the calico printing and cosset her mother. Now, in bitter grief, they should have comforted one another, but he turned away. Charlotte wished she, too, had drowned. As the days passed, it became clear he was travelling beyond rational thought or reason . . . and yes, the works, the very business he had nurtured, that, too, had turned on him. They would, he decided, all suffer as he was now suffering.

Charlotte begged to be allowed to run the business until he was well but despite a visit from Mr Caxton, the family lawyer, and interventions from friends, it was all in vain. She listened in dazed unbelief to her father's 'last word'. He took the already purchased brass plate – which in three months' time would have borne her name – and dropped it into the Irwell. That was his last and final word. The next day he laid off the men and shut down the works, sealing it like a tomb – leaving her alone to adjust her shattered life.

Losing the print works on top of the bereavement was almost more than her capable shoulders could bear. If ever she needed the solace of work, it was now. Bereft of her mother, and with her father losing his mind, she thought herself likely to have followed suit, if Mirabelle Moxham, the Honourable Mirabelle Moxham, had not invited her to London.

Then, a year to the day after the accident, her father's desperate footsteps took him to the New Bailey Bridge, where, filling his pockets with stones, he stepped into the river and the dark waters closed peacefully over his troubled head.

Returning to Smedley Vale for the funeral, entering the house which had once been her home, was ordeal enough for Charlotte, but the reading of the will in her father's study was worse. Everything – house, money and business premises – was left to the Humane Society. At first Charlotte was stunned, utterly unable to comprehend.

"Surely," she asked Mr Caxton, of Ainsworth, Caxton and Crabtree, "I could contest the will on the grounds of failing reason?"

"Not in this case," he replied. "Your father, at the time of adding this codicil, was of so sound a mind, that he took the precaution of having his sanity vouched for by two eminent doctors."

There was a long silence. Mr Caxton gathered his papers together. "What will you do?" he asked. Tears, rage or even abuse, he could understand, but not this . . . silence.

"I will keep you informed," came the eventual reply.

In the twenty years since walking out of the house in Smedley Vale, Charlotte moved into Manchester and found both solace and salvation in building her own business. People regarded Etherington's Enterprises as something of an overnight success. How it had happened was a mystery, and the source of capital a matter for speculation.

In reality there was no mystery at all; Charlotte borrowed just a little to get started from the Moxhams – who thought she'd gone mad – and repaid every last farthing from the sweat of her brow and the burning of quarts of midnight oil.

Deals were done. Acting when the time was right, she bought into schemes; she had a stake in the dye works and the tannery. She employed quality piece-workers. She bought a theatre at a knock-down price and built it up with cheap Irish labour. She read all the commercial and artistic papers and was constantly on the look-out for innovation and flair. Miss Etherington was on the way up.

All the anger and frustrated energy of the last year found an outlet; it cleansed her of self pity, of dwelling on the terrible injustices of the past. Her own brass plate. That had been her dream. A dream of utter independence, of never having to plead, beg, or be beholden to any – man.

And now, twenty years on, she looked down at the two little girls, at the faded kimono; and Jancie, looking up, recognised that Miss Etherington was a firm believer in dreams.

Chapter 5

Manchester had undergone changes of great magnitude
since the *Clive of India* had rammed the New Bailey
Bridge, but these were nothing compared to the changes
which took place in the lives of the Ridley girls.

Miss Etherington had wanted someone to attend the
door, take messages, to do anything that came under the
title of 'general duties.' She had wanted an able person,
preferably to live in, not young girls, street urchins at
that, who scarce knew their right hand from left. Still,
in a moment of . . . not charity . . . and certainly not
weakness . . . in a moment of she knew not what, she
had asked Bob to send them round. And the woebegone
little pair were here, and she was ushering them inside
out of the wind and offering food and a night's rest,
before gauging their potential on the morrow. No one
could do themselves justice in so poor a condition; and
should they not be suitable . . . well, a little hospitality
never did any harm.

Fortunately, Mrs Hallam the housekeeper, had not yet
gone home. Her husband often complained about her
working late. "You'd better take yer bed to Shude Hill,"
he grumbled. "Yer spend more time there than 'ere!" She
was too kind-hearted to tell him that life at Shude Hill
was far more interesting than his "war reports". Since
the 72nd Manchester Regiment had left to re-enforce the
Peninsular Campaign he thought of nothing but the war,
and how Sir Arthur Wellesley was more than a match
for Boney.

Mrs Hallam's red, chunky face always wore a harassed expression, brought about by being over protective of her mistress. Not that Miss Etherington had ever showed signs of needing protection. But Mrs Hallam, having taken on this role some fifteen years before – just until a male protector in the form of a husband took over – now found it difficult to shake off. Although there had been many male admirers, her employer remained unmarried.

The harassed expression was more pronounced tonight for Mrs Hallam, having raised a family of daughters, knew that however good Miss Etherington's intention, she would never, in a month of Sundays, be able to cope with the girls in this state. She pursed her lips, shook her iron-grey head, and decided to give that Bob Smollett a piece of her mind for wishing these two on her mistress – hadn't she enough with running her enterprises?

Mrs Hallam's form of registering displeasure was to clump, instead of walk. And all that evening the flagged passages and wooden floors echoed with the clumping as Jancie and Violet were scrubbed and fed, their rags burned – except the kimono which Jancie fiercely refused to give up – and both were nestled warmly with blanket in the hayloft across the yard.

After reporting the completion of these events, Mrs Hallam said she would bring some suitable clothing for the girls in the morning. Bidding her employer a good night, she added, "I hope you know what you're doing, Miss Etherington. You've undertaken some odd things in yer time, but this beats the lot!"

"Violet?" Jancie called softly, eager to talk now they were alone, about the turn in their fortunes. "We'd better say our prayers for tomorrow . . . you'll not say anything about my eyes at the interview? You promised . . . I didn't see Miss Etherington properly with it being dusk . . . what does she look like? She

33

sounds nice . . . Violet?" And louder. "Violet?" There was no response.

She sat up indignantly, and reaching out in the darkness, poked the recumbent mound. "Oh, Violet! How can you be asleep already! Honestly, I've never known anyone so incurious!" How can you sleep at all, she thought, on the eve of this great adventure.

She slumped back into her blanket, disappointed, and staring up into the darkness thought of the Admiral. He'd always been there by the fire to talk to . . . At Jepson's they had said prayers regularly – the Lord's Prayer. "Our Father which art in heaven . . ." If anything was instilled into the young at Strangeways, it was the saying of prayers. They hadn't said them much since leaving Jepson's, and neither did they call each other 'dear' anymore. Perhaps it was a sign of growing up. She thought of the interview on the morrow. Oh, how she hoped they would be able to do what was required and that she could prove herself to be invaluable before the eye defect was noticed.

Having slept soundly, both girls were wakened at dawn by the strident crowing of cocks and the whinnying of the horse stabled below. Violet nestled comfortably down from the draught enjoying the comfort and warmth of the moment. Jancie wriggled with excitement; although the day had not started, every pulse in her body was already working up to making a success of this

A blustery cold draught announced the arrival of Mrs Hallam. She swung the stable door open briskly, fastening back the top half; then, hanging up the lantern and setting down the basket of clothes, she yelled "Come on, look sharp you two! I've not got all day!" And as the girls scampered down, naked and shivering, she added, "These clothes'll do, though what Miss Etherington's thinking of, I don't know."

Despite her reservations, she was touched by the obvious pleasure and reverence with which the girls handled first the small clothes and then the woollen-mixture gowns; a heather colour for Violet and a sombre brown for Jancie. The gowns were simply cut, gathered into a yoke high above the waist and falling in folds to mid-calf length.

Mrs Hallam was puzzled – as she had been last night – at Jancie's inability to fasten the laces of her petticoat, and she noted how quickly Violet turned from her own dressing to do them up for her sister Yet the girl looked bright enough and seemed to have all her wits about her.

She watched them pulling on stockings, revelling in the grey warmth. "Shoes!" breathed Violet, admiring the brass buckles which relieved the plain, black leather. "Oh, don't we look the best, the grandest!" Standing up, she clapped her hands in sheer pleasure, then twirling under and about the loft-ladder, immediately felt as though she had always been like this – as though Jepson's, the Admiral and the quayside community had never been part of her experience.

Jancie felt different too. Although not having the magical properties of the kimono, the gown, so obviously for a young girl about town boosted her self-confidence and made her feel tall and efficient.

"We've got Miss Etherington to thank for all this," she said, the gratitude ringing in her voice – and for Bob Smollett's part in it, too; though he never said anything about clothes or living in . . .

"You 'ave, that." Mrs Hallam's crisp tone took up her thoughts. "And don't you forget it, either of you!"

"Oh no, ma'am," promised Jancie. "How could we?"

The housekeeper nodded her satisfaction. Then she glanced quickly at the small window. "Lawks, it's daylight, already," she chided, and beckoned to Violet. "Come 'ere, while I put a brush to your hair." Violet, to whom the untangling of tangles represented torture, submitted unwillingly, only to be told, "Yes, cringe and

35

wriggle as much as you like, my girl, but you're not having any breakfast 'till every hair is unravelled. So, you may as well be still!"

Mrs Hallam's terse monologue continued. "Now, you do this every day, both of you, d'you hear?"

"Yes, ma'am."

"Got to look decent, like, for Miss Etherington." She applied the tortoiseshell brush until Jancie's hair gleamed like copper. "Goes a lot on appearance, Miss Etherington does. Won't tolerate slovenly habits – and neither, I might tell you, will I!"

Having groomed them to her satisfaction, she led them across the yard. There was no kitchen at the Smallware Manufactory, for Miss Etherington always dined out, mainly at the Seven Stars across the way. The housekeeper's room was the nearest to a kitchen, it was here that the sweep, coalman, charwomen, stable lad, the widow who came for the laundry and the indoor and outdoor workers called for refreshment.

The ceilings in the premises at this end of Shude Hill were low and heavily beamed, and the Smallware Manufactory was no exception. The walls were whitewashed, the floor flagged, and a cheerful fire burned between an oven and a hob, where a cooking pot of porridge simmered.

At the end of the table nearest the fire, the girls, perched on stools, were scraping the last morsel of porridge from their bowls, when they heard footsteps along the passage. The steps were short and purposeful. It must be . . . They glanced apprehensively at Mrs Hallam, and Mrs Hallam nodded.

Laying down their spoons, and getting up from the table they said, as previously instructed, "Good morning, Miss Etherington."

A curious dignity rested on them as they stood there, solemn-faced and uncertain; their cheeks, rosy from warmth and food, contrasting nicely with the white pinafores.

Obviously pleased with the scene before her, Miss Etherington nodded her acknowledgement. "You've done well, Mrs Hallam – I'd scarce know they were the same."

"Thank you, ma'am. They seem to be good girls, there was no scrapping – which for sisters is saying something. And," she cast a stern glance at the awestricken figures, "They did as they was told and gave no lip. But how long that will last remains to be seen."

"It does indeed. Well . . . thank you, Mrs Hallam, and now," she smiled encouragingly. "Jancie and Violet, is it? Will you come with me to the office?"

Walking behind the tall, elegant figure, Jancie and Violet exchanged glances – a mixture of anxiety and excitement. They looked about curiously, realising they must have passed the office last night, for it was at the front of the premises and to the left of the entrance. The street door, painted a dark crimson, seemed very grand. It stood open and was wedged against the wall by a gleaming brass umbrella stand. Jancie had never seen such a display; a dozen or more umbrellas all clustered together like summer flowers, with the occasional black and brown gamp sticking up like the bare branches of winter trees. The three steps had been washed so well and the brass nameplate and door knocker polished so brightly, that the sisters wondered how anyone could pass without calling.

They followed her into the office and gazed about in bewilderment. The press of business was in the air, drawing attention at once to a fine French writing table with cabriole legs. This was the one exception to commerce; but even its crimson leather top was busy with papers, pens, brass ink-wells, artists' sketches, theatre bills, and a newspaper. At the back of the room to the left was a high desk with a ledger already open and a spike of bills acting as a page marker. To the right stood a hexagonal table, a deep rim keeping mounds of pamphlets and sheet music in order, and that, in turn, was supported by a neat set of drawers beneath. A club-footed, highly polished wall cupboard of black oak faced the window; two high shelves were lined with books, but on the gleaming ledge beneath stood another concession – a large brass bowl of bright yellow chrysanthemums.

Always, whatever time of the year there had to be fresh flowers. Two high-backed chairs completed the furnishing, along with an ornate brass fireguard and fender; the floor was carpeted, but the walls, being bare, offered a relief to the ceaseless energy.

Miss Etherington had by now closed the door, and with a swift look for space on the table, perched on the side edge. With slim dark eyebrows slightly raised, she contemplated the two girls, standing a respectful distance away by the mantelpiece. No quill-driving clerk could have faced an employer with faster-beating hearts than theirs. Oh, I hope she likes us, thought Violet, who, seeing her in light of day, considered the pale, oval-shaped face to be the most beautiful, the most refined. She wore her hair – and it had been dove grey for as long as Mrs Hallam could recall – shortish, and beautifully waved. The white frilled shirt contrasted with a thigh-length jacket, nicely relieved by a colourful waistcoat. Being perched at an angle, the severely cut lines of her skirts cascaded over dove grey boots – and oh, Violet almost ached at the sight of it, the underskirt was embroidered with pink rose-buds. She was enchanted; the thought of working for and living in with so lovely an employer filled her entire fancy, and fired her recently discovered ambition to one day wear an embroidered underskirt.

Jancie had guessed from the sound of Miss Etherington's voice last night that she would be some kind of wonderful person; this being confirmed, her mind was solely on the interview. "Now, which one of you is

38

going to tell me all about yourselves? – a truthful account, mind."

"Me," said Jancie, feeling her face go hot. "I remember most, because I'm a bit older than Violet . . ."

"Very well . . . I'm listening."

Far from being the dull, stammering catalogue of events usually recited by those looking for work, this was a lively, graphic account of their lives. Jancie related it all with the ease of a raconteuse, from her first memories of making daisy-chains on St Peter's Field with their parents. Once started, it was easier to go on; just as at Tinker's Tea Gardens wearing the kimono, once people gathered it became easy to put on a show. This was like a show. She lowered her tone and spoke feelingly of Jepson's: the disappointment of missing the Ardwick Green display on Trafalgar Night . . . a graphic description of the fire . . . a hop, skip and a jump to imitate Aberdaron Dick's loping walk . . . a touch of mimicry related to Mr Capper . . . and solemn truthfulness as to the stealing of the kimono and pumps; the Admiral was acknowledged fondly; and, by way of a finale, she quickly removed her shoes and went into a performance of the Japanese Dancing Act. Her small feet, her childish grace, and the total absorption with which she danced left Miss Etherington astounded. She was also moved. She never looked back to her own childhood. Life for her began when, with Mirabelle Moxham's promissory note in her pocket, she had arrived from London, and walked about Manchester looking for suitable premises. She had created Etherington's Enterprises, nurtured them, and proudly watched their growth. But, her heart told her, it was not enough. She had fulfilled her dream when the brass plate was fixed to the door. And now, twenty years on, Miss Etherington's blue-grey eyes were suddenly bright. Jancie and Violet, too, would have a chance to realise their dreams.

Chapter 6

For the first week of their employment, the girls, at Mrs Hallam's insistence, continued to sleep in the loft over the stables. "See how they gets on," she warned. "Really, Miss Etherington, to 'ave 'em under your roof when they're not proved or tried is – well, it isn't like you to be so rash."

But after the first week she changed her mind. "Eh, it's a reet pair o' treasures you've copped for, ma'am. They say, in the workroom, that Jancie's feet scarce touch the ground!" She had never spoken a truer word. Jancie went anywhere, did anything to keep herself busy in case she was asked to perform some close-worked task.

"Your duties for the present," Miss Etherington had nodded toward Violet, "will be to answer the door and receive both customers and travellers – courteously. Customers you take to the showroom, and travellers, who usually have an appointment, take tea with me – which you will serve, and Mrs Hallam will teach you how to infuse it. You will go to the market every other day and purchase fresh flowers." She indicated the chrysanthemums. "In between these tasks you will make yourself useful to anyone – those in the workroom, Mrs Hallam, or myself. Is that clearly understood?"

"Yes, Miss Etherington."

"This making yourself useful also applies to you, Jancie. In addition to which, there will be errands to go and messages to deliver. There will be mail to collect from the Post Office, and when you have proved yourself capable, letters and parcels to take."

While delivering a swatch of ginghams on St Mary's Gate, Jancie, on an impulsive surge of gratefulness, hurried down the three steps of the barber's shop. "Bob! Bob! Look at me!" She swung herself about, showing off her brown dress, braided hair, and buckled shoes. "Miss Etherington's taken us on – and it's you we've got to thank. Oh, thank you. Thank you a hundred times!"

He turned swiftly from lathering a bristly chin to receive a wild kiss of gratitude. Although momentarily startled, he felt the impact of her thin, child's body, and responded with a quick hug. "Is this really Jancie?" he teased, dotting the end of her nose with the soapy brush. "The little lass as was 'ere only last week to warm her toes?"

"It is! It is!" she laughed, brushing off the soap with the back of her hand. "I'm delivering a sample of ginghams," she added importantly, and realising the men waiting on benches were looking at her with curious amusement, became embarrassed. "I'd better go . . ."

Out on St Mary's Gate, she hurried away. This wild exuberance was a new feeling. What had come over her? A deep blush warmed her heart. She had never felt the urge to hug or kiss anyone other than her sister. She recalled the pressure of Bob's quick returning hug – the feel of his smooth-skinned face . . . and he smelled so nicely of soaps and scents. She recalled all these things, and not knowing what to make of them, changed her thoughts to how amazed Aberdaron Dick would be when he returned.

Jancie often looked in the direction of the river and paused sometimes on the bridge, wanting to rush and tell the Admiral about the upturn in their fortunes; but no, it would not do; no one, dressed as she now was, entered the derelict warehouse. "We comes and we goes" he had said, touching the side of his crooked nose. The quayside

41

community was now as much a part of her past, as the workhouse, as Jepson's.

Then, after only the first week, Miss Etherington made up her mind. The girls were to live in the house, share a bedroom, and take their meals with her in the Seven Stars. This astounding news was totally eclipsed by her next words. "You will have observed that each department in the manufactory has what we call a putter-out; for example, in the frieze and tassel department the putter-out is responsible for counting the moulds, weighing the silk and worsted that the outdoor workers take away, and then entering the quantities in a ledger . . . Jancie?" Miss Etherington looked questioningly at Violet, and back again at the distressed expression on Jancie's usually eager face. "Is something the matter?"

"You mean we'll have to learn to read, and write, and do figures, an' that?"

"Yes, Violet, I do."

"Jancie can't see close up, ma'am." The forbidden words rushed out, followed by an abrupt silence in which Violet fought down a sense of betrayal. "She's not blind or owt – just couldn't see the bobbin on the loom at Jepson's."

"Why did you not tell me this before?" Miss Etherington looked from one face, crestfallen and pale, to the other, now flustered and poppy red. Jancie dared not speak lest the words choked her.

Hoping to redeem the situation, and not daring to look at her sister, Violet continued recklessly. "We thought you'd stop us, ma'am, before we had a chance to show how useful we can be. But with the book learning, you'd be bound to find out . . ."

Miss Etherington had asked the question gently and with some sense of relief, for Mrs Hallam had put Jancie's peculiarities down to a streak of dim-wittedness. Not that she had agreed; the child was far too alert.

She rose from behind the writing table, and stooped

42

to touch Jancie's face; the slim, jewelled fingers moving over her hot cheeks and tracing lightly the contours of the troubled eyes.

"You mustn't be anxious on that account," she said softly. "Tomorrow I shall take you to Mr Battye the oculist." Seeing a shadow of alarm at the sound of the last word, she paused to qualify it. "Mr Battye makes eyeglasses," she explained. "Surely, you've seen, or know what spectacles are?" Their faces were blank. "You haven't . . . Well, this time tomorrow, with the aid of a pair of spectacles you will be able to see exactly what is in front of your face." Her thoughts hovered, seeking a comfortable word, something to quell the obvious apprehension. Ah! She settled on the very thing. "In fact, you'll be able to sit at the dressing-table to look at yourself in the glass, instead of standing a yard away!"

"Will I, ma'am, honest?"

"You will, I promise. There, that's something to look forward too, isn't it?" She stood up and, turning to Violet, put both hands on her shoulders. "You did right to tell me . . ." Then with a smile, and a rise of one slim eye brow, she added, "Are there any more secrets tucked away?"

"No, Miss Etherington," came the swift assurance. "Honest."

Despite heavy rain they attended the oculist in Deansgate under a large, fashionably striped umbrella. While Miss Etherington stood in the doorway, first shaking and then closing the umbrella, Jancie's gaze was drawn immediately to the jumble of scientific instruments displayed. It was not so much the pictorial advertisements of 'Venetian green spectacles for tired and watery eyes' which caught her attention, nor 'Concave spectacles for short sighted persons'; but, nestling among telescopes, microscopes, and magnifying glasses, was an oblong dish containing a pair of enamelled, artificial eyes. The pupils, painted brown, and sheltered by long, curling lashes, stared up from among trays of spectacle frames, lorgnettes and quizzers.

She thought of the last Sunday's text. 'If thine eye offend thee pluck it out,' and shuddered. As though that were not enough, the backcloth to the window portrayed St Lucia, patron saint of the blind, bearing her eyes in a dish.

It was a relief when the door opened behind them. "Come in, come in, Miss Etherington," beamed Mr Battye. "Not a very good morning, I fear."

"No, indeed – but I'm not one to deprecate the rain!"

The interior of the shop was long and narrow; its walls festooned with harrowing pictures of eye diseases, styes and squints; and above the glass-topped counter hung a rosewood wall cabinet containing vials, tinctures and ointments.

Dragging her gaze from the awful fascination of the eye diseases, and feeling thankful Violet was not here to see them, Jancie obeyed Mr Batty's request to be seated at a table. With a quick glance at Miss Etherington, who nodded reassurance, she rested her chin on the wooden sight-testing device. Curiously Jancie peered through the eyepieces.

"Now, child, tell me what you can see." Mr Battye placed a box of lenses on the table and stood beside her.

"Nothing, sir."

"What can you see, now?" He dropped a lens into the wooden slot.

Jancie saw the familiar haze and was swamped in immediate disappointment. Miss Etherington had said she would be able to see – and she couldn't!

"Child?"

"Mist," she answered in a small voice. "It's always there . . ."

"And can you still see nothing?" He dropped another lens in place. The clang startled her. She screwed up her eyes lest they fall out like the picture of the saint in the window. "Child?"

She peered through barely prised lids and immediately forgot St Lucia. "There's something! Something in the mist!"

"And that?" The lens clanged into place.

"I can see letters!"

"Describe them. You can do that, can you?"

"Oh, yes sir. There's one shaped like a ring – and another straight like a stick . . . and a stick with a dot on top – and two together like this." She placed two fingers together to form a wedge shape. "And—"

"That will do." He held up a hand to stem the torrent of description.

As he removed the lens the mist returned, and although Jancie could see the usual distance, her hand went up to be sure both eyes were still there.

Pleased to have trade so early in the day, he began to make up the spectacles. "A new assistant, eh, Miss Etherington, or did you say you had taken on two?"

Jancie stood by the table trying not to look at the pictorial inflamations on the wall, while the drone of conversation went from the completion of the new Exchange to General Wellesley taking the title of Lord Wellington, and had Miss Etherington heard that Mr Macready, of the Theatre Royal couldn't pay his way?

"And that, Mr Battye, is like to be the fate of us all if that madman Napoleon isn't stopped."

"Precisely," said the oculist smoothly. "Now, what would you like for your assistant's spectacles? Silver, gold, would you say, or tortoiseshell?"

"Silver – and a tortoiseshell, Mr Battye. If one gets misplaced both the job and her lessons would be held up – and in a recession we can't have that!"

"Indeed," he smiled. "And, now, young lady. Clip this to the bridge of your nose and tell me what colour my eyes are."

Jancie fixed the spectacles and stared at him almost in unbelief. There was no need to stand back. He was there in focus, a gentle face, thin, silver hair. "Blue, sir!" she exclaimed. "Your eyes are blue! Oh, Mr Battye, thanks! It's like having new eyes! I'll learn to read ever so quickly. I'll be able to weigh the silk and worsted, and enter it all up, honest, I will! Oh, Miss Etherington!" In her excitement, she flung her arms about her employer's neck, as she had done with Bob Smollett. Miss Etherington, who had never held anyone in her arms for the past twenty years, rocked on her feet with the impact, and realised that twenty years had been too long.

It was spring time. It had to be. "Eh, Aberdaron Dick's back!"

"Is he, by Jove?"

"I say, did you see—"

"Course, I did. Saw the old buzzard at the Swan yard."

"No . . . couldn't 'ave, he was sweeping the crossing in Market Street!"

Dick's plurality, or even multiplicity of jobs, was always the subject of good humoured banter. His energy and amazing alacrity seemed to rub off onto the town; it began to perk up; look more lively; the larks soared over St Peter's Field, and the oak tree outside Lady Egerton's town house in Quay Street was coaxed into bud.

No one could sweep a crossing clear of horse manure with as much aplomb – and speed – as Dick, nor swill the thoroughfare to make the cobbles gleam and glisten. Even the regular street and market cleaners, known as 'scavengers', deferred to him. Yes, Aberdaron Dick's singsong voice and cheerful manner had been missed – and no one realised it until he was back.

Jancie and Violet heard the news while breakfasting with Miss Etherington in the Seven Stars, and Violet caught up with him a little later while buying the office flowers at the market. He still looked a scarecrowish figure, even in his new coat, which, although not yet frayed at the cuffs, was too short for his long arms. His pleasant face screwed itself into a state of delighted pleasure. "So, this is what you get up to when me back's turned!" he teased. "My stars, Violet, I'd never have known you!"

"Wait till you see Jancie, you'd not know her either, even with the red hair!"

Well, who'd have thought it, he mused, listening to Miss Etherington did this, and Miss Etherington did that, and Miss Etherington had taken Jancie to the oculist . . . and had arranged lessons with Parson Brookes. "We seem to spend most evenings there. Jem calls him a slave-driver – we go with Jem Clowes from the sugar bakery in Half Street," she explained. "Well he's not Mrs Clowes son, really," she said in a confidential manner copied from Mrs Hallam. "And he's more interested in cock breeding than arithmetic – gets many a clout off the parson!"

"Well, I hope as Jem does right by Mrs Clowes, heart o'gold, she has. Took him from the workhouse and raised him as her own. An' there he is, large as life this morning at the cock breeders instead of attending to his duties at the sugar bakery."

"Wonder you didn't see my sister there as well."

"Not still cleaning pens?"

"Oh, as if she would!" declared Violet, as though the idea was utterly preposterous. "You got her into that!" she said in mock exasperation. "And that's what set her off as a bird fancier! Mrs Hallam disapproves, says cock breeding's no pastime for young ladies. I'm only eleven . . ." she gave one of her long, despairing sighs. "It'll be ages and ages before I'm a young lady."

Then, glancing down at the mauve and white chrysanthemums, she looked up at Dick incredulously. "Just imagine having these in the office . . . Oh, Dick, it's ever so nice with Miss Etherington. She lover flowers, the living rooms upstairs all smell of lavender, and in summer Mrs Hallam says there are window boxes filled with fragrant violas and stocks – and even the yard has tubs with scented roses! Oh," she lifted her eyes, partly to Dick, but mostly to heaven. "I hope we can stay there for ever and ever!"

In that summer of 1808 Jancie learned more than in her previous twelve years. The eye defect being corrected, self-confidence grew apace; natural curiosity gave her a head start, and out of sheer thankfulness for Miss Etherington's generosity she wanted to do more than her best.

These newly acquired interests filled her sharp eyes with a vivid intelligence. No one had to repeat an instruction or explain anything twice – as for weighing out the worsted and silk, she caught onto these so quickly as to be available when there was a rushed order.

Violet's interests lay not at all in the commercial aspect of the Enterprises, but in the artistic side of it. And now that the children had settled down to life at Shudehill, Miss Etherington allowed their inclinations – despite Mrs Hallam's warning of spoiling them – full rein.

"Ay," Mrs Hallam had to admit, "Violet's a proper little hostess . . . lays a good tea tray, I'll say that much for her, but where she gets her fancy ideas from, God only knows – flower petals floating on the tea! And sometimes, a rose lying by the seed-cake, 'brightens it up,' she says – cheeky young madam – as though my seed cake needs brightening up!"

"We can lay the blame for that on the latest pamphlet from Miss Bohanna's circulating library. Violet's only just learned to read and she's never out of the place!"

"That's education for you!" came the tart response. "What with one 'queening it' and the other 'swanning it' . . ."

*   *   *

48

While going about town on business with their employer, the sisters became as familiar with the inside of the crowded circle of warehouses, hotels, shops, and offices surrounding Piccadilly, as they had been with the outside.

However 'hostess-like' Violet was at the manufactory, or however 'business-like' Jancie looked in her sombre brown and spectacles, they reverted to childhood when visiting their favourite Enterprise. This was the small theatre on the corner of Deansgate known simply as 'Etherington's' where they sat in the side boxes enthralled at auditions of third-rate talent, and screamed with delighted shock at all the trickery of trapdoors, trip and trapeze wires.

Having learned to read, and progressing nicely with writing and figures, Jancie liked nothing better than to stand at the tall desk in the office, quill in hand, ledger opened, imagining herself to be a secretary, able with the aid of Parson Brookes's dictionary, to decipher the language of bills, delivery notes, invoices, and business letters.

It was only a matter of time before she realised Miss Etherington signed her letters in the name Charles.

"My first name is Charlotte," she explained. "And Charles is merely a shortened version. You would scarce believe it, but after setting up the manufactory I learned to my cost that a female name affected credibility in business. As an experiment I took to signing orders, contracts and letters, as Charles and was so amazed at the expeditious attention, that I kept it that way – I even think of myself as Charles!"

Miss Etherington's next step was to ask Mr Crabtree to start proceedings at once to make the girls her wards and she their legal guardian.

Chapter 7

"London!" Violet's delighted surprise echoed about the cosy sitting room, where Jancie had set down a tray of tea. "You mean we're going to celebrate Waterloo with the Honourable Mrs Moxham?"

"Not forgetting Mortimer," Miss Etherington smiled mischievously, "for without the Honourable Mr Moxham, there'd be no Honourable Mirabelle!"

"I can't believe it!" Violet took her tea to the window-seat and sat down carefully, as though to do any other would somehow jeopardise the news.

"Thought that'd make your eyes pop! You missed the last national celebration of Trafalgar, so we'll make up for it in style!" Although Napoleon Bonaparte's defeat by the Duke of Wellington was as good a reason to visit the metropolis as any, it was not the only reason.

Mirabelle Moxham – while telling herself she ought not to be surprised at anything her cousin did – had been astounded to receive a letter bearing news of the Ridley girls. 'Guttersnipes' Mirabelle had called them in her reply, and gradually progressed to 'your little urchins', then 'the waifs', and finally 'Your wards, Charles? Good God!'

Despite repeated invitations to introduce her protégées, Charles had deferred until the girls, at eighteen and nineteen, were sufficiently sure of themselves to cope with Mirabelle.

Although regular correspondents, the cousins had met but half a dozen times, because Charles felt uneasy at leaving the manufactory in these troublesome days, and Mirabelle dreaded travelling north. She reckoned that if there was to be a revolution, as in France, it would begin in the north; it was bound to happen when she was there, and as a titled person her head would be first to the block!

Also, and this was a big also for Charles, she thought it time her girls broadened their outlook. She wanted their experience of men to be wide, wanted them to be aware of the choice. For the past few years Violet had been casting boys in the role of lovers, creatures to dance attendance, to crush her in their arms and give her unimaginable pleasure. Wooing, courtship and marriage to a handsome man was all she wanted.

As for Jancie, many a sigh was expended over Jancie; nothing Charles could put her finger on, but the last thing she wanted for so promising a businesswoman was to end up breeding fighting cocks with Jem Clowes, or haranguing Reform meetings with Bob Smollett. Not that there was anything wrong with either of these young men . . .

Although Charlotte Etherington's youthful passion had been spent on calico printing and her dreams had been, not of knights in shining armour, but of nameplates in shining brass, she understood that the voyage into womanhood could be stormy and difficult. She had never thrilled to the touch of a man's hand or gone silly because of a man's smile, but she knew it happened.

A deep sense of compatibility had developed between the girls and their guardian over the years. For Charles the spontaneous hugs and kisses acted like a salve, soothing, but not healing the scars left by the *Clive of India*, scars that had gone too deep for too long.

The sisters wanted to be like their benefactor and thought her beautiful and wonderful – she was no longer ma'am or Miss Etherington, but simply Charles. Of the two, Violet's affection was worshipful, and Jancie's

51

practical; she sensed there had been a terrible tragedy in Charles's life, and unconsciously knew how to cope with it. She never discussed her suspicion with Violet, whom she knew, would blow it up dramatically into a romantic betrayal. It may have been, for all Jancie knew, but she reverenced her guardian's privacy and, in any case, Charles's past was no concern of theirs.

The journey to London, then, was to complete their growing up – a widening of experience. Mrs Hallam had set her mouth firm when hearing of the proposed visit. She clomped along the passage and put her head round the office door. "It'll put fancy ideas into their heads," she said. "You see if it don't!"

"When are we going, Charles?" breathed Violet. "Just imagine, we're going to where the Prince Regent lives!"

"And to where the working classes appeal for justice and get ignored," Jancie said.

"Don't you want to go?" Violet asked, in amazement.

"Of course I do. Just redressing the balance, that's all."

"Arrangements have been made," Charles explained, "for us to go down next week on the Coburg; it isn't the fastest coach by any means, but by far the most comfortable."

"The Coburg! I can't wait to tell Aberdaron Dick – oh, and everyone!"

"But it's parasol season," declared Jancie. "We can't leave when there's such demand."

"We're celebrating the end of nearly twenty years of war! It's over. London will be awash with hi-jinks all season, or so Mirabelle assures me." Charles raised a jewelled hand in a helpless gesture. "And all you can think of is parasols! All's well with the world, Jancie. All's well, at last."

"For a while, anyway."

"Oh, take no notice of her, Charles. She's always like this after reading Cobbett's *Journal* to those whiskery old bores in Smollett's!" Violet got up from the window-seat and stood looking down into Shude Hill, her mind already a week ahead, already in the Moxhams' great house, listening to the rattle of carriage wheels on the cobbles of St James's, looking down onto Green Park.

"How long will we be away?"

"Oh, a month of London is as much as an old rustic like me can tolerate—"

"A month?" echoed Jancie.

"Well, it's scarcely worth going for less, and a week of that will be travelling, including the return of course. Besides, it's a very interesting place, especially in celebration. And Mirabelle has heard so much about you over the years, she'll not take kindly to anything less."

"That's settled, then!" Violet hurried off to see what clothes she should take.

"We'll have to leave everything right downstairs . . . there'll be a lot of arranging to do . . ." Jancie placed Charles's cup with the others on the tray.

"Why the reluctance?"

"I suppose I'm set in me ways!"

"What, at nineteen!" They both laughed, and the humour defused Jancie's first anxious moments. She had grown tall and slender; vivacious both in looks and manner, her sleekly brushed hair was piled on top of her head, twisted into a Grecian knot, and held in place by combs the colour of her spectacles. Seeing that spectacles were to be part of her life, she made a fashionable feature of them and chose the colour of her clothes accordingly.

"I don't think we need worry too much about the business," Charles reassured. "Everyone will be glad of the chance to show how well they can manage without us! And, of course, Clogger is more than capable of running the theatre."

53

At the mention of Clogger Jancie brightened. She had been responsible for a few innovations at the Manufactory, such as the taking on of male labour. The theatre manager, who doubled up as chucker-out on occasions, was a big man called Clogger. The other was a runaway chimney sweep's lad, called Sampson. He was small and afraid of the dark and lived in the room over the theatre with Clogger.

It wasn't that Jancie didn't want to go to London, but, as she told Mrs Clowes at the sugar bakery in Half Street, she didn't particularly want to leave Manchester!

"Eh, I don't know what to make o'that!" laughed Mrs Clowes.

"Anyways, how's trade been lately?" Jancie peered over the top of her spectacles at the pile of toffees waiting to be wrapped in twists of paper.

"Got through nigh on three ton o'sugar this week," Mrs Clowes volunteered. "Our Jem's done nothin' but boil and stretch."

"Well, if he's too busy . . ."

"Did I say so?" Mrs Clowes demanded sharply. "He's never too busy to see thee."

Lifting the flap of the long mahogany counter, Jancie passed through, along a flagged passage, then down further steps to a rough wooden door.

"Heavens, Jem, it's like an inferno!" she gasped as the blast of sweet, sickly heat set her pores agape. Through the steam she saw him clad only in breeches, sinewy arms pulling and twisting long ropes of boiled sugar. As the apprentice stirred a vat, the pungent aroma of aniseed, peppermint and liquorice, seized her throat and brought tears to her eyes.

"Won't be long," he shouted over the boiling.

"Don't be or I shall melt!"

"Not the way I'd like yer to!"

With her clothes clinging uncomfortably, Jancie closed

the door and hurried along the passage, wishing she was
on the way to the Infirmary Baths at Piccadilly. That was
another point against London. She'd miss the weekly –
and sometimes twice-weekly visit to the baths, where
Charles was a member and had taken out subscriptions
for Jancie and Violet. Thinking of the cool spring water
in an apartment so large they could swim made her feel
even hotter and stickier. As she opened the end door
the cackle and chuckle of hens was a reminder that she
would miss these too.

Their chuckling soothed her spirits, for in saying
goodbye to Bob Smollett, she had not been prepared
for the way he viewed the venture. "Moving in society
circles, eh!" He had winked at the customers waiting their
turn. "Oh, dear . . . foot in both camps; bound to colour
your judgement, y'know. Come back a raving Tory, I
shouldn't wonder. I bet that's what Miss Etherington's
on about. Thinks you're getting too cosy with reforming
principles. An' who'll read Cobbett's pamphlets to the
fellas, while you're gone?"

"You!"

"Wouldn't be the same, lass. You do it real – with
feeling, like."

"Seeing you've got so little faith in me," she challenged, moving toward the door, "it'd serve you right
if I didn't come back!"

"Off already?" He looked up, realising he'd gone too
far. She recalled him standing there, in white full-sleeved
shirt and scarlet waistcoat, eyes anxious and shaving
brush poised. Trying to redeem the situation, and yet
aware of the amused glances of the waiting customers,
he said humbly, "Don't I get a kiss?"

"What?" she echoed, over the half door. "From a
prospective turn-coat?"

In retrospect, she thought Bob's teasing in bad taste,
especially in front of the customers. She was disappointed
in him. Her political mentor he may have been, but that

didn't give him the right to jump to conclusions. Jancie wasn't all that keen on going to London in the first place, and he had made her feel even worse . . .

Jem pulled on a shirt and joined her as she leaned over the pens, admiring the young cockerels.

"I'll miss you, Jem," she said simply. "We're going in the morning."

"I'll miss you, an' all . . ." They did not stand close, but a couple of feet apart, she near the top of the pen, he at the bottom, and across the heads of the strutting birds they looked at each other in silence. Jem was a muscular young man of twenty, sturdy as an oak tree, with broad shoulders, eyes as deep and tawny as an owl, and a thick mass of hair the colour of forest bark.

"These," she indicated the cockerels, "will be grown when I'm back. I'll miss these an' all."

"Jancie?"

"Yes?"

"When you come back, shall we be sweethearts?"

The birds paused in their chortling, heads to one side, awaiting her answer; and in the silence, she heard the faint river noises, and for some reason thought of the Admiral.

"I'm not sure . . ."

"You never will be," he said gruffly, "unless we try it out. We get on well enough – good friends, like. And you don't mind me arm around your waist when we're at Tinker's Tea Gardens." While talking he moved nearer, until, standing in front of her, he stretched out a hand and with the intention of kissing her, gently removed the spectacles. She looked so very vulnerable without them, he could have sworn his heart moved in his chest.

Unable now to see his face, she felt the warmth of his body, smelled the aniseed in his hair, and felt the blood rush to her cheeks. She was hot again, longing for the cold spring water of the Infirmary Baths. He was right, she didn't mind his arm about her waist, either at Tinker's or now.

He held her closely; could feel the fast beating of her heart, and knew it wasn't for fear of his mother coming on the scene. It was all terribly improper, kissing in the back yard, but she was going away, and she didn't want to go; and Jem was so dear. They kissed again and again.

"Yes, Jem," she said weakly. "When I return, we'll be sweethearts."

Chapter 8

The early morning was fine, and the sky rose-coloured with promise as Miss Etherington and her wards entered the gaily decorated coach yard of the Swan Inn. The colourful bunting and gaudy flags festooned about the archway added a holiday spirit. The bugle announcing the approach of the Coburg had already been heard in the distant streets.

"The coach!"

"It's coming!"

Violet and Jancie could hardly contain their excitement; they chattered and smiled and recalled with Aberdaron Dick how they had stood about, hoping to be of service to passengers – and now they WERE passengers! He laughed with them, enjoying their pleasure, teasing them about the Waterloo celebrations.

Clusters of people had gathered. Perhaps only one was travelling, but it needed three or four to see them off. Inquisitive dogs prowled silently round trunks and boxes. A couple of merchants awaiting the arrival of important mail talked with Miss Etherington, discussing Napoleon's imprisonment on St Helena in loud, confident voices. A woman with a canary in a cage was sniffling a protracted farewell on a man's shoulder.

"The coach!"

Bugle still blowing, the great coach, with thundering hooves and lumbering wheels, lurched through the arch and ground to a shuddering halt. A quick turn-round was the essence of good timekeeping, and no coach company could ever accuse the Swan of being laggardly. Even before the passengers alighted two men in dirty white aprons dashed forward and began to wash the red and blue bodywork; ostlers, with whom swearing and shouting was synonymous with speed and efficiency, ran to lead away the sweating horses. Grooms hurried out a fresh team of four, their hooves clattering smartly on the cobbles. In next to no time they were harnessed between the shafts, and raring to go.

Luggage was unloaded, and the passengers, having travelled overnight, stumbled out. Blinking like owls, they made their way to the Swan's dining room. A small boy moving with the speed of a ferret leapt inside the cab, turfing out the damp and dirty straw, like an animal refurbishing its nest. He then scuttled off for a fresh load, scooping it inside, and trampling it down to a depth of six inches. He re-filled the lamps with oil; hung sweet smelling pomatums to disguise the disagreeable odour of mildew, and, as the loading began, darted away.

Aberdaron Dick energetically thrust bags and boxes into the cavernous boot; and the woman with the canary took her place opposite Violet. Those riding on top scrambled up the ladder cheerfully.

"Beautiful mornin', ma'am," said the relief guard to Miss Etherington, as he and the driver, in their red and blue livery, appeared for duty.

"Yes," she replied briskly. "It is indeed."

"Coburg's ready, ladies and gentlemen!" roared the guard. "All aboard, please!"

The bugle sounded. The whip cracked. Bridles jangled; and the great coach lurched forward. Friends of the travellers jumped hastily out of the way. Clogger and Little Sampson who had brought the luggage, raised their hats. Dick loped alongside, and Violet waved frantically to him.

"Mind yer 'eads on the archway, gents!" yelled the

guard. The spectators cheered, the coach pulled out of the yard, and with another blast on the bugle rattled away up Market Street and out of town by London Road.

Having left the fine houses of Ardwick Green behind, the territory was all new to Jancie and Violet. First one and then the other, peering out of the little windows, would turn and engage Charles's attention with a look of amazement at some unusual sight which took their fancy.

Seated between her wards, Miss Etherington derived much happiness from their pleasure, and as the thunder of sixteen hooves and the rumbling of great wooden wheels rendered normal conversation impossible, there was great fun in misinterpreting the signs made to each other. Their obvious amusement was a source of intense study to the three passengers opposite.

The woman held the canary cage against her breast and frowned. A prim-looking man in cloth boots sat with his knees close together opposite Violet, and between him and the canary sat another man; plump, clean, and rosy, his small hands folded neatly on the ledge of his stomach. Although strangers, they immediately had something in common; they found it very agreeable to be seated opposite three attractive and interesting females, and occasionally to exchange a glance, a nod, a smile with them – although to be looked at over Jancie's spectacles made the rosy face a shade rosier, and drew the cloth boots even closer together.

Charles had hoped there might have been a fashionable young miss – or man, for Violet's interest, for as soon as the town was cleared, the distance between each would be longer, and miles and miles of green fields were tedious to the young. But Violet's thoughts centred on London and she was anything but bored. Jancie fretted about the Manufactory, and about Jem who had not been at the Swan to see her off. "Bad enough you going," he had said. She fretted over Bob viewing her London visit as some kind of defection, and was only saved from these worries by Violet's comical expressions of hunger.

On the third day, Charles and the girls were relieved to be arriving in London. After slow progress by the Fleet market, and much blowing of the bugle and rowdiness from those on top, it ground to a halt in the yard of the Royal George.

The Moxhams' carriage was waiting. Violet knew it was theirs; it had the smartest crimson bodywork with a crest on the panels and a driver in the same colour of livery. The carriage was capacious, and the wide, clear windows afforded the most comprehensive view of their progress from Holborn to St James's. And what a progress it was. First Violet and then Jancie would exclaim.

"Charles, did you see that?"

"Charles, wherever have all these carriages come from?"

"Oh, and the size of the houses . . . oh, and aren't they grand!"

"It's like a dream!" gasped Violet. "Oh, Charles, it's wonderful of you to bring us. Oh, the gowns, the fashion, the style . . ."

"St James's!" Jancie eyed the red brick of the handsome four-storeyed house; the delicately panelled door; the semi-circular fanlight above; the pillars either side and the tall, dignified windows. "Good Lord," she exclaimed, hand to her mouth. "Oh, we're here!"

The carriage came to a halt. Violet feverishly smoothed the skirts of her creased travelling coat. "Darling Charles, how do I look? I feel as though I've been dragged through a hedge backward!"

"Calm down, girls. Take a deep breath and be composed. We don't want Mirabelle to think we're country gobbins come to town," she smiled, and added, "even though we are!"

The footman had let down the step and was extending

a white-gloved hand to assist them out, but Jancie, not knowing the procedure, was out already. Turning, she saw Violet alighting gracefully as to the manner born, but before the embarrassment reached her cheeks, another footman stood ready to conduct them indoors to his mistress.

The footman took their travelling coats, while yet another led them to be imperiously announced. Everything about the Honourable Mirabelle was abundant and liberal. Choked in pearls, wreathed in smiles, and wearing a satin day gown of a peach colour, which Jancie thought quite inappropriate for her colouring and age, she rose to receive her guests.

"Oh, darling, darling Charles, welcome to London." She opened her arms and, drawn by threads of the past, they embraced silently, closing their eyes as they stood gripping each other. "Oh, it's so good to see you," Mirabelle added, with a catch in her voice. "I was beginning to think you'd never come – that I'd never, ever see you again!"

"But you're often in my thoughts, dearest cousin," breathed Charles, adding softly, "I can never forget your generosity, your understanding. Without you and Mortimer I would have no doubt gone the same way as . . ." Even now she could not bring herself to say the word 'Father'.

"Shh, Charles . . ." Mirabelle chided. "Who's being a silly goose!" She held her at arm's length, inspecting the thin face with tender curiosity. Suddenly they laughed together, a familiar, private laugh, excluding the others, signifying understanding and superiority and love. Then, standing beside Charles, she eased the others into the intimacy of the reunion. "She's scarce changed at all – commerce seems to suit her constitution admirably – doesn't it, Mortimer?"

Plump, goutish, and fair-skinned, he put down the book he had been toying with and stepped forward to take Charles's hand. Affected by the emotion of the past few moments, he cleared his throat. "Yes, by Jove, suits you well."

"And it will suit me even better," Charles said, regaining her composure, "if trade picks up. Peace, I fear, will bring another crop of problems."

"What, even though we've nailed that jumped-up little Corsican good and proper?" said Mortimer heartily. "He'll not escape St Helena like he did from Elba, y'know!"

"He talks of nothing, but Waterloo!" declared Mirabelle. "I forbid any mention of the subject until Charles has introduced these handsome gels of hers – you've got all of three weeks to discuss the war and talk of trade!"

"Of course, my pet . . ." he turned to where the sisters were standing. "So, these are your waifs, eh?"

"My wards, Mortimer."

"Of course." He acknowledged them with an incline of his head, and retreated to the safety of his book.

"Let me guess," smiled Mirabelle, moving away from Charles. "This is Violet, a name to match such saucy eyes. You're not the shrinking kind, I hope," she teased. "Which is well, for I want you to enjoy yourself heartily."

"Oh, I will, Mrs Moxham." Violet, always one to relish an emotional scene, swallowed hard." I've thought of nothing else but coming here ever since our guardian told us!"

"And talked of nothing else, either!" laughed Charles.

"I thank you greatly for your hospitality, ma'am," Violet said, surprising everyone by sweeping the prettiest curtsey.

Even Mortimer applauded, and Violet, archly, through tear-bright eyes, sought Charles's approval. See, her glance seemed to say, not bad for a country gobbin!

Jancie, too, had been overwhelmed, and following on that, was surprised at their guardian's depth of emotion, wondering what sorrows and hopes had been shared to promote it. The cousins could not be less alike, and being curious about the Honourable Mirabelle, Jancie pushed the spectacles higher on her nose.

Mirabelle was pleasantly large, her body looking soft enough to absorb all who came in contact with it. Her features were affable, hazel eyes nicely set and her hair, a little too golden, was arranged in an elegant filigree headpiece. Her hands were small, reminding Jancie mischievously of Rosy Face on the coach. No doubt, in moments of repose, Mirabelle's hands could be folded as neatly on the ledge of her stomach!

"It's very kind of you, Mrs Moxham," she said with an incline of her head, "to include my sister and me in our guardian's visit."

"Jancie . . ." Mirabelle found the spectacles a little disconcerting. But they could be an asset, if handled properly, she thought – not that she's doing too badly as it is. "What a distinctive colour of hair. You possess reforming principles, too, I understand?" She cast a glance toward the long window. "Some of the greatest names in England stroll in St James's park, and are members of Mortimer's club. Lord Castlereagh's town house is in the Square, 'Goody' Sidmouth is round the corner. You might even glimpse the Duke of Wellington! Yes, – you could keep your Radicals amused for hours with what you observe from that window!" She glanced at Charles. "They are a credit to you, my dear, no one would ever imagine their humble beginnings."

Gathering the girls with a smile Mirabelle added. "There's a positive whirl of entertainments lined up for you – Waterloo has provided a capital excuse, if we ever needed one, for jamborees and junketings! And there's no shortage of handsome escorts! As you know, Moxham and I have no family, but we love to have young people about. We entertain a lot, but it isn't the same . . . Ah, here's tea. Be seated now, and after

64

you're refreshed, I shall conduct you on a tour of the house. No doubt, Charles, unless you've changed over the years, you will head straight for my bathing room – or one of them. We've had another installed. Beau Brummell is so very keen on bathing and advocates cleanliness to such a degree that we felt compelled to comply with fashion." Jancie watched in unbelief as a maid came forward to pour the tea – they didn't even pour their own! "Seeing you're so taken with the bath, Charles, why don't you have one fixed at Shude Hill?"

"I did consider it, not I might add on the same scale as yours. But firstly, the old timbers wouldn't stand any more interference; secondly, there's no room; and thirdly, we in Manchester have one of the most complete and elegant public baths in the kingdom – to which I've taken out subscriptions. You can enjoy any kind of bath – sometimes we're stuck for choice, aren't we, Jancie? There's hot and cold; sulphur, Turkish, Buxton; there's a Matlock too, but only in summer – and the compartment for swimming is kept remarkably cold by an underground spring. It's so clear and pure – positively rejuvenating!" She caught her hostess' pained expression. "You needn't look so horrified, Mirabelle, it's all very civilised."

"If you say so, darling . . . but, swimming at your age!" She sighed as though Charles were a lost cause, and enquired brightly, "More tea?"

After what the sisters regarded as an eye boggling, breath-taking tour of the principal rooms, Mirabelle took the girls to their bedroom. It was large, lofty, elegantly furnished and draped mainly in a rose colour. Long sash-windows reached almost to the floor, a cheerful fire crackled in the hearth; flowers and fruit were massed on a sideboard, and to their embarrassment, a maid was appointed to attend exclusively to their needs and clothes.

"First thing tomorrow," said Mirabelle, having caught sight of their Manchester clothes, "we shall get you some suitable outfits and I shall promenade you, and perhaps later a drive about the town."

While Violet, overcome with the shock of so different a life style, reclined on the rose-coloured sofa in their room, Charles and Jancie reclined at either end of a great marble bath in one of the Moxham's bathing rooms.

Chapter 9

From that moment on, every day was novelty and amusement. And every day the company was a little different. Just enough for Violet to enquire with a pretty frown, "Where's Captain Noakes today?" or for her to remark, "George would have liked this," or, "Has Neddy taken a chill? Oh, poor man!"

"If we keep moving 'em about, ring the changes," winked Mirabelle to Charles, "there'll be no breaking of hearts when the girls return north!"

Charles was not too sure about Arthur Thistlewood. He was tall, ramrod-straight, dark-haired and seemed of a passionate disposition in anything he undertook, putting twice as much effort into things as others did. At first, when there were gardens to see, a picture gallery, an arcade, he seemed to be on the periphery of the circle, but by the end of the first week he was noticeably attentive to Jancie.

"Oh, nothing to worry about there, Arthur's not an adventurer – his intrigues seem to be of a political nature. He's well into his thirties," informed Mirabelle. "Must be. He has served in the army, the militia, and has been in France with the militants. Gambler – a widower now, I think. Your ward is probably flattered by the attention of an older man."

"None of which is very reassuring. He even has a nickname for her – of which I don't approve. Calls her Citizeness – a joke, she says – a term used by the French for the militant women of the Revolution."

"Rest easy, darling, if they talk about anything seriously, it will be politics. Arthur Thistlewood is obsessed with extreme politics, so Mortimer tells me, which after a while can become quite tedious. Being outside our circle, he does not attend society events – neither does he own a carriage, so he's not likely to make off with her!"

"The general air of excitement could render even the most level headed a trifle silly – and if anything were to happen to either of my girls I'd suffer agonies of remorse, I know I would."

Was it the general air of excitement which woke Jancie the following night? She turned on her side, envying as always her sister's facility for sleep. Dear Violet, curled up like a dormouse, no doubt dreaming of the next ball, the new gown, a different young man . . . There it was again! A rattling on the window . . . shale being thrown up by someone below. Moving quietly out of the bed, she parted the curtains. There, on the lawns at the back of the house she recognised, with a thrill of utter amazement, the tall figure of Arthur Thistlewood. What was he doing here at this time of the night? She stared down, her eyes widening in disbelief. He was dancing. Hand on slender hips he executed the steps of the waltz.

Seeing her, he glided across the moon-shadowed grass, moving sinuously, invitingly, head up, arms held out. The sheer theatricality of the scene captured her imagination. She had to go – had to be part of the magic. She quickly put on her bathrobe, snatched her spectacles from the dressing-table, and without shoes or slippers, hurried down the darkened stairs and let herself out onto the terrace and into the summer night. She placed her hand in his, and passing into his arms waltzed rhythmically, silently, across nature's ballroom; whirling and twirling beneath the moonbeams, her small feet caressing the grass effortlessly. No thoughts came into her head, no words to her lips. Nothing could convey the wonder of the experience.

At last their imaginary music faded, and Arthur led her to the seat by the sundial. She sat down and he remained standing, eyes focused on the silver-painted nails of her toes beneath the bathrobe. "You're so different," he smiled, his gaze travelling up the slender figure, taking in the filigree spectacles astride her short, straight nose; the tousled hair, the rise and fall of her bosom.

"You're not exactly the ordinary type of man yourself," she countered, aware of his gaze. Why ever did I sit down, she suddenly thought. I must be mad to have left my room in the first place! Waterloo Fever was the current name for giddy behaviour – and it seemed that most people were suffering from it!

He leaned forward, and taking both her hands raised them slowly to his lips, and her to her feet. She felt again, as she had at the window earlier, a wild feeling of compulsion, as though some mystic power were tugging at her limbs. The magic had not altogether gone, it was still there, in the moonbeams, in the dappled clouds of night, and the faint rustling of leaves.

As in a dream he drew her slowly into his arms. Their bodies came together. Eyes closed. They stood shadowed by the great elm tree. The muscular strength of him through her robe gave her a delicious, euphoric sensation; bringing startlingly to mind the fact of him being fully clad, and she not. This fact had also not escaped Arthur Thistlewood. The suppleness of her young limbs made him tighten his hold. He wanted to feel the fast beat of her heart, to feel it beat even faster at his touch, but just then, she lifted her head from his shoulder, her lips parted tremulously. Ardent and passionate by nature, Arthur Thistlewood's kiss in no way resembled that which had passed between her and Jem Clowes by the hen pens. An owl in the tree above hooted. Jancie shivered.

"I must return," she said, breaking free. "If Violet's awake she'll think I've taken leave of my senses."

"Does it matter," he said softly, "what other people think?"

"Violet is not 'other people' and she'd only tease me. But, yes, on the whole I do value good opinion."

"Does that mean," he said as they walked across the lawn, "you'll not allow me to accompany your party to Vauxhall Gardens?"

"Does that mean," she countered, "that some people don't have a good opinion of you?"

"Would it matter?"

"No, why should it?" she said frankly. "You are splendid company, Arthur. Quite a refreshing change from the quips and masculine giggles of the younger men . . . you know, Neddy, George, and Algy . . ."

"In other words, you're more at ease with men in their dotage!"

"Now you're laughing at me!" Arrival at the terrace cut her words. To signify silence she placed a finger on her own lips, and then touched his, allowing it to remain, teasing the contours slightly. Before he could catch at her hand she had fled into the house.

During the Waterloo celebrations there seemed to be a perpetual military festival, with regimental bands playing at all hours the favourite 'Rule Britannia' and 'The Girl I Left Behind Me'. There was even a martial accompaniment to the boat trip on the Thames, from which Charles excused herself. Mirabelle resisted the temptation to explain why to her wards.

After the visit of the Moxhams' party of young people to Vauxhall Gardens, Jancie declared at breakfast the following morning, "Vauxhall's all right, but it can't hold a candle to Tinker's!"

"Take no notice, Charles," said Violet, crunching toast. "It was absolutely, brilliantly, wonderful!"

70

"And I suppose," returned Jancie, "you saw it all from the ballroom; dancing with that George, or, was it Neddy?"

"Yes, I did. The ballroom is open to the sky, and the hundred thousand extra lamps lighted to celebrate peace would've knocked Tinker's into a cocked hat! Oh, and Charles, fiddlers in fancy costume played ravishing melodies under gilded cockle-shells; a signal went up to announce the ascension of gas balloons, and then bells tolled to announce yet another firework extravaganza, oh, it was divine! And where my sister was when all this was going on, I don't know. Tinker's indeed!"

The young people had made the most solemn promises to keep together during the evening at Vauxhall, but parties at Vauxhall always did separate, only to meet at supper-time to discuss their adventures. Not that Jancie discussed hers, she didn't know quite what to make of them herself.

Her heart had quickened to feel the pressure of Arthur Thistlewood's hand on her arm, guiding her to one of the solitary walks between avenues of dimly lit trees. Once within the shadows, his arm was about her waist as they strolled.

He had not referred to the moonlit dancing, and Jancie was filled with relief that so mystical a scene was not to be reduced to language. At the same time she was filled with a curious kind of caution. She, who in Manchester considered herself to be well informed about Radical matters, felt almost gauche when he had found it easy to tie her in knots in their arguments; and the Sunday School she had set up to teach mill children their letters, and her work with the Female Reformers, appeared wispy and fragile. Moreover, her lifelong interest in Reform, which had been so absorbing, now seemed exceedingly limited.

"Of course I'd heard of you," he was saying, as the firework display began. "Why else d'you think I

71

tagged on to the silly merry-go-round of the rich? The Manchester Rads – Sam Bamford, the Middleton weaver, was down here some time ago, presenting a petition – had heard about you from a revolutionary barber called Smollett. A redhead, they said, "only a slip of a lass, but knows her Cobbett backward!"

"So, your curiosity was aroused?"

"Sidmouth and Castlereagh are not the only ones with a spy system, y'know."

The word 'spy' fell from his lips in a precise, crisp manner. He was always dropping hints of subterfuge and undercurrents, and then immediately fending off any probing; for which she was thankful. There was, she thought, in Arthur Thistlewood's mind, a lot that she was happier not to know.

Her steps became more reluctant. "I think we ought to return, my sister will be—"

"Having the time of her life! Oh, my dear Citizeness," he laughed softly. "Has my talk of government spies upset you?"

"No it has not!"

"Why go back, then? We were getting along capitally and now you want to return to Neddy, and Teddy in his tasselled boots!"

"I don't!"

"Well?"

"I don't know what to think – yes, I do. I shouldn't be here in a situation like this, with a man I hardly know."

"You didn't seem to mind the other night."

"The other night . . ." she stopped and turned direction, thus removing his arm from her waist. Sensing her change of mood, he offered his arm, she slipped her gloved hand within it, and walking toward the supper rooms, began again. "The other night was a delusion," she sighed, watching the glow of the firework display in the sky. "Part of the unreality of London Society . . . of Waterloo

Fever. If anyone had told me, three weeks ago, that I'd spend an evening in a Park Lane mansion, brilliantly lit and extravagantly furnished, flooded with cockaded footmen, and awash with white-calved flunkeys, I wouldn't have been able to understand – and now I've had the experience, I still can't comprehend!" Her voice rose above the whoosh of rockets. "So much food – and so many people starving . . . children crying for a crust of bread. No more Park Lane affairs for me, I protested – my social conscience pukes at the disparity!"

"Well said, Citizenness!"

"Poor Violet was panic-stricken at my refusal! 'Take no notice!' she exclaimed in terror. And imagining her entire social life at stake, she pleaded, 'My sister speaks only for herself – she gets like this at home, after reading the *Leeds' Mercury* to a crowd of whiskery old bores!' Fortunately, Mrs Moxham indulges us to ruination!"

She thought of Bob's last words – light-hearted, but barbed – about having a foot in both camps. She'd give him defection! Her spirits rose, as they always did when a good idea presented itself. She paused for a moment. "Arthur? Between yourself and Mortimer Moxham I want to spend my last three days in London seeing places, and people, likely to be of interest to the Manchester Rads."

"That will give me immense pleasure." An annihilating flash commemorating Borodino lit up the sky. "But there is a price for my services."

"A price!" She had recovered her nerve now. Was it, she wondered, because there were only three days left? Three days, and they could go home . . .

"One kiss . . ." he stopped by the shrubbery. "Surely a word with Major Cartwright . . . a glimpse of Sir Francis Burdett, the darling of Reform . . . is worth a kiss?" He gathered her into a hard embrace.

And on the last night, having attended a farewell gathering at the Moxhams', which spilled over onto the terrace and gardens, he waited impatiently until she was free of Neddy, Teddy, Algy, Penelope and other muslin-clad young women with whom she and Violet had become acquainted in the last three weeks.

"We are surrounded, darling Citizeness." His dark intense gaze held hers. "And I may only kiss your hand . . ." Her glance shifted to the elm tree, remembering the ethereal quality of that special night, and she was thankful for those who thronged the garden. His tone changed to speak quickly and seriously about Sidmouth's spy system, and begged her be careful and cautious.

"Oh, you do exaggerate, Arthur, there's nothing about me that could possibly interest their Lordships. It's you, who ought to be more circumspect."

"Well," he said expansively. "We must all be on our guard. I could," he lowered his voice, "be in danger of falling in love with a certain red-haired Citizeness."

She shook her head and pulled the ivory tasselled shawl about her shoulders. "These are words spoken in the safety of parting."

"Ah," he placed a hand on his heart in an extravagant gesture. "You will never know the truth of the matter unless you come to London more often. And, my dear Jancie . . ." he bowed over her hand to whisper, "never forget that it was with me you danced on the lawn to the melody of moonbeams and in the magic of moonlight." His dark head lifted and he was gone.

She watched him out of sight and hurried into the house for a moment of reflection. The drawing-room door was open; she peered inside. Charles, Violet and Mirabelle were standing about the fireplace. The atmosphere strained and silent. "What's happened?" she asked.

Violet lifted troubled eyes. "I've been presumptuous enough to ask Mirabelle if I can stay here . . ."

"Stay here?" Jancie frowned. "You mean another few weeks?"

"I mean . . . for ever," came the quiet reply.

"For ever?" echoed Jancie. "But that's impossible . . . isn't it Charles? It has to be. She's my sister – we can't live without her."

"Please, Jancie. Don't make it more difficult for me. Mirabelle has graciously agreed, and Charles has my happiness at heart. Do say you don't mind?"

"But I do mind. Of course I mind!" Jancie heard her father's voice coming over the years. "Stick hold of yer sister's hand," he had said.

"Charles, how can you agree to this?"

"How can I not? If Violet's heart is set on staying, she'll not settle at the Manufactory – and I couldn't bear to see either of my girls unhappy, or stand in their way of making more of themselves. Besides, she's with Mirabelle, and it will be an incentive for us to come more often."

"But what," Jancie asked her sister lamely, "what of Aberdaron Dick?"

"What of him?" Violet replied.

Chapter 10

The return journey to Manchester was more doleful than the parting with Violet; it was beset by thoughts, memories, and imaginings of what might have been. The last night shared by the sisters was a silent one. Violet had wanted to talk, to chatter on and try to make her sister understand how exciting and unpredictable life in London was; how delicate and refined this life with Mirabelle and Mortimer. Companions, people of her own age, were in abundance. Oh, couldn't Jancie see how impossible it was to swap St James's and the Moxhams for Shude Hill and Mrs Hallam! But, realising her sister would never understand, she curled up and went to sleep.

Jancie could have borne the parting better if Violet's bright eyes had been just the least bit tearful; if her ringlets had not shaken so jauntily with the turn of her head; her lips more ready to crumple in tears than in a farewell smile. Violet had no thought of pretence or artifice. How could she be so ungrateful, unthinking of their guardian?

Charles had thought it best to say goodbye in the drawing-room.

"*Au revoir,*" Mirabelle had corrected, her arms about her cousin. "Surely, only *au revoir.* Violet is my guarantee of seeing you again . . ." She held her away and regarded the thin face tenderly. "And you are not to worry about your ward, Charles. Mortimer and I will care for her as if she were our own. We cannot thank you enough for the loan of so precious an object."

Jancie stared miserably out of the coach window, thinking how different their last journey was. The Coburg had practically jingled with anticipation; every moment had been charged with pleasure, and every new sight with surprise. Their fellow travellers on this occasion were three elderly men, who assuming there to be sorrow in the women's lives took refuge in silence.

"Oh, Charles!" Jancie turned helplessly to her guardian, and above the noise of travel gave vent to the latest wave of misery. "Did you hear what Violet said about Aberdaron Dick? I could scarce believe it! she was always so fond of him. Oh, how could she?"

"It's her way of letting us know, my dear, that she's breaking completely with the past. I, too, am grieved, Jancie; cut to the heart, if I'm to admit it. I've grown very fond of you both."

"I won't leave you, Charles. I'll never go away. Never. Never!"

"Sshh . . ." Each wanted to comfort, to reassure, but no words came.

And yet the misery was not total. The full sum of it was waiting at the first overnight stop. The sense of loneliness in the empty room Jancie should have shared with her sister was overwhelming. She stood for a few moments as the door closed, clinging to the sound of the servant's footsteps receding along the passage. The silence was awful. It reminded her of Trafalgar Night. The stillness of Jepson's factory, with no candle, no lamp. Alone for the first time with scurrying rats and the slinking shadow of a predatory cat. Her heart beat uncomfortably against her ribs. The gaunt, spectral outline of the bed took on the appearance of St Mary's graveyard at night. Thoughts of hell and hauntings crowded in. Grabbing her overnight valise she ran along the passage. "Charles! Charles!"

"Whatever's the matter?" The door swung open quickly.

"Oh, Charles," she burst out. "I cannot stay in that

room by myself . . . I've never slept alone before . . .
I'll be all right when we're back at Shude Hill. But
I'd never sleep – not alone in a strange place. I can't!
I can't!"

"Sshh . . . you don't have to – there's no need. Come
along inside . . . oh, you poor dear." Charles knew about
silence and loneliness, and about being suddenly bereft.

"I'll not disturb you," said Jancie, seeing that her
guardian was already in her nightgown. "I'll sleep on
the chair – or the floor."

"As if I'd let you! What's the matter with the bed?" She
resumed the combing of her hair, patting it into shape. "I
know I'm not Violet, but perhaps I'll do until, as you say,
we are back on familiar ground. There's some water left
for washing – here take the candle. And before you come
to bed open the window."

As Jancie began brushing her hair, Charles wondered
what Violet was doing, if she was yet asleep between the
silken sheets at the Moxhams' house or still being whirled
round the ballroom by Neddy – or was it George? She
wondered how they would manage without her; the three
of them had been together . . . what was it, ten years?
While being aware that her girls would leave her some
time, this first parting had come as a shock. How long
will it be, she thought, before Jancie leaves, too?

The room was pitched into darkness as Jancie opened
the window, and blowing the candle out, felt her way to
the bed, turning at once into the protective arms of her
guardian. They lay gripped together, motionless, cheek
against cheek, bosom against bosom, in an anguish of
sorrow. The warmth of their bodies released the fragrance
of lavender from Charles's nightgown. Inhaling it Jancie
sighed softly and remembered that Violet had loved
the fragrance too. "You won't go away, Charles?" she
murmured. "I mean – you won't get up first and go out
or anything?"

"Of course I won't, darling."

"I'd hate to wake and find you gone, and an empty space beside me."

"Oh, you are an imaginative girl," she said comfortingly.

"There won't be an empty space, I promise . . . now, go to sleep. You're here with me, and all's well . . ."

The arms about Charles's neck slackened. Jancie's breathing became soft and rythmic, and Charles's heart was flooded with a strange happiness. "You're here with me," she repeated softly. "And all's well . . ."

She felt a great sense of gratitude for the chance to have brought these splendid girls up. That Jancie had needed her, had come to her when frightened, like little children do. No one had ever needed Charles Etherington before. I'm becoming maudlin now, she thought, over-sentimental, because Violet has stayed in London.

All the same, this brave and talented young woman, with her impulsive ways and immense affection, made her feel . . . more tender and protective than before.

By the time they arrived in Manchester, the worst was over. After all, Violet was not at the other side of the world, and they could visit Mirabelle at any time. Violet might even, they thought in a good moment, come to visit them!

The Swan yard had never looked so good, so welcoming, so familiar. It was the afternoon of a hot, sultry day, and the curdled sky, a mixture of yellow sun and black factory smoke, resembled a custard that had gone wrong. Jancie would not have exchanged it for all the blue skies above St James's. She looked around half-expecting to see Jem. A surge of disappointment went through her. She had hoped on the journey home to have had time to sort things out in her mind, to see, or gauge, her attitude to the brief encounter with Arthur Thistlewood, and to what had happened to her in the past three weeks. Because, undoubtedly, she was different. But Violet's defection

79

had coloured all the journey home, and to have seen Jem's sturdy, solid figure would have gone a long way to putting things in their right perspective.

Above the bustle of arrival, the scuttling of ostlers and exchange of horses, she heard their fellow travellers bidding Charles farewell. And there was Aberdaron Dick with his scarecrow clothes, and that odd loping walk!

She rushed forward to greet him, and seeing his anxious look at the absence of her sister, explained it all brightly, saying that Violet was staying on a little longer; and how Violet wished to be remembered to him. She knew that would please him, and it did.

Cocks were crowing half-heartedly in the heat and she wondered how Jem's cockerels were coming on. And from a distance she saw the red and white barber's pole indicating Bob Smollett's shop . . . yes, she wanted to talk to him about other things than Reform – although that figured high on the list – she wanted to discuss the dressing of her hair. Not so much dressing it, as colouring it. Mirabelle had suggested that a more becoming colour could be obtained by an application of henna powder. "Auburn," she had said, "shines up like burnished copper. Very fashionable. Try it, my dear."

Before they rounded the corner to Shude Hill, Jancie gave her guardian's arm a squeeze. "I shall leave you to explain about Violet to Mrs Hallam," she said mischievously.

"I thought you would!"

"She'll clomp about all day, and fix you with her 'I told you so' look!"

Both women, despite the camaraderie, pondered on what life without Violet would be like, now they were home. Would there be delayed reaction; little awkwardnesses – or big ones; unspoken recriminations; possessiveness; over-protection? Would there be the same cheerful, bantering atmosphere? Violet would be missed without a doubt, in more ways than one. When she had been there things just happened. There had been no pattern to their time when the Manufactory closed for the night, but now, ward and guardian, with no Violet in between, wondered how it would all work out.

Having first paid her respects to Mrs Hallam, Jancie hurried anxiously upstairs to the room she had shared with her sister. She turned the doorknob slowly, and pushing open the door, stepped inside. The large bedroom, with its white plaster walls and heavy beams, was warm with summer's heat, rich with memories, and fragrant with the scent of lavender. The polished floor-boards creaked a welcome; and the summer curtains, caught between the draught from the door and the open window, fluttered an acknowledgement.

There, everything is fine, she thought, and added, quite untruthfully, I knew it would be! She slipped off her shoes, wiped the sweat off her forehead, and padded about the room, eyeing the furniture with appreciation, touching the dressing-table, the chest of drawers, pausing by the desk – and a novel of Violet's to be returned to Miss Bohanna's circulating library. Yes, she concluded her little survey, all was well.

Suddenly stifled with the heat, she padded down the stairs and pushed her head into the office. "Charles? It's far too hot to do anything constructive – let's go and bathe?"

Her guardian, flowery waistcoat discarded, was sitting at the French writing table, face flushed, cuffs turned to the elbow. "I had the same idea, but we'll have to wait until this evening. Women's hours are six to eight today."

"Oh, I'll have melted by then! I can't wait that long."

"There's no alternative – except the river. And the Irwell at this time of year . . . well, you don't need me to elaborate on that!"

81

"How about the pump in the yard?"

"You wouldn't?" Charles's lips curved, one eyebrow rose. "Mrs Hallam will have a seizure!" And as the idea took hold, added: "Not in your bathing dress? You wouldn't stand in the yard in your bathing dress?"

"My muslin. I shall wear the cream muslin which Mirabelle bought for me. Come on," she cajoled. "Come and join me?"

"Now that, Mrs Hallam would never survive!"

"Be a darling and work the pump for me then? I'm just going to change."

"Miss Etherington," declared the housekeeper a few moments later. "Whatever is Jancie up to?"

"Cooling off, Mrs Hallam. She needs refreshing after the tedious journey, and with the catching up we have to do in the office it isn't at all a bad idea."

"Well, I never," Mrs Hallam murmured, as her employer, positively skittish, she thought, hurried through the kitchen and out into the heat of the yard.

The housekeeper clomped to the door, hearing shrieks of laughter, as Charles pumped fierce gushes of water over the muslin-clad figure, occasionally letting out a dignified yell of surprise when splashes backfired. Jancie stretched out her arms.

"Oh, it's lovely, Charles. Reminds me of Jepson's."

"Thank you," came the smart reply, accompanied by as smart a pull on the pump handle. "Thank you for the comparative compliment!"

"I'm rinsing the smell of London off my skin, out of my hair."

"And Arthur Thistlewood?" The probing was gentle. "Are you rinsing him away, too?"

"Shall we say I caught a touch of Waterloo Fever – don't worry." Jancie flashed her mischievous smile. "There's no danger of me eloping – not while I'm cross-breeding Jem's cockerels!"

"Thank God, then, for Jem," was the dry response.

"Oh, come under," urged Jancie. "It's so exhilarating. You'd love it. Just like the shower bath only fiercer! Come under, while I operate the pump. Go on, the workers aren't here. No one'll see you. And we'll get through the evening's work a lot quicker."

"This is madness," laughed Charles, who, through heaving on the pump handle was now hotter than ever. She recalled Mirabelle's comment over their first taking of tea. "Swimming, Charles, at your age?" That did it. Not even bothering to change her skirts and white ruffled shirt, she kicked off her shoes. "Right," she laughed. "Quick, before I change me mind!"

The yard was filled with laughter as Charles, who always gasped on contact with cold water, inched herself, little by little, under the pump.

"Brr. Don't know about refreshing, it's damn cold!"

"Cold? Good heavens, three weeks in London has softened your constitution – ouch!" It was her turn to yell at a well-aimed splash. "Charles! I'll get you for that!"

They splashed and laughed together, their old familiar water-antic laugh, a mutual, intimate laugh. The resumption of normality was complete. This first strand of her life had been picked up, and any residual awkwardness over Violet gushed away, to trickle into the gutter.

Leaving the pump, Jancie combed her wet hair with her fingers, pushing it to the nape of her neck and screwing her eyes up against the curdling sun.

"What are you thinking?" asked Charles.

Jancie stepped forward and put a hand out to touch the sleek dove grey head. "I think everything's going to be all right," she said simply.

After the first surprise of Violet's staying in London, all their acquaintances regarded it as an obvious outcome. Charles and Jancie had by tacit agreement shelved any deep discussion about Violet. They talked over supper at the Seven Stars of immediate things; of how trade could buck up now the war was over; of materials to be stocked; of orders which had not been delivered; of travellers who had made appointments; of arrangements. "Will you trust me," said Jancie, carving herself a lump of Cheshire cheese, "to find someone to take over Violet's duties?"

"Of course, I've every confidence in your ability, you know that. And the theatre. You will look to Etherington's? According to Clogger there are a few gaps in the bill which need to be discussed."

Jancie was awake before dawn the next day. She had slept well, and was impatient for the light. Hurry, hurry, she thought, the cocks are already crowing, there's work to be done and Jem to see. He would know she was back and would be expecting her at the pens, for birds were at their best first thing. He never came to the Manufactory, for in Miss Etherington's company he felt clumsy and tongue-tied. Besides, it suited her, suited Jancie and himself, to meet before their respective premises opened. They had talked of birds and trade, but now they would talk of being sweethearts. The trouble with being sweethearts was that an engagement usually followed, and eventually marriage. And Jancie was not ready for marriage. It had not been easy, in Jem's strong arms, and under the emotional impact of parting, to argue with his theory of giving love a chance by becoming his sweetheart. London had broadened her outlook – and Arthur Thistlewood's brand of passion had certainly opened her eyes. But she and Jem were friends, they had grown up together. They had many things in common – and, surely, that counted for a lot.

She always joined Charles for breakfast at the Seven Stars at eight o'clock, but these two hours were for her and Jem. The morning was fairly sweet, for as yet the chimneys were not putting out much smoke, and the sun

84

looked a lovely buttercup yellow. Few people were afoot, and even Aberdaron Dick was obviously elsewhere. As she turned into Half Street the sight of St Mary's church reminded her that Parson Brookes, too, would be waiting to hear about London.

"Jem!" she opened the yard gate, but he hadn't heard above the crowings and cawings, the chuckles and cackles. His back was turned, and the shirt bloodstained.

"Jem?" she repeated, running forward and turning him to face her. "What happened to your back?"

"Jancie! Eh, little Jancie!" His eyes, as deep and tawny as an owl, lit up in pleased surprise.

"Your back, oh, your dear back! You've been flogged, Jem. Why? What happened? Oh, Jem, you poor, poor lad!" She went into his open arms, placing her own about his neck. "Is it still sore?"

He nodded. "Mrs Clowes," he always gave his step-mother her title, "keeps rubbing salt in. Very healing is salt, she says, but the pulling and stretching of that bloody boiled sugar opens 'em up again!"

"Was it Constable Nadin?"

"Who else, in this town?"

"What for? Honestly, Jem, I've got to drag everything out of you – for goodness sake, explain!"

"Well . . ." he smiled sheepishly, aware of her scrutiny through the spectacles. "There was another bread riot and I opened me big mouth too wide. The constables were there in no time. Smollett says they were waiting in a house round the corner, and that the riot had been organised, so they could make an example of trouble makers. Me, a trouble maker, Jancie! Disturbance of the peace, the magistrate said, and ordered five strokes – but the worst was, to be flogged in public, at the tail-end of a bloody cart!"

He indicated the house. "And she's still going on about it. Reckons it'll ruin trade, that Nadin'll have it in for me now. That I'm a marked man!"

"We'll have to prove her wrong, Jem. She's every right to be worried. People have been transported for as much, and without you she couldn't run the business. Anyway, I've returned now to keep an eye on you." She touched his strong, sinewy neck. "I've only to turn me back," she teased, "and you're in trouble."

"Seein' that you belong to the Female Reformers, and that we're sweethearting, like, I thought I'd better get some practice."

"Oh, Jem, you don't have to at all! It's a matter of us all doing what we know best, and what we feel to be right. You know about birds and sugar baking. I know about Reform, what to say and how to say it, how to be circumspect so that Nadin can't lay a finger on me. Just because I do what I do, Jem, doesn't mean that I'd expect you to fall in with me."

"I'm glad you said that," he squared his shoulders, and grimaced.

"Dear, dear Jem." She kissed him lightly, and turned her attention to the cockerels. "How's progress?"

"I was going to ask you about your progress in London."

"We can talk about that any time – Etherington's tonight? I've got to see Clogger about artistes, and besides, I've missed the place."

"Did you miss me, though?"

"Of course I did."

He put his head to one side, in the manner of the birds he bred, contemplating her with his bright eyes.

Chapter 11

Miss Etherington was never far wrong in a propounded surmise, but she was the first to admit that her hopes of trade bucking up were in vain. The peace which followed Waterloo instead of bringing plenty, brought more distress. In the new year of 1816 the army and navy off-loaded half a million men onto an already depressed labour market. Steel and iron works, gunsmiths, food contractors and cloth mills all suffered from the coming of peace. The only good thing about it was the abolition of the five per cent income tax.

Most people in Manchester agreed that an unreformed, unrepresentative parliament was at the root of the country's troubles, and Radical agitation, which had been simmering for as long as Jancie could remember, was now beginning to bubble.

She forgave Bob Smollett his uncalled for remarks only if he would agree to the colouring of her hair, which he did, on the understanding that she would continue her weekly readings of Cobbett and the *Leeds' Mercury* for his customers. At which they both laughingly accused each other of driving a hard bargain.

It was a hard bargain so far as Jancie was concerned, for time was in short supply, but she realised the opportunity was not to be missed.

The barber's shop, by tradition, was an all-male preserve to which she had been given regular access as a child; she had been accepted as part of the shop fittings, and wanted to keep it that way. Firstly, because the discussion and comment were a useful gauge to male opinion. Secondly, if she was going to be of any use to the Rads, it was the men she had to impress; and thirdly, she had to prove her credibility by overcoming the accusation of having a foot in both camps – both her feet were firmly in the Radical camp, and it must be proved without a doubt.

The readings were illustrated by graphic descriptions of political personalities in London. How Mortimer took her on a tour of the House of Commons; of listening to Major Cartwright, one of their champions in Westminster, giving a speech; of how she was but a cock stride from the two most unpopular men in England, Lord Castlereagh and Viscount Sidmouth, as they strolled arm in arm down St James's. The men cheered to hear she had actually spoken to Sir Francis Burdett, the darling of Reform, and heard from his own lips an utter condemnation of Sidmouth and Castlereagh's spy system – they might not, she thought, have been so impressed if they knew of his foppish habit of being rouged and wearing a lace cravat and cuffs. It was not until the discourse ended that Jancie realised there was one name she had not mentioned – that of Arthur Thistlewood.

As for the colouring of her hair, that, too, was to be conducted in a conspiratorial manner. Bob insisted she enter the back way, after hours.

"You're afraid of what your customers will say, aren't you?" she teased, as he took her cloak.

"Well, my clientele are not renowned for artistic appreciation, as you well know! Best we keep the arrangement to ourselves, or I'll never live it down!"

Two hours and a cup of coffee later, he stood behind her chair, surveying his handiwork in the mirror, and nodding approval. How handsome a lass she is, he thought. Like one of those heroic girls in romantic pictures. And those green eyes, so bright with sincerity, peering through silver filigree spectacles with a slightly anxious manner, as though apprehensive of missing something – not that she ever did! He had swept the long thick hair back from her brow and into a knot on top of her head, finally securing it with a decorative pin. The colour gleamed, rich and shining in the lamplight . . . different, it was. Trust her to come across something different! He thought of the kimono, the fan, and the little black pumps . . .

"Yes," he said eventually. "I like it. Auburn, you say? It's certainly striking. Your complexion needed a slightly darker frame."

"More definitive?"

"My words exactly!"

"Liar!" They laughed together as she stood up and shook the creases out of her skirts. She had enjoyed his attention, the almost sensual experience of having her hair lathered by strange, strong hands, masculine hands. Thick fingers, slippery with soap moving about her ears, her neck, with a rhythmic, practised precision.

Then as he draped the cloak over her shoulders there came an unexpected awkwardness as whether to kiss him, as she always had, on the side of his face. As they stood looking at each other, it was clear the same thought had passed through both their minds. His round, brown eyes were deeply intent. She fiddled with the clasp of the cloak, using it to break her gaze, to think upon the setting of precedents. There was an intimacy about the henna operation which she had not anticipated; and Mirabelle said it would need renewing several times a year . . . In thinking of a kiss, she remembered Arthur, and remembering Arthur . . . She lifted her hand, touched Bob's cheek, and was gone.

She walked quickly through the darkened streets, glad of the watchman on his rounds, cheered by the light of his lantern. Once on Shude Hill, the windows of the inns and taverns were bright, and people were thronging in to suppers. She and Charles had already dined, so she let

89

herself into the Manufactory, and hurried upstairs to the sitting-room.

Over the past year a routine between ward and guardian had somehow been established. How it got there, neither was quite sure. In the first place, it had to do with a traveller, who, expecting Charles to be male had presented her with a box of small cigars. To his amazement, she accepted with no show of surprise and assured him they would be appreciated. The cigars were smoked in the evening, either as they discussed the day's affairs, or, being of a competitive nature, as they pitted their wits in a game of cards, This was accompanied by a glass or two of canary wine for Charles, and, as Jancie preferred the sharp edge of ale to wine, a pewter of the Seven Stars best was brought over by the pot boy at nine o'clock every night.

This preference had been a source of argument between the sisters; for Violet, at sixteen, developed a liking for Charles's canary wine, and accused Jancie of not cultivating a more sophisticated taste in order to impress rank and file Radicals. It wasn't for the want of trying; in London she had endured Mirabelle's table wines; red and white, mulled and spiced; she had spluttered into brandy, choked on rum, and suffered frequent headaches as a consequence.

She paused outside the door of the sitting-room, and having put both hands up to be sure her hair was still in place, made an exaggerated entrance. Charles looked up from a game of Patience, seeking the cause of exuberance. "Oh, your hair!" she exclaimed. "You've had it done, at last!"

"I went out like a carrot, and have returned with a head of burnished copper! Tell me," she swung round, showing off the back. "What difference does it make to my looks?"

"Oh, the vanity of the young!"

"Not so much vanity, Charles. I want to look older, more mature and responsible – and nice."

"Why this obsession with maturity? Time will come when you'll want to knock a few years off!"

"I'll cross that bridge when I come to it . . ." Jancie, having first reached to the sideboard for the pewter, sat down opposite her guardian, took a drink, and leaned forward, elbows on the table, chin in hands. Then, with a flick of a finger, she pushed the spectacles higher on her nose, bringing the distinctive features into focus.

"Oh, dear," laughed Charles, gathering the cards together swiftly, her rings sparkling in the light of the candelabra. "The game wasn't working out, anyway – and I'm sure whatever you have to say will be far more interesting."

"Oh, it will Charles, it will. You know how Clogger's been having trouble this past year with artistes letting us down at the last moment? Well, I came across the tattered kimono the other day – fallen to the back of the linen cupboard – and it presented me with two marvellous ideas. Firstly, to extend and polish the Japanese Dancing Act, so that I can fill a gap at short notice. Clogger has only to send little Sampson round – that is if I'm not already in the theatre. The Japanese Dancing went down well, when Capper's Circus brought it to town – and it wasn't so bad either, when I used to dance in Tinker's Tea Gardens. I could carry it off, Charles, I really could. What d'you think?"

"What a marvellous idea! You'll make Clogger a happy man, darling, for he's the one who takes the catcalls, and dodges anything the audience cares to throw on those occasions." Having leaned forward, she now leaned back in her chair, and sipped the canary wine. "But, what would you use for an outfit?"

"Reconstruct my old kimono. Take a pattern off it."

Charles nodded approval, then prompted. "And secondly?"

"I think . . . only think, mark you, that the kimono could add yet another line to Etherington's Enterprises."

"In what way?"

"As boudoir wear. I know trade is in a depression of sorts. But there's money about. Look at the number of cotton mills going up and investment in new industries, if you need proof. The well-to-do are still living in style, hence our trade in parasols. Sales have never been higher. People will pay for a diversion, for something different, and if I wear a different kimono every time I do a turn, news will soon get about. Women will love to wear them as wrappers, dressing gowns – as I said, boudoir wear."

"What about the design?"

"Look at these . . ." she jumped up from the table, and bringing a sketch-pad from the window-seat, laid it briskly on the table. "There. Just imagine these in bold colours; lustrous colours; gleaming silvers; scarlets and golds; and broad black sashes – so narrowing to the waist!"

"This is very exciting," said Charles. "I must admit, looking back, that it was partly the romance of your faded kimono that went straight to my heart, when you and . . . Violet, stood looking up at me from the step . . ."

"Yes, I'll warrant Violet would write more often if she knew we had something exciting afoot! I heard all about kimonos from the old sailor we called the Admiral. He had been to Japan and told me about the colours and the stories behind the designs; how some kimonos were quilted – which means we could have a winter range! There's no end to the possibilities!"

"Accessories – in matching material. Slippers. Covers for stools!"

"And we'll need to take people on. More outdoor workers. We'll be putting labour in the way of fabric printers!"

"We must buy our silks and satins at the lowest possible price! My goodness, it's all quite breath taking!"

"I'll spend a few days in Cheshire – price up silks at Macclesfield and Congleton – see what the Rads are up to, while I'm at it. There's another thing, Charles, I need to look older, if I'm to get anywhere in Reform—"

"But, why d'you need to get anywhere, dear heart? Thousands of people settle for supporting Radical interest. I do myself."

"That's all very well, but someone has to do something, and that someone is me . . ." She took a hefty draught from the pewter and continued, "You know Margery – Jem's cousin?"

"That nice young woman who's sweet on him?"

"Margery? Sweet on Jem?"

"I see you didn't know. Still, the paths of life," she said quietly, "are littered with the remnants of unrequited love."

"Oh, dear . . . anyway," Jancie toyed with the handle of the pewter. "How do you know all this? Did Mrs Clowes tell you?"

Charles nodded.

"Now," began Jancie, her voice all alacrity. "Margery – the very one," she smiled, "who's sweet on Jem, is one of the Female Reformers. And as part of a countrywide movement to consolidate Reform, we have to get ourselves into properly organised clubs or societies, with the usual offices to be filled, you know, secretary, treasurer and president." Charles nodded and sipped her wine. "Margery put my name forward for president, and there was opposition on the grounds that I lacked maturity! What has age got to do with it? Have any of the others spoken to Sir Francis Burdett? Set eyes on the House of Commons? Been farmed out from Strangeways to the factory system? And come to that, how many can sign or even read their own name? And they hold lack of maturity against me!"

Jancie's ideas had not stopped at the Japanese Dancing Act or the manufacture of boudoir wear. "You see," she said to Jem, the following morning, after he had expressed delight with her darker shade of hair, "this improvement of colour got me round to thinking that it wouldn't be without the realms of possibility, for us to breed a fighting cock with the most glorious scarlet feathers you've ever seen."

He scratched his forest brown hair. "Why would you want to do that?"

"Scarlet is the Radical colour?"

"Yes."

"So . . . we breed a bird, Jem, which will appeal to the Radical fancy. It will be an encouragement, a fillip. And if we can breed fierce, really fierce qualities into the strain – a good, clear, clarion call for example – we could have a champion and make your fortune!"

"*Our* fortune," he amended, lifting her chin, forcing her to look up. "And we've not had our morning kiss, yet!" He gathered her into his hard embrace, to which she went willingly. There was no awkwardness, no reason to hesitate. Being with Jem was a pleasurable rather than an exciting experience – and she'd had enough excitement with Arthur Thistlewood. Perhaps it was the workhouse background which tied them, or learning with Parson Brookes, or just growing up on the same streets; whatever it was that bound them Jancie found it very reassuring and satisfying.

"*Your* fortune," she emphasised, returning to the subject. "This will be your enterprise, not one of Etherington's."

As Jem held her in his arms, her head on his chest, he recalled his dream. In it, he summoned up enough courage to ask her to marry him. 'Yes, Oh, yes, Jem!' she had answered. 'You will leave Miss Etherington!' he had persisted, scarce able to believe his luck. 'To come and live with me?' But even as he asked, the dream began to fade. Best, not to rush things, he thought, looking down onto her copper head. I can't bear to think of life without her.

Chapter 12

Jancie, returning from an early morning meeting with Jem, lingered on Blackfriars Bridge, stopped to lean her elbows on the balustrade, watching the dawn swirling in on a cloak of river mist. In this year of 1817, she had come of age, and although Violet could not attend the celebrations, she had sent a long and loving letter, which almost made up for her absence.

Charles had presented her with what she had always fancied and never thought to own – a smart, two-wheeled van; black-lacquered, small, lightweight; and a fine black horse to pull it, called Morocco. Having become proficient in the handling of it under the guiding hand of Mr Hallam, she already enjoyed sitting on the box and urging Morocco out of town to collect or carry goods. And with the boudoir wear having taken off grandly, her own transport was a boon. The only disappointing aspect of the kimono success was that it left no time for her and Charles to visit Mirabelle. The more pleasurable aspect was the coining of a pet name for Jancie, that of Charles's 'Geisha Girl'.

Jancie had also achieved her goal of becoming President of the Female Reformers, because, although not lacking courage, most women, for family reasons, were scared of the new laws pushed through by Lord Sidmouth making it illegal to hold a public meeting of more than half a dozen people without permission of the magistrates. Habeas Corpus had also been suspended, which meant anyone could be in prison without trial for an unlimited time. Leaders of organisations were now the target of government spies and *agents provocateurs* – so, suddenly, Jancie discovered her lack of maturity was now no bar to the office she gratefully accepted.

She and Margery had got to know each other better and through this knowledge a deeper friendship evolved. Jancie's curiosity had been aroused when Charles had mentioned her being 'sweet' on Jem; and Margery's supportive interest in Jancie's presidential aspirations had consolidated the friendship – but not to the extent that Margery admitted her passion for Jem, or that Jancie admitted her knowledge of it. Their friendship was further advanced by Margery's father – a cousin of Mrs Clowes and a brush maker by trade – allowing the Female Reform meetings to be held secretly above his premises.

But the bond which really drew them together was their interest in Jem. Margery, a self-effacing young woman, with blue eyes, fluffy, flaxen hair, and given to wearing gingham, had been admitted to Jem's company, and for that she was immensely grateful.

Here, she could clean out pens, and worship Jem in safety and security. Just to be near him filled her with pleasure. Not that she was jealous of Jancie, for in the mysteries of this relationship Jancie was necessary to Jem's happiness and revered as such. She and Jancie could tease him, indulge him, and humour him when anything went wrong at the pens.

As for Jancie, she had not, at first, thought it at all strange to make a friend of a potential rival for Jem's affections. But, as time went on, Margery had, without knowing it, made her gradually aware of the difference between loving someone . . . and being in love.

At twenty-one, Jancie reflected, looking down on the broad sweep of the river, you no longer needed permission to marry. She had taken refuge somehow in the knowledge that her guardian would have given no such permission. But, as soon as this new bird was launched,

Jem would broach the subject of marriage, which was lingering beneath the surface of their relationship, and she could no longer hide behind Charles's permission.

Marriage seemed so final . . . yet most women of her age, with the exception of Margery, were already married. What irked her about the whole marriage question, was being harnessed together like a pair of carriage horses; forever holding claims over each other and generally getting in each others way. From what she had observed, most of the men, after a while, lamented their loss of liberty; and women discovered they had exchanged one lot of restrictions for another . . .

But, just now, she and Jem were anxious that the new breed should be ready for the Fancying season which started in May. Jem had done well, especially in the magnificent scarlet feathering. In fact, all that was needed for champion status was to increase its fierceness – and that was why she was out so early.

Miss Bohanna, from the travelling library, knowing of Jancie's interest in birds, had come across Markham's book on the subject, which stated that a fighting bird fed on Markham's Mash was guaranteed to beat all comers. One of the ingredients of this magical mash was to be found in freshly procured, early morning urine. Jem had experimented, using his own and that of several other suppliers. But apparently hers – due, she reckoned, to the Seven Stars ale – had the best results. So, here she was, destined until May Day, to get up before dawn and hurry over to Half Street to use his mother's chamber-pot!

"Really, Jancie," her guardian had remarked. "Don't you think that's going a bit too far, even for political principles?"

She smiled at the recollection; apart from the mash it was worth turning out so early to converse with Aberdaron Dick, before he disappeared on his various jobs, and just to stand here on the bridge and watch the town wake up.

97

Raising her head, she followed the line of the river bank to where the derelict quayside warehouse, weakened and rotted with worms and damp, had finally sunk into the river and was now being redeveloped as a cotton mill; she wondered what had happened to the Admiral and the rest of the community.

There was always, while standing on this bridge, a feeling of affinity with her surroundings, for the growth and progress of the town had in a way marked her own. The country lanes where she and Violet had picked wayside blackberries were now highways bustling with traffic; and the road makers, as though, having started could not bear to stop, were still in progress of widening streets. Great spinning-sheds were visible on every approach to the town; and jerry-builders were throwing together shops, houses, and factories. Mills seemed to be the thing, cropping up like mushrooms on a dungheap. Three and four storeys, higher and higher they grew, employing four hundred hands, then seven hundred, until Murray's monster mill enclosed over a thousand – working fourteen hours a day, for two pence an hour. And glad to, for there were thousands more just waiting for the opportunity.

The majestic cloak of river mist was now lifting, like the curtains on a stage, to reveal a rosy blush of crimson, making a glorious backdrop for the soaring chimneys. It was a brief appearance; the curtain fell, and the crowing of cocks was overtaken by a different sound; more urgent, more clamorous. Claxons and factory hooters vied with each other. Strident, insistent. Come on, come on, they urged, wake up, wake up! At once, at once!

Later that day, after tea, Jancie and Charles, while driving to the bleach works, laughed uproariously at the sight of the London coach, the prestigious Flyer held up on its way into town by, of all things, a donkey cart – and a small one at that.

Pitt Caxton, glancing out of the coach window, did not share their amusement – neither did the driver. If anything aroused the ire of a fast driver it was to be thwarted of a dashing arrival. The guard blew impatiently on the horn. But, instead of scattering people, they all rushed to see what was amiss. Aproned shopkeepers shouted advice from their doorways; traders with trays attempted to entice the donkey out of the way, and lads with baskets, tiered like the tower of Babel on their heads, swore at the obstruction.

Pitt Caxton's grey eyes widened, eyebrows shooting almost to his hairline at such ineptitude. Coaches had right of way at all times, but not here it seemed. Was this a sample, he wondered, of a bumbling community? What a fitting end to so boring a journey. He sighed. Unless you had an interesting companion, travelling was tedious to say the least. He thought of his fiancée, Selina, the reason for his coming to Manchester. He wanted to be successful, to make money. Oh, she never tired of pointing out they could live off her money, but he wanted to be his own man, to bring an equal share to the marriage. While travelling, he had found himself wondering how long it would take to earn sufficient money. And having made it, would Selina be happy to live in the north? For that matter, would he? The journey might not have been so tedious if he could have ridden on top; the better view added interest, the air was keen, and there was always the thrill of uncertainty, of being unseated as the coach rounded corners, or careered down a hill, jolting and bucking as though the horses had gone wild. Indeed, he had booked a seat on top, but the other passengers who joined at Derby were delegates returning from a Reform meeting – reliving it all at the top of their voices! The same old theme of hardship, Corn Laws and Parliamentary Representation. And the same old names of Cobbett, Cartwright, and Hunt – Sidmouth and Castlereagh came in for a right rollicking! It had been enough to drive him inside – not that there was much improvement, for those inside were manufacturers, and talked of nothing but wages, overheads, militants and trade! And when you looked out of the window there were chimneys stacked to the skyline!

"Manchester's the chimney of the world," he'd been warned. "But," he had defended his decision to rejoin the family firm of lawyers. "Where there's muck, there's money – brass, as they say up there."

While being held up by the donkey cart, and indeed, before. Pitt Caxton's fellow travellers had given up directing conversation toward him, beyond the time of day. He knew his manner was not encouraging. He had several manners to suit different occasions, but on the whole he had little patience for small talk; he did not suffer fools gladly, and was intolerant of those who did.

The town didn't seem all that bad, he thought. The old parish church looked interestingly ancient . . . there were banks and business houses – yes, the streets had a brisk and lively look. He shifted his position, hunching himself, impatient of the hold up. So, this is where the family firm of lawyers had started – the chambers were in Marsden Square, and he wouldn't know where that was until the morrow . . . Ainsworth, Caxton and Crabtree. The Caxton concerned was his uncle, whose ambition had taken him, twenty years ago, to a lucrative practice in London. Ainsworth had died of the pox, the plague, or something equally virulent. So there was only old Crabtree left – not for long though.

His thoughts were interrupted, as the way was cleared and the Flyer, quivering with indignation, was set for a rattling run along the narrow Market Street. Pitt braced himself against the seat, and the others, alarmed, reached out to grab the cords. The Flyer, with the thunder of its great wheels filling the air, lurched recklessly between tall, thin, black and white houses, arriving in the yard

100

of the coach office with a flourish that made up for lost dignity.

As the passengers sank back on their seats with relief, Pitt smiled; it was a good smile, all the more pleasing for not being readily given. He could afford to be generous now he had arrived. Cramped and glad to stretch his long legs, he stepped lightly down, and having collected his hand baggage, the rest to await collection, enquired about a decent supper.

"The Seven Stars in Withy Grove, sir," answered Aberdaron Dick, in his capacity as trade-tout. "Guy Fawkes had a room there, once," he announced as though it was the hallmark of recommendation.

As Dick loped off, Pitt stooped under the low entrance of the inn and entered the public room. Looking beyond the Dutch kegs arranged in rows on shelves, and bottles sunk in old oaken pigeon-holes, he passed through to the dining-room.

"Mind the sauce and gravy!" Waiters, holding trays aloft, thrust their bodies sideways to the dining booths. "Mind yer backs, there, I say, mind yer backs!"

After an early supper of jugged hare and braised parsnips, Pitt sipped a glass of port and considered the other arrangements. Lady Egerton, who had known his uncle and was still in occasional correspondence, suggested Pitt stayed at her town house in Quay Street for as long as he wished. She was seldom there and it would keep the servants occupied looking after him. Being in residence, too, would help get him integrated into the social and business life of the town. It was a fine evening and he decided to walk to Quay Street.

The town was quietish, the pleasure seekers were not yet afoot, the offices had closed, and he, mellow with port, wandered to the upper end of Market Street looking with interest at the confused medley of shops and houses, from rickety tenements opening onto the street, to fine mansions standing well back, cordoned off with chains on posts. Harrap's press was still clattering . . . perhaps it was newsday tomorrow. What would they be reporting, he wondered, yet another riot, or the forthcoming May Day attractions?

The large square of the Infirmary Gardens bright with daffodils caught his eye. Who said Manchester was all mills and muck? Selina, he was sure, would be as impressed as he was by the fine houses in Mosely Street and Portland Place. The gardens and pond of the Infirmary set them off beautifully; as a residence these would take some beating . . . costly, no doubt. He could do without the view of stocks and pillory, but, then, you can't have everything!

He had entirely lost direction by now, not that it mattered. Lights began to glimmer here and there, and already the watchman in his brown coat and broad-brimmed hat with a yellow band, was patrolling the streets, swinging his lamp. He paused to light one of the ten street lamps, and with a cheerful, "Fine evenin', sir," was gone.

Pitt retraced his steps down Market Street, past the barber's shop on the corner of St Mary's Gate, where Bob Smollett was still lathering chins, and onto Deansgate. Quay Street he was sure, could not be far away. But he turned right instead of left and found himself outside Etherington's theatre.

'WATERLOO!' announced a bill pasted on the wall. 'AN AMAZING EXTRAVAGANZA!'

What? he thought, looking at the small, flat frontage, an extravaganza in a place this size? Then, in the light of a small oil-lamp flickering above, he noticed the smaller, qualifying letters beneath. 'In Mime and Sketch.' His lips twitched in amusement . . . there was always something to catch the gullible! On impulse, he paid the entrance fee at the small window in the street and went inside.

Chapter 13

Making his way to a pew-like box at the side of the stage, Pitt would have felt conspicuous, if it had not been for an over-enthusiastic application of battle smoke which, even though the Waterloo sketch was ended, had not cleared away. The acrid smell of cordite had risen to the short gallery where some coughed and spluttered and had to be revived with a glass of ale.

"The skylight!" someone behind stage yelled. "Open the bloody skylight!"

The opening of the skylight served to clear the air and Pitt looked about him with amused interest. Apart from the front row of armchairs, bench seating rose sheer and in tiers to beneath the gallery. In London, this kind of place was referred to as 'intimate' – a euphemism for being too small. True, they filled easily, and artistes preferred a full house to one half empty . . .

He admired the decor; despite the smoke it was bright and different – oriental in some way; he was not artistic, but appreciated something other than fat cherubs blowing golden trumpets.

Although the coughing in the gallery was getting less, the panic behind stage had increased. Clogger was anxious. He hated it when people let him down; and after being almost choked to death the patrons were not likely to be in an accommodating mood.

"Eh," he addressed a diminutive boy who had been sweeping the floor. "Sampson, go and tell Miss Ridley the Oldham Players haven't arrived. Ask her to give 'em one of her turns."

"Why do I have to ask her?" the boy mumbled. "She won't like it. Comes 'ere for a rest – away from trade."

"And Miss Etherington won't like it either if the takings are down!" He gave the lad a push. "Be sharp, or you'll have 'em yelling for their money back!"

Pitt's attention was drawn to the hoarse whispers on the front row. He saw Jancie quietly leave her seat and slip through the side door. What next, he wondered?

"It was no good hanging on any longer, Miss Ridley . . ."

"You're right, Clogger," she answered from behind a changing screen, "it isn't. But once on that stage I'm not coming off – so if the Oldham Players do arrive send 'em packing with a flea in their ears! Etherington's will not tolerate slackness. And, Clogger?"

"Yes, Miss Ridley?"

"On no account book them again." She stepped from behind the screen and surveyed her slender figure in the long glass. "How do I look, Clogger?"

"Ravishin', miss!"

She caught his cheeky smile. "Go on, then, tell 'em the worst!"

The manager, unfastening his coat, strode onto the stage, and held up his hands against the good-natured abuse which came his way.

"The management," he bellowed, "convey their regrets for the inconvenience caused, not only in the scene of battle . . .," he paused while the laughter settled, ". . . but for the delay in presenting the last act, which, has not turned up. But Etherington's has never disappointed an audience yet. So, standing in at the shortest notice possible, I give you, ladies and gentlemen, your own, your very own, Japanese Dancing Act!"

The curtains opened to cheers and stamping of feet, and Jancie stood for a moment, head bowed, to acknowledge

104

their greeting. A sleek black wig covered the coppery hair; and the ivory kimono, shot with silver temples and golden trees, was secured by a wide, black sash. On her feet were soft, black pumps, and in her hand a colourful fan of oriental design. The figure was self-effacing, the manner deferential, but the eyes beneath the black fringe were bold and gleaming.

The dance began. There were no stereotyped postures, no fixed smile or mechanical techniques. With fluttering fan, little mincing steps and graceful movements, enhanced by the flowing lines of the kimono, she fluttered like a butterfly. The only music was a single instrument which sounded like a stringed tambourine; and all too soon it was over.

The Japanese dance, Pitt discovered, was by way of introduction to the rest of her turn, and the sketches which followed were as different in mood as it was possible to be. From behind a tapestry screen strode Queen Boadicea, wearing a helmet and carrying a shield; fiercely, she addressed the audience, abusing the enemy in colourful language and urging her troops to "knock hell out of them there Romans!"

Another quick dash behind the screens produced feathered cap and ruff; she was at once imperial, majestic; she was Elizabeth Tudor delivering her speech at Tilbury. The sincerity and fervour brought a flush of national pride to every heart and cheers from every throat.

A change of mood sent the audience wild with laughter, for she staggered across the stage as 'Brandy Nan' – Queen Anne, with a brandy bottle in one hand and ecclesiastical symbols in the other. Pitt was now beginning to view the act in terms of euphemism and innuendo, part of which he did not grasp. His mind could scarce keep pace with her versatility, and he began to realise that both she and the patrons had scant regard for the Establishment. The finale left him in no doubt. It was a daring burlesque of the present Queen Charlotte, who in guttural accent and full wig, sent the Mancunians into fits of hysterical giggles with spicy anecdotes about the Prince Regent.

The performance over, she pulled off the wig, and stuffing it beneath her arm, bowed her head in acknowledgement of the tremendous applause. Pitt was not sure whether to applaud or not, for those sketches had sailed a little close to the wind for these troubled days of 1817. Instead, he decided to redress the balance and end the evening on a fine patriotic note, by leaping to his feet, raising his hat high in the air and shouting, "God save the King! Three cheers for his Majesty!"

Utterly astonished at the lame response, he demanded incredulously. "What's the matter with you all? I said, God save the King!"

"God damn the King!"

"Lot o'guzzlin' Germans!"

"Damn the Regent – and Parliament. To hell with 'em. That's what we say, isn't it lads?"

The lads roared, and spat their agreement on the sanded floor.

"Who is this fella?"

"Throw him out!"

"Let me get at 'im – I'll give him God save the King!"

"C'mon, lads, let's clog him!"

A child began to wail; a thin, eerie sound against the backdrop of sudden, hostile silence. Women screamed and surged toward the door. Men shouted and surged toward Pitt. Not waiting to be cornered, he vaulted lightly over the side of the box onto the stage, to be met by a big knuckled fist. Reeling from the impact he turned toward the other wing. Too late, an outstretched leg brought him down. Rolling over he dodged a narrow-toed clog. The dust rose like a cloud; his chest tightened, and he was about to charge the owner of the clogs, when he sneezed violently, and the man, with a vicious swipe struck first.

Pitt's hat which only a few moments ago had been raised in so patriotic a manner was now with equal fervour rammed firmly down onto his head. The pack closed in. Snapping. Snarling. His fine coat was ripped like a rag from his back. The cambric shirt tore like paper. His ears sang. The lamps danced, and the arrival of the yeomanry was the last thing he remembered.

"Eh, that were a close shave," whispered the diminutive boy, peering through a crack in the curtains. "A reet good idea, miss, to pull the curtains."

"My second impromptu act of the evening," muttered Jancie as they stood round Pitt's body. "I'm full of good ideas, Sampson," she smiled impishly at the boy. "That's why I am where I am!"

"Yes, miss. But it were daft of the soldiers not to look on t'stage. I'm glad they didn't, though, I were terrified."

"Don't know why we didn't get out and let the yeomanry trample on him," grumbled the manager. "He's nothing to us, bloody nuisance his sort. It was him started it all, yelling for the King—"

"You know as well as I do, Clogger, that if the yeomanry had found this man they would've taken him to Constable Nadin and a highly exaggerated report would have found its way to the Home Office." She held up an admonishing finger. "And Miss Etherington would not be pleased to have the theatre closed down as a rowdy house. Were that to happen, you, Clogger, would find yourself back with the travelling fairs, down to your drawers, bending iron bars and making the girls gawp at the size of your . . . muscles!"

"D'you think he's a spy?" asked Sampson hoarsely. "One o' them *agents provocateurs* . . . I mean, have any of us seen him before?"

Jancie, with an alarmed glance at the boy, took from the pocket of her skirt a slender box; opening it she removed a mother-of-pearl pince-nez. With finger and

107

thumb she affixed it to the bridge of her nose and stooped quickly to peer at the dishevelled body. She shook her head. "You could be right Sampson. He is a stranger, I've never seen him about the town."

"Looks like a gypsy to me," suggested Clogger.

"What with clothes like that?" She raised an eyebrow in comic concern at the scattered fragments of a sleeve, a cuff, part of a collar and a few buttons. Sampson giggled, and Clogger, with a feeling of some kind of justice having been done, grinned.

"What the hell are we going to do with him, then? Let's douse the lamps and clear off before that jackass, Nadin, gets wind of it."

"We can't leave him here all night," said the boy, who was afraid of the dark and thought everyone else was afflicted in the same manner. "We can't leave him bleeding like that – got a bad gash under his hat, miss. He's taken a terrible beating."

"Looks a reet tuttle," observed Clogger, "lying there half naked with his hat on!"

"Wouldn't like to be inside his ribs tomorrow," Jancie said dryly. "King fever, that's what ails him. Time he was cured."

"Happen this'll cure him?" suggested the boy.

"I think not," she replied. "A virulent fever like this needs Radical treatment!"

"Ay," observed Clogger, fastening his coat. "And if he's a spy, he's like to get it. And spy or not, he'll be off to lay charges the minute he's on his feet."

"I'd lay a groat to a farthing he won't," she said, brushing the dust off her skirt.

"Why are you so sure?"

"Because he's a fool. Who, but a fool could be so imperceptive as to call for the King after my performance?" She removed the pince-nez slowly, and remembering how Jem was unjustly whipped by the Constable, added, "What did you say, Sampson? Did

108

you say we can't leave him here all night?" She closed the slender box with a snap. "I cannot for the life of me see why not."

Two days later, Pitt Caxton left Lady Egerton's house in Quay Street feeling much better than when he had stumbled out of Etherington's. The earlier drizzle had given way to a fine breeze; a thrush sang in a sycamore tree, and Market Street smelled fresh as Aberdaron Dick, the water-man, poured barrel after barrel of water on the cobbles making them shine like large, rounded crystals.

He followed directions, and a narrow thoroughfare brought him to Marsden Square, a busy place, but small. The buildings were tall and oldish; mostly boasting two, or even three, brass plates. Some of the doors were smartly painted in a glossy crimson, another of a deep blue. Pitt looked at these hopefully, but none bore the name plate he was looking for.

At last! 'Caxton, Ainsworth and Crabtree'. There it was, brightly polished; a shining, brilliant eye; winking and twinkling – from the shabbiest door in the square. Instead of being wide open to suggest business, it was standing slightly ajar. He went in, and rapped on a glass panelled door marked 'Chief Clerk'. Poking his head inside, he announced himself.

Thomas, the chief and only clerk, who retained his title from former glorious days, almost fell off the tall stool in his eagerness to take Pitt's hat and cane. "We knew you was comin', sir, but not exactly when. You're lucky to catch Mr Crabtree in without notice . . . eh," he smiled shyly, trying to conceal his surprise at the bruised face. "It'll be grand to have a Caxton about the place again." Pitt, merely nodded. "The fire up in Mr Crabtree's room needs replenishing," went on Thomas, lifting a scuttle of coals. "Come, sir, I'll show you the way . . ." his face creased into another smile. "Eh, you favour your uncle, sir, when he were a young man . . . apart from the plaster on your forehead, that is . . . hope it's not too painful, sir."

Not half as painful as it's going to be getting up these stairs, Pitt thought, and a dustier set of stairs he had never seen. Thomas knocked on Mr Crabtree's door, announced the coals first and then the junior partner. Somehow, the introduction took place without the shaking of hands. The senior partner was already seated, and with a glance at plaster and bruises declared heartily, "You'll find us a cantankerous lot in these northern parts."

"So I've noticed," agreed Pitt, with feeling.

"Ah," Mr Crabtree wagged a finger. "But we've got something to be cantankerous about! D'you know the price of bread?"

"The price of bread? What's that to do with it?"

"There!" he pounced with satisfaction. "You don't know the price of bread. It's one shilling a loaf, sir. One shilling a confounded loaf!"

"So . . . people are cantakerous," said Pitt with exaggerated calmness. "And bread is a shilling a loaf . . ."

"I'm merely pointing out that when economic conditions are low, emotions run high – and as a lawyer you should be aware of the situation. Fancy, brawling already, and coming in here as though you've gone half a dozen rounds with a prize fighter! Your uncle wouldn't like it. No . . . he wouldn't at all."

"Brawling!" echoed Pitt, his crescent-shaped eyebrows shooting up indignantly. "It was clearly a case of self-defence."

Mr Crabtree smiled, and indicated the clients' chair. Pitt waved aside the offer. "I doubt whether my ribs would survive the ordeal."

"You've laid charges, of course?"

Pitt turned from the inquisitive gaze. "As you say, feelings run high."

"Hmm . . ." said Mr Crabtree, who considered a prefix of some kind gave weight to a sentence, or an extra

110

second or two to change it entirely. "If you are hoping to be a citizen of some consequence in the town, that was not very wise."

Pitt said nothing. He felt himself already compromised. For some obscure reason he was not mentioning the Etherington's affray to Mr Crabtree. The office was small. He was beginning to feel cornered.

"You're a Tory?" observed Mr Crabtree.

"A high Tory," corrected Pitt.

"Personally, I'm middle-of-the-road. I have no real political opinions. Indeed, I admire those with strong views."

"Before leaving London, I took the trouble to scan the Home Office list of agitators."

"Tell me," the older man leaned forward over the writing table. "What made you do that?"

"There's a lot of talk and speculation . . . I wanted to know the truth of the matter. Whether the town was really seething with unrest. And, did you know there are clubs of Female Reformers?"

"And why shouldn't there be? Half the operatives are female." Crabtree shrugged. Our young Mr Caxton, he thought, was in for a lot of surprises.

"Another thing," Pitt crossed to the fireplace. "The list referred to one particular female by the name of Ridley. A militant; a troublemaker it seems, with strong opinions."

"That's the trouble with opinion," the comment came on an easy smile. "If you have any, there's always someone wants to change 'em. This lady sounds like a regular . . . Boadicea."

Boadicea! Pitt squirmed inwardly. He had heard her voice echoing about his half-conscious mind. "He's a fool," she had said. "Furthermore, he's a Tory fool." He eyed the older man narrowly, but knew it was too late to say anything now without losing face.

"You'll take a glass?" Content to ignore a warning

111

twinge from his gouty leg, Crabtree crossed to a wine cupboard. It was a fine piece of furniture, beautifully carved and as highly polished as the brass plate. Pitt, still with a foot on the hearth, compared the glory of the cupboard to the rest of the dismal office. Ancient bookcases, great dusty tomes, whose titles had long since cowered back into their bindings. The green baize surface of the table was devoid of any documents, or even a pen; the table itself crouched on a threadbare square of carpet – and the sight of the dust made him want to sneeze. The office looked as though it hadn't seen a decent client in years. He would alter all that. Manchester was an expanding town, there would be even more buying and selling of land and property – and who in their right mind would bring business to dilapidated chambers like these?

"So, the Home Office have heard about our Miss Ridley, eh? Shouldn't take too much notice, informers have to exaggerate to justify their existence."

Pitt rubbed his chin thoughtfully, eyeing the dapper figure standing between cupboard and table. Bet he's quite a card, our Mr Crabtree, with his shirt fine and frilled, his waistcoat white and patterned, and his blue-skirted coat bright with silver buttons. Come to think of it – he brought his survey to an end with a glimpse of gleaming buckles on high-tongued shoes – there was even a gleam in his eye. Was it, he wondered, for Miss Ridley?

"You sound as though you admire this woman," he prompted. "Tell me about her?"

"There's not a lot to tell," came the muffled answer as Crabtree searched in the cupboard for a bottle of his choice. "Lives with her guardian . . . is President of the Female Reformers, an astute young woman. She is respected by most, and especially the working Rads. She's full of ideas, plans, campaigns and enterprises – a young woman who values her independence . . ."

"And the guardian?"

"One of the town's . . . eccentric, but well-respected business women. But, enough of questions, sir, you will know all about everyone in due time." Mr Crabtree found a bottle to his liking and cradled it protectively in the crook of his arm. He mischievously kept the name Etherington out of the conversation, for he already knew of the theatre incident, and would dearly love to be present when his junior partner realised Miss Jancie Ridley and Boadicea were one and the same.

He poured the wine, lifted a glass reverently, and handed it to Pitt. "Now, now," he prefixed. "To what shall we drink? I hear you will be going out to Heaton Park on May Day?"

"News does travel fast. Yes, I'm there for the Main of Cocks to be fought."

"Are you any good as a handler?"

"Lord Derby seems to think so, he's asked me to set his best bird, the Knowsley. It's a champion fighting cock which hasn't been beaten this season."

"We'll drink to the Knowsley, then – and good luck to you, Mr Caxton." And by heaven, Mr Crabtree thought, you'll need every drop!

Chapter 14

When Pitt arrived at Heaton Hall for the May Day sports, the scene was already one of holiday spirit. The park was alive with colour; bands were playing the gayest of tunes; the fashion and wealth of Manchester strolled the greens; kerchiefs waved, heads nodded and eyes sparkled in anticipation. Apart from a huge maypole, stands and platforms had been erected for spectators to view the cavalcade of horse sport, boxing, and wrestling.

The day being fine, Lady Egerton had decided to lay the refreshments for her personal guests, not in the orangery, but on the long terrace by the shrubbery wall. It was here that Pitt, seated beside her ladyship on a white wicker garden seat, paid his respects; passing on the regards of his uncle. And she, after enquiring, firstly about Mr Crabtree's health and then whether he found her Quay Street residence satisfactory, went on to explain that the May Day Main of Cocks to be fought this year was to be a little different.

"I hear you're the one who is setting Derby's bird, Mr Caxton?"

"I . . . was, ma'am, before you informed me of Lord Derby's novel idea."

She smiled, an indulgent smile. "Come, come, now. Where are your sporting instincts?"

"I don't regard a 'Tory versus Radical' contest as a novel idea. Since leaving London, it seems to be the only topic of interest."

"Tea Mr Caxton?"

114

"If you please . . ." He paused to take the cup, wondering whether he had caught a gleam of amusement in her eyes. "Whoever heard of such a thing?" he persisted. "Inviting all those ragamuffin Radicals!"

"All those," she echoed. "There's only a couple of dozen from the cocking fraternity, and it is a sporting occasion – the rivalry being of a good-natured kind."

"I wouldn't mind so much if the opposing bird belonged to a Radical of my own standing – my equal. But to discover that I'm sharing the mat with a tradesman, and his mangy fowl from the dungheap—"

"Don't underestimate the Radical setter," Lady Egerton interrupted smoothly. "Trade, he may be, but Jem Clowes is a respected breeder. His mother owns a sugar bakery in Half Street, by the church, y'know – and she's worth in excess of £30,000 – rather more than you've got in your pocket, I think."

She's damn right, conceded Pitt, accepting a slice of seed-cake.

"You see," she continued, "a sporting man like Lord Derby is always on the look-out for something to heighten interest, to make the betting brisk. Besides, we in the north have not the same aversion to commerce and trade that you have in the south."

"Oh, I can see the novelty of the idea . . . just wish it wasn't me on the mat that's all."

He finished the tea, took a watch from his waistcoat pocket, glanced at it hurriedly, and like a drowning man clutching at a straw, said with an air of desperation, "It isn't too late to withdraw! I can go now! Take my leave – or pretend I never came!"

"The sporting fraternity won't like it, Mr Caxton . . . and it will give the Radicals something to crow about – if you'll pardon the pun. Besides, if Derby's bird wins, the resulting publicity will do you some good. Manchester society goes very much on recommendation.

Having agreed to set, my dear man, you must stay and see it through."

"Very well," he breathed on a sigh of resignation, and felt again the anxiety of being cornered. He asked grudgingly, "What do they call this . . . Radical bird?"

"The Clowes Scarlet – scarlet being the Radical colour, you know."

"No, I didn't know, Lady Egerton, and I don't want to know. I prefer very much to keep to my own side of the fence! Now, if you will excuse me?"

He strode out from the shrubbery wall which sheltered the terrace and crashed into Jancie Ridley. He withstood the impact without losing an inch of balance, but swore at the legacy of pain, inherited from the theatre fracas. Was nothing to go right this day? he asked himself, on a swift intake of breath. He had caught her easily as she crashed against his body. In releasing her, the apology died on his lips. Etherington's! The recollection flashed through his mind on a whiff of acrid 'battle smoke'. The Japanese Dance! Boadicea! Subversion!

Both stared in amazement. He found himself surveyed through scarlet-enamelled spectacles; surveyed by wide, green eyes. White skirts clung about her legs, fastened by the onrush of the breeze from the shrubbery. The neck of her gown hung provocatively open, straggling laces white against a scarlet over-tunic. It was the fluttering of scarlet hair ribbons that brought him bewilderingly back to the present. What was she doing here? Was there to be no end to these astonishing events?

In the moment of being momentarily winded, a slightly pungent fragrance, like a herbal concoction, which emanated from his clothes, jerked Jancie into awareness. Having overheard part of the conversation, she had recognised the voice, and knew the features would be gypsy-dark; the hair raven-black – and on his brow would be a scar, barely healed. Their eyes met for a brief, unguarded, uncomprehending moment. She turned

116

and walked briskly away, not lessening her pace until well behind one of the spectator stands. As her pace slackened, her mind began to race. With so much else at stake this day she could have done without an extra complication. *I was right about him being a Tory.* – Pitt Caxton, oh, what a fine Tory name! She recollected the window-tax jingle she and Violet had sung as children:

> 'God gave us light and saw it was good,
> Billy Pitt taxed it, God damn his blood!'

Yes, and God damn this fella's blood as well, for what he said about Jem, and trade – oh, Lady Egerton set him right there! As for the 'mangy fowl' from the dungheap, she recalled all the time and effort, all the knowledge that had gone into breeding the Radical bird – not forgetting all the early morning trips to use Mrs Clowes' chamber-pot! Jancie had no doubt at all that Mr Pitt Caxton – so very much on his dignity – would have the surprise of his life! Clogger had been right, she concluded, *we should've left him for the crowd and yeomanry to trample on.* But was Sampson also right? she wondered. Was this stranger a government spy, an *agent provocateur*, or just an over-enthusiastic Tory – and was there all that much difference?

Some little girls ran by, skipping and frolicking like lambs; dresses of muslin, sashes of silk, hearts excited and eyes asparkle for the maypole dancing. Her mobile lips parted into a smile, recalling two beggar children's enchantment with the dresses and sashes of the young girls in the Whit Week procession.

The evocative moment passed and her thoughts plummeted to the contest again and to the conversation she had overheard. Had she and Jem done the right thing in accepting Lord Derby's challenge? she wondered for the hundredth time. Bob Smollett had been very much against it.

117

"Why should the Rads go to Heaton Park?" he asked. "Why not have the Main on neutral ground? What's wrong with the cockpit in Shude Hill? And if that's not grand enough they could rig something on St Peter's Field. But, no, his lordship wants the Rads to go trooping up there!" He had lifted her chin, and teasingly stroked the end of her nose with his forefinger. "I tell you, my little cock-o'-wax, being with the gentry will put Jem off his stride – we'll lose the contest, and humble pie has a rotten taste!"

"I wouldn't know," she had replied. "I've never tasted it – and I never intend to!"

After a lot of discussion at the Radical Clubs, the decision was left to Jem. But it was Jancie who pointed out that Lord Derby would on no account come to the town pit, for the May Day Main at Heaton was traditional. This challenge was a chance in a lifetime, and if Jem didn't take it, someone else would.

Oh, dear, she thought, I could do without all this speculation on today of all days. And yet the speculation went on, the thoughts kept going round, until they had brought her to the pens, where the cackle and chuckle of fighting birds challenged the martial strains of 'Johnny Went To War'. She pushed the spectacles higher on her nose and, leaning over the rail, thought again about her latest idea – a travelling school.

She and the Reverend Brookes – Jotty, as Mancunians affectionately called him – had for some time been discussing the possibility. He believed passionately in education and his response to her innovative idea was both enthusiastic and encouraging. Not that there was any shortage of schools in Manchester, or any lack of tutors and governesses willing to impart knowledge for a fee. But for the beggar children, and those down coalmines, up chimneys, and in factories, there was nothing. To get the scheme afoot, she needed time and money – more to the point, she needed the backing of Etherington's

Enterprises. Charles's birthday gift of a horse and van had made the scheme more viable, and at the same time more impossible, for, in order to travel with the school, she would have less time for the promoting of the boudoir wear and less time with her guardian. Although Jancie had talked about the idea generally, there had not seemed a way of broaching the subject specifically – until yesterday.

While indulging in their after supper ritual of a hand of whist and a cigar, Charles had opened the subject: "Parson Brookes called today. He told me – as only he can – that my Geisha girl is seriously intent about this travelling school?"

"Yes, Charles, I am."

"So, you want time off from the Manufactory? A lot of time. And for what? You are an excellent tradeswoman with an organising ability next to none. You have just that something extra – that I never had. And you want to minimize it. You want to diversify your talent, to travel about like an itinerant, taking education to those who don't want it – to the indifferent, the poor, the unsociable!"

"Like I used to be!"

"Oh, my dear, you're wasting your time and your talents for an ideal, a will o' the wisp."

"Mr Brookes thinks it worthwhile . . . and haven't you told me often enough how his crippled, cruel, foul-mouthed father didn't care about his education, and how his benefactor begged from the gentry to send him to Oxford? And see what a great scholar he is! Children ought to have at least the opportunity."

"Besides, this is not the time to let you go, with the summer parasols to be designed—"

"Oh, but it is the time! I feel it! D'you remember Shakespeare writing about a tide in the affairs of men – and women – when taken at the flood?"

119

"Spare me," Miss Etherington had said, closing her eyes in mute appeal. "Spare me the analogy!"

"But, Charles, I'm twenty-one. I know my own mind – I've served ten years—"

"You sound as if I'd press-ganged you! I suppose we've got the Radical Movement to thank for this."

"You mustn't drag that into it," Jancie had burst out. "After all, it was you who encouraged me to read the works of Cobbett and Tom Paine to the men in Smollett's when I was young!"

"That was to develop your voice, gel, and give you an audience to improve your reading expression – if you can arrest attention with Cobbett and Paine, you can make anything sound interesting!" Charles's lips softened into a smile, Jancie had taken it up and they had giggled like schoolgirls.

"I tell you what," Charles had said, laying down her hand of cards. "Let's dice with Fate, my sweet."

"Fate?" Jancie asked in bewilderment.

"Yes." Charles was pleased with the astonishment she had created, and continued, "If Jem Clowes' bird wins the contest, we'll launch your travelling school with all the weight of Etherington's behind it." Her hand reached out across the table. "Should Derby's bird win, however, will you take it as a sign that you are to stay in commerce? Come now, what d'you say?"

Jancie had agreed, and here she was, her ideal wrapped up in a bundle of feathers.

Jem joined her. She watched his bright eyes follow the striding of the bird. Leaning against the breadth of his shoulder, she could almost feel the excitement thrilling through him.

"Not nervous, are you?" he enquired, putting an arm round her. "Something's up, I can tell. Have you been arguing with Miss Etherington about this travelling school? Or is it me you're vexed with?"

Jancie shook her head. How could she tell him about last night's conversation?

"You're a strange lass," he said. "You set your heart on summat, and when you've got it, you're off on to summat else. Many a fella would give his eye-teeth to get on as well as you in trade."

"But I want to pioneer this scheme for literacy. I can do it, Jem I know I'm the woman for it – and I'll be damned if I'll do 'owt else!"

"Eh, you're a right rebel, Jancie." His hand on her shoulder slipped down to tease the scarlet ribbon blown across her breast. "But not rebel enough to marry me, eh? Miss Etherington doesn't think me good enough for her Geisha girl."

"If I knew for certain I wanted to marry you, dear Jem, all the guardians in the world wouldn't stop me. You ought to know that by now."

He sighed and moved his arm to the rail of the pen. "It's Mr Crabtree, isn't it?" he said resentfully. "Fine clothes and gracious manners won't keep you warm on a frosty night! Or, it could be Bob Smollett with his fiery Radical ways, you spend enough time in there with that bloody warbling nightingale! Or, for all I know, you could finish up with Jotty, – old enough to be your grandpa – look at the hours you spend in his house, with his cats and pet monkey, his pigeons and Latin verbs . . ."

The string of mild jealousies trailed to silence as Jancie gently pressed her finger to close his lips. She nodded toward the Scarlet.

"Sssshh! You know that fighting birds are extra sensitive."

He regarded the bird swiftly. "Ay, and he'll be up against a top bird, Derby's Knowsley."

"Can you doubt that he's a champion, Jem Clowes?"

"No. No doubt at all!" A great confident grin spread across his face. "Eh, you make a fella feel reet good. Anyone can see he's a champion!"

You'd better be, thought Jancie, directing her mind to the magnificent fowl. You must win for Jem – victory here at Heaton will assure his place among the breeders. You must win for the sake of your supporters; dressed in their Sunday clothes they've rallied in droves. We can't have them slink away in defeat. You must win, Scarlet, you must, for on your victory hangs my future as well.

An audacious idea, which had been vaguely circulating since the encounter with Caxton by the shrubbery, now broke over her with an overwhelming clarity. She turned from her mental deliberations with the bird to face Jem. "I want to set the Scarlet against the Knowsley."

"You what?"

"I want to set the Scarlet."

"You mean to go on the mat instead of me?"

"What else?"

"Bloody 'ell, Jancie, there is nothing else! You've reached the sky . . . it's impossible."

"Why is it impossible? Whose idea was it to breed a specially fierce fighting cock to rally the Rads? Whose idea was it to produce this singular scarlet colouring – and a clarion call to be heard all over Manchester? It was my idea, Jem. I've handled it, helped in the training, and the Mash was my idea, too. I realise I've not got your years of study and experience – but I've got a rapport with the Scarlet. I must set him, Jem!"

He ruffled his forest brown hair in an agony of indecision.

"Why are you bringing this up, now? Why didn't you say something before?"

It was too late now, to explain the wager with Charles; about wanting to be in control of her future. If the Scarlet lost, she would only have herself to blame. And for another thing, she wanted to gather the goodwill, the co-operation and respect of the male Rads.

Jem was still in an agony of mind. "What if it . . ."

122

the word stuck in his throat, "if it loses. It will be the ruin of us both."

"You mean, if it loses while I'm on the mat, the ruin will be more sensational, and the Rads will call you all kinds of a fool for allowing a woman to lead you by the nose!"

"Y'know how it is, lass, how it always has been . . ."

"Jem? Have you no faith in me?"

His bewildered gaze took in her eagerness, her enthusiasm, and he knew he was lost. His emotions, should he refuse her, would be in such a mix of turmoil and remorse that he would be no good in the pit. It was she, and not he, who was in the right frame of mind to encourage and urge the Scarlet on. Yet, still he prevaricated.

"It isn't a matter of faith," he wavered helplessly. "What will Lord Derby think? What will his setter say to be confronted, without notice, by a female? No woman in the history of public cock-fighting has yet been on the mat – women don't even come to watch . . ."

"I shouldn't worry about Lord Derby," she cut in, recalling the words by the shrubbery. "He'll think it quite novel. What the opposing setter thinks I neither know nor care. As for your last point, there's a first time for everything."

She thrust her hands deep into the pocket of her skirt to jingle a pair of silver spurs. "Come, Jem. Don't hedge. Give me a straight answer. Do I go on the mat or not?"

The words worked painfully up and down the sinewy throat, the answer emerging on a half strangled sigh. "Alreet, if that's what you want."

"It is," came the breathless reply. She touched his hand. "Thanks . . . oh, thank you Jem!" Then more briskly, "Not a word to a soul or we'll lose the element of surprise. That must be preserved as part of our strategy."

He shook his bemused head. "Eh, you're never short of an idea, are you?"

"No," she replied cheerfully, "that's why I am where I am and not still begging in Tinker's Tea Gardens! Come on." She tugged the sleeve of his smock. "Put the fowl in the travelling bag, it'll have to be weighed in. They do things properly here, y'know – we're not in the town pit now."

"I wish to God we were," muttered Jem fervently. "I wish to God we were anywhere but here."

Chapter 15

As they approached the cockpit Jancie's heart beat faster.

While Jem was weighing in the bird, she glanced into the room. It was crowded. Men were everywhere, talking, shouting, bragging and swaggering.

Already eight cocks had fought to the death, and excitement was running high. Fanciers and breeders clucked and spluttered like the birds they were discussing. Radicals in best coats stood by the door in groups; Tories, fashionably dressed, lounged in wicker chairs at the front, smoking, drinking and scattering guinea wagers as if they were dandelion seeds.

Jem had said women never went into the pit, and no wonder. The odour of birds' blood and damp straw was nauseous; language was rough, and jests were coarse. Dear heaven, she thought, what have I done? What if they bawl me out of the pit? What if they throw things like they do for an unpopular turn at the theatre? It had been hard to persuade Jem to let her set – and if they bawled her off he'd be too embarrassed to show his face. It could all go wrong . . . it could all go so very wrong.

Then the familiar figure of Aberdaron Dick, stepped down to dampen the matting, and the sight of him raised her spirits.

"Clowes Scarlet!" yelled the teller, "weighing in at six pounds . . ." He resumed his seat on a wooden stool, consulted the list in his hand and jumping up, shouted to Jem. "Is this 'ere name," he waved the list, "correct? Thought you were settin'?"

"Last minute change," came the subdued reply.

"Shout up, Mr Clowes!"

"Last minute change, I said!"

Pitt looked about for the replacement, and stared in utter unbelief. Silence followed the corporate gasp of astonishment as Jancie stood forward. Even the birds were silent. There was not a chuckle, a chortle; and if a feather had dropped it would have been heard. Jancie stood rooted to the spot, to be released the next moment by throaty cheers from the Radicals and a flurry of speculation from the fashionably dressed. They watched with interest the placing of the mother-of-pearl spectacles on her short, straight nose, and sat back curiously.

It was customary for the setters to shake hands. Pitt stood stiffly. He felt so stiff he thought he would never move again. Boadicea in the cockpit! He groaned inwardly. It was too late to quit. He would have to see it through. He glanced at Lord Derby. How could he allow all this interchange with the lower orders? It was unthinkable. Why me? he asked of Fate. But Fate was dumb. He gathered his wits to see her standing before him . . . scarlet ribbon, scarlet over-tunic, and even the blasted fowl would be scarlet! If he was not so angry he would have laughed, but there was no levity in what Jancie saw.

Not a one to hesitate on the brink of indecision, she extended her hand first to meet his. Each hand was firm, cool and unyielding. Each face well guarded. This contest was more than just the last item in a Main of Cocks.

A buzz of speculation rippled as attention focused on the cocks still in their travelling bags. Jancie pulled on her gauntlet and drew out the bird. With a flourish she held it up high on her wrist.

"The Clowes Scarlet!" yelled the teller.

Oh, you're a beauty, she thought, as it perched there

126

like a royal falcon. It turned its head to give the spectators a view of the large, vigorous beak; short, strong wings were opened, poised, and brought down with a ferocious flap. But the display was not yet over. It lifted a dark blue sinewy leg to slyly show off the silver spur secured to the heel with scarlet thread. The militant beauty brought roars of applause, to which it responded with an impatient, muscular chuckle. Flushed with excitement, Jancie looked up and smiled at Jem who was leaning over the rail, his face strained and anxious.

Pitt took off his mulberry-coloured coat and threw it on the low wall. Turning back his cuff, he pulled on a black and ivory gauntlet, which matched the embroidery on the Knowsley's bag.

The Knowsley, she realised was not going to be brought out with a vulgar flourish. His approach was much more subtle. He withdrew the bird, slowly, gently, almost coaxing, until it was perched on his gauntlet without a feather ruffled. Jancie's heart plummeted. Derby's bird was a Black Breasted Red. Not only did they possess good looks, but a skilled fly and powerful drive. If the contest hadn't been arranged so quickly, Jem could have trained the Scarlet to cope with these attributes, but never, never in his wildest dreams, did he expect to match their creation with one of Derby's.

At a signal from the teller, the setters began to prime their birds, whispering, fondling, encouraging. Jancie spat on her finger to wet and tighten the cord on its heel. The birds were held up, face to face, pecking at each other, taunting, and teasing. A little strike, a little thrust, until, too fierce to hold, they were placed on the mat, beak to beak. They darted at once into an attitude of combat. Screeching and squawking; sparring and dodging like wrestlers for the first cut. Wings fluttered ferociously as they rose into the air; the first fiery leap over, the birds descended onto the mat with a dull thud which sounded like a wet umbrella being opened.

127

"He's throated!" yelled Jem from the gallery. "T'Scarlet's throated!"

"Knowsley's drawn first blood! Two to one on the Knowsley!"

The setters ran to examine their birds; Jancie wiped the blood off the Scarlet's feathers. "Go in and get him," she urged, making the hoarse clucking noise which she had used to train it. "Put your spurs in, Scarlet!"

"Game is he?" asked the teller.

"Game!" confirmed Jancie.

"He's game!" yelled Aberdaron Dick. "Who'll give us two to one on Scarlet? Three cheers for the Radical bird!"

"Three cheers be damned," answered Pitt. "Who'd give three cheers for a mangy fowl! Four to one on the Knowsley!"

The shouts, the yells, and the excitement fed the maddened birds. Already incensed by the drawing of blood, they danced frenziedly, rearing to and fro, chortling savagely, chuckling madly. Jancie, her mouth dry and gaze fixed, thrust her hands beneath the tunic and concentrated with an intensity which hurt. She wished desperately for the Scarlet to win. It must win. It must. And she mustn't get anxious . . . fighting birds were sensitive to mood.

"Scarlet," she gasped, as the Knowsley reared its neck. "Look out! Look out!" The opposing bird struck.

"He's blinded!" groaned Jem. "Oh, the Scarlet's blinded!"

The setters ran forward. Jancie, with heart pounding and stomach churning, stemmed the flow of blood. She knew it would be like this; but thought she was more prepared for the viciousness . . . for the fighting to the death. It had to go on. The contest must continue. Taking a deep breath, she smoothed the ruffled feathers. "Go to it, lad," she whispered softly. "Tha's a grand bird . . . you're not finished yet. You just show 'em . . ." And

128

as an after thought, she moistened the cord on its heels. "Get your spurs in, eh?"

"Is he game?" asked the teller.

"Game." Confirmed Jancie.

"He's game!" yelled Aberdaron Dick. "Did you ever see such courage – who'll up the odds on the Scarlet?"

But the odds mounted for the Knowsley. As the sightless bird tottered across the mat, Jancie's confidence tottered with it. Bob Smollett had been right, she thought miserably, we shouldn't have come. The Black Breasted Red had only to leap now, and Jem's bird, the Radical's bird, was done for; finished. Her lips pressed grimly together and sweat trickled onto her face like tears. She wanted to pick the Scarlet up, to save it, run off with it. Oh, Scarlet . . . She closed her eyes to the dreadful sight. She heard the crowd yelling, going mad for Derby's bird. She imagined Caxton preening himself, Jem crestfallen.

The Knowsley, sensing his adversary's blindness, closed for the final drive, and leapt. The Scarlet veered and with unswerving accuracy seized the Knowsley's throat. It struggled furiously; but the massive, vigorous beak retained a tight hold. Jancie opened her eyes.

Excitement ripped the smoke-filled air. "Great O, Scarlet!" she shouted, as it gathered strength for the final kill. All eyes were on the lift of the dark blue sinewy leg. Spurs gleamed with scintillating wickedness. The spectators caught their breath. The spurs struck . . . struck . . . and struck again. The Knowsley dropped to the mat, but was not done for. The grim tenacity of the fighting cocks imposed an awestricken silence. Pitt's eyes narrowed; Jancie's rounded; and Jem's in the gallery stared in shrewd assessment. With a courage born of desperation the Knowsley made a valiant attempt to heel. The Scarlet, loss of sight, inducing greater perception, brought down a glittering spur again. It was a stroke to kill. But still the Knowsley staggered after its blind opponent . . . tottering on its breast, sinking on its tail. The Scarlet delivered a final stroke. The Knowsley dropped. It was finished.

The victorious cock, droplets of blood running off the eagle-like beak, feathers puffed, stretched out his wounded neck and gave a mighty crow of victory which was heard all over the park. No one moved. Then, an imperceptible wave of relief surged into cheers. Jem was at her side. "Great O, Jancie. Eh, tha's a reet good lass!"

"Congratulations!" Lord Derby had stepped into the pit and addressed Jem. "Splendid fowl!" And to Jancie. "Well handled, Miss Ridley – a female on the mat," smiled the sporting earl. "Quite novel – a Main to remember!"

Thrilled for herself, for Jem, for the Rads, Jancie revelled in the victory, letting it wash over her, wallowing in it, enjoying it. She felt proud and vindicated. The opposing setter pulled on his coat with an impatient gesture. Jancie, stepped toward the low wall. He turned to her, not meeting her eyes, but presenting his face stiffly. He was not angry or upset, merely mortified – an emotion he wasn't used to. He knew she would say something, her kind always did. It was not enough to win, she had to crow over it!

"Not a bad performance, Mr Caxton, considering the Scarlet to be a 'mangy fowl from the dungheap'?"

He bowed his head in acknowledgement.

"Well worth straying from my side of the fence for."

Up came his head. So . . . she had overheard his conversation with Lady Egerton. A dull flush mounted his temples. "I should not make a habit of it, Miss Ridley. Straying from your own side of the fence may prove dangerous."

"Is that a challenge, or a warning?"

"Why should it be either? But, if your militant nature requires it to be one or the other, I would suggest you interpret it as a warning."

Chapter 16

The Radicals, having agreed beforehand not to be rowdy or boisterous if the Scarlet won, kept to policy, and with the utmost decorum and haste, exchanged the holiday atmosphere of Heaton Park for a boisterous 'knees up' at Tinker's Tea Gardens.

Since Waterloo, Tom Tinker had tried to upgrade his business by renaming it Vauxhall Gardens like those in the metropolis, but Mancunians still referred to it as Tinker's. Here a supper of eel pie and Eccles cakes cost only tuppence; life and limb could be risked on swings and flying boats for a penny. They could dance the Denton two-step, watch bareknuckle boxing, drink Tinker's Unadulterated Ale, or go sweethearting among the avenues of trees, subtly and enchantingly illuminated by coloured flares on top of poles.

Jem and Jancie were cheered, and chaired round the gardens, down the avenues, past the maypole and into the Concert Room where the events at Heaton Park had to be told again, properly. In detail and more detail. Jancie, seeing Jem was likely to be there for hours, slipped away to Shude Hill.

Her thoughts gathered about the travelling school, the preparations for it, and approaches to be made to sympathetic employers. Her Sunday School held at the back of the Manufactory was run on the lines advocated by the Radical writer, Mary Wollstonecraft. At first, the fact of boys and girls sharing the same room and lessons, incurred the displeasure of the clergy and Watch Committee – and the suspicion of Constable Nadin, who from time to time searched the premises in hope of finding subversive material.

One of the scholars turned teacher was Fancy Macdonald, whom Jancie had employed to help Mrs Hallam, who, getting older, was thankful to hand over the task to someone who regarded the running of Etherington's with as much esteem as herself. Fancy, being younger, quicker and cleverer, combined the tasks of overseer, housekeeper and anything else that came to hand with apparent ease. Fancy had been a pretty child until falling victim to smallpox, which had left her features badly scarred. She was a thin, wiry young woman, brown-eyed, black-haired. Her chief glory was that, strangely, she did not care about her disfigurement or people's reaction to it. She did not care about anything other than Reform, Etherington's and Clogger. As yet the latter was not aware of her concern, but she was working on him.

Being a holiday, neither Fancy, or the boy, Sampson, were at the Manufactory. Shude Hill was fairly quiet and the town free of workaday noise. Jancie let herself into the Manufactory and hurried up the black-timbered stairs, calling a greeting as she went. Unwashed and grimestained, she entered the parlour, and standing behind the highbacked chair, put her arms about her guardian's neck, looking at the game of Patience before her. Her cheek brushed the dove grey hair, the caress slowly misting her thoughts . . . now the travelling school was a reality, she would miss being home, the evening game of cards, the wagers, talk of trade, the Enterprises. From the moment she had stood in a ragged kimono looking up into Charles's refined features, there had been an immediate attraction – a recognition of similar spirits; someone who understood the necessity of a kimono, about a child holding onto her dreams. The atmosphere between them was one of easy and extravagant affection. It had developed into a

132

dear and jolly relationship, carefully tended so as not to introduce any kind of disorder into the harmonious pattern of their lives.

"Oh, Charles," she whispered. "The Scarlet won . . ."

Her guardian's hand came up to touch the side of her face and smooth away her rush of remorse.

"Charles," Jancie said. "Your mind isn't on the game. That hand will never work out in a month of Sundays!"

"I was beginning to think that meself . . ."

"Good. You put the cards down, I'll light us a cigar, and tell you all about Heaton Park – and by the time I've finished you'll wish you came!"

Charles Etherington listened to her ward's animated account with delighted and yet mixed feelings. They took immense pleasure in each other's achievement and were totally blind to each other's follies. Charles felt a sense of pride and fulfilment in having brought up those two little girls. Violet had already gone, and the other, her Geisha Girl, was now talking of spreading her wings. Not that she was leaving entirely, like Violet; but, with her quick and able mind withdrawn from the Enterprises, how long before the downward trend? Not that I'm in my dotage, yet, she thought philosophically; with the help of Fancy and the outdoor workers, umbrellas, parasols, and boudoir wear of distinction would be available from Etherington's for a little while longer . . .

"You didn't!" Charles's voice echoed with pride. "You mean you actually persuaded Jem? That you set the Scarlet? That you were on the mat?"

The copper-coloured head nodded; lips parted in a mischievous smile, for they always tried to outdo each other.

"And, that's not all," she moved to the table, handed her guardian a small cigar, and, drawing contentedly on her own, leaned forward. "Derby's setter turned out to be the man who caused the trouble at the theatre. The one Sampson thought could be a spy. Honestly, when I heard him talking to Lady Egerton, I could scarce believe my ears! And guess what his name is? Pitt. How d'you like that for a good old Tory name – Pitt Caxton?"

"I think I can go one better."

"Try."

"Ainsworth, Caxton and Crabtree."

"What? That Caxton? I always thought the other two were dead!"

"One, it seems, is very much alive. Intent on making his fortune, would you believe! Crabby called to tell me – wouldn't say anything before on account of putting Jem off his stride. I don't think Caxton can really be a spy, my dear."

"It seems very odd to me, that a stranger should come to Etherington's – out of all the theatres and concert rooms in town. Just when the Oldham Players don't turn up. Which means I stand in with Boadicea and Queen Charlotte – then he gets on his hind legs and starts a riot by calling for the King! If that isn't suspicious, I don't know what is. Besides, why take up the family business now?"

"It's as good a time as any, I suppose."

"What did Crabby say about him?"

"Takes himself very seriously . . . wants to succeed. They only had a short interview, it seems. Reading between the lines, my sweet, Crabby's not at all happy about suddenly acquiring a junior partner!"

"Dear Crabby!" They both laughed, and as the hilarity settled Jancie's tone turned serious. "You don't mind," she asked, hesitantly, "about . . . losing?"

"We agreed to let Fate decide, and, never a one for reneging on a contract, I abide by Fate's decree. If you want your dream to come true, my dear, I'm the last to stand in your way. All the weight of Etherington's behind you, I said – and so it shall be."

"You're too good, Charles," Jancie's throat tightened. "I . . . don't know what to say."

"That makes a change!" Charles gathered the cards. "Don't say anything – go and change your clothes, and instead of having supper sent across we'll go over and dine at the Seven Stars – we shall carouse!" she said with flourish. "And drink to Jem's Scarlet – Oh, I almost forgot. Fancy left a message that your revolutionary admirer—"

"Which one?"

"Bob Smollett. He wants you to call on him first thing tomorrow."

It was still early when Jancie closed the door of the Manufactory. The street scavengers, stiff brooms across wiry shoulders, had just cleared Shude Hill from the May Day rubbish. Aberdaron Dick set about filling the horse troughs, and the cocks were crowing. Never again would she hear a cock crow and not think May Day 1817.

In a few moments she was at the barber's shop. Despite the early hour there were half a dozen men sitting on the benches. Her heart warmed to the smell of soap; to the hum of talk; to the tame nightingale. Stopping to talk to it, she rewarded its attention with some mealworms from the box hanging on the wall. Then, in answer to the questions which poured from the stubbly chins, she gave an animated account of the Clowes Scarlet versus Lord Derby's Knowsley. She worked hard to gain the approval of the working Rads, for many were conservative by nature and would not allow their women to join the Female Reformers. "It wasn't all my doing," she ended, "the Scarlet's a wonderful bird!"

Bob, having finished a shave, endorsed the sentiment by stropping his razor with a dashing, slashing air. Jancie eyed his striped, crimson waistcoat. He never wore a stock, but wide-collared shirts of the kind preferred by artists. His round face was topped by a head of

135

well-groomed brown hair, dressed this week in the style of Lord Byron. "You look very dapper today, Bob," was her verdict.

He grinned bashfully, and to ward off comment from the benches, lengthened the grin into a laugh. "Just harken to her! Who'd have thought when she was a little 'un – her and that little sister, both as skinny as laths, crouching by that very stove for warmth – who'd have thought she'd end up with Etherington's—"

"Hold on, Bob," Jancie interjected, with mock indignation. "What d'you mean by end up? I've only just started!"

The laugh changed to a smile; the vulnerable, uncertain smile that reminded her of the decision that there could be no more kisses . . .

"Bob," she pitched her voice lower. "You left a message for me?"

"Ay, an' it's not so good, me little cock o' wax."

"Why, what's up?"

"You remember how Bradshaw's cut the women and children's wages by half, last week?"

"Yes. A delegation from the union were appealing to Mr Bradshaw himself yesterday."

"Ay, well, they did, lass. And Bradshaw's sacked 'em all. Not even been given the chance to continue working for half pay."

"Oh, no!" Jancie was appalled.

"Some of 'em went to the Manufactory last night . . . thinking you'd be there . . . waiting to hear the result."

And I was carousing with Charles in the Seven Stars, she thought. I was so taken up with the Scarlet's success I forgot about Bradshaw's.

"They're looking to you, lass, to do summat about it."

Struck with remorse, she answered. "Yes, Bob, I shall. Oh, I shall."

She looked up to see the Reverend Joshua Brookes

MA thrust himself through the door. Pleasure at seeing his protégée was heavily tempered with disapproval of her presence in a barber's shop. "Thou art a blockhead, Miss Japanese Dancing Girl . . . ay, a blockhead! But you did well yesterday." He winked his reference to the wager; but straw-coloured eyebrows frowned to admonish. "When I was teaching thee thy grammar, girl, I never thought to hear of thee in so God-forsaken a place as a cockpit."

"It was merely a stepping-stone, Mr Brookes."

"Time tha was stepping up to the altar, never mind on stones. Women and politics are not meant to go together."

"But," she teased. "Who introduced me to Mary Wollstonecraft's *Rights of Women*?"

"Ay," he conceded, settling himself onto a bench. "She's a very enlightened woman, but methinks she'd draw the line at a cockpit!"

"What I did, Mr Brookes, I did for the travelling school. Our scheme can go ahead – and I'm that excited! We'll discuss the details later – I'll call on you, Mr Brookes. Got to go now."

She was up the steps in no time, and on her way to Half Street, where the bow-fronted, many-paned window of the sugar bakery displayed its mouth-watering wares.

The ear-splitting clang of the shop doorbell added to the shouts and cries of the grammar school boys racing each other down Long Millgate. Mrs Clowes, stout and mob-capped, was already in the shop, supervising everything; from the wenches polishing brass weights, to the maid polishing the mahogany counter, and the clerk filling his ink well.

"The militia's on t'moor," volunteered Mrs Clowes without preamble. "And we're ran off our feet, we are. D'you know how much we've been boilin' since they went up there?"

"No, Mrs Clowes."

137

"Nine ton o' sugar a week – fancy that, nine ton! Y'see, all the folk are going up to watch the militia, and they want summat to suck – and then the militia come down 'ere, and they want summat to suck! An' that means our Jem and the apprentice are boilin' and stretchin' . . ."

"Well, if he's too busy, Mrs Clowes."

"Did I say so?" she demanded sharply. "He's never too busy to see thee. As for yesterday, Miss Jancie," she raised her short, fat arms in an expression of horror. "To hear you'd been in the cockpit – and on the mat an' all! Eh . . . I doan't know what young women are up to nowadays – and what must poor Miss Etherington think . . ."

"Women of all ages have to get up to all kinds of things, Mrs Clowes, to earn for their sex the right to such elementary things as being able to read and write. You and me, and Miss Etherington and all the other businesswomen of the town are privileged, and that privilege should be extended to—"

"Ay . . . well." Mrs Clowes interrupted by lifting the counter flap. "Come through, Miss Jancie."

Going along the flagged passage, she pushed open the rough wooden door. Through the steam she saw him clad only in breeches, sinewy arms pulling and twisting long ropes of boiled sugar. The sweat poured off him, and the heat had raised the weals of Constable Nadin's whiplashes. She stepped forward and put out a hand to touch the scars, but withdrew; he would mistake her motives.

"It's me, Jem," she shouted above the boiling of the vats. "I'll wait in the yard."

Pulling on a shirt, Jem joined her, his arm going about her shoulders as she stood watching the young cockerels strutting about their pens. "Missed you yesterday at Tinker's. They said you'd left."

"I could see you'd be there for hours, and I had to see Charles."

He followed her gaze. "What's it to be, then? Are we going into business, you and me? Orders are pouring in already for the new breed."

She took his arm from her shoulders.

"What's up?"

She told him briefly about the lay-off at Bradshaw's.

"What do they expect you to do about it?"

"Oh, I'm not short of ideas."

"Your ideas will get you into trouble one o'these days. You and Bob Smollett between you. Real trouble, that Mr Crabtree won't be able to get you out of." He lowered his head to hers. "When I asked what's up, I meant why did you move me arm?"

"It was hot and sticky, that's all, and I'm just cooling off."

"Ay, I can see that."

"You can see no such thing, Jem Clowes. I told you from the outset I was only interested in breeding the Scarlet as a symbol to rally the Rads. I'm not for staying in trade, Jem." She then told him about the wager between Charles and herself. "This travelling school means as much to me as your birds to you. If it hadn't have been for the contest, the whole thing might still be a dream."

"Glad I came in useful, then."

"Oh, Jem," she coaxed. "We really can't go on seeing each other. I can't bear it when everything I say and do is misconstrued. It makes even makes friendship difficult . . ." her voice trailed away helplessly. After a few moments' silent contemplation of the strutting birds, she tried again. "Your cousin Margery's very fond of you. Spending her time embroidering the cocking bags, and always about to help you clean the pens. She's even volunteered a pot of early morning urine – and for a young woman so modest that means only one thing!"

"I don't want hers – it's yours they were reared on – no wonder the Scarlet was fierce."

"Well, you're going to have to change your supplier. I'm not dashing over here every morning for the rest of me life just to use your mother's chamber pot! Markham's Mash apart, you've your stepmother to consider. She has quite a business and you owe it to her to marry."

"Not so quick, lass, not so damn quick. Thou'rt trying to arrange me like you arrange them demonstrations and scholars' lessons." His throat muscles tightened. "If you won't marry me, I'm not marrying anyone. You're full of ideas, but you've no idea how much I love you . . ."

"Jem . . ."

"All right. All right. I had to say it. Had to tell you, so you can never say you didn't know. I suppose I've always known it wouldn't work." He took a deep breath and continued on a quieter note. "I'm not staying in the sugar bakery all me life . . . stretchin' miles and miles of bloody sugar. Nay, the Scarlet's started something, and I'm going to make a name for myself in the cock-breeding world."

"So, it doesn't matter about your stepmother? After all, she did take you out of the workhouse, educate you, and brought you up as her own son."

"What about you, then, leaving Miss Etherington? And after all she didn't only take you, but your sister, from a life of beggary – and Violet's already gone and you're next."

"I'm sorry, Jem. I had no right to suggest or interfere. Like me, you must do what seems right for your own life. I came to give you an answer about the partnership . . . with the cocks or anything else."

"And what if we'd lost the contest?" he asked pointedly. "No doubt you'd have come in with me then, seeing it as another way to win Radical esteem."

"If the Scarlet had lost," she replied evenly, "you would not have asked me. I'm not daft, Jem."

He shrugged his wide shoulders, and tossed her a good-natured grin.

"So, you see, dearest Jem, things have come to this between us."

"And this leaves you free?"

"My wings were never clipped."

Chapter 17

The following day Pitt rounded St Mary's Gate and came across what he thought to be a funeral procession, but there would be about two hundred people. And they were all silent. And those who watched were silent. Children near the front shuffled; thin, white faces ghastly against their black smocks. Black-shawled women, gaunt and hollow-eyed, trudged past, brought up at the rear by crippled and maimed soldiers – cast-offs from Waterloo. There were banners:

'BRADSHAW'S THE WAGE CUTTERS'
'BREAD – NOT STARVATION'
'TRADE WILL NOT REVIVE WITHOUT BREAD'
'A SWINISH MULTITUDE OUT OF WORK FOR APPEALING TO BRADSHAW'S'

'Swinish multitude' . . . he recognised Viscount Sidmouth's description of the working classes, and realised this sepulchral affair was no funeral procession, but one of those protests he'd heard about. Hurrying to the head of it, he stopped in astonishment. There was a solitary figure leading a horse and cart; the figure wore a black-cowled robe such as a monk would wear – or a medieval executioner. On the cart, bound tumbrel-style, were two fashionably dressed effigies, features drawn from caricature, of those considered responsible for defective legislation – Lord Castlereagh and Viscount Sidmouth. The women carried empty cooking pots . . . the children empty plates, and the significance dawned on him.

The procession halted at Blackfriars Bridge. How quiet it was. The silence became heavy, pronounced, sinister – threatening almost, as though something terrible could happen. Pitt looked about. The entire town, it seemed, had stopped to watch. Street vendors, clerks, button-nosed errand boys, and even the dogs. The black-robed figure by the horse threw back its cowl. Pitt stared. Miss Ridley! No wonder the dramatics were effective! Surely this was asking for trouble? But then, had the Home Office not listed her as a troublemaker? Why she was taking such risks, he'd never understand. Northern women, it seemed, were of a different temperament than those in the south. Selina and the women he knew would never dream of banding together in societies and clubs, still less get involved in acts of civil disobedience. And as for demeaning themselves in the cockpit!

The lone figure walked with deliberation to the cart, lifted Castlereagh, and although the effigy was obviously light weight, made a show of dragging it to the parapet of the bridge, before tipping it over into the Irwell below. The silence was broken. Cheers ripped through the air. Cooking pots clanged and tin plates clashed as she dragged Sidmouth off to a similar fate. And, as the medieval executioner dusted her hands together in an extravagant gesture the crowd roared with satisfaction.

Jancie, filled with remorse at not being home when the Bradshaw workers called, had insisted on leading the procession herself. Margery and Fancy Macdonald, as an extra gesture, had wanted to walk beside her carrying cardboard axes. But Constable Nadin would see that as 'provocative'; Miss Bohanna had suggested they use empty pans and pots, and that had carried the vote.

The cheers were fading now – into hoarse cries of "Yeomanry! Yeomanry!"

The procession broke ranks instantly. The women scattered like a flock of low-flying starlings wheeling this way and that, some settling here, others there. As

143

pre-arranged, the twenty or so Female Reformers joined hands and created a barrier, giving the starlings time for flight.

Long Millgate was suddenly ablaze with the conspicuous uniforms of the loyal Manchester Yeomanry; a bevy of constables snapping and yelping at their heels.

"Got you, my beauty! Caught red-handed!" A terrier of a constable seized Jancie, who had remained at the parapet. His fingers nipped her arm as he closed in. "Just an innocent bystander," he leered. "Just happened to get caught up in a nasty incident, eh?"

"No. I just happened to be leading the procession."

"Eh, don't you get clever with me, miss!"

"The procession was orderly – and quite silent," she gasped. "It's your interference that's caused trouble. Look at the gallant yeomanry harassing helpless cripples and chasing children!" She struggled. "Let me go! You little, jumped up Napoleon!"

"I don't like that!" he snapped. "By God, I don't!" He jerked her arm, twisting it behind her back. "Move. I'm taking you to Mr Nadin. Hurry up, or you'll get Napoleon's boot in yer backside!"

Pitt rushed forward. "Constable, release that woman!"

The tone of the command had the desired effect, and the terrier, recognising authority of some kind, tried to justify himself. "She was resisting arrest, sir!"

"Don't add lies, Constable, to your other distasteful traits."

Jancie, rubbed her arm, and looked from one to the other.

"You don't know these 'ere Rads, like I do, sir. Crafty, they are—"

"I'm not suggesting you deviate from your duty – merely pointing out that such rough treatment of women is quite unnecessary – pray proceed in the normal manner."

Without acknowledging her he went on his way calling

himself all kinds of a fool for having intervened – after all, she had left him on Etherington's bare boards all night, and he would never live down that affair in the cockpit . . .

He walked quickly on his way, eager to confront the senior partner with the escapade and to report that justice was taking its course. See how he took that piece of information!

But when he arrived at Marsden Square, Mr Crabtree was already out. Thomas, the clerk, took Pitt's hat and stick, and settled to talk of the refurbishing of the chambers which had not been touched since Pitt's uncle had vacated them. "And, I've ordered a new name plate, sir, deleting Mr Ainsworth's name, God rest him . . ."

While clerk and junior partner talked of likely firms to undertake the refurbishing, the senior partner, flushed with port and triumph, had persuaded the magistrate, the Reverend Hay, not to lodge Miss Etherington's ward in the New Bailey Prison, but, with himself and Miss Etherington as surety, to confine her to her own premises until the authorities decided which action, if any, to take.

The following morning Pitt settled himself for a day of consultation and costings with furnishers, decorators, and joiners. The street door opened to admit a small boy in a large smock. It was Sampson, who, recognising Pitt from the theatre riot, appeared suddenly nervous.

"Yes?" demanded Pitt.

"A letter for Mr Crabtree, sir."

Thomas, seeing the boy, left his desk and extended a mittened hand. "I'll see he gets it."

The look which passed between the two made Pitt impulsively intervene. His long fingers closed over the letter. "I'll save you the trouble, Thomas. I'm going up to Mr Crabtree's rooms."

Mounting the steps to the top floor, he flipped open

the unsealed note. It began, "My Darling Crabby . . ." Realising it was of a private nature, he read no further. His lips curved into a smile . . . a billet-doux for the old boy – what next!

Mr Crabtree was but two generations above Pitt's twenty-seven years, and that was every reason to think of him as 'the old boy'. Pitt was still smiling when the door opened.

"Ah, good morning, to you, Mr Caxton. "What? You've brought me a note – and I was, as you see, on my way down." His entire person gleamed, beamed and shone. Recognising the handwriting, he beamed even more and tucked it tenderly into his pocket.

"I was coming to see you about Miss Ridley," said Pitt eagerly, as they were on their way down.

"Were you, now?"

They descended to the first floor in silence, and entered the antiquated office. Both men stood by the shabby baize table, and Pitt continued. "Yesterday I was witness to what they are calling the 'Bradshaw Demonstration'."

Crabtree shook his head. "The magistrates are no longer referring to it as a demonstration," his mild, jocular voice took on an edge, "but as 'Incitation to Riot'."

"But, if they are taking so serious a view of the case, ought I not to place myself as a witness?"

"No, my dear sir, you ought not."

"But why? We are in the legal profession."

"For two reasons," came the brisk reply. "Firstly, because the magistrates, in order to impress the Home Office with their vigilance, have invested the incident with such overtones and colour that there are bound to be charges; and secondly . . ." he paused, wanting to relish this moment of disclosure. "Because . . . we are Miss Etherington's lawyers."

"What!" Pitt was astounded. His eyebrows shot up; his eyes stood out; and colour flushed his temples. Mr Crabtree was well satisfied. What would Fancy

146

Macdonald call that expression? Gob-smacked! Ay, he chuckled inside himself, young Caxton was gob-smacked, all right – and I've not finished with him yet!

"Why?" demanded Pitt. "Why didn't you tell me this before?"

"Me, tell you! It was your place – as junior partner – I may remind you, to enquire for a list of clients – but you've been too busy running the chambers down to even ask! Miss Etherington's father put a lot of money your uncle's way – enough to buy into that lucrative London firm. I was, at the time, junior partner, like yourself."

"I . . . Oh, I didn't mean any disrespect, sir. It's just that, well . . ."

"You need not concern yourself about Miss Etherington and her wards. Their legal interests and those of other long standing clients will remain in my hands." He turned to the door, "And there's another point to remember."

"Yes?"

"Should you offer yourself as a witness, there are those who would see your motive as that of petty revenge for being bested on the mat at Heaton Park!"

When he had gone Pitt sank into the unyielding embrace of the clients' chair, his fingers tapping the brass studs which rounded the edges. He wasn't used to thinking in a panic. Life had once given him time, but since coming to Manchester it had been one damned thing after the other. He was even now thinking of breaking from Crabtree, just as he'd thought of quitting the Main at Heaton. But, as Lady Egerton had pointed out, Manchester folk relied a lot on recommendation . . .

On his way down Pitt paused at the outer office. "Thomas, where was that diminutive boy from?"

"Etherington's Smallware," came the reply. "On Shude Hill."

And who, thought Pitt, from Etherington's would address the senior partner in so affectionate a manner?

* * *

The late spring evening was close to darkness when Pitt was almost ready to leave the chambers. The day had gone as well as could be expected, with the refurbishers organized to come in on the morrow and the furniture arriving at week-end. Thomas had already gone, and as Pitt was thinking of following suit, the outer door slowly opened. A thin man with red-rimmed eyes pushed his head inside furtively.

"Mr Caxton?"

"Yes."

"I am clerk to the Reverend Hay, stipendiary magistrate to the township of Manchester."

"I am just about to leave," said Pitt, warily. "What can I do for you?"

"Oh, not for me." The man stepped inside, "For the Reverend Hay, sir, for the cause of law and order."

"Yes. Yes, whatever you say."

"I have called with instructions for Mr Crabtree, regarding one, Jancie Ridley."

"Mr Crabtree is not in."

"You are his partner?"

"Just about. But, I know nothing of the person you mention."

The man closed the door and stood holding a document as though it were a prayer book. "The Reverend Hay has a reputation for dealing quickly in these matters. Squash 'em, good and proper, like at the Blanket March."

"Blanket March?"

"Ay, last year. Nine thousand fellas set off from St Peter's Fields, to petition Parliament in London – with a blanket to sleep in, like. But, the Reverend Hay was quick to realise the danger."

"Danger?"

"Yes, from more joining in as they went through other towns. It'd be a veritable army that eventually got there. But, as I say, the Reverend Hay was quick, he had the yeomanry after 'em in no time."

"What has any of this to do with me?"

"You asked about the Blanket March, sir. And I was tellin' you as how Mr Hay is quick."

"Very well," sighed Pitt. "We have ascertained, beyond doubt, that Mr Hay is quick. May we proceed?"

"You are requested with the utmost expedition, to lay an offer before your client."

"What d'you mean by utmost expedition? Will the morrow not do?"

"No, it will not," declared the clerk pettishly. "I've just been tellin' you that the authorities have to act quick. If Miss Ridley will sign this undertaking not to declare Radical sentiments in public or cause further breach of the peace, all charges will be dropped."

"And if the client will not sign the undertaking?"

"Then to London she goes – on the criminal coach at noon tomorrow from the New Bailey. The Reverend Hay wishes you to act quickly. He has," the red-rimmed eyes engaged Pitt's, "a lot of influence with the gentry . . . you understand me, sir. Do you follow?"

Pitt snatched the document and almost pushed the furtive creature out into the square. He took a turn about the office and wished Crabtree would come back, then he could push the document onto him, and go to a splendid supper at Quay Street. But it would not happen that way. He knew it wouldn't. And, if it did, it would not please the Reverend Hay – and he could ill afford to antagonise him!

Where was Crabtree, he wondered? She's his client, had he not said so only this morning? While waiting, he thought of Miss Ridley . . . what if she had not been of Radical persuasion? What if she had not been on the mat at Heaton? What if he had not been so zealous – stupidly zealous, it now seemed – at the theatre?

What, he thought irritably, am I doing speculating on the impossible? He supposed he was missing Selina; missing the social life within the circle of their friends.

He would ask her to come up when the chambers were in decent order . . . take her out to Heaton Park, introduce her to Lady Egerton . . .

These musings had somehow lessened his former truculence at the possibility of having to go to Shudehill himself. If he could get Miss Ridley to sign this document, it would be a feather in his cap. The magistrates would be pleased, word would get about – as that disgusting little man had implied, trade would take off and a degree of social life with it. The opportunity was too good to miss. He put out the lamp – and set out for Shude Hill.

Chapter 18

After mounting the steps of the black-and-white-timbered Smallware Manufactory, he stood for a full two minutes before pulling the doorbell. He heard it echo in the house and then a scampering of feet. It was Fancy's night off and the door was opened by Sampson, who lifting the lamp higher, surveyed Pitt with the same round-eyed expression as he had at the office.

"Is Miss Ridley at home?"

Still the boy stared.

"Well, is she or isn't she?" Sighing with exasperation he took a card from his waistcoat pocket. "Present this to your mistress and tell her my errand is urgent."

Sampson placed the lamp on the window-ledge and ran up the creaking stairs. It was some time before he came down, and at first Pitt amused himself by wondering what their reaction was to his card. They might even not see him. And that, he readily admitted, would be disappointing, for, having got so far, he was curious. Then a worse thought occurred – had they forgotten him? Chosen to ignore him? Was he to be left on the doorstep like a tradesman? Then everything was normal again. Sampson came down to usher him inside, close the street door and take the lamp.

"Sitting-room's up there, first on yer left, sir." With that he scampered off, and left Pitt to go upstairs alone. The place smelled of lavender and beeswax, a combination which he found very pleasant. His footsteps reverberated along the polished oak floorboards, filling the passage in the quiet of the evening with creaks and clatters. It was only by light showing through cracks in the dried out panelling, that he could tell which room was occupied. The reason for his errand would be obvious. Somehow he felt no sense of satisfaction that it was he this time, and not she, who held the whip hand. He rapped on the door with squared knuckles.

It opened and Miss Etherington stood to gesture him inside. She saw at once the resemblance to his uncle, and a flash of memory went back over twenty years; to Smedley Vale after her father's funeral, and this young man's uncle explaining to her shocked mind why it was impossible to contest the will. 'What will you do?' he had asked. She had thought at the time he was embarrassed by so long a silence. "I will keep you informed," had been her reply.

Pitt was not familiar with the notion of living over business premises. It did not appear unattractive. The cosy opulence of the Brussels carpet, polished Jacobean furniture, the small fire in the gleaming grate, and the sparkle of several candelabra made him realise Mr Crabtree would not be amiss among the general shininess. But Mr Crabtree was not here – and he was. This was the lady, then, whose father had put so much money his uncle's way. He experienced a fleeting astonishment at the distinctive figure, so slender and straight of shoulder, looking so well in waistcoat and cravat – and what a fine diamond she sported in it. With a movement of her jewelled hand she dispelled his momentary astonishment, bade him be seated and state his errand.

She had not intended to seat him, but the opening of old wounds had made her legs seek the sanctuary of a chair. The bringing of bad news, it seemed, ran in the Caxton family.

"I prefer to stand," he was saying. "My visit will be brief."

She nodded and indicated the small table. "My ward and I are engaged in a particularly vicious game of cards . . . and are anxious to resume play as soon as possible – are we not, my sweet?"

He transferred his glance to Jancie, half expecting the medieval executioner, and felt again a fleeting astonishment. She was wearing a dark green kimono, which was as lustrous as a peacock's tail; and about her waist was a silver sash. Which of these women, he wondered, wrote 'My Darling Crabby'?

"My goodness, Mr Caxton." Jancie looked at him over the top of her spectacles. "You are straying from your side of the fence."

Yes, he thought, she would not make it easy, her sort never did. "If your call has anything to do with the Bradshaw Demonstration," Jancie continued, "Mr Crabtree, as I'm sure you are aware, is my legal representative."

"Yes, I am well aware, Miss Ridley. But, he has been out of the office all day, still is. And as Mr Hay requires your signature on this document . . .," he withdrew it from his coat, "with the utmost urgency. I had no choice but to bring it myself." He explained the legal requirements, and how the magistrates were using their powers of discretion to act quickly and avoid further unrest.

He stood, hands behind his back, on the same spot he had entered, and waited. Charles leaned forward to the box of Redtzkys, but Jancie, who had been scanning the document, looked up. "I'll get them, Charles." The kimono swished in the silence, as with a waxen taper she lit the cigars, drawing on each while he stifled the urge to cough. The kimono swished again as she returned to place the cigar between her guardian's lips.

"If you have any influence over your ward, Miss Etherington, please use it to persuade her to sign – otherwise Mr Nadin will be here in the morning to escort her to the New Bailey – in time for the criminal coach to London which leaves about noon, I'm told."

"Criminal coach! My ward is not a criminal, Mr Caxton."

Pitt was going to say she would be if she didn't sign, but Miss Ridley would construe that as a threat—

"London! Why, in the name of heaven would Mr Hay send her to London – and why the hurry?"

"Discretionary powers, ma'am. To set an example. And the Reverend Hay has a reputation for being quick, I believe."

Seeing them reminded him of a tableau, or a pose for a painting. Their dress, the cigars; the older woman sitting in her high-backed chair, one hand across the table holding that of the rebel. Crabtree had not exaggerated to say the relationship was extravagant. Pitt looked from them to their things lying about the room; the decanter and wine glass near Miss Etherington; the pewter by Jancie. Their books; flowers: a dish of toffee; drawings and charcoals; a copy of the *Leeds' Mercury* – and the layout of cards.

While Pitt was bewildering himself, Jancie was trying to summon a fierce bravery. So, it had come to this. Somehow she thought Mr Crabtree would be able to get her off, as he had before. She wondered if the Pentrich riot out Derby way had set the magistrates on edge – if so, she was certainly in trouble. She glanced at Charles; it wasn't fair to do this to her, not with Violet gone. To sign meant freedom. But for what? What was freedom without freedom of speech? How can you be a Radical and not want to talk about it? But with Habeas Corpus being suspended, she could be kept in the New Bailey for ever, and that amounted to the same thing.

"If there are any questions?" he prompted, anxious for a feather in his cap.

"Questions? No, Mr Caxton, merely an answer." Quick as the rustle of a kimono she lined the document up with

154

the fireplace and aimed it at the grate. Helpless in the grip of astonishment, they watched its flight. It landed on the embers, raking them into awareness. Once alerted, the flames caught on quickly; chuckling and crunching into the vellum, digesting it to a film of grey ash.

Whether Pitt choked with astonishment or on their cigar smoke he never knew. He gasped his way out, spluttering that she would regret so flagrant an action, and should hold herself in readiness for the New Bailey Prison at noon on the morrow. "Whence the criminal coach will bear you to your fate!"

"Was that wise, my dear?" asked Charles, after the street door had slammed.

"No," came the small-voiced reply. "It wasn't, but what is wisdom? How could I, as President of the Female Reformers, have appended my signature to that document? What a field-day they'd all have. I feel I'm on trial with the Rads as it is, and to fall at the first hurdle would just about finish me in that direction – half of 'em don't trust me, anyway." Jancie pushed back her chair, and going over to the hearth looked down on the grey ash that had once been proud vellum. "As I was saying, dear Charles, I couldn't sign as President of the Female Reformers, but I was sorely tempted as . . . as ward of the best, the kindest, the most beautiful guardian in all the world. That's why I burned the document – out of frustration, I suppose. First Violet, and now me – a nice pair we've turned out. She leaves you for the grand life, and I leave you for . . ." she shrugged. "Who knows what will happen? In fact, I'm proving more of a worry to you than Violet. At least she's safe and happy with Mirabelle . . ." She turned from the hearth as her guardian came over. "Did you hear what he said? They'll take me to London. Oh, dear God," she laughed shakily as tears brimmed over.

Charles put her arms round her ward, and drew the copper head to her shoulder. It was on her lips to ask . . . to beg, oh yes, her heart was not above begging that they send now for another document, that Jancie should sign it for her guardian and sister's sake. There was no doubt in Charles's mind that Jancie would comply – and for that reason she dared not even suggest it.

"Oh, to think there was never time to go to London – and now, I'm going as a criminal! Just when I've formulated plans for the travelling school as well – oh, everything will be interrupted. What a mess . . . meetings, plans, the autumn designs; they'll all have to manage without me!"

"And I'll have to manage without my Geisha Girl. Oh, darling, you're so young to be doing all this. Why you drive yourself on and on is a mystery." The suspension of Habeas Corpus made Charles sick with terror, and not wanting to pass any of it on, she said with forced brightness. "Let's be practical and engage our minds positively by making preparations for your absence, short though it will be. What I cannot understand, is why Crabby isn't here . . . I know," she said on a flash of inspiration. "I shall send Sampson round to Marsden Square with a note for his return, asking that he attend us at once – he'll travel down with you as your legal adviser, of course, but I need to talk to him about this . . . so-called charge."

Apprehension forbade sleep, and a lively imagination would have rendered the existing hours anguish, had not Charles – whose nerves and emotions had not undergone anything like this for the past twenty-odd years – taken the situation in hand. "I'll go and rouse Fancy – if she's in yet."

Fancy spent most of her late evenings at the Rover's Return, the next hostelry down from the Seven Stars, where she drank like a trooper, yet never showed signs of inebriation. The lamp was burning in the loft above the stable, and hearing her employer call, Fancy was at the sitting-room door in a trice. "What the 'ells going on, ma'am?"

156

When Charles explained, she let out a whistle of unbelief. "The swine!" She had stopped begging people's pardon for her language long ago – they had to take her as they found her. "Leave it to me, ma'am," she said with her usual competence. "I'll summon Margery, and the others will rally round." she turned to Jancie. "You did right not to sign their damned document – I'm proud of you. We'll all be proud of you. Let the scurvy swine know they can't muzzle the President of the Female Reformers, eh!"

Before anyone could answer, she was clattering downstairs. After rousing Clogger out of the Rover's Return, she woke Margery who, on the way to Shude Hill, woke Jem and was thrilled to walk alone with him through the darkness. She then threw pebbles up at Bob Smollet's upper window.

He put his head out. "What the—"

"Get yer arse over to Etherington's, quick, they've got Jancie!"

"Oh, my little cock o'wax." He muttered his pet name for Jancie, and yelled out that he would come at once.

When they were all there, all talking animatedly in the sitting-room where the unfinished game of cards was still displayed, Charles's emotions took on a frightening aspect. Their presence certainly cheered and encouraged Jancie, but it did nothing to reassure Charles. Such talk, she thought, would be considered inflammatory, subversive, vengeful – to say the least. It alarmed her that she hadn't realised how fiery it all was, and made her think of Arthur Thistlewood, and his revolutionary nick name of Citizeness for Jancie . . . not that Jancie was revolutionary; oh, why couldn't they make an example of people like Thistlewood? Why couldn't Mr Hay and that galoot Nadin pick on someone their own size?

Despite the awfulness of the situation, Charles, who had never seen either Smollett or Jem interacting with her ward, observed their obvious concern with interest. Jancie, for some reason, never discussed the men in her life, not in an intimate way, but Charles would 'know' when the right man arrived. What she would do about it was another matter.

Jem, tousled and tawny, looked stunned. He greeted Jancie shyly, eyes full of anxiety. He had warned her often enough that this might happen, really warning her against Bob Smollett – and if truth be told, he thought, Smollett was to blame. Now his warning had come true and he was confused and angry that someone so vital to his existence was being taken from him. Rather like when he was a schoolboy and the Reverend Brookes used to confiscate his humbugs.

Bob, in white shirt and breeches, had obviously found time to brush his hair. He was incensed at the injustice, and his incapacity to do anything about it. At times, his brown eyes, brilliant and fiery, would seek Jancie's, with a kind of half challenge as to whether she was able to run the course, as well as a fierce resentment against the magistrates. He knew she would rise to the occasion. You must, his look seemed to say, like the Scarlet, go through with it, for the sake of the Rads, the Female Reformers, for yourself; all this she caught from his glance, his manner, his dashing, slashing stance. His very confidence made her feel stronger.

Charles, her observation completed, reflected on the times she had read about Reformers being arrested and taken off to London. But you didn't take an awful lot of notice when it happened to someone else . . . perhaps even murmured that 'there was no smoke without fire'. But, when it affected your own it became possible to see things in a different way. After all, Jancie had only dramatized a procession, no harm was done . . .

The dawn light of a summer morning, with cock crow and bird-song, brought a dimension of normality to the frenzied speculations of the night. The gathering dispersed quietly, agreeing to meet at the New Bailey gates.

"I've missed our morning meetings," said Jem huskily when saying good-bye "When you're about town the thought of our accidental meeting often cheers me . . . but knowing you'll be—"

Jancie closed his lips lightly with her forefinger, and kissing him on the cheek, whispered, "Wait for Margery, there's a dear, and see her safely home."

Jancie had already told Margery that she and Jem were no longer sweethearts. Not that the news had been cheerfully accepted. "Jancie, how could you? He worships the ground you walk on. You're made for each other . . . Oh, you can be so cruel."

"It would be cruel," she had answered, "to have him live in hope. And besides, it would be unfair. You want a lot more from him than I ever would. You, Margery, will make him a better wife than ever I would . . . honestly." Such plain speaking had sent her friend's fair cheeks so crimson and her lips moving so speechlessly that Jancie had changed the subject.

This morning, as they parted by the door, her eyes sought the soft blue of Margery's, and touching the flaxen hair, she said earnestly, "Do what you can for Jem . . . he'll depend on you more, now that he's getting busier."

When they had all gone, Jancie realised that the women's time for bathing at the Infirmary Baths was from seven until noon; the times for male and female bathing alternated weekly. Making jokes about this being her last wish, the two were first through the Porter's Lodge.

Already news had spread, for the Bath Mistress, handing out soap, towel and wrapping gowns commiserated on the outcome of the popular demonstration in so doleful a tone that Jancie hurried on to the Shower Bath. Flinging off her clothes, she wrenched

159

at the handles of the water cocks, until she could scarce keep her feet against the ferocity of the jets. It was here Charles found her, lithe as a Spartan, head thrown back, eyes tightly shut, long hair streaked over neck and shoulders. Charles reduced the flow of water, then turned it off. "Come along, my dear," she said gently, holding out the wrapping gown. "Let's go and swim."

Jancie's body began to glow. Her mind felt more buoyant. Their wet feet, echoing down the flight of steps to the Lower Bath, quickened in pace. The hum of the Great Engine and the water noises began to work their magic. The slight smell of sulphur, of water on stone, the anticipation of the swim . . . all intoxicated their senses. Suddenly nothing seemed so important or urgent as slipping into that expanse of bubbling water. The Lower Bath itself filled most of the room. It was oblong in shape, bordered by two rows of classical columns and a narrow outer area of stone, with two simple wooden benches at either end.

The ritual was always the same, Charles prowled about in her gown, nerving herself. "Getting used to the idea," she would laugh. Although bathing dress was coming into vogue, it was by no means common, and those using the Lower Bath swam naked. As more men swam than women, Jancie and Charles often had the entire compartment to themselves. Leaving her gown on the bench, Jancie stood on the edge, tensing her body for the dive, squaring herself up. This observation never ceased to give Charles pleasure, not unmixed with the secretive tenderness experienced at the inn, en route from London. Her Geisha Girl would not always be with her . . . and she must be thankful for at least a few years of her company.

Charles inched herself in by the steps, gasping on each one, and murmuring, "It's damn cold, this!" But once in, she swam purposefully, head underwater, thrilling to the

160

movement of her limbs, the outhrust of arms, the smooth gliding through the green, clear depths.

"Oh, Charles." Jancie surfaced, shaking the water from her face, to exclaim, as always, "Isn't it exhilarating!"

They swam like otters, and behaved like children, their animated yells, at being ducked and splashed echoing beneath the lofty pillars, until, playtime over, they emerged laughing and nicely exhausted, to their wrapping gowns and a welcome breakfast at the Seven Stars, where Fancy was waiting to say she had seen Mr Crabtree arriving at Marsden Square.

Everything from then on was conducted with frantic haste. Clothes and food were packed; reams of paper filled with a long letter to Violet; another one with instructions for the Sunday School; notices for the Female Reformers urging them to support Fancy Macdonald, whom she had chosen to hold the reins until her return; notes were left for various business arrangements. Finally, when it could be fended off no longer, there was the moment of parting.

They were in the office, and Jancie, having closed the door of the club-footed wall cupboard, glanced about her with tears which could be held back no longer. Oh, how she loved this office. She wanted to remember everything about it, even to the spike of bills on the high desk. And Charles perching, distinguished and distinctive in coat and skirt of dark grey, on the edge of the writing table just as she had when she and Violet first came to the office. Charles had sat at an angle then, the severely cut lines of her skirt cascading over dove grey boots – yes, Jancie even remembered the colour. How Violet had ached with envy at the sight of a sliver of underskirt embroidered with pink rose-buds, and how it had fired her ambition to own one herself. And now Violet had dozens . . . and their beloved guardian was going to be left

161

alone . . . while Jancie, her right hand in the business, her companion, ward and friend, was going to prison – for a principle.

She moved across to her guardian and they embraced silently. Charles, with tears overflowing, drew the copper head close to her cheek. She wept out of sympathy for Jancie, and wept for herself, for the eternity of loneliness ahead.

"Come," sniffed Charles. "Time to get your things."

They moved apart, drying their eyes and silently gathering bags and a cloak. "You'll be back soon," said Charles, as they went out to the yard where, at the sight of Morocco standing patiently between the shafts, Jancie choked again with tears.

"Oh, Charles, I'll never be able to go through with this!"

"You mean . . . you've changed your mind?"

"No. No."

"Oh, damn you, Jancie – No, I didn't mean that. I'm sorry, I'm sorry."

On the way to the New Bailey, they called first at Marsden Square to collect Mr Crabtree, to save him a journey and to give Charles the opportunity to discuss the charge against her ward. But although they knocked loudly and it was half-past eleven already, the door was closed, and no one answered.

"He'll be waiting at the New Bailey – or perhaps he's gone to have a last word with Mr Hay . . . it's odd though that even Thomas isn't about . . ."

Afterwards Jancie called on the Reverend Brookes at Long Millgate to bid what she hoped was a temporary farewell to him, his cats, pet monkey and the pigeons. She could tell at once that he was in a bad humour – probably blaming her behaviour for the temporary shelving of the travelling school – and if she had expected anything resembling a blessing or a word of comfort, she was disappointed.

"Eh," he said sadly, ruffling her scarlet hair ribbon, "thou'rt a blockhead, Miss Japanese Dancing Girl! Ay, thou'rt a blockhead, indeed!" And with that he went into his house.

Jancie, dressed in a summer skirt of dark green and a white blouse with a scarlet overtunic, joined her guardian who was at the reins of the little, black van. "So, dear Charles," she said soberly. "Let us go now, as Mr Caxton said, to keep my appointment with Fate!"

In silence Charles drove from Long Millgate, crossing the Irwell at the Old Bridge, into Salford, and along Chapel Street which they noticed was becoming more populated. "It's the Rads, Charles!" exclaimed Jancie. "Oh, they've turned out in fine style!"

But the fine style was of no help when she stood alone before the criminal coach.

"Get inside!" yelled the officer!

"You can't go, yet," she gasped. "My lawyer hasn't arrived."

"Neither has theirs," he jerked his head toward the other prisoners; a mad youth, a murderer, and a female bigamist. "It don't make a pennyworth of difference, whether he's here or not. Waste o' money lawyers."

"Oh, please just another moment?"

"God love us, you're going to prison not on a bloody tour!"

"Team's in, sir."

"Right. Off with you, driver!"

The guard pulled up the step, slammed the door, locked it and applied a great padlock. The coach jolted forward. Springs creaked. Bridles jingled. They had not got so far as the great archway, before the prison officer was angrily racing after them. There was more cursing and fiddling with lock and padlock. The door was pulled open, a figure thrust into the empty seat, the step pulled up, door slammed, the ostlers shouted again, and the prison

163

officer danced after them roaring, "Be off with you! Off with you! Out of my sight!"

The coach lumbered under the arch and was out onto the street. Jancie pressed her face to the window. Although gatherings of people outside the prison gates were not allowed, people lingered on Chapel Street. Some were hoping to catch a glimpse of the criminals – but Charles was there, with Jem and Fancy Macdonald. They waved handkerchiefs feverishly, faces contorted into the fixed cheerfulness of people saying goodbye. Jancie waved, tears of desperation blurring her vision, until they were out of sight.

The coach was over the old bridge before she could bring herself to address the dark figure in a many caped coat. "Where?" she asked faintly. "Is Mr Crabtree?"

Less than an hour before, all had been chaos at Marsden Square. Unknown to Mr Crabtree, Pitt had gone to the furnishers, and Mr Crabtree had sent Thomas to Quay Street to see where Pitt was. And, when Pitt did arrive, Thomas thrust a bundle of documents into his hands. "Your first client, sir."

"But these are the Ridley papers," he had protested. "What is Mr Crabtree thinking of? Where is he?" Without waiting for an answer he raced up the stairs. The office was empty, so he ran to the top floor.

"Come in."

But Pitt was already in, already demanding an explanation. "May I remind you, sir, that neither Miss Etherington or her ward are my clients."

"You are a partner of this firm, and, as partner, you are going to London to conduct whatever defence they will allow."

"But, she's your client!"

"I know that, you fool. Do you think I'd trust her with you – oh, to the devil – it's me gout! Look at this leg. It took the cabman half an hour to get me up here

164

last night. I couldn't bear to be jostled to Piccadilly in a sedan chair, still less London in a coach. Move man!" he had urged. "Oh, for heaven's sake, hurry!"

So Pitt had hurried, and here he was. "Mr Crabtree is nursing a severe attack of gout – damn his eyes!"

"And he sent you?"

"I'm sorry to say, Miss Ridley, he has." He removed his hat and placed it on his knees; he watched the raindrops trickle off it and glanced at the woman opposite. He had suspected from the very first that she was sailing close to the wind, but had never thought he would have to put up her defence. Did I read law, he asked himself, to keep ragamuffin Radicals from the gallows? He shifted his gaze to the other occupants, one in chains the other two suitably manacled. A journey to London in a criminal equipage! No overnight stops. Just time enough to change horses, relieve the bladder and snatch a hunk of bread and beef . . . and the interminable jog . . . jog . . . The damp would no doubt set his asthma off, dear heaven! He leaned back as waves of desperation washed over him. What about the refurbishing of his office? Workmen had to be stood over, watched. He ought to be there for consultation. He had been due to give an after-dinner speech at the Pitt Club and Lady Egerton was expecting him at Heaton Park this weekend. The coach already smelled of dank straw and sweat – oh, and the conversation for the next three days would be scintillating!

That it was not Mr Crabtree's gleaming personage sitting opposite her was an awful shock to Jancie. Although not of Radical opinion, he would die in her defence. But what could she expect at the hands of this man? Of course, Crabby had done his best, poor dear. And she supposed that Pitt Caxton was better than nothing. After all, the thought of going to London with no legal representation had been daunting. She failed to see how there could be any client-lawyer understanding between herself and him. She did not trust him, did not even like him. But, with Habeas Corpus being suspended, he was better than nothing.

Chapter 19

Jancie never knew how long she had stared out of the mud-splashed window of the coach. She was impervious to the iron bars across; impervious to the countryside beyond Ardwick Green; to the timid who stood and gazed open-mouthed at the grim-looking vehicle; or the lads who ran alongside to catch a glimpse of the prisoners, cheering the guard riding shotgun.

Already she was cut off, isolated, incarcerated, imprisoned. Cooped up like Jem's cocks, only in conditions not half as clean. That she was here through her own choice only served to deepen her reflection, but, if the magistrates were out to get you, it really was only a matter of time. But that they should choose this particular time – after the victory at Heaton Park, and just when the travelling school was almost on the road . . . Oh, if only Mr Crabtree were here, she wouldn't be thinking like this, he wouldn't let her.

"Prisoners out!" yelled the guard. "Come on, look lively, there!" Anything less lively than the shackled, shuffling trio Jancie had yet to see. With a series of shoves and pushes with the butt of the blunderbuss, the guard chivvied them first to the privy, and then to an allowance of bread and water in the yard.

Due to being in the company of a lawyer; to the possession of money; and to the rare event of having a young woman of manners as a prisoner, the guard allowed Jancie to buy her own food and to use the privy unaccompanied. The privy was foul, the food poor and the ale adulterated, but none of that mattered – the glimpse of normality, of people going about their everyday tasks revived her spirits.

The prisoners had remained silent throughout the day, but the hours of darkness encouraged the murderer to sob and sniffle his remorse, and the mad youth to startle them all with his screams, which in turn set the bigamist rattling her chains. Jancie, despite the warmth of her cloak, shivered. Her heart beat fast with fright. She did not like darkness. It reminded her of Jepson's factory floor when the others had gone to the fireworks; of the deserted looms standing stark like gravestones. She fixed her gaze on the windows, eager for a sight of a lamp, a lightening of the night sky, a glimpse of the moon from behind the clouds.

She stirred, opened her eyes, sniffed. There was a woody fragrance, sharpening the damp, mildewy odour of the coach. She glanced at the opposite window, expecting to see Caxton's hunched outline. She put on her spectacles and peered through the shadowy darkness. Caxton was crouched on the floor.

"What on earth's the matter? What are you doing down there?" Her voice, though raised, was lost in the babblings and ravings, the creaking of the coach, the thundering of wheels and hooves.

"Are you ill?" she yelled.

"Can't breathe . . ." His fingers clawed at the neck of his shirt. "Asthma . . ."

Jancie grabbed his arm and half-hoisted, half-pushed him onto the bench. "What are you looking for?"

Between gasps and wheezes, she gathered he was trying to ignite a herbal pastille to help him breath when the coach jolted the tinder-box out of his hand. She stooped to the squelchy straw, spreading both hands swiftly over the surface. She found the tinder-box at once. "Quick. Where are the pastilles?"

There being no answer Jancie searched, running her

168

mud-stained fingers over his heaving chest, until locating the small box in his waistcoat pocket. Still stooping over him, balancing herself against the motion of the coach, she struck the tinder; in its lurid light his raven black hair fell jagged across a pale forehead, droplets of sweat glistened, then hurried down his jawline to be absorbed into the loosened stock. She quickly ignited the herbal concoction, fixed it into the lid of the box, and again bracing herself against the movement of the coach, held it for him to inhale. The aromatic fragrance sweetened the air; calmed the prisoners, and after some moments eased Pitt's breathing. In the darkness his chilled fingers brushed her warm hand as he took the box. "My thanks . . . Miss Ridley."

At the morning stop, having staggered out into the dawn light, limbs stiff and clothes crumpled, Jancie gulped a hasty breakfast, and was escorted back to the coach.

"Thought you'd be on the box Mr Caxton, enjoying the good air."

"Last night . . . I lacked the breath to thank you properly for your assistance."

"I have a vested interest, remember."

"Precisely. Which brings me to the reason I'm travelling inside, uncomfortable and damp though it be." The end of the ghastly journey now being only a few hours away, Pitt was in a better humour, and having been struck by her uncomplaining fortitude and the unfussable manner in which she had dealt with his asthma, found it possible to discuss the legal situation amicably.

Not that Jancie was for amiability. She was glad now of the rattling coach; it gave her the opportunity to raise her voice. "I'm not guilty. It's a trumped up charge organized by the magistrates. You were there. I did not incite a riot. If those stupid roughnecks of soldiers hadn't interfered, we would have all dispersed in silence. I'm looking to you to get me off," she shouted.

"I'm afraid that is not up to me! Listen, Miss Ridley, a defence, in proper terms of law does not apply in your case. I am instructed to lodge the papers with the Home Office, or rather – with the Secret Committee—"

Her heart lurched with fear. The Secret Committee consisted of Lord Castlereagh and Viscount Sidmouth, the two most hated men in England . . . the very men whose effigy she had cast into the Irwell!

"Then," Pitt continued, "their lordships will set a date for your interrogation and, depending on their findings, you could be released and charged in court with an offence – that is where my services would come in. On the other hand, you could be set free. And, then again, Habeas Corpus being suspended, they have the power to "detain you in their pleasure, which," he concluded, "is another way of putting dissidents and rabble rousers out of the way for a year or two."

"Will you do something for me, Mr Caxton?" Jancie was suddenly terrified.

He turned toward her, eyebrows raised. "What is it you wish me to do?"

"Will you take a letter to my sister, Violet? She lives in St James's with my guardian's cousin, the Honourable Mrs Moxham."

"Yes, I owe you that much at least . . . Tell me, is there an Honourable Mortimer Moxham?"

"Yes. Why d'you ask? Are you acquainted?"

"My fiancée is."

"Your fiancée?"

"No need to look so amazed!"

Amazement momentarily overcame her fear, especially to see him smile. On the three occasions she had seen him his lips had never once curved into anything resembling a smile – but then, recalling those circumstances, there had been nothing to smile about! As he concentrated on the documents, she peered at him through her spectacles; noticing the olive-coloured skin; the hair, thick and springy, curbing neatly the nape of his neck. No wonder Clogger had thought him a gypsy! Heavily-fringed lashes, shielded slate grey eyes, and these were topped by an expressive pair of slanting eyebrows.

Reaching into her valise which was now on the seat beside her she withdrew the letter previously written to Violet and held it on her lap until the country roads turned into the busy streets of London.

"Where . . . Where are they taking me?"

"Were you not informed?" He turned his head to reply, and then added, "To Newgate."

Newgate! How dare they? She thought of the magistrate; the Reverend Hay was more concerned about advancement and his fashionable flock than the merciful dispensing of justice. And William Hulton, so pretty a fellow as to be nicknamed 'Miss Hulton', always chose the least line of resistance. But then, she thought, indignation waning, why should I expect them to treat me differently simply because of my guardian's social standing?

Entering Newgate Yard, she handed the letter to Pitt, and said with a small smile. "You will keep Mr Crabtree informed – and the Moxhams?"

He had just bowed his acquiescence when the turnkey came to conduct her to the office. He consulted a list. "Civil disobedience eh? Incitation to Riot? Trouble maker?" He glanced at her apprehensive face. "Come for a little 'oliday have yer? Newgate by the Sea . . . London's best resort!" Then, taking up a lamp, he led the way into a narrow passage, his keys clanging like church bells at a funeral.

Water glistened on the walls, and breath turned to vapour in the chill. Footsteps echoed, and shadows leapt in the lamp's glare. Jancie experienced a curious taste – it was blood. She had bitten into her lip. Faint sounds of weeping impinged on the silence. Coming from where? From dungeons below; behind heavy padlocked doors?

171

Emanating from the walls? Muffled groans and cries of anguish mingled with screams of laughter . . . or madness. The man stopped, unlocked the door, and pushed her inside. She heard the door slam, the key grate in the lock.

Jancie stood with her back to the door and tried not to inhale; the stench was overpowering. It, too, was imprisoned. She mastered her nausea and remained still. The sepulchral clanking of iron keys faded, leaving her with the lesser sounds . . . muted movements . . . the catching of breath . . . the closeness of bodies.

As her eyes became used to the semi-darkness – for there was a grating admitting light – she saw a ghastly tableau of grey figures; about thirty women, gaunt like spectres, others frail like wraiths. Children, their little faces already old and hunger pinched.

The surroundings, she tried to reassure herself, were not unlike the derelict warehouses by the Irwell, and the inmates not all that much different from the vagrants and villains of the riverside community who came and went – only these, like herself, would not have that privilege. One of the wizened children, unused to silence, began to whimper.

"Well, I'm glad someone's got a voice," Jancie said. Immediately, the tableau, moved by a collective insight, closed in. Hands reached out; begging, touching, tugging.

Jancie stayed where she was, clutching the valise, not yet ready to accept a position in the tableau, not yet able to comprehend fully that this was actually happening to her. To stay by the door was a comfort, a last link with the world beyond these terrible walls. She would stand here until sleep cast its shadow over her eyes . . . until her body slowly drooped onto the straw. And when that happened, she knew from her beggar days, they would close in, like crows over a corpse, pecking here and picking there, haggling with hushed fury over her

172

possessions. Come the daylight, she would take up her position in the tableau as if nothing had happened.

And indeed it was so. Coat, hat, shoes, stockings, gloves, money, ornaments out of her hair, a ring off her finger, and spectacles were gone. It was the stealing of the latter which affected her most, reducing her to the old eyesight problem, to the old uncertainties. When thoughts of home intruded, she pushed them aside. But she wondered constantly if Mr Caxton had delivered her letter to Violet. Why had he not communicated with her? Why hadn't Mrs Moxham at least sent a message?

Chapter 20

The longest, the most miserable week Jancie had ever known ended with the turnkey escorting her to an early morning interrogation by the Secret Committee. Once out of that foetid, overcrowded atmosphere, her personality gathered itself together. In the swiftness of this summons she recognised the intervention of the Honourable Mortimer and Mirabelle Moxham. They had no doubt portrayed her to their lordships as a deluded, idealistic female who needed a quick reprimand to bring her to her senses.

"I need water to wash," she said urgently. He was about to refuse, but she added, "Their Lordships will be offended if I tread this sewer filth before them."

The turnkey considered for a moment, then indicated a bucket of freshly drawn water. She quickly plunged her head and face in its depths, clearing her mind, washing away the apathy. Then she vigorously rubbed the caked dirt off her arms before attacking feet and legs. She cleaned the hem of her gown as best she could. Water . . . oh, lovely, refreshing, invigorating water! She permitted herself to think of the Infirmary Baths, of swimming with Charles . . . of the Moxhams' bathrooms.

She was taken to a more civilised part of the prison and the lofty room of interrogation.

"Stand forward," commanded the usher. "Step to the table and acknowledge their lordships." She bowed her head before each, her gaze falling first on Castlereagh, for of the two, he was the most unpopular.

174

Lord Castlereagh was every inch an aristocrat, tall, fashionably dressed, with fine, dark eyes now fixed on Jancie as though she was the first of a species. She glanced at Sidmouth. He, too, was tall, and wore a plum-coloured coat, and was inclined to stoop. He bore the air of a High Church cleric, and, due to the intonation of voice, was referred to by his colleagues as 'Goody Sidmouth'.

"Ah, the Manchester woman . . ." breathed Viscount Sidmouth. So . . . thought Jancie, there is such a thing as the Home Office List. There were so many stories circulating that you never knew how much was truth, invention, or rumour circulated by government agents to frighten people into submission.

"It is a measure of our concern for the state of the country," Sidmouth was saying, "that we have formed this Committee, to ascertain the truth. You will, therefore, answer all my questions truthfully. Do you understand?

"Yes, your Lordship."

He sat down while a clerk read out an account of the "silent, sinister procession" to the point where the effigies were hurled over the parapet, and the charge of "Incitation to Riot" and "Wilful Insubordination" in not signing the magistrates' bond.

The silence, carved by the scratching of quills as the clerks prepared to record all the proceedings, did nothing to reassure her. Every word would be sieved and sniffed for the slightest speck of . . . what?

"That you stand thus, before us, is entirely your own doing?"

"Yes, lour Lordship."

"You are, I understand an advocate of the views of Mary Wollstonecroft, a Radical writer and an atheist, who studied in Revolutionary Paris. She lived in an unmarried state with an American and bore a child out of wedlock. Then, after an equally sinful liaison with William Godwin, she married him. He has been called the 'prophet of anarchy'. Do I understand your views to be an echo of these revolutionary persons?"

"You have omitted, your lordship, to mention her views on the rights of women, with which I am in total agreement."

"Rights of women?"

"The basic right, your lordship, to exercise choice and judgement; the right to such education as is available; and rights over their person and property."

The sound of her voice, forthright and purposeful against the scratch, scratch of the quills, increased her confidence and reduced the previous terror to handleable proportions.

"Rights! Rights!" his voice rose higher with each word. "Over persons and property! Why, the very words smack of revolution. The choice and judgement you have exercised, Miss Ridley, are highly questionable. Female Unions, marches, demonstrations and petitions . . . furthermore," he leaned forward as over a pulpit, "the particular freedom you enjoy as ward of a wealthy guardian enabled you, under cover of visiting that very guardian's relatives here in London, to make contact with political persons and attend assemblies of a Radical nature."

"May I respectfully point out, Your Lordship, that those assemblies were perfectly legal, and that eminent people were present. Sir Francis Burdett, Lord Cochrane, Major Cartwright—"

"And may I point out, Miss Ridley, that His Majesty's Government will not tolerate insubordination from within its ranks; and infinitely less, riots and disturbances! In the recent insurrection at Pentrich, near Derby," he continued with mesmeric vehemence, "a man was killed and arrests made. Here, on Spa Fields, in the nation's capital city, shots are fired and blood is spilled. In Greenock and Birmingham the militia are on stand by. Property is attacked, weapons are stolen. The French Revolution,

176

Miss Ridley, is not going to be repeated this side of the Channel – not under the guise of Reform or anything else!" Jancie stood transfixed as the fearful, vein-inflating crescendo reached its peak. "To return to the political assemblies," his voice came down the scale. "You were introduced to Henry Hunt, from the west country, once a devout loyalist, now a raving Radical, a mob orator; riding about the kingdom in the company of another man's wife . . . and then," his tone took on a cunning softness, "there is Arthur Thistlewood."

Arthur! Her eyes widened in astonishment. How long, she wondered had they been collecting this information?

"Ex-lieutenant in the militia," he intoned, "a firebrand, Miss Ridley, who escorted you round the Waterloo Celebrations. Thistlewood, who actually assisted the French in their Revolution. He has already been on trial for treason."

Put-up treason, thought Jancie, recalling the newspaper account of the jury throwing out evidence of government spies because it did not tally. She was amazed. How low could nobility stoop to recruit spies of so little intellect as to present conflicting evidence.

He was off again. She gave a mental sigh to hear the petty aspects of her life brought up as evidence. The purchasing of Cobbett's *Journal* . . . the reading of it in a public place – Smollett's! Every bit of tittle tattle . . .

"The effigies . . ." Sidmouth was saying. "Those thrown into the river, bore a striking likeness, so the informant assures, to myself and Lord Castlereagh. What have you to say, Miss Ridley?"

Her green eyes came to meet his directly. "Whoever the informant is I suggest they look to their sight."

"Perhaps you will acquaint us with the true likeness?"

"The Bradshaw brothers," she lied.

After a short silence, he inhaled deeply through flared nostrils. "I put it to you, Miss Ridley, that you would not sign Mr Hay's bond because it would interfere with your indoctrination of tender minds?"

"I did not sign the bond, Your Lordship, because of the basic right to speak freely."

"A right, Miss Ridley, His Majesty's Government is about to curtail."

Thirty minutes later she was released. Turned out. There were no other words to describe it, she thought, an anticlimax after all the fear and dreadful anticipation which had preceded the questioning. Out through the big gates and into the early morning street.

Jancie leaned for a moment against the railings. She felt drained. Having stood too long, weak from too little food and too much adulterated gin, she had only faintly heard Viscount Sidmouth's decision. "It would grieve me," he had said, "for the sake of your connections, to incarcerate you for a long time. Lord Castlereagh and myself, put these charges down to an over idealistic enthusiasm engendered by the hardship of your younger days. We also detect a lack of maturity, something which a good marriage will put right. Should you come before this committee again, you will not be so fortunate. Furthermore, we shall inform the Reverend Hay of our decision that you relinquish all matters of education. You have, through your own folly, placed yourself for the marked attention of this Committee. Therefore, Jancine Ridley, you are dismissed, and abjured to conduct yourself in a manner conducive to the state of womanhood and the position in which you have been fortunate enough to find yourself."

Standing outside, relief was tinged with bitter disappointment . . . "that you relinquish all matters of education . . ." So, she thought, I might as well have signed Mr Hay's bond in the first place . . . There would

178

not be any travelling school . . . any Sunday school or any other school.

Her hand on the iron railing was cold and wet. She peered into the fog, expecting any moment to see the outline of the Moxhams' carriage. It was not there.

And what about Mr Caxton? A wave of despair swept over her. Oh, it was all too much. Tears welled up, she brushed them away with the back of her hand and moved slowly off into the fog.

After a while she became conscious of footsteps, muffled yet close. She sighed with relief – someone had come for her. She turned, and called into the greyness. "Violet? Mr Caxton?"

A figure emerged from the fog, looming up like a genie. Another man followed quickly on his heels, and roughly seizing her arms, propelled her along quickly.

"Who are you?" she gasped.

"Never mind who we are, Miss Ridley. You're among friends. Come quietly now – or I'll cut yer throat!"

Chapter 21

Immediately they plunged into a maze of mean alleys. It was a silent maze. No one passed. No one seemed to be living in the mean, little houses. It was as though the world were dead and they were shuffling through it. No scavengers came to sweep the thoroughfares. No waterman with his barrels to sweeten the streets. The place was as desolate as Jancie felt. The men were too close for her to see them clearly, but the grip on her arms and the threat on their lips was enough to keep her compliant.

Inwardly she railed against Pitt Caxton, against the Moxhams and Violet. Oh, if only one of them had been outside the prison, these men would not have dared to abduct her. Is that what was happening? Was she being abducted? By whom? Who would want her? She had nothing, not even a shoe to her feet . . . and where were they taking her?

The fog, thinning since they left Newgate, was now almost clear; the men suddenly halted in the yard of what had been, in its time, a fine coaching inn. It stood balustraded and bedraggled, a couple of broken carts in the place where the Taunton Flyer used to stand. One of the men, who boasted a fine crop of mutton chop whiskers, broke away and pulled open a trap door by a gathering of deserted barrels. The other man pushed Jancie toward it. "Oh, no," she cried, teetering on the edge.

"Aw, the lady said she ain't goin' down!" mocked the

man in the pepper-and-salt jacket. "P'raps she's afraid o'the dark . . ."

"Pray set foot on the top rung," said a voice from the cellar. "You are among friends, Miss Ridley, and there is a lamp down here."

She frowned, hesitated, trying to peer into the depths, and then, catching sight of the knife, began to let herself down.

"Steady . . ." A warm hand grasped her firmly about the bare ankle, and as she stepped lower the hand moved higher, until it was now just below her knee.

"I'm quite capable of descending a ladder," she said briskly, "without any familiarity from . . . whoever you are."

"Well said, ma'am, and as pert as ever!" Strong hands reached up to her waist and pulled her down the last few steps.

"What's amiss," he said. "Last time my arms were round your waist you were a lot warmer than that!"

"Arthur!" she exclaimed. "Oh, Arthur Thistlewood, you must be raving mad!"

"So were you at one time." He made a grand sweep of his arm. "We were all gloriously mad, caught up in the fervour of Waterloo, and the passion . . . of Radical gatherings."

"What have you brought me here for?" she demanded. "And at knife point? I would never have believed it of you."

"Would you have come otherwise?"

"No, I would not. As you are obviously aware I have just been released from the Secret Committee."

"Yes, and that's the reason for bringing you here," he said earnestly. "I need to know the gist of their questioning. It is important to me, Jancie. For the sake of old times . . ." His smile was one of roguish cajolery. "Or if that won't do, for the sake of the movement we are both pledged to."

Her thoughts moved quickly. There was no harm in relating the interview, she'd be telling the Manchester Rads anyway, and the sooner he was in receipt of the information, the sooner she could be up that ladder and off. "Very well . . ." She quickly related the interview, including the remarks about himself.

"You showed spirit, Citizeness."

"Don't call me that again."

"You liked it at one time."

"It pays to be more careful nowadays. Besides," she leaned against a barrel for support. "I've no stomach to go to prison again."

He signalled the mutton chop whiskers. "Fetch the lady a noggin of . . . ale. You see, I have remembered your Radical taste. Oh, Jancie, we had good times, didn't we? So spontaneous, a thing of the moment. A marvellous romp – one of the happiest . . ." he lowered his voice. "the happiest three weeks of my tempestuous life."

She recalled their parting. "Never forget," he had said, "that it was with me you danced on the lawn, to the melody of moonbeams . . . and in the magic of moonlight." It seemed now to have been in another world, another life.

He had changed; he was thinner and looked a lot older, she thought. To judge by the state of his clothes, he seemed to be down on his luck – even so, he looked a sight better than herself! And, as before, her own suffering and sacrifice seemed wispy and fragile compared to his.

"Ah, here's the ale," he smiled, passing a jug and eyeing her speculatively. "I have an excellent toast – to the revolution!"

"To Reform," she replied, and after a long drink, wiped her lips on the back of her hand. "Oh, this is good, Arthur, almost worth coming for!"

"Do you remember my great ambition?"

"If you're referring to that mad scheme of blowing

182

the Prince Regent off his throne, I don't want to hear about it – now or ever again!"

"You make me sound like Guy Fawkes."

"And you know what happened to him."

"Do I detect censure?"

"All you detect is me being in a hurry to get away from here."

"Because the talk grows hot?"

"Oh, Arthur," she said faintly. "Can't you think of anything else! Because I'm exhausted, hungry, and cold! I've told you about the Secret Committee, and now I'm going to try and find the Moxhams—"

He moved closer to where she leaned on the barrel; so close that she could feel the pressure of his leg. Then, taking her hand, he raised it almost to his lips, and then spoke urgently. "I must be able to count on the support of the Manchester Rads. You must persuade them, Jancie. Revolution is coming. We already have a committee – an army." He held her astonished gaze with glittering eyes, before pressing a gentle kiss on her lips. "I must have their support," he repeated.

"Caught you!"

Arthur sprang back as if he had been shot.

"So, you wanted to interrogate her, did you?" A woman of about thirty slowly emerged from the darker parts of the cellar and made her way to the pool of light. She stood before them, breasts thrust forward, hand on hip, dark head tossed back, and eyes flickering with suspicion. Jancie recognised the attitude of a jealous woman, and what was worse obviously Arthur's woman. "You said you wanted to question her . . . this marvellous woman from the north! Close questioning, is that it? And I saw yer 'ands up her skirts as she came down the ladder."

"Susan, my dear—"

"Don't you 'my dear' me!"

"Whatever you think—" began Jancie.

"No one's asked for your opinion! And don't you

183

forget I'm his lawful wedded, Miss Fancy Drawers. Oh, I know all about you. Gutter girl raised above her station. Playing at Reform; playing with fellas; a foot in both camps."

"What did you say?"

"You 'eard, but I'll say it again. A foot in both camps."

Jancie stared, momentarily stunned. To think she had lost forever her grand scheme of a travelling school; suffered that awful journey in the criminal coach; enduring the filth of prison; almost dying with fright under Sidmouth's cold eyes, and this creature had the sheer—

Quick as a snake's tongue Jancie's hand shot out, and sent Susan sprawling backwards. She clambered slowly to her feet, seizing a piece of rusty, iron hoop.

Jancie grabbed the jug – now emptied of ale – smashed it against the barrel, and held it out in defence. "Don't you dare to suggest that ever again. D'you hear?"

Susan heard and stepped back uncertainly, her dark eyes moving slowly to the jagged edge of the jug. She could ill afford any loss of beauty. It was her only asset; but no one had ever got the better of her before. It went against her nature to back off, but she did so, reluctantly . . . there would be other times.

Jancie indicated the piece of iron. "Put it down."

Susan hesitated.

"Put it down, damn you!"

As the iron clattered among the barrels, she turned on her husband. "And you stood there and let her humiliate me! Listen, if she's so genuine, get her to supply them ferrules."

Jancie looked from one to the other.

"You're in smallware; umbrellas and parasols?"

"What if I am?"

Arthur came alive again. "We need weapons. And a pike with a ferrule stuck in the top makes a crude,

184

but effective bayonet. The London Rads want you to supply 'em."

"I can't. What you're asking is impossible! To begin with, we never send ferrules to London. And if we start now, Miss Etherington would become curious, and the magistrates, already bristling on account of the insurrection at Derby, would have Constable Nadin onto me in trice. No," she declared firmly. "Too much is at stake. The risk is too great."

"Risk!" Susan lurched forward. "Risk! The whole Reform is a bloody risk!"

"When you have been before the Secret Committee, Susan Thistlewood, you'll have room to shout about risk. So, till then, keep your big mouth shut and your lying teeth closed!"

"See, Arthur, I told you Miss Fancy Drawers wouldn't help." And seeing Jancie was already on the ladder, she felt it safe to yell after her. "Prison could have been a sham, to give you esteem in the eyes of the Rads! That's why you got off so lightly – a sham, that's what you are – a bloody sham!"

But Jancie was up the ladder, and Arthur, pushing Susan aside, shouted frantically, "Think of it, Citizeness. A Radical army of six hundred, unmemployed navvies. They can't fight the military without a weapon. You can provide 'em! You must act, Jancie. Strike a blow for Reform!"

But she was up the ladder, flung open the trap, and ignoring the mutton chop whiskers and his cohort, hurried away, letting the noise of traffic direct her to the main thoroughfare.

After many enquiries Jancie found her way to the Moxhams' house in St James's. Not that she recalled much about her arrival. Sheer necessity had kept her going, but once on the doorstep, she alarmed the footman by collapsing at his feet, and was only saved

185

from being put back on the street by the parlour-maid recognising the colour of her hair.

She woke from a twenty-four hour sleep to find herself in the big four-poster bed she had shared with Violet; nestling within apricot silken sheets; propped on frilled pillows; and with Mirabelle and Violet sitting on either side.

"Oh, my dear girl," Mirabelle stood up, putting her hands together. "Thank God you have survived!"

"Oh, Jancie—" Violet threw herself on the bed, and into her sister's arms. They hugged each other silently, eyes closed, bodies strained; and for a moment they were little girls again, calling each other 'dear' as their father had; embracing against the darkness, the cold, the cruelty of Jepson's cotton factory.

At last, when tears were dried, and they felt safe within the old intimacy, Jancie related her experiences.

"Don't tell me any more!" Violet begged. "Oh, you poor, poor thing!"

"But, you knew I was in Newgate? Mr Caxton did bring you my letter?"

"Yes, of course," answered Mirabelle. "We could not get permission to visit. Viscount Sidmouth's Secretary told Mr Caxton that a short, sharp week in prison, with no visiting, would do you no harm and was guaranteed to bring you quickly to your senses. He said that he relied on both Mr Caxton's and Mortimer's co-operation. Mr Caxton, they said, would be informed of your release and, of course, we would have sent the carriage for you. He called yesterday, news of your collapse on the doorstep having got about, full of apologies, and apparently, knew nothing of your release. Really, my dear, this is all extremely terrible – the Secret Committee, I believe, are a law unto themselves. But I've already written to Charles, post-haste, telling her that you are free and here in safety and comfort."

"Thank you, Mirabelle," said Jancie simply, holding

186

out both her hands. "Thank you for your intervention, and your hospitality. I hate to think what would have happened otherwise."

"All I ask, nay, beg of you, my dear, is that you tread carefully and moderate your views . . . for Charles's sake, at least. I think you owe her that much. And now . . ." with a conspiratorial glance at Violet, she moved toward the door. "I shall have some coffee and muffins sent up . . . you two will have a lot to talk about."

"What are you and Mirabelle up to?" Jancie smiled. "Here I am still in the after-throes of prison. Surely you are not thinking of social engagements?"

"Pray don't mock Society, Jancie, if it had not been for the intervention of Mortimer, you might have finished up in Van Diemen's Land – and what would that have done to our guardian?" Her violet eyes clouded. "I hate Reform and anything that reminds me of those years of beggary . . ." The cloud quickly passed. "Anyway," she brightened. "There is one little engagement, only one."

"No."

Violet's hand fluttered bewitchingly, as she braced herself for argument. "I really cannot allow your social graces to wither, they don't get much of an airing in Manchester, and after Newgate . . . well!"

"You don't understand, Violet. I want to return home as soon as possible."

"To your raffish Female Reformers! Oh, Jancie, darling, you are stubborn! Now I shall have to tell you, and I wanted it to be a surprise. Mirabelle is holding a soirée in your honour – although disapproving of your Radical antics, we are really quite proud of you, and are looking forward to showing you off. But what I wanted to keep as a surprise, was an introduction to my new beau at the soirée."

"Oh, Violet, I'm delighted for you! Do I know him? Don't tell me, let me guess. Is it George, or Teddy of the tasselled boots?"

187

"Oh, they're mere boys . . . Dyson is more mature, a proper man. Dyson Edwards is his full name. Oh, and he is good looking; wears elegant clothes, and the most stylish Wellington boots – puts the Iron Duke in the shade! He talks well, is witty and so attentive. I've told him all about you."

"All?"

"You know what I mean."

"No, Violet, I do not."

"Does it matter?"

"It could . . . but," to smooth the alarm from the oval face opposite, she added, "Oh, it's just me being nervous after my rendezvous with the Viscount!"

"I'll never understand why you let yourself in for all this . . ." said Violet on a note of petulance. "It really is so disagreeable." Almost at once her mood changed to one of delighted anticipation. "Now, what are you going to wear? We'll have the dressmaker in – she's wonderful at rigging up on short notice . . . and tomorrow we'll visit the optician and get you some more spectacles. Can't have you stepping back to look at Dyson – he'll think you're odd!"

The sisters walked along the passage to the top of the wide stairway. Jancie stared in amazement. "Soirée! It's more like a jamboree." She drank the wine in her hand at one draught. "Oh, Violet, all this is on too grand a scale for my comfort."

"Mirabelle does tend to overdo things, but, as she said, 'nothing is too grand for Charles's ward.' What could I say? She means well."

The conversation took them into what the Moxhams called the 'marble drawing room' on account of the marble fireplace and sculpted overmantel, where Jancie, on being approached by a man wearing a magnificent pair of Wellington boots, rallied herself for Violet's sake.

"I know who you are," she smiled a greeting. "Dyson

188

Edwards. Your boots proclaim your fame. Without your boots, sir," she chaffed, "you are nothing!"

"Indeed, I ain't much with 'em, Miss Ridley."

Through the marcasite spectacles she saw a man of at least thirty, attractive in an easy, careless way. Good looking, as Violet had said, even though smallpox had left its mark on his lower jaw.

"Reform proclaims your fame," he countered, "a much nobler cause than mere fashion."

"I'm pleased you think so, sir, there are not many here would agree with you."

"You are from the north, Violet told me. Manchester, I believe?"

"And where are you from, Mr Edwards? I don't recall Violet actually mentioning it."

"I travel," he replied evenly. "My business, although mainly in London, takes me about the country."

"If it brings you north," said Jancie, wanting to end the conversation, "we may perhaps meet up some time."

"We may indeed, Miss Ridley. Ah, our hostess is coming to carry you off."

"Oh, been lookin' for you, everywhere," declared Mirabelle, leading her out into the hall, where from the green drawing-room, came the mellow, yet plaintive sound of a harp.

"Mirabelle, do I see Mr Caxton playing the harp?"

"Oh, yes. Don't be misguided by his clever face and sombre clothes. He is quite a romantic, I believe. Not that you're likely to come against that side of him. All the Caxtons are High Tories. Detests even the Whigs. Sworn to bring down Reform," she slid a sideways glance, "so, he's not likely to flirt with Citizeness Ridley."

"Nor she with him neither. He's supposed to be my lawyer – and did damn all to help me!"

"Moderate your language," whispered Mirabelle, pulling her away from the drawing-room. "Pay attention instead to the big blond man with the strikingly beautiful woman."

"That's Henry Hunt! Arthur Thistlewood took me to one of his meetings when I was here with Charles. Oh, Mirabelle, have you asked him here on my account?"

"Especially on your account." She hunched her soft shoulders, "Told Violet to keep it a surprise."

"And who is the good-looking woman?"

"Catherine Vince, his mistress. Mortimer and me, we simply adore her. Went overboard for Hunt several years ago. Cut herself off from county society through leaving her husband and eloping. She's one of the Bishops of Parham House . . . look well together don't they? He's always all eyes for her, and she openly adores him. When the Bishops saw her sporting Hunt's Radical colours at the Bristol election they were shocked. Will Cobbett didn't like it either. Bad example and all that guff. Accused him of 'riding about the country with a whore.'"

"Like the Prince Regent," said Jancie sharply.

"Oh, naughty, naughty. I heard that, ho, ho!" laughed a fulsome man in a green stock. Heads turned. People clustered curiously.

"So this is the young lady Reformer?"

"She'd like to flood the country with cheap corn?"

"And end all our sinecures?"

"Not forgetting the rotten boroughs," added Jancie.

"And you agree with voting by ballot, I believe?"

"It is the only democratic way."

"It would be chaos. Absolute and utter chaos!"

"And of course, there's universal suffrage."

"Did you hear that?" The man in satin breeches addressed the cluster, and turned again to Jancie. "Would you seriously give women a vote, Miss Ridley?"

"Of course. It's one of the tenets of Reform."

"Then, God help us!"

In the shocked silence which followed, Jancie noticed

190

the harp was not being played and that Mirabelle was ushering her toward a tallish young woman, fair and sophisticated, with not much of a chin, whom she introduced as Selina Lansdowne. Jancie, whose own chin was firm and rounded, and squared with stubborness in times of strain, did not care for the chinless.

"How d'you do, Miss Lansdowne?" She thrust out her hand. Selina regarded it with a startled expression. "In the north we shake hands when introduced," Jancie explained.

"In the south," Selina inclined her head, civilly, "we do not."

Not sure how Jancie was going to take this snub of Selina's, Mirabelle lunged out for Henry Hunt's arm as he passed. "Henry, and dear, dear Catherine . . . " In the warmth of new introductions, she breathed more easily.

Pitt was a shade embarrassed by Selina's conduct – though he failed to see why – and under cover of ladling two cups of punch, observed Jancie in conversation with Hunt and Catherine Vince.

She was quite the centre of attraction from her high-collared gown to her bare feet and painted toe-nails; like a priestess of some Grecian cult. He recalled the dishevelled prisoner sluicing her face in horse troughs . . . the crimson and white clad figure of the cockpit . . . strident Boadicea . . . the black clad figure throwing effigies into the Irwell. He wondered about the Secret Committee and the legality of it. Their lordships had not consulted him at all – not even about her release, and that rankled. That he was in this invidious position at all was due to the feckless, reckless conduct of not his own client, but his partner's. And he supposed, when he returned to Manchester, she would be on the doorstep to complain to Mr Crabtree. After supper, while Dyson Edwards was singing a duet with Selina Lansdowne in the music room, the sisters met briefly.

"I saw you tête à tête with Henry and Catherine, what plots have you been hatching?" Violet asked.

"I've been sounding out the possibility of him coming to address a meeting in Manchester." Jancie replied excitedly, "and he's game – on the understanding that I address the Female Reformers at Camberwell, and canvass for the Rads at the Westminster election!"

"Oh, dear," sighed Violet. "I thought you were anxious to go home?"

"I was. But Bob Smollett would never forgive me if I passed this up."

"And you'll enjoy telling them!"

"Of course, they'll love a first-hand account of the personalities. Henry Hunt is one of their heroes you know, and he has nominated the father of Reform, dear old Major Cartwright – not that he'll get in, even though he is popular. Then the Tories are putting up Lord Byron's friend, Cam Hobhouse; and the Whigs, George Lamb, and seeing he is Lord Melbourne's son, there are no prizes for guessing the outcome. Still we have to start somewhere and we start canvassing after tomorrow!"

"Is this wise, Jancie, so soon after Newgate?"

"They've forbidden me to teach, but I'm not muzzled altogether! Besides," she absently folded and unfolded her spectacles, "I was so inadequate and apathetic in prison, that I'm ashamed . . . and somehow feel as if I'm condoning this terrible inequality by my being here."

"Oh, Jancie . . ."

"So, dear Violet, the canvassing is a chance to claw back some self respect . . . a chance," she recalled Arthur Thistlewood's parting words, "to strike a blow for Reform and, ironically enough, it's Mirabelle I have to thank for inviting Mr Hunt in the first place!"

"And," said Mirabelle, later when in receipt of Jancie's overwhelming thankfulness. "I want you to talk to Violet before you return to Manchester. I'm not given to anxiety, m'dear, and I don't want you to make Charles anxious, but your sister's latest beau, this Edwards fellow, seems to have commandeered her in a way I don't like. She won't hear a word against him – and indeed he seems exemplary, but she's very much smitten, and needs to exercise a little caution. He's also curious, for some reason, about you. Try and talk sense into that pretty head of hers before you go north."

Chapter 22

Jancie wrote to her guardian:

'Darling Charles,

Thank you for your letter which reached me yesterday, and the news of Jem and Margery's engagement. It's very curious how quickly they have come to an agreement in my absence – I am intrigued!

The campaign here is continuing at a feverish, chaotic, and corrupt pace. Bribes are bandied about, evictions threatened, and there are brawls on every corner. For fear of the opposition rowdies following me to the Moxhams' and attacking their house, I am staying at the Swan With Two Heads.

I have seen some rough goings on in Manchester, but for sheer, vitriolic abuse this campaign beats all. Henry Hunt (the Radical orator mentioned in my previous letter) had his private life held up as a scandal on account of Catherine Vince, but gave as good as he got, and was challenged to a duel! But the scandalous life of Lady Caroline Lamb, who is canvassing with the Whigs – in flesh-coloured tights, would you believe? – is referred to as "eccentric".

There is, of course, lots more, dear Charles, which you shall hear over our cigars. Mirabelle and Violet insisted I send their regards each time I write, which I do. My next letter will be a conclusion of the campaign, and please do not be anxious for me. The constabulary are far too busy protecting property to bother singling out individuals. Mr Caxton, accompanied by his fiancée, has left town for Manchester.

Your Geisha Girl, J'

On the last day of the campaign all London appeared to be on the streets. There were flags and trade banners getting in the way of sweating, swearing constables. Horses backed and carriages blocked streets. Children, excited by the turmoil, were fractious, and errand boys squabbled. Dogs barked and chased a pig who added its outraged squeals to the clamour of the yeomanry's fife and drum.

Jancie wrote again to her guardian:–

'Darling Charles,

Such excitement – words fail me, so you can judge how it is! Already, the Prince Regent, out in his coach has been publicly insulted; anyone, it seems is fair game on this last frantic day. Despite the jeering or cheering of paid mobs, and the attendant fisticuffs, there are some lighter moments. I must be one of the few who has not fallen victim to pickpockets; but you should have heard the applause when Henry Hunt had his watch and seals returned – before he realised they had been stolen! The Tory, Cam Hobhouse, was not so fortunate, and Lord Byron was quick off the press with the following:

> "When to the mob you make a speech
> My boy, Bobby O,
> How do you keep outside their reach
> The watch within your fobby O?
>
> But never mind such pretty things
> My boy, Bobby O,
> God save the people, damn all kings
> So, let us crown the mobby O!"

195

The crown, dear Charles, on this occasion went to George Lamb, our poor Major Cartwright coming last, but still the Rads have made their presence known, and will continue to do so. The committee regard this as a beginning. And I feel much restored in spirit for having played a small part in it. I shall give this letter to the post boy en route to the Moxhams, for once there I shall spend hours in that lovely marble bath and so miss the last collection. Will be travelling home alone, for Violet, alas, cannot be prised from her beloved Society – and I cannot get away from it quickly enough!

Your Geisha Girl, J'

Jancie arrived at St James's bubbling over to relate all the anecdote and scandal of the campaign, to discover no one at home. Puzzled over this, she spent an hour in the great marble bathroom. By the time she emerged Mirabelle had arrived and sent for her.

"Ah, dear gel," she greeted. "You had an excitin' campaign by all one hears?"

"It seemed as flat as yesterday's ale when I returned to find no one at home; the house silent as the tomb; and servants who can't answer a simple question."

"Come and sit by me," she soothed, extending a hand and patting the sofa. There was no kiss, no embrace.

Jancie sat down slowly. "It's Violet, isn't it? Has . . . has something happened?"

"She has . . . prepare yourself for a shock, m'dear, eloped."

"Eloped? You mean gone off with a man?"

"Well, she'd hardly go off with a woman. Though even that wouldn't raise an eyebrow nowadays."

"Dyson Edwards?" Jancie felt sick with sudden anxiety.

"I . . . I was not at first alarmed, for Violet has been absent for two or three days before – she's in demand

196

for house parties y'know – and returned so full of smiles and giggling accounts of the hilarious times she'd had, that it was clear she had forgotten to inform me of her intentions in the first place. When five days had passed I was really becoming anxious, and then this note arrived by messenger."

"Mirabelle! You've had this over a week. Why on earth did you not inform me?"

"Mortimer insisted we were not to ruin your campaign – and anyway, what could you have done?"

"I don't know . . . I would have thought of something . . ." Jancie adjusted her spectacles and quickly read the note. "That doesn't tell us much, and the handwriting is his," she observed in dismay. "Oh, why didn't Violet have the consideration at least to add her signature, or a postscript, to stop us worrying?"

"We must face it m'dear, consideration is not really one of your sister's strong points."

"But, why did she think it necessary to run off? No one would have objected to a marriage or even a liaison—"

"It's easy to say that now," pointed out Mirabelle.

"Yes . . . I suppose you're right. But, I can't really see her going off like this. Oh dear, if only I'd taken time to speak to her, as you suggested, before the campaign and not after."

"Darling gel. Do you really think it would have made any difference?"

"I would at least have the comfort of knowing I had tried."

"Not necessarily. You might have assumed your talk was the reason for her going."

They spoke in random sentences scattered across a chasm of fearful apprehension.

"She has only known him some three months or so . . ."

"And I didn't care for his asking questions about me."

"Especially after your Newgate experience."

"I can't imagine she would want to get married without having me, her only relative, present . . ."

Their eyes met and held, each wanting to reassure, to comfort, to say there was really nothing to worry about . . . until another aspect dawned. "Charles . . ." Mirabelle's hand fluttered to her lips. "Oh, how are we going to tell her? She'll never forgive me. I remember her saying at the Waterloo Celebrations that if anything happened to either of you, as a result of her bringing you to London, she'd never forgive herself."

Jancie's strong hands took hold of Mirabelle's limp fingers. "Charles must not know – not until we hear the outcome. There's no sense in all three of us worrying. As you say, she'll no doubt return when the novelty has worn off. You will write to me the very instant you have news of her?"

They sat for a long time, and outside the evening shadows fell across the lawn.

Before travelling north Jancie had one more task to undertake. Since her release she had been summoning courage to call on Sir Francis Burdett, for according to the *Leeds' Mercury*, he was campaigning to bring an end to Sidmouth's Secret Committee and network of spies, and was willing to hear from victims of the system. On the strength of hearsay that he never turned a Reformer from his door, she put it to the test.

Sir Francis Burdett, the darling of Reform, lived at Number Eighty, Piccadilly, a mansion twice the size of the Moxhams', and potently more lavish. She hesitated, hovered by the railings, approached the steps. What would she say? If her heart didn't stop hammering like this, she wouldn't be able to say anything! Quickly, she mounted the steps and pulled the bell.

The door opened, and asking if Sir Francis was at home, she presented her card to a manservant dressed in the baronet's yellow and crimson livery. Intimidated by the opulence, she stood by one of the ornate pillars, until bidden by the manservant to a leather-walled study, the size of which made her office at Etherington's seem like a cupboard.

The *Leeds' Mercury* and other Radical papers littered the desk from which Sir Francis rose to acknowledge her entrance. Of middle years, he had rouged cheeks and was handsomely dressed, from his lace-edged frills to his exquisitely fashioned coat.

He indicated a chair on the other side of the huge desk, and Jancie, conscious of taking up the baronet's time, quickly related her experience from the Silent Procession through to the Secret Committee. While signing a document as to the veracity of her statement, he saw the Moxhams' address, and his tone became less formal. They discussed the Westminster election, and it was not long before the conversation turned to the subject of spies.

". . . you have no doubt heard of Oliver, Sidmouth's crack spy?"

"The *agent provocateur*? Who has not? Parents used to threaten naughty children with Boney, they now threaten them with Oliver! The Radical newspapers, and even some of the others, reckon he's the paymaster for informers. Hasn't it come to a pretty pass, Sir Francis, when English folk are snooping on each other? They say Oliver stirred up that dreadful riot at Pentrich near Derby."

"Most unfortunate. Most unfortunate," said the baronet, rising from behind his desk. "For in the resulting fracas a man was shot, and three are likely to be hanged for it. And, of course the stranger in town, who set it all up – none other than Oliver – has vanished, disappeared."

"The awful thing is no one knows what he looks like."

"Apart from the smallpox scars on his lower jaw."

Jancie put a hand behind her, feeling absently for the

chair, and slowly sank into it. "Is he, despite the marks, good-looking? Tall, accomplished, and given to wearing . . . Wellington boots?"

"Why, yes. Are you acquainted?"

"Briefly. Under the name of Dyson Edwards he has eloped with my sister . . . please, Sir Francis, tell me all you know about him."

"It will be no comfort to you, Miss Ridley."

"It isn't comfort I want, sir."

"Very well. I must warn you that he is not a tuppeny informer like those who made a fiasco out of the Thistlewood trial. He is clever and plausible. A thief, bigamist, womaniser, embezzler, and, I suspect, a murderer – in the course of his duties, that is. His style of living is financed by Sidmouth, and because of the connection, Oliver is above the law at present. A big spider at the centre of an immense web of spies and paid informers . . . Hence my campaign, Miss Ridley. No one should be above the law. I shall not rest until Oliver stands in the Old Bailey – and the ensuing scandal will put an end to the Secret Committee – and possibly the government."

Jancie never recalled how she took her leave of the baronet, or how she parted from Mirabelle and Mortimer without them suspecting anything was wrong.

Coaches, Jancie reflected, from the window-seat on her journey home, are a melancholy mode of transport for me, apart from the first, that is. At least, there'll be plenty of time to get used to the sinister revelations. And, sinister they were, for if Violet became aware of Dyson's profession, he would scarcely let her return to her family because of the intelligence against him. On the other hand, maybe Violet would not want to return. Perhaps Dyson really loved her and they had eloped so as not to embarrass her own position as a Reformer. Her lips curved a little – Susan Thistlewood could make capital out of that. "Sister of the President of the Female Reformers goes off with Oliver the Spy."

Not that Susan Thistlewood mattered. A trembling sigh escaped her lips, and despite the other passengers, she felt terribly alone. The overnight stops would be spent in strange beds, in dark rooms . . . wondering, where would Violet be staying? She hoped that if there were no silken sheets, Dyson Edward's arms would make up for the loss. Oh, Violet, dear . . .

"Always stick hold of yer sister's hand," she heard her father's voice spanning the years, echoing across St Peter's Field, as she and Violet had run to pick daisies. How could he, or they, have ever envisaged there would be a such a gulf over which no hands could ever reach?

Safer perhaps, to think of home – she had been away scarcely a month and it seemed like years. Safer to imagine sending Sampson for a pewter of the Seven Stars' best; of lighting cigars for herself and Charles to smoke over their game of cards; and wearing . . . well, what should she wear? Her scarlet kimono or the dark green shot with silver flashes? Perhaps Mr Crabtree would call . . . Perhaps Jem and Margery . . . And there was Mr Caxton of course . . .

Chapter 23

The London coach entered Manchester with a show of dash and verve, and Jancie, hanging onto the cord by the window, sighed with sheer delight. Home! Home!

Children ran alongside shouting excitedly. Sleeping dogs leapt up, barking angrily. Laggardly errand boys quickened their pace, and suddenly the whole street perked up; curtains parted at windows; people came to their doors; and Constable Nadin, thumbs hitched into his belt, fingers splaying his paunch, noted Miss Ridley's return with interest.

Ostlers sprang to life; servants scurried; and Jancie, seeing the scarecrow figure of Aberdaron Dick, almost stumbled on her overnight valise, in an attempt to descend the step quickly.

"Dick! Oh, it's lovely to see you! To see the town! To be home! But where . . ." she glanced among the crowd, as he took her bag. "I . . . expected Miss Etherington." His loping stride had taken them beneath the arch and into Market Street. "Perhaps," she glanced at him anxiously, "my letter did not arrive? Dick?" she tugged his sleeve, trying to keep pace. "Where is everyone?" They were now half way down Market Street . . . past St Mary's Gate. She had almost darted to the barber's shop when Dick grabbed her arm and hurried her along. "If you'll pardon me, Miss Jancie," his sing-song voice rose in desperation. "No . . . you can't go just yet, see."

"No, Dick, I don't see!"

"Welcome home, my little cock o' wax!" She saw a

vivid flash of scarlet waistcoat, felt herself hugged and whirled.

"Bob, thank God! I was beginning to think something terrible had . . ."

She turned to see Jem, was held gruffly in his arms . . . oh, never had the odour of birds and toffee smelled so good.

"Eh, c'mon, lass, up tha goes!" They hoisted her onto their shoulders, and carried her past Mrs Clowes bow-fronted shop to where a cheering crowd had gathered in the churchyard.

"Miss Etherington told Fancy you'd be home today," grinned Clogger, "an' it went on from that to this!"

Eyes bright with tears and voice trembling with emotion, Jancie was overwhelmed. She shook hands, was patted on the shoulder, squeezed on the arm, kissed on the cheek, embraced:

Miss Bohanna had closed her cellar bookshop for an hour. But Pitt Caxton, on the pretext of showing Selina the magnificent carved-oak screens of St Mary's church, kept a distance, standing with Selina by the door. Then Jancie, giving her guardian a great hug, noticed her fine features were thinner. "Charles," she chided. "Oh, dear Charles. You mustn't worry, so."

"They want to hear about your experiences, Jancie, stand on the wall there, and," she glanced in the direction of the Constable, "just watch what you say, or he'll have you on that dreadful coach again!"

Jancie had leapt lightly onto the low wall of the church yard in front of Mrs Clowes' shop, when the Reverend Brookes appeared, leaning heavily on gnarled walking stick, prepared to berate what he assumed to be a set of rowdies. "Eh . . ." he quickly perceived his mistake. "If it isn't Miss Japanese Dancing Girl – I've come across some capital books for the travelling school of thine."

"There . . . will not be any travelling school, sir." She said. "Viscount Sidmouth has forbidden it. But I'd love to see the books . . ." and leaning forward, added in a lower tone. "May I call tomorrow?"

"Thou'rt a blockhead," he declared, in his old-fashioned speech, "Tha shouldn't be meddlin' in politics. I've told thee, politics and women don't work . . ." There was a short silence, but as neither she, nor anyone else, rose to the bait, he set off toward his house in Long Millgate. "Ay, come to thee tea," he shouted over his shoulder. "Mrs Platt has turned out a gradely seed-cake."

"Speech!" yelled someone, as Parson Brookes left. "Speech!"

"Tell us about London!"

"C'mon, Miss Ridley!"

She faced the crowd swarming irreverently over the grave stones, and gave a graphic account of her experiences. Only a few of her listeners had ever been outside their native town, and they listened enthralled; gasping in horror at the grey figures in Newgate; jeering Sidmouth and Castlereagh, cheering Henry Hunt and Sir Francis Burdett. And when it came to the Westminster election their delight at her mimicry knew no bounds.

"Eh, it's as good as a turn on the boards!"

"Game, isn't she!"

Charles, looking cool in a lavender-coloured skirt and white blouse, stood with Mrs Clowes in the shop doorway. Although proud of Jancie, and God knew how thankful for her safe return, she viewed the 'heroine's welcome' with apprehension. Constable Nadin wasn't standing on the corner for the good of his health, and in her view the Reformers should have staged this in a less public place.

"And Orator Hunt has given his word," Jancie was saving the best until the last, "that he will address a meeting on St Peter's Field when we are ready!"

"Much good it'll do!" Constable Nadin's voice boomed above the cheers. "Yer can't not hold a political meeting without the magistrate's permission – and if the Reformers think Mr Hay will allow a rabble-rouser like Hunt into town they're very much mistaken!"

"In other manufacturing towns," Jancie countered, "permission has been demanded on so large a scale that the magistrates have had to comply!"

"So . . .," breathed Pitt Caxton, seeing her scarlet ribbon flutter in the light, summer wind. "Boadicea has returned."

"Do speak up, darling." Selina lifted her wide, blue gaze. "What did you say?"

"Oh, nothing. Just amazed at the foolhardiness of the woman. Look at her. Just released from the Secret Committee and bandying words with Nadin."

"If she's as troublesome as you make out, why did Sidmouth release her – unless, as Mirabelle said, it was on account of so brilliant an advocate."

"Really, Selina."

"It's all very well to adopt that tone, but if you are not interested in her progress, what are we doing here?"

"Precisely." And with that, he swung sharply away from the church steps. It was the movement of Selina's highly coloured parasol which drew Jancie's attention – dear heaven, her heart paced up a little. Pitt Caxton was straying from his side of the fence again, and dragging Simpering Selina with him. Why had she thought of Selina as simpering? Well, why not?

Jancie returned to trade on a surge of energy – surge enough to dowse her anxiety about Violet. Movement and purpose filled her mind. When not at the Infirmary Baths with Charles, she was driving about the town, drumming up trade, delivering, bargaining, as pleased as Morocco to be in harness again.

The first evening, Mr Crabtree joined them for supper at the Seven Stars to explain that Mr Caxton was not at fault in London. The Secret Committee had used his "lack of knowledge in these affairs" to their own benefit. "Had

I, dear Charles – being much longer in the tooth – been there, I'd have played merry hell. But young Caxton . . ." he shook his head.

Later that evening Charles and Jancie waved goodbye to Mr Crabtree from the window-seat of the sitting-room above the manufactory. The perfume of night-scented stocks wafted through from the window-box, and the street noises came up from below. "That was a pleasant evening, Charles; you and me and darling Crabby . . ."

"Yes, he was quite angry that Sidmouth squashed your educational schemes. Knew how much it all meant . . ."

"It did mean a lot, but I've raged and wept . . . and there are other challenges."

After a pause, Charles said hesitantly: "I couldn't help wishing Violet had been with us . . . our celebration would have been complete."

"I know, dear Charles, I know. And I did try to persuade her." Violet's elopement was the first secret she had ever had from her guardian; the first deception she was about to practise, and she feared it might show. Her own imprisonment had sharpened the delicate lines of Charles's features, and sometimes there was a bluish hue to the exquisitely shaped lips. Fancy said it was a sign of a faulty heart, but Charles had never consulted a physician in her life and had no intention of starting now. There was no one with whom Jancie could share the knowledge of her sister being at the mercy of the notorious Oliver. This was something her guardian must never know.

"I'm sure you did . . ." Charles was saying. "But somehow I have a feeling you're uneasy about it." She touched her shoulder and shook it a little. "I understand, darling, and don't think I hold you responsible for her not wanting to swap St James's for Shudehill – even for a few days!"

The following morning Jancie descended on Mrs Clowes like a whirlwind. Down the steps into the sugar bakery, skirts aswish, under the mahogany flap of the counter and along the passage. She poked her head into the inferno of boiling toffee and yelled.

"Jem, I'm out in the pens."

"Eh, Miss Jancie?" Mrs Clowes had shouted after her. "You'll be comin' to the wedding – banns is in, you know?"

"Already?"

"He's tying the knot too fast for my liking." Then, in a hoarse whisper. "I did think at one time, I'd have thee for a daughter-in-law . . ."

The sound of Jem's footsteps saved Jancie further embarrassment, and Mrs Clowes returned to the shop.

"I didn't congratulate you and Margery yesterday, so much was happening. But, I'm happy for you, Jem. And how's trade?"

"Eh, God save us," he grinned. "After all you said against trade at Heaton Park!"

"Sidmouth and Hay have put an end to my educational schemes, so I've got to make the best of what's left."

"Yes," he said, looking down at her solemnly. "We have. They say a fella's got to wed sometime, and if I can't have Miss Etherington's Geisha Girl, I'll settle for Margery." He grinned ruefully, "Didn't think you'd be home so soon. Wanted to be a married man when you returned – happen it'd stop me thinking, hoping that one day . . ."

"Jem . . ." She touched his arm, conscious of the hard sinews, the tackiness of boiled sugar, of the aroma of a dozen sweetnesses.

He swiftly gathered her to the breadth of his chest, lowering his head; she did not, could not, avert her face, and their lips met in a kiss, so gentle, so full of the flavour of sorrow, that their cheeks were wet with tears. She felt the massive strength of him shudder on a great sigh. Why is he not enough for me, she thought. He's so good, so very dear, and yet, not dear enough to marry.

It was as though for a brief moment of time they

had occupied another world, for this one was suddenly ajangle with the crowing, chuckling and cackling of hungry birds.

"C'mon," she smiled weakly, in an attempt to restore normality. "I'll help you with the feed."

The attempt proved successful, for as they approached the last pen, he leaned over the railings and said proudly. "There, what you d'you think of them cockerels?"

They leaned over the pens. "Fine feathers," she squinted up at him. "Very fine indeed."

"It was Mr Caxton put me on to 'em. Brought Lord Derby's breeder round he did. And," he grinned bashfully. "He were reet impressed. What's up? You look vexed."

"Of course I'm vexed," she stood away from the pen. "How you can have any truck with Tories," she demanded, "after the Anti-Reform League – of which he is leader, mind – has advised employers to dismiss, 'root out' were the words, 'root out' all Radicals in the interests of town and country."

"If I'd been marrying you instead of Margery, I'd have stayed with politics. But now, I'm all for trade. Times are hard and Tory money's as good as anyone else's. As for Caxton, he's on the same tack, circulating, touting for business. Even patronises Smollett's, attends your theatre." He straightened up and tilted her chin with a sticky finger. "If it weren't for the Tories, lass, I bet your order book would be well down. Did something happen in London to turn you against Caxton?"

"Oh, Jem, you are short-sighted! If it hadn't been for him and his repressive brand of politics I wouldn't have been arrested and muzzled in the first place! See," she laid her hand on his sinewy forearm in a farewell gesture. "I came to congratulate you, and ended up arguing . . ."

Yet still his little jealousies persisted. "But you'll continue the argument with Bob Smollett, won't you?"

"I will just – when I think of how he tried to stop us going to Heaton Park . . ."

And at Bob's she hissed into his ear as the shaving water boiled, "Patronage you called it then – and now you are accepting Caxton's patronage!"

"Don't be hasty now, my little cock o' wax," he whispered, indicating the crowded benches. "They've all been shut out of the foundry – come to chin-wag about what the *Herald* calls a 'witch hunt'."

She looked at the rows of faces, gaunt, thin and determined. These were men being driven further and further onto the rocks of desperation. She thought of Arthur Thistlewood and his army of unemployed navvies.

He turned to the benches. "C'mon now, let's be havin' yer," he called in the manner of the market men. "Anyone for a shave or a trim?" And then in an aside to her. "Henna's wearing off," his round, brown eyes twinkled. "I've time this evening. After you've had tea with the parson. What d'you say?"

Later that evening Pitt Caxton, passing St Mary's Gate on his way to the Pitt Club, paused to observe a crack of light between the curtains separating the window – back from the shop, and through it he saw the jaunty outline of Bob Smollett with his hands about Jancie Ridley's face. Their movements took them away, and Pitt continued thoughtfully to the club, wondering what Boadicea was up to.

"It was him," declared Jancie, "I distinctly saw him. The white stock he wears stood out against the darkness. It was Caxton!"

Bob tugged at his ear-ring. "What does it matter? He has surely seen a man and woman standing close before – or happen you don't want him to see us together?"

"Oh, I don't know Bob . . . it's just that freedom is at a premium. Newgate has set me on edge. And Nadin's always had an eye to this place."

"And you care?"

"Of course I care," she patted his well-shaven face, "for who else can apply my henna to so good an effect?"

209

"And who else," he replied, untying the scarlet ribbon, "enjoys doing it so much?"

It was wedding day at St Mary's church, the bell-ringers swung and sweated in the July heat, and the Saturday being a half holiday, there was no pall of smoke to cast its shadow.

The Reverend Joshua Brookes, MA, impeccably dressed in silken robes, hair neatly powdered, and spectacles on the end of his nose, swept down Long Millgate, to join Jem and Margery, and some two dozen others in the bonds of holy matrimony.

Entering the church packed with guests and well wishers, he strode toward the Etherington pew, greeted Charles, and seeing Jancie, commented testily, "Time tha was up there, Miss Japanese Dancing Girl . . . I could have baptised thee half a dozen by now."

He bowed in the direction of Mrs Clowes; exchanged further greetings with some, and ignoring others, swept on his way to begin the ceremony.

"Now, now," he rapped, coming down from the altar. "What's all the commotion?" And swishing his way along the couples who were hurriedly lining up before the sanctuary steps, discovered the commotion was caused by a woman who could not find her intended groom. "I can't keep all these folk waiting until tha' sorts out thy man," he declared irritably, and gathering straw-coloured eyebrows together pointed to one of the guests in the centre aisle. "Here, you?"

Startled, the man at once looked for some way of escape, but there was no escaping the parson's harrowing tones. "Come along and stand proxy for this lass? C'mon, now, it won't harm thee."

Selina Lansdowne, looking beautiful in salmon-pink, nudged Pitt Caxton. "What a debâcle! I hope you're not intending that awful man should marry us?" She threw a significant glance at the orange peel littering the flagged

210

aisle, at children playing, and the churchwardens sorting out their bets audibly on the time it would take the parson to perform the ceremony. "And," she continued, "I'm certainly not getting married in this church!"

The ceremony had begun. Jancie contemplated Jem's stocky figure beside that of his bride in yellow taffeta, with an upsurge of emotion. They belonged together; they were suited. She closed her eyes and prayed for their happiness.

When she looked up there was a further altercation taking place in the line of couples.

"Can't tha see her finger's swelled with the heat," a young man declared. "the ring won't go any further. Leave her be!"

"Art thou telling me my business," roared the parson. "Thou'rt not man and wife till I've pronounced the blessing!"

"An' a reet blessin' that'll be!"

The blessing, when eventually bestowed, sent brides and grooms into each other's arms for the traditional kiss. In the excitement, Margery was whirled round by the man on her left.

"Eh, hold on, lad," the Reverend Brookes warned. "Tha must dip in thy own treacle!"

Selina nudged Pitt again. "Such vulgarity – it's like a scene from Molière!"

"I'm glad you're amused," said Pitt drily. "We are now expected to take wine in the rooms above the sugar bakery."

"I could say, how sweet," she giggled.

"You mean you want to go?"

"It could be very amusing. The bride decked out like a spring chicken; him all puffed up and fine-feathered; and the ward whom you so brilliantly defended!"

"Damn it, Selina, I've told you a hundred times," his voice came knife-edged above the exodus. "Mirabelle was mistaken. I did nothing. I would not have gone if it hadn't have been for 'darling Crabby's' gout!"

211

"Darling Crabby?" Saucer eyes tilted.

"Oh, never mind." He guided her through the crowds. "Let's get this ghastly affair over."

Although it was her son's wedding, Mrs Clowes had not closed the sugar bakery, and customers paused to stare at the folk who passed through the shop and up the narrow stairs to the long, low-ceilinged room where a bashful Jem and Margery stood to receive congratulations.

Selina gravitated at once to sip canary wine with Jem's quality guests; Beadle Hapgood, Lord Derby's setter, and a prominent sugar-dealer. Pitt stood beside Mr Crabtree, as dark and austere as the other was light and gay, watching the company and drinking great bumpers of a fine ruby port.

Pitt found himself watching less of the company and more of Miss Ridley, who stood with her guardian and Margery's people. She was hatless, and wearing a simple cream-coloured gown of muslin with a wide, crimson sash. Good God, he thought, she even brings the Radical colour to a wedding! His glance travelled from the sash to the curve of her breasts; the sweep of her throat to the dark auburn hair. It was done up in a large, heavy pleat, and added a fine sculptured look to her profile.

He watched her drinking, the pouting of her lips against the rim of the glass, the tip of her tongue flicking to catch the last drops, the uptilt of her throat . . . and resting provocatively on her breast was a crystal quizzing glass.

"Oh, for a metamorphosis into a crystal quizzer!" quipped Mr Crabtree, who had been watching him.

"If you are quoting Ovid," commented Pitt, "It was not an eyeglass suspended on a chain, but a ring." Warmth suffused his voice, as he continued the quotation, ". . . a ring to lie so close to her heart, to caress her bosom and to be held in her hand, to be placed near her lips, to be toyed with . . ."

"Upon my soul, sir," intervened Crabtree, "Pray leave off or you'll have me all of a passion." He surveyed the serious face of his junior partner in astonishment. "Didn't think you had it in you. It appears I've not the measure of you yet."

When the afternoon wore on and the wine ran out, Jem invited them all "to dance at our wedding – nine o'clock at Tinker's!" Beadle Hapgood decided to risk his dignity; Mr Crabtree his gout; Bob Smollett was to put up his shutters for the night; and the sugar-dealer to attend "for the sake of trade".

The night was warm and the grass dry, the atmosphere festive and convivial, in the more secluded avenues lovers strolled among lantern-lit trees. The staid walked the promenades, lads and girls larked, and shrieks of terrified laughter echoed from the swing-boats.

By the time Pitt and Selina arrived the dancing was in progress, led by three gypsy fiddlers. Waiters scurried to and fro with refreshments, expertly balancing trays, deftly weaving among bodies.

"No, Jem," Jancie said softly. "We cannot dance together on your wedding night, for Margery's sake, Oh, do understand Jemmy . . ."

"I can't," he said, with a shadow in his voice. "I can't understand . . ." Then slapping his great thigh he turned to where Pitt and Selina were standing. "Miss Lansdowne," he made a bow. "D'you fancy takin' me hand for the Romp?"

"You'll have to show me how to do it, Mr Clowes, but yes, I'd be delighted." Enjoying herself, and highly amused at what she referred to as 'the rustic society', she called out, "Don't stand there all night, darling. Miss Ridley, I am sure would like a romp!"

Startled, he could do nothing but comply, and warily, like sparring cocks they sized each other up. Cautiously, he reached for her hand.

"If you are game, Miss Ridley," he said, and why he

used cocking parlance he didn't know, "shall we take to the mat?"

The fiddles struck up and the couples, some twenty or so, faced each other in a long line. Jancie, rosy-cheeked and exhilarated from previous dances twirled opposite him. Her prancing feet were bare and her toe nails scarlet to match the sash. Charles, elegant in mauve with a purple waistcoat and polished boots, stood, hands thrust within skirt pockets, in conversation with Mr Crabtree.

Arms were linked, partners whirled, and holding crossed hands they romped down the centre and under an arch formed by the leading couple, who then became the last. Selina's face glowed with excitement, responding to the magic of the fiddles; there was, she fancied, something mysterious and abandoned about Tinker's Tea Gardens – Vauxhall was never like this.

Margery was happy and flushed, with Bob making the agreeables. Pitt too, became a victim of the wild music of the fiddlers, responding to them, responding to her. Raven hair fell recklessly across his forehead, dark eyes flashed through a fringe of even darker lashes; he smiled, tossing his head a little, laughed showing white, uneven teeth.

The music, he realised, was becoming progressively faster. Some had dropped out. Jem's sturdy frame, not built for speed, was soon puffed, and Selina, who had never danced so fast in her life, was glad to sit out. The others stood watching, clapping, shouting. The music was now faster, wilder. Feet flying, hair streaming in the light summer wind, gown soaked with sweat and thinking of the cool springs of the Infirmary Baths, Jancie was grabbed by the Clowes' apprentice. "Mr Caxton's out!" he yelled, and joining hands they galloped madly down the centre. All eyes were on the dancers, the fiddlers . . .

No one noticed Pitt's disappearance into the shadows. His chest had tightened with exertion, he could scarcely breathe, and was not for tottering in public like the Knowsley at the May Day Main.

They wondered where he had disappeared to. But could never have guessed he was in the shadows with Susan Thistlewood.

Chapter 24

Having ignited the asthma pastille, Pitt inhaled until his breathing became easier. He was then aware of someone calling his name. "Yes?" He turned to see a black-haired woman surveying him curiously.

"I've got something that will interest you mightily. An' it ain't what you think," she said. "I am Arthur Thistlewood's wife."

Thistlewood! He recalled the trial for treason and subsequent acquittal. He turned swiftly and answered almost as frantically. "I have no business with revolutionaries – or their wives."

"This concerns Jancine Ridley." Susan moved further into the coppice and leaned against a tree; he stood before her, coat over his shoulder and the fragrance of herbs about him. "I've certain information about her."

"Oh, very well," he said curtly, "but don't hedge. If you've something to tell me, tell me at once."

"For a price."

"Oh, I see . . . What kind of price?"

She held out her hand. "I like my money with a shine to it, a yeller, gold-like shine."

Intrigued now, he put his hand in his breeches pocket and withdrew a sovereign. "That is all I have about me."

"You can get more?"

"If your information is worth it."

She reached out and took the money, her fingers lingering across his. He pulled away sharply.

"Jancie Ridley's a spy."

"I don't believe it."

"I've got proof."

"Show me?"

"Not so fast – eager now it's taken yer imagination, eh?"

"I must admit to a certain amount of astonishment," he lied, for he had never been so astonished in his life. "But, why come to me?"

"As leader of the Anti-Reform League you've got what they call a 'vested interest'."

"Such as?"

"If the Rads knew the truth they'd string her up."

"And so?"

"Neither Sidmouth nor the Reverend Hay, nor the League are going to be pleased when one of their best spies is unmasked."

"You expect me to believe that Miss Ridley is a Tory and in the employment of Viscount Sidmouth?"

"I've got a written letter as proof."

"Let me see it?"

"Not so fast, eh. Not so bleedin' fast. I ain't got it on me. Come and search if yer want."

"Bring the letter to my office, then."

"Why d'you think I followed you here? I'm keepin' low since Arthur's trial. No, if you want to buy that letter, come to Dirty Dick's Chop House, by the Irwell. I'm in the scullery there and once I've got the money I'm going back to London—" she hitched her skirts and thrust out a begrimed foot, "on these. No fancy coaches for the likes of me. I'll expect yer Monday night. It's quiet then."

"And if I decide not to purchase this letter?"

"The newspapers, especially the *Leeds' Mercury*, would give their right 'and for news like this . . . think on it, Mr Caxton. You just think on it."

Pitt stood transfixed after she had gone. Thought, circumstance and recollection struggled to make some coherent pattern. One thing was certain, he could not possibly go back to the Clowes' wedding dance.

The next evening found Pitt wandering by the short streets and alleys of Blackfriars. Faint lamps clung like leeches to blackened walls. The low, mysterious plashing of water between gratings sent up the odours of the town, and Dirty Dick's Chophouse was just by the corner.

He pushed open the door, went down three steps, and almost choked on the acrid smell of fried chops. The waiter came to take Pitt's hat and short cane, and stared in disappointed silence when he ordered, not the best of chops, but Susan from the scullery. "Yes, sir. At once, sir."

She came from the scullery, face red, arms red, and clinging all about her the odour of fried fat. She sat, not opposite, but beside him in the high-backed booth.

"You found the place all right, ducks?"

"I wouldn't be here otherwise. You have . . . the letter?"

"You have the money?"

He nodded.

"We can do a deal, then?"

"If this . . . letter is worthwhile."

"You're an 'ard one, Mr Caxton. I wonder just how 'ard you are? You might be a match with the society wenches, but when it comes to a real woman—"

He stood up, face whitening in anger. "If you have brought me here under false pretences—"

"Oh," she rounded her mouth. "Keep yer voice down, or they'll have it round town that you've been tusslin' with a doxy at Dirty Dick's!"

He lunged forward in an attempt to get past, but she hooked the laces of her bodice onto his coat button.

"Damn!" he exclaimed in dismay. It was now impossible for him to move away without tearing her gown – or unhooking the laces.

He had an intense dislike of being cornered, and was

218

angry for being such easy prey. The warmth of fleshy thighs . . . the nauseating odour of burnt chops and stale sweat became instantly intolerable. He pulled sharply away, heard the sound of tearing cloth, and saw the insert of her bodice clinging to his coat like a frayed bat.

"Now, look what you've done to me!"

He looked at the blatant nakedness his panic had caused. He was conscious that were alone in the high-backed booth. Her bosom was completely bare before him; her eyes glittering; body trembling. She stood waiting for him to touch her, and that, he realised would be the end of any restraint on her part. His lawyer's mind saw clearly all that could be involved. There must not be a scene and he must not turn her lust into anger. Taking hesitation for shyness she snatched at his hands and thrust them against the softness of her breast. Her arms were about him, straining closer . . . now fumbling his breeches.

"Susan . . . Susan Thistlewood . . ." he admonished gently. "Not now. Not here."

"Where?" She slackened her hold. "Where then?"

"Come now, be seated." He lowered her gently to the bench, all the time talking softly as if to a restive animal. It was on his mind to vault over the back of the booth and be gone, but there was the letter . . . and the frayed bat hanging on his button.

"Where?" she repeated, conscious that the music of his voice was altering her mood.

He removed the insert from his coat, and handed it to her with his handkerchief. She snatched it off him and made up her bodice as best she could.

"Why?" she asked mutinously.

"Because you would despise yourself afterward."

"Me?" She cut in. "That's rich!"

"You wouldn't betray your husband . . . with a Tory?"

"I hadn't thought of that . . . but still, yer don't when you've got it on yer." She was calm now. "But, yer right. Arthur deserves better. Married me and took on me bastard

219

son, as fond of him as if he were his own. You're a bit like him, y'know. Black hair, deep eyes, good with the talk – and, well . . . gentle, like. I suppose that's why you took me fancy. I've been away from me man for three weeks an' that's a long time when yer frisky."

"Yes," he ventured. "Now, shall we conclude the business that brought us together? And if you're that frisky, I'll throw in the price of a coach to London."

She quickly took a letter from the pocket of her skirts, and slapped it on the table. He noticed at once the free frank of the House of Commons, the seal of Viscount Sidmouth, and it was addressed to the Reverend Mr Hay, JP. He read:

'The bearer of this letter is a person well acquainted with the designs of the Manchester Reformers. It is possible that much information maybe obtained, the early communication of which to a magistrate on the spot maybe of material importance. This letter will serve as a warning to you of what is afoot. This person is intelligent and much deserving of your confidence.'

Pitt looked up. "Where did you get it?"

"Well, I've got no scruples for a start. Second, I hate her guts. Third, I'm jealous of a romantic connection she had with Arthur. And when she got out of Newgate so quick, I knew something was up. I got an acquaintance to smuggle me into the Moxhams'." She shrugged cheekily. "And in the room she shared with her sister, there was a locked bureau."

"And the letter was in there?"

She nodded.

"And what about Thistlewood?"

"Oh, he won't believe a word. Thinks the sun shines out of her fancy drawers, he does. I pretended to burn it; and now it's out of my hands."

He shook his head wonderingly.

220

"Notice that it says 'person', not a man."

"But a female spy. It's hardly credible."

"Who would suspect a woman? Who has entrance to the town's affairs; information about Reform? 'Well acquainted with the Rads', it says. If she ain't I don't know who is! As for the charges that took her to Newgate, they was all trumped up to gain the confidence of the Rads. Gave her a decent excuse to come to London and make terms with Sidmouth. Why else was she out so quick?"

That would explain why I wasn't called to her defence by the Committee, he thought. "In other words," he tapped the letter. "She's a turncoat."

"Oh, they're all at it. Makes me puke. Henry Hunt's a loyalist turned Rad; Burdett was for all the tenets of Reform, but has now decided he can't go along with 'universal suffrage'. What else will he find he can't go along with? An' William Cobbett, first he's all for Tom Paine, then against him. And then he clears off to America to avoid paying his debts. There's only people like Arthur that stick to their aims and ideals. As to what made her turn spy, I don't know and I don't care. Just so long as we know who our enemies are." She stood up. "Do I see the colour of yer money?"

"Five sovereigns, and the price of a ticket to London."

Out in the night-black street, he walked slowly, mulling over the astounding intelligence. He now had the means to finish Miss Ridley. With this letter he could throw her to the Rads – and yet he couldn't because she was on his side. Was 'darling Crabby' in on this? he wondered . . . and what about the romantic connection with Thistlewood? She had more strings to her bow than he'd thought.

She had probably obtained another letter and presented it to Mr Hay by now. There was no use in confronting her, for that would imply a degree of intimacy, and even the smallest degree between two such opposing poles would be suspect. He felt lightheaded with the discovery. She was a Tory! Sly little fox with her green eyes and auburn hair. Fighting the Rads on their own ground. The risk she was taking! A double game!

In some strange way possession of the letter gave him leave to think of her openly, to let his imagination in. He felt like God, for in his hands rested power to wreak havoc or let events take their natural course. Exhilarated, he quickened his pace. He would watch the drama play itself out as though he were in the stage-side box at Etherington's. Boadicea. Everything about her was militant and free . . . and yet, this very freedom covered a tissue of lies and duplicity. A foot in each camp, some said. By God, they didn't know the half! The network of spies he felt sure was justified to save the country from a bloody revolution. That she should be one of them gave him a vague sense of disappointment. People like her had a natural cunning, an opportunist outlook. No wonder she lingered behind closed curtains with Bob Smollett. The Thistlewood woman was right, they'd lynch her if they found out. They must not find out. And she, too, must not know that he knew – until he saw fit to arrange otherwise.

The summer sun had given way to the mists and drizzle of autumn, and as there was still no news of Violet, Charles had been told of the elopement, but not of the darker side of the affair. The fact that Jancie had met Dyson Edwards and found him agreeable was as comforting to Charles as his real identity was as alarming to Jancie. She found herself becoming preoccupied with Oliver's whereabouts, listening to or reading with avid interest the alarmist rumours that he was here and there, responsible for this and that.

Reform was on the upsurge, from Henry Hunt manufacturing Radical coffee to avoid the tax on it, to interest in the treason trial at Derby referred to by Sir Francis Burdett. Radicals countrywide had collected money to pay for a defence.

"Manchester's done well," said Margery, when Jancie called to buy eggs. "Clubs and unions have given what they could. Miss Etherington's been right generous. And, you'll never guess who else has stumped up?"

"Constable Nadin? No . . . the Reverend Hay, I bet he put himself down for ten guineas!"

"I'll tell you. Miss Lansdowne."

"She didn't."

Margery nodded her fair head vigorously.

"I've not seen either of them since your wedding. Wondered whether I'd danced the breath out of him – he suffers from asthma," Jancie added.

"Does he?" Margery's eyes widened in enquiry.

"He had an attack on the Criminal Coach. Not that I've any sympathy – especially as he did damn all for me."

"But, she's nice. Quay Street buy all their eggs here. We aren't turning good money away – although, I've a feeling she's making sport of us, really." She placed the last egg in the shallow basket. "Are you sure about taking this money to Derby?" she asked with concern. "According to the papers it's like a garrison town. The authorities have really got the wind up – think there's going to be an attack on the jail to get the men out! As if it was likely. Sometimes, y'know, I think we ask too much of you. Expect you to do it all – take all the risks."

"Seeing I'm practically the only one with no husband – still less one out of work; no children round me skirts, and not on short time meself; of course, I'm favourite."

Chapter 25

"Just been to the post office, Miss Jancie," yelled Sampson entering the Manufactory. "Letter . . ." He let the sound echo along the passage.

"Yes, yes. I'm not deaf! Thank you."

Putting on her spectacles, she saw the circular post mark bore the name of Derby. Who, she wondered, from that ill-fated town was writing to her? Slowly, Jancie opened the letter and read:

'Your sister and myself in Derby town. Appeal for costumes and an equipage to to travel. Come in haste and with the utmost discretion. Instructions at post office in name of Timothy Wise.'

Perching on the tall stool she stared at the note for a long time. When in London, she and Mirabelle assumed Violet would return or write. When it became obvious that neither was the case, Mirabelle could no longer keep up the pretence. 'Your guardian must now be informed,' she wrote. But, Jancie, out of concern for Charles, insisted on giving the impression the elopement had recently taken place and was more to be viewed in the light of a fashionable escapade, rather than a regrettable instant.

"Did I hear Sampson shouting news of a letter, earlier?" asked Charles, over their game of cards that evening.

"It was from Jake and Hetty Mawson at Derby," she lied, determined not to involve her guardian in the darker side of the elopement. "Remember, they were the first to

224

lose their jobs for being in a union, and went weaving stockings at Nottingham, but were then sacked for being Rads, so they ended up on parish relief in Derby – and are in charge of the Defence money."

"I see."

"Your Geisha Girl is merely boarding the coach to Derby and calling at the Mawsons' with the banker's note – and hey presto, I'll be home before you've missed me!"

Charles crossed her elegantly skirted legs, and leaning back in her chair, said with exaggerated resignation. "Light me another Redtzky, my sweet, for it seems I'll be lighting my own for the near future."

Lying awake in her bed, the lamp still lit, Jancie wondered for the hundredth time what had taken Violet and Dyson Edwards to Derby. The little society flower, she thought tenderly, would not like the discomfort and terror of being in hiding. For, reading between the lines, that was obviously the case. "Costumes" were, of course, a euphemism for disguise, and "travel" meant escape. And escape for Violet meant escape for Oliver! Jancie thought of him now as Oliver and not Dyson Edwards . . . and she, as President of the Female Reformers, would be making his escape possible. The list of crimes reeled off by Sir Francis Burdett rose up in her vision like bright lights. Awful as it was, she had to go along with his demand for her sister's sake. Had he taken up with Violet, she wondered, to use herself as a kind of guarantee? What if she arrived too late, and the Rads had already dealt with him – and with Violet, as an accomplice? Then again, what if something went wrong, such as being caught in the act by the Rads? Dear God . . . what a state to be in. She would be finished for sure. If not dealt with on the spot, as Oliver's accomplice her credibility as a Reformer would be shattered; the 'foot in both camps brigade' like Susan Thistlewood would be vindicated.

Popularity, which meant a lot to Jancie, would fade, and as for what effect such disclosures would have on trade . . . oh, duplicity was a terrible thing. She felt haunted, afraid, just like the night before boarding the criminal coach. Sleep was impossible. She hoped Violet, who always slept like a dormouse, was curled up somewhere comfortably. As for her, practicality asserted itself: she had letters to write.

The damp, drizzly dawn, found her already gowned and cloaked. Unrefreshed, she headed toward Etherington's theatre, feeling herself to be as taut and strung up as . . . Pitt Caxton's harp! What made her think of that, she wondered, then went on to speculate if it was installed in the Quay Street house . . . funny how you could think of something so trivial with so much at stake.

Letting herself into the theatre, she quickly kindled a lamp. It was strange being alone in a place usually so alive with illusion and spectacle. Dusty, deserted and cold, it now seemed as dull and grey as the reality outside.

She hurried to the robe room. Robe room! Big cupboard more like! Her footsteps echoed; round, up to the gallery and back again. The costumes looked shadowy, disembodied. Wigs, she thought quickly, a couple of wigs; hats; whiskers to hide the telltale pock marks on Edward's face. A gown? Yes, and shawl. Stuffing them into a large canvas bag, she doused the light and returned to the street.

Lifting her skirts a little with one hand, and clutching the bag with the other, she made her way to St Mary's Gate. Bob would be disappointed if she left town without saying goodbye.

Reaching his shop, she peered over the half door. Good; too early for customers. Going down the steps, she tossed a couple of mealworms, from the box hanging on the wall, to the tame nightingale, and shouted. "Shop! Shop, Mr Barber!"

He appeared from the back room, resplendent in scarlet

waistcoat and Byronical shirt, his round face glowing from a recent shave. "If it isn't my little cock o' wax, and so early in the day. Bags, cloak and all, off to to the rescue."

"What d'you mean?" she repeated, startled.

"The Derby men! The Defence money – what did you think I meant?"

"Sorry, Bob. I must be a little nervous."

"Not surprising, for it's quite a responsibility. No money – no defence. But," he grinned. "When have Etherington's not delivered on time! Put your baggage down, and I'll toast us some muffins, eh?"

"Yes, Bob," she said, warming, as always to his geniality. "It's quite cold out there. What they call 'raw'."

She stood by the stove, watching him thrust the long-handled fork toward it. "D'you remember toasting muffins for me and Violet when we were little?"

"I'd toast 'em for you for the rest of me life, given the chance. There," he surveyed the muffins simmering nicely in pools of butter, with satisfaction. "The coffee's hot, so draw up a chair, lass, and we'll have a minute to ourselves before you go."

The next call was to send one of the letters she had written to Sir Francis Burdett's private address in Piccadilly, London; and the last call was to Marsden Square. In the outer office Thomas, wearing black mittens, took her cloak and bag. "Nasty morning, Miss Ridley, is it Mr Crabtree you're wanting?"

"Of course, Thomas, who else?"

She heard him ascending the stairs to the senior partner's rooms, and sneaking a glance at Caxton's office door, was startled to see it open and him in the door way watching her. She was hatless, and strands of damp hair hung in little corkscrew tendrils about her face. He saw folded spectacles tucked between the buttons of her bodice, and thought how he and Crabtree had discussed Ovid's poem at the Clowes' wedding. What, he wondered, was she wanting with 'darling Crabby' – and if he could glance within those stout boots she was wearing, would the nails be tipped with copper or crimson?

"Good morning, Miss Ridley." He had deliberately avoided her these past weeks, to give him time to get used to the new situation. He wanted to be able to face her with equanimity, but he was still uneasy. He rubbed his chin with the back of knuckles.

"Good morning," she replied and, indicating the new furnishings, "you have, I see, made some radical changes, Mr Caxton."

Before he could reply, Thomas struggled down with an empty coal-scuttle. "Ready for you, now, Miss Ridley," he panted, and with an incline of her head to the figure in the doorway, she mounted the stairs.

"My dear," greeted Mr Crabtree, rising from breakfast. He smiled, and not merely his lips, but his eyes, twinkled and his entire face beamed. "Come and sit by the fire, your hands are cold." And when she was seated. "Tell me, to what do I owe the pleasure of your visit?"

"Now, you mustn't be anxious," she began – not that he knew about Oliver and Violet – "but, if anything goes wrong concerning me at Derby . . . I want this letter to be in legal hands, so you can act on it if necessary. Just a formality to make my mind easy, that's all."

"And quite understandable after that fiasco in Newgate."

"You will look to Charles?"

"Of course, I shall call every day . . . But when are you going?"

"Today. There's only one coach . . . Why," she giggled at the face he made. "What's up?"

He stabbed a forefinger with ferocious significance in a downward direction. "He," he mouthed with another stab below, "is boarding the same coach. That's why he's in the office so early."

Dismay covered her face. "He isn't involved, surely?"

"No, but John Cross and Thomas Denman are part of the

defence, and Cross suggested Caxton went with 'em for experience." He leaned across from his chair. "Denman is ambitious. Made a name locally for defending the Luddite trials and he hopes to make his name nationally at the Derby trials – finish up as Master of the Rolls I shouldn't wonder." His voice sank lower. "Denman is out to prove that Oliver, the *agent provocateur*, is at the bottom of the insurrection. He insisted that Oliver, who is the government's key witness, should return to Derby, to swear on his written evidence to the four judges. Rumour has it that Oliver, after complying, is virtually a prisoner in the town, with the Rads ready to kill him if they find him, and the militia on street corners, ready for trouble."

"All that doesn't really bother me, Crabby, but I don't want to share a coach with him," she pointed a finger in the downward direction. "He will tell 'em I'm a Rad, and I'll have to endure patronising comments and sly pokes at Female Reformers – and I'll end up being blazing rude and put Miss Etherington to shame." Her frown suddenly lightened. "I've got it." She took his chubby, pink hands, pulled him up and danced him round the table, only stopping to whisper. "I shall disguise myself!" It would do for Derby, as well, for she realised her copper hair and wearing of spectacles tended to draw attention. "I've got some stuff downstairs already. Thomas?" she called running to the door. "Thomas, please bring my bag and cloak?" And when he brought them, she whispered. "Let me know the moment Mr Caxton goes out?"

At half-past ten, the yard of the Swan was already packed with Radicals come to cheer the lawyers off. The coach prepared to leave. Parcels, and bags had been swallowed by the boot. The guard was poised and passengers scrambling, for even the most sedate and calm of people, when confronted with a coach at the ready; horses rearing to go and the guard with the horn to his lips, felt the impulse to hurry, lest unable to hold back any longer, it should suddenly take off.

The King's Counsels, Cross and Denman, occupied a window seat facing each other, and Pitt, beside Denman, was bordered by their clerks. Jancie, disguised as an old man, who from the name on his box was a hatter from Denton, occupied the other window-seat.

"Not that the fees of this case will make anyone's fortunes," Mr Denman told them, when the coach was on its way, "for all of the forty-three on trial are destitute, and the ringleader who fired the shot, has been in receipt of parish relief for years."

"I really don't think Sidmouth wants them all to swing," declared Cross.

"But an example must be made, sir," said Pitt.

"Not if I can help it; we have to convince the jury, Mr Caxton, that Pentrich was a riot set up by an *agent provovateur*, and not insurrection or revolution, which the evidence of Oliver maintains."

"You'll never convince me," said Pitt. "Men willing enough to carry guns and use them are well on the way to anarchy."

He leaned back, folding his arms across the words. This was his opinion to be held and cherished. Having excluded himself from the huddle, his dark-fringed eyes surveyed the other passenger, idly at first, and then keenly. Despite the hatter's age, the eyes peering from under the shaggiest eyebrows were young – and green.

After the luncheon stop, further observation convinced him the 'hatter' was indeed Miss Ridley. Obviously, she was coming to Derby with the money collected for the Defence Fund – to which Selina, merely to annoy him, had contributed handsomely.

It was dusk when the coach swung into the George at Derby, and he, agreeing to meet the others for dinner, suddenly had an idea. This was an ideal opportunity, too good to miss. First out of the coach, and swiftly seizing the hatter by the arm, he helped the shuffling figure

230

into the George's Public Room, and the most secluded corner alcove.

He pushed her in first, then sitting down himself made her a prisoner. She observed, with a vague sense of disappointment, that he had seen through the diguise, but short of making a scene, she was forced to accept the situation.

"Smoked lenses would have hiden the colour of your eyes," he said softly.

"Yes," came the tart response, "I must remember next time."

"Do you make a habit of this?"

"And do you make a habit of abducting people? For that's what you are doing. Forcibly detaining me against me will?"

"I'm not, believe me, I am not, Miss Ridley. You are free to go . . . in a moment." Then he saw the funny side of it. The smart, the stylish Miss Ridley, designer of distinctive boudoir wear – baggy breeches on her slender haunches and a brown coat hanging about her like an old umbrella. "It's the whiskers," he spluttered. "Are these what every fashionable young lady will be wearing next season?"

"I know it seems odd to you," she answered coldly, "that I am dressed like this, but I have my reasons. Please allow me to leave." She lowered her voice. "My time is money, sir."

"So you are here on business?"

"Yes."

"Don't tell me – let me guess." He made a theatrical gesture. "Install the Clowes Scarlet in your farmyard, and you too, will have Radical eggs! Or perhaps Etherington's are breaking in on the false whisker trade! You must pardon me . . . oh, dear heaven, false whiskers, what a ticklish subject!"

"And what rotten humour."

"Yes . . ." he sounded chastened. "Forgive me. The reason I brought you here . . ."

"Yes?"

"Come, come, Miss Ridley, let us stop hedging about," he leaned forward, and whispered, "I KNOW." He placed emphasis on the word, and repeated, "I know that you and I are on the same side of the fence."

There was a silence. He's mad, she thought. Something has turned his brain. She reached in her pocket for an eyeglass, which quickly changed his blurred image into features of the utmost sincerity. Of dire seriousness. The dark-fringed eyes looked deeply into hers . . . She lowered the eyeglass at once.

"You can trust me, Miss Ridley," he said earnestly. "I have not, and will not, on my oath, breathe a word to anyone – even Miss Lansdowne."

"I think you're very wise," her voice almost quavered with incredulity, "for they would think you had taken leave of your senses."

And it wouldn't do my reputation any good, either, she thought. Her mind whirled before his gaze. At least, the whiskers hid most of her alarm and astonishment. But, why should he assume something so remote? A clock struck half-past the hour of seven. She had to get away. Hetty Mawson would be waiting. Violet and Oliver would be waiting.

"Mr Caxton," she said, "I trust you will never refer to this matter again?"

He bowed his dark head in submission, and indicating the whiskers, asked on a smile. "I trust you bear me no malice?"

She answered frankly from the shadow of the hat. "I'm not sure, Mr Caxton, not sure at all."

Outside the George, she first hurried to the Post Office, noticing the militia, and a cavalry presence on the streets. Rapping smartly on the window, Jancie asked and paid for the letter, which bore only an address, 'Mallinson's Barn'. Disappointment welled up. She had expected . . . something from Violet . . . not for the first time, she wondered if Violet was really with him.

But first, before anything else, she had to get this bank note to the Mawsons who lived by Broad Gate. Acting on directions from the postmistress she shuffled her way to the cottage, and rattling the latch, called, "Hetty Mawson? Open up. Open up!"

There was a great noise of unbolting from behind the door. "I'm from the Manchester Reformers," she told Jake. "I know it doesn't look like it, but tell Hetty I'm Jancie Ridley."

But Hetty, large, fair and freckled, was already there, smothering Jancie in her arms and rocking to and fro, laughing about the whiskers.

When they had calmed down, Jancie, feeling greatly relieved, produced the bank note for two hundred pounds from a body belt beneath the breeches.

"Eh, but you're a good lass," said Jake, then looked from the note to the bare table. "And there's not a bite to give thee. What little money we had has gone toward me brother's defence."

There being no chairs, they perched on a straw mattress on the floor by a small fire, and talked into the hour, Jancie relating all she had overheard in the coach concerning the trial. After changing her clothes and removing the whiskers, she left five sovereigns on the bare table. "Not for the fund," she insisted. "This is for you both – for old time's sake."

Having ascertained direction previously at the Post Office, she walked briskly along the deserted road, her fear of the dark swallowed in rehearsing her plan of action. After about a mile, she arrived at Mallinson's Barn.

There was a smaller door within a large one, and, reaching out, she lifted the latch and pushed it open. She stood by the door, breathless, uncertain.

"Miss Ridley?"

"Where is my sister?" she called into the darkness.

He appeared with a rushlight, his hat at the ready to shade it. "Can you imagine the pretty Violet blooming in a barn?"

"Your note gave me to understand—"

"I have to be wary. Once united with your sister, you could have thrown me to the Rads."

It sounded feasible. "Where is she, then?"

"London, which ensures you conduct me there in safety. Should anything go wrong and we do not reach London, you will never know where to find her."

"Why hasn't she written to us?"

"You can ask her that yourself. Come now, what have you brought?"

"Whiskers, wig, breeches, dancing pumps – they were the only footwear I could lay hands on. Your Wellington boots might be recognised."

"Did you arrange a conveyance?"

"Before I conduct you to any arrangements, there are conditions."

"What?"

"I also, have to be wary. There is nothing to stop you, the moment you have transport, from throwing me into a ditch and making off."

"What conditions then?" he snapped.

"Before we leave this barn you will pay me ten guineas for my trouble and expense; plus, another ten, being the price of a chaise waiting in Derby, with a crack driver to London."

"Twenty guineas!"

"There's always the alternative."

"You're a cool one, Miss Ridley."

She pocketed the money, adding, "And you will agree to be handcuffed; both your hands, which will be linked to my left by a short chain."

He was instantly sullen. "If attention is drawn to us, and I'm caught, you'll be finished, too. Imagine it. 'President of the Female Reformers assists Oliver the spy escape the net he's laid for others!' Pretty newsprint."

"I must see my sister, and if that means getting you to London safely, I'll risk the pretty newsprint." The letter to Sir Francis Burdett, posted this morning, had outlined her plan. Oliver must not escape.

"If we are to be chained together for the best part of forty-eight hours, the situation may become awkward at times."

"Not as awkward as the forty-six men awaiting trial here in this town."

In the light of early morning, a bearded man, hatted and cloaked, with a young woman on his arm, strolled past County Hall where the trial was to take place. Oliver was nervous, and when they reached the carrier to find the chaise not ready, and the stable staff asleep, he was both angry and suspicious.

"I couldn't give them an exact time," Jancie declared. "We'll just have to wait. Besides, it'll do you good to sweat it out for a change."

Not that they waited long. Men in gaiters and tightly rolled sleeves appeared like a swarm of ants. Out came the chaise, in went the horses, a man took the reins, travellers got in, and the ants swarmed back to the nest.

For the first five miles Jancie was apprehensive of pursuit. But as the horses became thoroughly warmed they worked in good style. She thought of Etherington's lazy horse, Morocco, and wished she was back home.

As for Oliver, it looked as though she might get him to London. What a triumph for the Rads if she did – and what a come down for Sidmouth and Castlereagh. She sat as far distant from Oliver as the chain would allow, and after locking the hand-cuffs had thrown the key away. As in holy matrimony, she was bound to Oliver for better or worse, until they reached London.

Chapter 26

"We're being followed," said Oliver, tersely.

Jancie's heart sank. She looked out of the back window. "There is someone, but it's not the militia."

"What's the matter with this chaise?" he demanded. "Are the horses lame? Ten guineas for a crack driver to London, you said, and it's crawling like a louse! Faster," he implored. "Faster!"

She looked again. The rider, leaning forward over the horse's neck, was hatless; the wind tossed his raven black hair, and she knew it was Pitt Caxton. Jancie's thoughts were thrown from panic to turmoil. She glanced at the hunted look on Oliver's face without satisfaction. They were linked together in more ways than one. Nothing must prevent her and Oliver arriving in London together. Nothing must prevent her taking him in these chains to Sir Francis Burdett, and nothing, absolutely nothing, must stand in the way of her reunion with Violet.

"If he does catch up with us," she said. "Leave all the talking to me."

"Catch up!" yelled Oliver. "He's driving us into the side – damn fool!" The horses, now alarmed, took off onto the heath; the chaise, constructed lightly for speed, was at risk among tussocks and burrows. It swayed and bumped. A sudden lurch threw Jancie and Oliver across the juddering chaise. It's going over, she thought wildly. Away rolled a wheel and over went the chaise. Horses plunged and reared. And when at last all was still, Jancie felt herself extricated from the wreckage by Oliver pulling on her wrist.

The driver, who had succeeded in freeing the horses from the shafts, stood white-faced, a hand on each bridle.

"You deliberately drove us off the road," he accused Pitt. Wait till the Company hears about this. What did you do it for, eh?"

Taking advantage of the attention focused on Pitt, Oliver quickly took up the slack of the chain, and jerked Jancie close up against him.

"Everyone stay where they are," he commanded. "If you care to look, gentlemen, you'll see I've got a short knife – but wait, best to take her word for the sharpness of it."

Jancie stood rigid. The knife-point tore into the flesh of her ribs. She gasped with pain and terror.

"I don't know what your game is," he addressed Pitt. "But one move and the knife goes right in. You, there," he indicated the driver's lad. "Find something to break this chain. Hammers, tools, a file in the driver's box. Be sharp with you. One wrong move and she's dead." The boy quickly appeared with a file. "Put your brawn into it, lad," he snapped, "and no tricks."

The desperate breathing close to her ear and the threat of the knife made Jancie angry with herself. Oliver would arrive in London without her. Why, oh why, had she not searched him in the barn? The filing stopped. The chain was cut. Flinging Jancie to the ground he swung himself up onto Pitt's horse, and was away to the road.

In silence they all watched the horseman into the distance.

"Right," said the driver, "and now, your card, sir? Such reckless 'orsemanship I never did see. Your card? I must have it for the company – they're not going to like this." He took the card, offered with an impatient gesture. "Oh, that's rich," he grinned at the lad. "He's a lawyer – will yer settle out of court for all this damage?"

"Cut the comedy and allow me a horse to take this lady to the nearest inn – apart from her injuries, this has been a distressing experience."

"And whose fault is that, eh?"

"A horse, if you please?"

"But they're chaise horses, sir. I can't do that, it's against Company rules."

"I'll settle with the Company, and stable the horse at the inn." He reached into his pocket. "Here's a guinea piece, and a florin for the lad. Your Company would not leave a lady in the middle of nowhere?"

"Certainly not, sir. The Coach and Horses, sir, is the nearest inn, some ten miles back."

When they had gone, Pitt turned toward her from the horse. He saw she was pale, but not from injury; anger flashed, lighting up the brilliant green of her eyes. It was too late to stop her fury. She lashed out, the chain on her wrist crashing into his lower jaw. Turbulent tears of bleak disappointment and frustration clouded her vision. "You have ruined everything," she yelled. "Everything I ever cared for, cared about!" She would have struck again, but for the pain in her ribs. Its sharpness cleared her vision, allowing her to focus on the blood trickling onto his white shirt.

As she made a predatory examination of his jaw, his voice cut across the bedlam of her emotions. "I realise," he began grimly, "that my actions have ruined something of extreme importance, but before we leave this spot, Miss Ridley, you will listen to my reasons." She remained silent. "One of the forty-six Radicals awaiting trial has escaped. The only vehicle equipage to leave town so early was a chaise hired by a young woman who couldn't see to sort her money without putting spectacles on, and a male companion." He fingered his jaw. "The description fitted yourself. And presuming you to be abducted, I acted in

238

your interest. What else was I to do? As a lawyer Miss Ridley, I am given to reasoned judgement, but it appears that where you are concerned, I am constantly wrong." He brushed back his hair. "I must be mad."

"And an idiot to be talking. Keep your jaw still and the blood will clot."

Neither spoke for a long time. As by common consent they fell into a truce.

"Shall we move off, it will be dark soon?"

She nodded, and stood regarding the horse. "I'll hold him, while you use the box as a mounting block. C'mon," he chivvied. "Up you go!" Up she went to find herself clutching the horse's mane with both hands. Her thighs tortuously strained across the broad, silky, back. She remembered Violet wanting her to learn to ride – the saddle and stirrups held terrors enough, but to ride bareback and straddle-legged! The horse reared slightly as Pitt jumped up behind. Her cloak was creased and ruckled, her skirts shrivelled, and the knife wound throbbed with the effort of mounting.

"To keep our balance," he said urging the horse forward slowly, "you must lean back into me . . ." He did not take up the reins until he felt the pressure of her body against his chest. The pressure came by degrees; at first she was stiffly cautious, then, because of her ribs, she gave herself up to the comfort of his body.

Progress was going to be slow, thought Pitt. Used to saddle, stirrups and spurs, he was no good without. But he was not impatient. Indeed, he fancied her tangled hair bore healing properties as the wind brushed it against his sore jaw. Miss Ridley and he riding together was quite pleasant – despite a split jaw!

It was dark when they reached the Coach and Horses. He leapt down and gave the ostler, who had clearly hoped to have finished duties for the night, the Company card as the driver had bidden him. The man stared at the blood-stained neckcloth. "Nasty accident, sir."

"Yes, you could say so."

"Inn's full. But you're welcome to spend the night in the Travellers' Room. Only benches to sleep on, bit 'ard, but better than under a hedge."

Pitt turned to assist Jancie and found her already dismounted. She had slithered down, and, leaning against the horse, rubbed her thighs and seriously wondered if she would ever walk again.

There were only two other couples, and a man with a spotted dog, in the Travellers' Room; it was warm, white-washed and furnished with benches. The main wall boasted a big-faced clock, a cracked looking-glass, and in the corner a washstand with tin bowl and pitcher.

A hurried glance in the mirror convinced Pitt of the alarming spectacle he presented. Quickly pouring water, he removed the neckcloth and used it to bathe his jaw. He noticed the scar on his forehead received in the fracas in Etherington's theatre. Now it seemed he would bear another! And what a bruise there'd be tomorrow! His lips curved into a smile. He would have to prepare a good defence to satisfy the curiosity of his colleagues. Having finished his ablutions, he called the attention of the pot boy. "Rum and pineapple!" he shouted up the flagged passage. "Sharpish, mind – and hot."

Jancie, cold, hungry and tired, put on her spectacles and settled into the bench nearest the fire, contentedly watching the steam rise from her russet-coloured skirts. Pitt, poured the pineapple and rum and handed her a glass, and they sipped it slowly, in silence.

The pot boy returned. "If you want to keep the fire in all night, sir, you'll have to pay for coals, tuppence a scuttle, but they're large scuttles, sir. An' don't turn down the lamp, or you'll have beetles all over yer boots. Supper? There ain't much left . . . cold pie, beef, pickles."

"Add to that a bottle of port and a jug of your best ale."

While waiting for supper he watched the steam rising

from her skirts and his boots. Selina would laugh at the notion that steam from crumpled skirts and muddy boots could arouse such interest, such pleasant interest. She would say he was going 'rustic', and maybe he was. Where was the fault in that?

Supper was eaten in the same easy manner of silence and the occasional observance. "We couldn't do this in Manchester," he reflected over his port. "The Radical Ridley and the Tory Caxton, closeted all night in the Travellers' Room at some God-forsaken place in Derbyshire. Compromising to say the least!"

"There'll be nothing compromising," she laughed, "about this night, I assure you."

"With my jaw and your ribs, Miss Ridley," he grinned, "It's highly unlikely."

"I . . . I'm sorry about your face."

"Shh . . ." he put a finger to his lips, fearing to wreck so pleasant a mood.

They moved from the table to the bench before the fire. Looking into the dancing flames, she called to mind the few occasions on which they had met, from the very first at the theatre, to the May Day Main and him in a mulberry coat; the asthma attack in the criminal coach; his dark head against the gilt frame of a harp at the Moxhams'; then at Jem's wedding dance, responding to the wild music, responding to her. Lastly in the George. He was obviously under a misapprehension which accounted for the change of attitude. And now . . . she thought, what now?

The silence between them had taken on a deeper quality. He raised a dark, slanted eyebrow and considered her. The wind had blown her hair into little corkscrews, which gleamed in the lamplight, making it the colour of burnished chestnuts; her complexion glowed, and her eyes were soft and contented. I must be drunk, he thought, helplessly, maudlin drunk.

She took up her glass and drank the last of the ale, tipping it up, as she had at Jem's wedding to catch the

241

last drops, her lips pouted against the rim, the tip of her tongue just visible. He watched, fascinated. Unable to resist, he leaned across the bench, and mindful of the knife wound, slid his hand behind her neck and lifted her lips to his. There was no demur, no coyness. He felt her free hand touch his good jaw, reaching round to the back of his neck, moving, caressing. The kiss was hesitant at first, then exquisitely explorative. They parted, and taking breath explored again. Traversing, searching, tasting. Kiss followed kiss, until Jancie with racing heart, put her hand on his shoulder and pushed him away. They sat there, side by side, sharing a strange kind of modesty. "A Tory kiss, madam," he teased softly, "is not so disagreeable?"

"Not at all," she smiled.

"And shall we talk well into the night?"

"No," came the quick answer. "I am going to sleep. We can talk tomorrow."

The bench was hard, her body bruised and tender. She slept soon and dreamed of Oliver in Mallinson's barn; of throwing away the key to the handcuffs; of vowing they would arrive in London together. Oliver was laughing, while she was . . . crying.

Chapter 27

Jancie was well on the way to Ashbourne market by the time Pitt Caxton woke stiffly from his bench in the Travellers' Room at the Coach and Horses. She had been aroused by the jingle of harness and, going outside, she saw a gig preparing to leave. The innkeeper's wife, sitting on the box, reins in hand, had almost started on her weekly visit to Ashbourne market when she saw Jancie, and welcomed a passenger to ease the tedium of travel.

At Ashbourne, a farrier removed the handcuff and chain from her wrist, and she boarded the mid-morning Flyer to Manchester. Her thoughts sped as swiftly as the wheels turned. First, recalling the misery of the time she and Charles travelled from London without Violet. If that was sad, this was worse. At least that misery was shared, but this was her own exclusively. She had imagined a heroine's return – having delivered Oliver to Sir Francis as the final proof of her integrity to the 'foot in both camps' brigade. She had imagined returning triumphant to Charles, with news of Violet – after having gloriously returned Violet to Mirabelle. But would it have been so simple? If Violet was so taken with Oliver, she would look upon her sister's act as damnable treachery, and no doubt cut all connections dead. She regretted the presumptuous letter to Sir Francis, who no doubt saw it as the impetuous zeal of a fanatic. What about Pitt Caxton's attitude? How could she ever face him again, not to mention Selina?

The trials in Derby would last another three weeks, which were time enough for her to settle into life as it had been before Oliver's letter; before Pitt Caxton rode so dramatically into her affairs. So, went the thoughts, round and round, circling, whirling, turning and eventually arriving at the Swan yard.

"I don't think I should let my Geisha Girl go away again if she returns in so badly a state," said Charles, her jewelled fingers bathing the torn flesh on Jancie's ribs, "a highwayman, you say, held you up at knife point. It's a wonder you're here to tell the awful tale! Now, come to the glass and see for yourself. No need to be stitched, its closing up nicely. But no swimming, for you, my dear!"

Lifting her arm slowly before the looking glass, Jancie saw her ribcage to be a mass of purple bruising; except for the white skin and red flesh where Oliver's knife had entered. She closed her eyes and shuddered. Violence so personal had not come her way before.

"Ouch!"

"Tender?" came the mischievous enquiry, as Charles applied a herbal ointment. "This may sting a little . . . there," she said, covering the linen dressing with broad bands of sticking plaster.

"At least I survived it all."

"And thank God you did. It's bad enough Violet eloping so suddenly and without a word . . . to lose you would be . . ."

She reached for a flannel robe which had been warming by the fire, and as Jancie slid her arms into it, the older woman made light of her anxiety by wrapping it about the slender body, tying the sash, and putting up the collar, as she had when they were children.

Jancie put her good arm about her guardian's shoulders. "Charles, oh, darling, Charles," she breathed against the elegantly waved hair, "don't upset yourself. We'll hear from Violet soon . . ."

Sufficiently rested, and radiant in chestnut-coloured gown and short worsted cape to match, Jancie's first reaction was to be busy; to see everyone and everything. In the room above Margery's father's brush works, where the Female Reformers met, she made her report, and passed on the grateful thanks of the Derby Rads, and then they talked of Hetty and Jake Mawson, and argued and laughed and drank Hunt's Radical coffee.

Then she called on Bob. The shop being full, they wanted to know about Derby, and on hearing the chances of the men getting off were slim, they cursed Oliver, and Sidmouth and Castlereagh. "That fella Thistlewood's got the reet idea," said one of the stubbly chins. "Revolution. That's what this country needs!"

Jancie was glad to get out and hurried to 11 Long Millgate into the comparative safety of the Reverend Brookes' company. There, with his pet cat on her knee, the monkey on her shoulder and his pigeons cooing in the loft, they talked not of Reform but of the alterations to the church and the removal of the steeple. "Not content with that . . ." He added emphasis by drawing bushy eyebrows together, ". . . they're meddlin' with the town. Want to build on St Peter's Field and widen Market Street. Where will it all end? Where will it all end, eh?" The world was moving too fast for the minister of St Mary's.

By the time Pitt Caxton returned to Manchester the country was plunged into mourning. The Princess Charlotte, a popular figure, and only child of the Regent and Caroline of Brunswick, had died in childbirth – and the hanging of three Radicals at Derby and the transportation of another ten was scarcely mentioned.

The overshadowing of the executions hardened Radical opinion; it hardened Jancie. She quarrelled with Charles about closing the Manufactory for the day of the princess's funeral; and although Charles had her way, Jancie refused to take part in any public token of sympathy.

"Miss Ridley!" Pitt exclaimed, when they accidentally met on the day of the royal funeral. He wore deepest mourning, and she the Radical scarlet and white. "You would have passed me," he said, with a hurt expression. "Like at the Coach and Horses, when I woke, you had gone."

"We have not a great deal in common, you and I." She indicated his clothes with a glance.

"I was under the impression we had."

"You were quite wrong."

"Miss Ridley . . . may I call on you?"

"No. Now, if you will excuse me?"

Christmas came and the old year passed into the new. Not that anyone expected 1819 to be an improvement. To make matters worse, Aberdaron Dick had gone to that mysterious place called Wales. The winter was grim, the town sullen and strikebound. Trade was at a low ebb which meant Jancie had to travel further afield for orders. This suited her Radical activities and being out of town she was less likely to meet Pitt. But avoiding him was becoming more difficult because Selina Lansdowne had taken to calling on Charles, sometimes with Lady Egerton and sometimes with her fiancé.

Jancie, wrapped warmly against the cold, and drawn by the strident call of the Clowes' cocks, called on Margery. Now that Jem was devoting more time to the birds than his mother's sugar bakery, she was a full-time assistant. After discussing the effect of the continual strikes, and the low morale of the Rads, the three of them stood by the pens admiring the young birds and the improvement in the strain.

"You've done well, both of you," congratulated Jancie. "Success in a recession of trade is something to be proud of."

"Ay, we bred a good 'un, there, Jancie, you and me."

"Oh, and Margery," she laughed. "You should have seen me hurrying over here at dawn to use his mother's chamber pot! 'Mixing the mash with early morning urine makes a fighting cock doubly fierce.' Oh, I can laugh about it now, but that bird was a symbol. There was so much at stake."

"Pity we can't think of another symbol," said Margery.

"But we can! Oh, Margery, we can! I've got it – a most marvellous idea!"

"Charles!" Jancie burst into the office. "I've got an idea for another line in Etherington's Enterprises! Say you want to hear it?"

"Oh dear," laughed Charles, gathering some bills together, her rings sparkling in the lamplight. "I've had enough of accounts, anyway. And yes, I do want to hear my Geisha Girl's idea."

"White hats!"

Slim, dark eyebrows raised in surprise.

"Mirabelle mentioned a craze for white hats in her last letter."

"Started by that Radical fellow, Henry Hunt?"

Jancie nodded. "It will catch on up here sooner or later. We must see that it's sooner. Clogger, Fancy and Sampson must be sworn to secrecy, and Etherington's must be the first to sell white hats in Manchester."

"But, my dear, making hats is a specialist trade."

"We can supply materials to the hatters. I can attend to that tomorrow – from velour to buckskin to cotton. They'll jump at the chance to go into production. Some are on short time, others have ran out of it. Charles, darling, darling Charles, what d'you say?"

Her guardian reached for the sketch pad. "Not just one style, that would be terribly dull."

"Hats for women, of course!"

"Why stop there? Bonnets, caps—"

"Hunt may have started it, but Etherington's can improve on it!"

"Just in time for spring as well."

"They'll look so good everyone will want one."

"Everyone?" Eyebrows shot up again. "Not Mr Caxton, surely. Selina, perhaps, just for fun!"

247

"And we'll launch it on the boards, like the kimono. I shall wear white breeches, knee boots, a scarlet coat and tuck my hair beneath . . ." she paused for effect, "the first white hat in Manchester!"

The sale of the white hats boomed. Every Radical who could afford it, had one. Entire families were fitted out. Spring sunshine helped. It was spring, it had to be. "Eh, Aberdaron Dick's back!"

"Is he by Jove?"

"I say, did you see—"

"Course, saw the old buzzard at the Swan yard."

"No . . . couldn't have been, he was sweeping the crossing in Market Street!"

The good-humoured banter about Dick's plurality of jobs filled the air, but there were some who noticed his long, loping stride had shortened, and although never fat, his face looked thin.

A week later Jancie was sitting at the French writing table in the office, when there was a knock on the door.

She called out, "Yes, Fancy, what is it?"

The door opened. She looked up. It was Pitt Caxton.

He stood for a moment contemplating the astonished angle of Jancie's auburn head; the hair smoothly drawn back to her ears, falling in bunches of corkscrew curls. The tortoiseshell spectacles were thrust into the buttons of her military-style gown – spare ones, he presumed, for a pince-nez was already perched on her nose. Behind one ear was a tattered goose quill, and the cuffs of her gown were doubled back across the forearm. Pitt Caxton thought to himself, why have I come to place myself in this absurd and terrible position? Why have I so improperly and undeniably fallen madly in love with Boadicea? He thought he might have been going that way, now he was certain.

"Good afternoon, Miss Ridley."

248

She covered her surprise by asking, "What can Etherington's do for you, Mr Caxton?"

"It's a case of what I can do for Etheringtons." He had prepared his opening speech well.

"And what can you do?"

"Warn you that the magistrates have begun a campaign against the white hats."

"Have they, indeed? Good. That will increase the popularity even more."

"You are going ahead with production, then?"

"Of course."

He turned to place his hat on a chair. She frowned. "Is there something else?"

"Yes . . ." Putting his hands on the edge of the table, he leaned toward her. "Something of a problem, I fear." Then with mock gravity, he continued, "It's like this, Miss Ridley. I have a suspicion that I spend more time than is good for me, as a man engaged to be married, thinking about another . . . Would you suggest I approach the other lady on the subject?"

Her eyes, widening with every sentence, responded to his ploy. "D'you think it wise?"

"Would this young lady object?"

Jancie considered for a moment. "She would consider the barriers—"

"Barriers," he interrupted, "can be surmounted. And, recalling my conversation in the George at Derby, with a certain bewhiskered lady, we both know that this barrier is not all that much of an obstacle." There, he thought, straightening up. I have used the word 'we' and she hasn't bawled me out!

He stepped round the table. Jancie, unprepared, leapt from her chair. He reached for her hands, and like a small girl, she thrust them behind her back. He remained in front of her, and she, like a rabbit watching a stoat, felt herself becoming entranced by the charm of him. Charm she never knew he had, but was discovering at an alarming

249

rate. His grey eyes were no longer the colour of wet slate, but smoky and warm. A lock of heavy, raven black hair had fallen onto his forehead. She saw the scar on his jaw, reminding her of how his interference had lost Oliver.

He was inches from her, taking in again the smudge of ink on her chin; the spectacles in her bodice; braided hair with a wisp or two out of place; cuffs turned back. This sweet disorder, touched him, softened his frustration. He wanted to take her in his arms, but reached out to touch her hair. She looked at him fiercely. He withdrew his hand.

"What you are suggesting is impossible," she said quickly, "and even were it not, there is still . . .," she was weakening, "there is still your fiancée."

The brief silence between them took on a new and sudden quality. She seemed to him, with her smudged chin and fierce brow, very beautiful and utterly desirable. They stood for a moment, perfectly still; entranced, their faces grave. Smoky grey eyes impaled on vivid green. The sounds of commerce from the workrooms at the back, from the street in front, hovered and fled.

Pitt took her in his arms, and her body yielded softly, taking her will with it in a bid to rekindle the exquisite emotion experienced in the Travellers' Room. Never mind that someone might come in. Never mind Selina. Never mind anything. Her arms were about his neck. The quill fell from behind her ear, to flutter like her resolve until it reached the floor, lying forgotten and crushed.

They kissed and paused, and looked upon each other in sheer delight. She cradled her head beneath his chin, listening to the thump of his heart, bewildered that it was beating so strongly for her. She heard him whispering her name, and never had it sounded so thrilling, coming from the depths of his chest, vibrating against her heart. "Jancie . . . Jancie . . ."

She lifted her face and they kissed again on a long and satisfying sigh.

"This is madness," she drew apart to tell him. "A

250

perverse trick of fate to throw two opposites like you and me together. It's just a . . ."

"Yes?"

"A passing attraction."

"We can put its durability to the test."

"There's too much against us." She untwined his arms from her waist. "Go now, return to Lady Egerton's house and Selina, and think about it."

"I think about nothing else."

"Well, think again!"

She was now anxious to be rid of him. If he continued with his persuasive talk and lover's looks through those long lashes, she might not be able to keep a level head.

"Very well. I will. And if I come up with a satisfactory solution?"

"I shall," her tone lowered, her eyes lifted, "be only too pleased to hear it."

He squared his shoulders, prepared to leave. "Your hand?"

She extended it across the table. He pressed his lips to the faint bruises still on her wrist, and with an incline of his head reached the door. "Your hat!" she called after him. "You've left your hat." and with a smile, "Would you be interested in a white one for a change?"

Pitt contrived to be talking fighting birds with Jem when she called to see Margery. Equally contrived was his presence in the outer office when she came down from a consultation with Mr Crabtree. Doesn't mind seeing him alone, he thought begrudgingly. He heard laughter up the stairs, the chink of glasses, the deep, earnest tones of the man, and the tinkling asides in her lilting, theatrical voice. Between the opening of the door and descent of the stairs, there had been a pause, a silence, before the bidding of farewells. Then she came down, sporting her white hat, radiant and sparkling as though some of Crabby's gleaming personage had rubbed off onto her.

251

When Selina called on Miss Etherington with her fiancé in tow, Jancie arranged to be home. They found the situation exciting, for each knew the other had schemed to be there and the knowledge added a piquant flavour to an ordinary call.

On these visits he always sat by the gnarled table, and, while sipping China tea, reflected that far from the frosty reception expected, he had been indulged and drawn into the circle of these afternoon calls with an almost imperceptive benevolence. He accepted the generosity gratefully.

While Selina was busy appreciating 'the rustic', he felt a strange sense of satisfaction in the guilty enjoyment of watching Miss Ridley in her scarlet and black kimono. She sat by her guardian, whose dress was as elegant as her ward's was unconventional. They did not smoke cigars in the afternoon, or play cards, or drink their respective ale and wine. For this he was glad, Selina would have poked fun.

The lull in Radical activity, due to the effect of the Derby trial, was over. Radicals country wide, incensed by the Home Secretary's refusal to present a petition of grievances to the Prince Regent, decided to achieve this by another method, and that was to call a spate of monster meetings in all the big manufacturing towns. To which Lord Sidmouth responded by urging all the Lord Lieutenants to proceed to their counties with haste.

Every day in Manchester some new outrage occurred to bring overfed mill owners to Pitt in droves. "The Anti-Reform League will have to act promptly," they told him. "A gentleman is not safe in the streets. We have no truck with unions and societies and reserve the right to lay off who we will. These Radical blaggards attack our houses, pull up the railings and shatter the windows. The Specials are overpowered, stones thrown, and Bradshaw has half a dozen stitches sewn into him. What is the League going to do about it, eh?"

The League formed an armed association to patrol the streets for the protection of life and property, but there were not enough recruits to make it effective. Bad masters were still marked and their property attacked.

Arthur Thistlewood's contribution to the whirlpool of unrest was to send firebrands like himself to preach the gospel of anarchy, to instruct in the making of weapons and to 'prepare' themselves by drilling in a military – like manner on the moors outside the town.

In keeping with the militant mood, Sir Francis Burdett introduced into parliament a scheme for the reformation of the House of Commons, and Henry Hunt agreed on a date to address the monster meeting in Manchester. How much higher, thought Pitt, anxiously watching the escalation of events, could the fence between himself and Miss Ridley grow?

Chapter 28

Sitting behind the serpentine desk in Marsden Square, the sounds of yet another affray in the distance, Pitt felt hemmed in and pinned down, entangled in a web of circumstances beyond his control. A good thing Sidmouth and Castlereagh's espionage system did not rely on him! This reflection led him to think how even more glorious Jancie was. And in turn, how life with Selina was becoming tedious. She knew he was avoiding the subject of their wedding – he was and he felt wretched about it. He wanted to be brave, to break the engagement and be free. Really, there had not been much call for bravery in his life . . .

Almost before realising it, he was out in the heat of the square, in search of bravery. He found the essence of it in Shude Hill, dressed in a white muslin blouse with a wide neck, and skirts of apple green. He followed her into the office. It was cool, the blinds were halfway drawn, and the shade a relief.

"Is Miss Etherington home?" He always referred to Charles in this manner, not using the word guardian.

"She's resting. We stayed overlong at the Baths – I think I tired her out, poor dear."

"Like you danced me into the wheezes at Jem's wedding! I understand how she feels!" He glanced at the door.

"We shan't be disturbed for the next few minutes."

"A few minutes! I don't want to be disturbed for hours, and hours!"

"You look hot and frantic," she smiled, and taking his hat observed, "a white one would be a lot cooler this weather."

"I'm not brave enough."

"At least you're honest."

"Much good it does me . . . listen," he caught her hand as she returned from the placing of his hat. "We need to discuss our lives, Janice. I need to discuss where this path is leading. Wait!" He stilled her lips, with a touch of his forefinger. "At the George in Derby, you gave me to understand something which you have ever since been denying. Under such circumstances we cannot meet openly to talk, so I am asking you to come away with me. I have in mind," he rushed on, "a very pleasant country inn, grey-stoned, with scented roses tumbling over the walls, quiet and peaceful – where we can talk and be ourselves, away from prying eyes and suspicion."

She perched on the end of the writing table, looking cool and unpeturbed, her will riding calm over her panicking body. Then, peering at him through fine-rimmed spectacles, she shook her head. "I would not have you betray your fiancée with me."

"Whatever there was between Selina and me has been wearing thin to threadbare."

"If there's nothing between you, then it isn't right to keep her on a string, is it? The sooner she is released to find herself someone more worthy, the better, don't you think?"

He rubbed his chin with the back of his hand. "I could suggest taking Selina back to London . . . but what reason can I give?"

"Merely point out the state of the town. The magistrates think we're on the brink of revolution, and really Manchester at this time is no place for a lady."

"That's a good idea."

"I'm full of good ideas, that's why I am where I am!" He touched the end of her nose playfully. "I love you."

He drew back, startled at having said it. But, by this time, Jancie knew he was the man she had waited for. These little startled shafts of uncertainty added a quaint and appealing pathos to his formality. His stability appealed to her, his solidness, and somehow, his belonging to the established order. He was to become her beloved enemy. For him she was throwing caution to the four winds. Heaven help her!

"So," he breathed. "We call a truce at last?"

"First we must fix a date," she said, practically. "Trade is never brisk on a Monday, so you have Sunday and Monday in mind? Now . . . Henry Hunt is addressing the County Meeting on 9 August—"

"He wouldn't be coming at all, if I had my way!"

"You haven't, thank God, besides, you must have time to take Selina to London."

"Shall we say the sixteenth, then?"

"Yes."

"So," he said again, "we call a truce, make a pact, strike a bargain . . . and seal it with a kiss." From her perch she was into his arms, feeling the warmth of his hands through the muslin blouse, the pressure of his body as they stood merged together. The pact was sealed with one kiss, and then another, longer. Yet, through the passion, the exquisite darts of delight, her intellect posed the question. Is this a man to give me love on my own terms? And even as the aromatic fragrance of his clothes, released by the warmth, filled her senses, she thought it wasn't likely. A few moments later, watching him go, she was entertaining grave doubts as to her sanity. Common sense told her all she would get from that quarter was trouble. But, as Fancy Macdonald said, when asking permission to move into the loft rooms over the stable with Clogger. "When you've got a yen for a fella, you've got it, and that's that!"

Pitt removed Selina to London, and settled her after breaking off the engagement, at which, to wound his vanity, there were no tears. Then he returned to Manchester.

Recalling the state of the town, he had been anxious about the county meeting, or more truthfully about Jancie's part in it. For the Female Reformers would be there in force, with banners from all the surrounding areas. Well . . . it must have passed off without incident or it would have been the topic of conversation in every inn forward.

As they passed the Halfway House, his anxiety dissolved in the overwhelming prospect of being in her company for two whole days. The weather was fair and he was riding on top, experiencing the thrill of freedom. The thundering of hooves in his ears, the jingling of bridles, the shouts of the driver and guard, put him in mind of the theatre. Etherington's theatre, and Boadicea . . . Once started on memory road, he was at Heaton Park blazing with anger at being opposed by not merely a Radical, but a female! That took some swallowing, and yet, looking back, his attitude had not been sporting. He was filled with remorse at his rudeness and unconcern in the Criminal Coach – but he would make it up to her; also for interfering at Derby. But what had she been up to? First disguised, and then racing across the country shackled to a mad man. At the Moxhams' soirée, she had looked so different from her sister; the high priestess of Radicalism! He smiled at the phrase and lingered over the vision. Best of all, though, he liked to see her as Miss Etherington's Geisha Girl, wearing a wide-sleeved kimono, secured about the waist with a broad sash. Their display of affection was evidence of obvious devotion, but what, he wondered, would Miss Etherington do, when he came to take away her Geisha Girl – as assuredly, he would.

An unbidden smile lightened his dark jaw. What recklessness! What great exuberance of spirit! There was no time to be lost. He recalled Andrew Marvell's poem. "Had we but world enough and time, this coyness, lady, were no crime . . . the grave's a fine and private place, but none, I think, do there embrace."

He had to admit, now that he was away from her, to

being a little curious as to whether Jem Clowes had been her lover. He was not sure, either, about 'Darling Crabby' – and there was a ripeness of friendship between her and the barber, for had he not seen them standing close together behind the curtains? Not that he would ever question her, for he knew her to be the kind of woman who would not question him. The past was the past. And the week-end just one glorious day ahead.

His arrival in Manchester at once plunged his glorious week-end into doubt. "You there! Aberdaron Dick!" he yelled. "Take this baggage to Quay Street will you?" And passing him a shilling. "What's been happening in my absence?"

"Date of the county meeting changed, sir, to the sixteenth."

Pitt swore and strode out of the Swan yard. It was dusk already. The atmosphere struck him almost physically. The town was charged with excitement, held down, it seemed, by the sultry heaviness of a hot August night. Men clustered together at street corners, outside the inns and tobacco shops; some rowdy, others sullen. And the Specials whom he had sworn in were patrolling the thoroughfares, stout batons at the ready, in case anyone should overstep the mark; here and there, among the specials, among the crowds, were a sprinkling of Yeomanry.

He hurried to Shude Hill which was as much athrong as anywhere else, and looked up. The window of the protruding bay was open and Jancie, at cards with her guardian, looked down, and saw him.

"It's Mr Caxton," she told Charles, trying to calm her fast beating heart. "I shall see him in the office."

"Not trouble again, I hope," said Charles, "the name of Caxton has never augured well for me."

"It hasn't done a lot for me either," she smiled. "It's probably some legality to do with the meeting, you

258

know what a stickler he is for what they call the letter of the law."

Down in the office he stretched out his hands, and announced. "I stand before you, dusty, travel-stained, but free – and I couldn't return to you quickly enough. Oh, Jancie, Jancie, my darling." He gathered her against him, murmuring endearments, to end in a kiss. She leaned against him, spectacles crooked on his coat button, enjoying, savouring his nearness. Oh, if it could be always like this, for ever and ever . . .

"You've heard about the meeting?" she asked on a sigh.

"So the date has changed. What does it matter?" A prickle of fear caught his heart. "Come away with me," he said quickly. "As we arranged? You will honour our pact? Leave all this intrigue. Oh, my dear love, you've done far more than anyone could reasonably expect. You will come?"

There was a short silence.

"I am pledged to lead the Female Unions." Her voice muffled against his chest was barely audible. It became firmer. "And, privileged to share the platform with Henry Hunt." She lifted her head, adjusting her spectacles. "They are calling it 'Our Glorious Monday'. I can't let them all down, my dear. Don't press me to do so, it isn't fair. I wasn't to know the magistrates would change the date."

As the chill of uncertainty took hold on him, so fear of the county meeting grew. He was afraid it would, in some measure, alter things between him and his newly found love. His fear made him say all the wrong words. "But we made a pact, called a truce. I have made arrangements, thought of nothing but our week-end together. Is this how you rate me, then, as second fiddle to a county meeting! Come, Jancie, you must make a choice."

"Must?" She was immediately on her dignity. No one ever used that word to her. She drew away, slowly.

"Yes," his voice came at her, hoarse as a crow.

259

"You must choose between me and the Radical meeting."

"Very well . . ." She removed her spectacles and closed them with a snap. "The Radical meeting."

Chapter 29

"At least," remarked Charles, after they had breakfasted at the Seven Stars, "it's a fine day for your meeting."

"'Our Glorious Monday'!" quoted Jancie, flinging her arms wide. And it will be glorious, she thought. No doubt, afterwards, I'll have second thoughts of sending Pitt off with a flea in his ear, but just now, Reform is all.

Charles, in the sitting-room, heard the hurried footsteps of her ward making ready for the meeting. Having watered the window-box, where night-scented stock and nicotiana, nestled among brightly coloured nasturtiums, she straightened a cushion, rearranged the flower bowl, moved the decanter . . . and turned as Jancie entered the room in a white gown, scarlet over-tunic, and broad-brimmed white hat, secured under the chin with a scarlet ribbon.

"What a lovely outfit for a warm day. Far too nice to wear at a Radical meeting! You will be extra careful, my sweet?"

"Dear Charles!" exclaimed Jancie. "You mustn't fret. It's only a Reform meeting, not the storming of the Bastille!"

"Don't fret! How can I help it? From the numbers you estimate, there's never been such a mammoth gathering in the country before, still less in Manchester. The town isn't armed to teeth for nothing. Look," she pulled aside the curtain, "the Yeomanry have been swilling ale since breakfast, and they're a loutish lot to begin with."

"It's all nerves and precautions!" Jancie dismissed her guardian's alarm with a smile. "You know how nervous

James Norris is, he'd jump with fright at his own shadow, and the other magistrates are not much better. Nothing can go wrong."

"What about the reports of drilling on the moors?"

"Merely to give a semblance of order to so many on the move. We want an orderly approach to St Peter's Field, and good timing – not a mad scramble."

"And what of the weapons, made openly, I was told?"

"I took Bob Smollett to task for that, but he made out a good case for self-defence. Would we have encouraged women and children if we expected trouble? All the same, to make you feel easier, Clogger has shuttered the lower windows, and I've asked Crabby to call and keep you company. I tell you what, book some suppers at the Seven Stars, for us and Crabby and Clogger and Fancy – anyone who cares to join us."

Another kiss, a last embrace, and Jancie, shouting for Fancy to join her, was out on Shude Hill, where, linking arms, they poked fun at the Yeomanry, on their way to St Peter's Field.

There were others in Manchester on this hot August morning who were not so light-hearted in outlook. Among them being the three magistrates, Ethelstone, Norris and Hay, responsible for law and order. The Reverend Charles Ethelston, a pompous poet, and one of the 'hang 'em' brigade, had sought to muzzle the *Observer* with writs for 'seditious libel' and was still smarting from the amusing, but vicious abuse which had come his way as a result.

The resident magistrate, James Norris, had written in a panic to Lord Sidmouth three weeks before, asking advice in case of insurrection. The advice had now arrived, stressing that "military and troops should never be used until the 'peace' is actually broken". The Reverend Hay, ambitious, smug and righteous with it, at once ordered the local Salford and Manchester Yeomanry to be at the ready.

Fidgety, nervous, uncertain of what to expect from a

gathering of upwards of eighty thousand, disenchanted people, addressed by a raving demagogue, they stationed the Cheshire Yeomanry in John Street. For extra safety they engaged professional soldiers; the 15th Hussars, to be placed in Byrom Street and Mosely Street; added to this was a contingent of the Royal Horse Artillery and two long, six-pound guns. With fifteen hundred soldiers in all, virtually surrounding the area, and an extra four hundred inexperienced specials, the anxious magistrates hoped to maintain law and order.

The drilling of which Charles had been nervous, was now in evidence in the steady tread of the crowds pouring into town. Mile after mile they tramped, some having been afoot before dawn. They walked in orderly procession like the Sunday School scholars on Whit Sunday. Bands played 'Scots Wha Hae' and 'Cherry Ripe'. Bugles, fiddles, and drums were in demand: anything that kept people in step, or to which they could sing. Colourful banners were staunchly carried. Those who had best clothes wore them, those who could afford dinners brought them. Men, women and children, even dogs were all set for "a reet good day".

The magistrates were in a house overlooking the platform with a good view of St Peter's Field. They were joined as the morning wore on by the delicate figure of William Hulton; the burly figure of Constable Nadin, accompanied by his runner known as Big Booth; the Borough Reeve, and other supporters, one of whom was Pitt Caxton as leader of the Anti-Reform League.

By noon Jancie had taken off her scarlet over-tunic and hung it on a corner of the platform, which consisted of several wagons pushed together and draped with Hunt's colours. There was not much grass on the field due to the recent hot weather, there'd be even less, she thought after today.

"Going to be a scorcher!" said Fancy, as they watched the arrivals. Banners of every hue were cheered on appearance, from the green and red silk of the Royton Female Union, with their motto 'Let us die like men, and not be sold as slaves' to the sepulchral black with white lettering 'Equal Representation or Death'. Stockport, always eager, had been first on the field; five thousand behind a massive banner with the words 'Annual Parliaments. Universal Suffrage. Vote by Ballot. No Corn Laws. Success to the Female Union of Stockport.'

Others followed. Thousand upon thousand. Latecomers, stragglers. Newspaper reporters from the *Mercury* in Leeds, the *Mercury* in Liverpool, and even the *Times* from London, milled about, asking questions, inviting opinion.

By one o'clock excitement ran high. Orator Hunt should be coming. Where was he? The band suddenly struck up 'See the Conquering Hero Come' and there he was, riding in an open barouche. In blue coat and white breeches, the flaxen-haired Viking of a man raised his white hat with a flourish. Cheers, and yells of "Bravo! Bravo!" filled the air. Every neck strained, and children were hoisted on shoulders, as Henry Hunt's barouche made its way, through a path lined with the Specials, to the platform.

Leaders of the Manchester Reformers, male and female, were all set to welcome their hero. Jancie, bespectacled and seated, thanked God the assembly had met without incident. All the swaggering militia, she thought, could now go away. The authorities had seen the meeting was peaceful and orderly. Here was Hunt! As he stepped onto the platform, her heart pounded with pride. In him lay hope of pushing Reform. He was the Clowes Scarlet, the fierce fighting cock of the Rads!

"Hunt!" they yelled.

"Bravo, King Harry!"

The shouts ascended to the open window where James Norris, and his black-gowned colleagues, dithered and twittered like so many starlings. Constable Nadin, thumbs hitched in his belt, fingers splayed over breadth of paunch,

264

positioned himself by the door. Prominent townsmen stood in uneasy groups, and Pitt Caxton paced to and fro. The heat of the day, of the moment, began to tell on the officials. Voices cut the hot, still air of the room.

"Never seen such a mob."

"Smacks of anarchy and revolution."

"It ought to be stopped now, before it's too late."

"It ought never to have started."

"D'you really think the town's in danger?"

"By God, sir, I do!"

"They'll break out any moment. Once Hunt gets going, they could, if the mood takes 'em, storm this house and cut our throats!"

"Let us act, then. Stop the meeting!"

"For what reason?"

"The town's in danger – is that not reason enough?"

"Quickly, then. A sworn affidavit to agree we adopt strong measures for the safety of town and people."

"Ay," said Norris. "It's all very well for Lord Sidmouth to preach restraint, and then go off to Broadstairs and await developments!"

"Be ready to read the Riot Act, sir!"

"But," protested Pitt. "No one will hear from this distance."

"Doesn't matter so long as there's witnesses to it being read."

"What about Hunt?"

"Arrest him!"

"Ay, that'll show the swinish multitude – a warrant, man," this to a harassed clerk, "a warrant for Hunt!"

"Caxton? Append your name will you? Where's he gone? Damme if the fellow wasn't here a moment ago!"

Pitt stood in the hall below, a hand on the door. He would not, indeed could not, put his name to that affidavit. Nadin lumbered down the stairs, hurrying past, out into the street, warrant in hand, to make the arrest. Some of the 'swinish multitude' referred to were people whom he

265

had come to know. Jem Clowes, Margery as fluffy as a chick; the clerk Thomas in his mittens; Aberdaron Dick . . . Etherington's apprentice, the little fellow with great saucer eyes. Boadicea! Oh, dear God. He remembered Susan Thistlewood's letter, and raced after Nadin. Jancie had said she'd be on the platform with Hunt, she could be arrested with him! He feared both for her being discovered as a spy and arrested as a Rad. And she was so unpredictable, likely to give as good as she got, and where would that lead! Hunt had began his speech. Nadin pushed on. Pitt was pushed back. The Specials near the platform fell back to allow an opening for the constable – and sixty mounted yeomanry.

"The soldiers!"

As the alarmed cry filled the air on one part of the vast field, a cheer went up from another. A great cheer to welcome the late arrival of the Blackburn contingent, who had walked twenty-five miles – and were soon to wish they hadn't.

Panic and terror gripped those near the platform. It had all happened with alarming rapidity. The yeomanry surrounded the platform. Hunt was arrested and stepped down with dignity. The rough hands of the drunken yeomanry pulled at the women's clothes, dragged others by the legs, women and men alike, with no consideration for modesty. Their 'Glorious Monday' was over.

Pitt, choking as the dust of the dry earth caught his throat, ran among the terror looking for Jancie. Even as he looked, the town's own Yeomanry in their blue and white uniforms rode, sabres drawn, into the densely packed throng.

"Radical swine!"

"I'll reform you – damn yer eyes!"

Sabres fell on unprotected heads. Horses, untrained and unused to crowds frothed and foamed, plunged and reared. Shouts and screams vied with the screech of horses, as folk trying to get out of the way fell back into the arms of those behind, pressing, pushing. The world had gone suddenly frighteningly mad. Pitt stood aghast, as the yeomanry fell upon the wagons, smashing, hacking, demolishing; then, seeing Jancie's scarlet overtunic, whipped it to shreds with sharpened sabres.

The raising of dust caused the starlings to flutter. "Good God!" cried Norris. "The mob is attacking the yeomanry. Call out the Hussars!"

Obeying the magistrates' orders, the 15th Hussars, resplendent in blue and yellow with scarlet plumes, rode onto the field with drawn swords. Unlike the yeomanry, they were trained and disciplined, and set about their task with cold detachment. Screams ripped the dusty air as they charged the unbelieving and unprepared mass. Women with babies, men with children on their shoulders, young and old, stumbled over already fallen bodies, to get away from the terror.

Stabbed, battered, pressed down and trampled over, the tide of humanity surged forward, pursued and harried relentlessly. On the outskirts of the field by the Quaker Meeting House, some of the Radicals had regrouped in brisk retaliation. From the roof; behind the garden wall; and from the top of the steps, they fought back, using for ammunition building materials from the property development deplored by Parson Brookes.

Some of the women had taken refuge within the Quaker House, but not Jancie. She stood on the garden wall and kept up a constant aim at the pursuers. Spectacles looped behind her ears, gown smeared and stained, white hat hanging by a string, and skirt tucked up as a receptacle for stones, she cheered as her aim knocked a narrow-headed lout off his horse.

Her attention was drawn to his comrades, tormenting at sabre point some two dozen or so terrified people huddled against the front of a house.

"Leave'em alone!" she yelled, sparring and dodging like one of Jem's fighting hens, aiming stone after stone,

267

until an officer of the Hussars rode up and, by sharply ordering the yeomanry away, put an end to the cruel harassment.

No sooner had the officer gone, when a grating over the cellar, having borne too much weight, gave way, and taking some of the frontage with it, plunged the victims into the cellar below. Pitt, coatless, hatless, and bare-throated, was in time to witness the disaster. He stared down into the great, gaping hole.

"Oh, God, dear God!"

He knew the voice and turned at her cry.

"What is it?".

She pointed to the cellar. "I saw Mr Crabtree. I saw him go down!"

"Crabtree – what's he doing here?" Seizing her hand, he ran with her to the house, where already one woman had been brought up dead. People pushed their way down the cellar, others stared into the hole, and all about were the cries from St Peter's Field, the wail of lost children, screams of the injured, shouts of the militia.

As they pushed their way down, moans spiralled up. Voices in hushed tones calling for a lamp, a candle. Rescuers tripping over debris cursed.

"There he is!" The gleaming personage was gleaming no more. He was dull and dirty. He had fallen awkwardly and lay still. "Mr Crabtree?" Jancie knelt on the rubble. "Mr Crabtree?" She unfastened the frills of his shirt and slipped her hand inside, moving it about his breast until locating a faint heartbeat. "He's alive," she told Pitt. "Find someone to help us get him upstairs."

Upstairs on the parlour sofa he answered at last to his name. Jancie gave him brandy. The eyelids flickered, then opened wide. Pitt leaning forward wiped the blood from his partner's dusty lips.

"My dear," he whispered, to Jancie, "you're not hurt, are you?"

"Not in the least – oh, I saw it, Crabby, I saw you fall!

Are you badly damaged, can you move?" And to Pitt. "More brandy, he's going again." She cradled his head in the crook of her arm. "Oh, why did you go to the meeting?" she asked on a whisper, "Why, darling Crabby, why?"

"I didn't . . . middle of the road man, you know that . . ." his voice faded, then rallied to add, "going to see Charles . . . heard the commotion . . . no sooner rounded the corner than the devils pinned me against the wall . . ."

"No good trying to get a doctor," said a man. "Can't get through for the crowds. But anyway," with a nod to the sofa, "looks as though he's past it, to me."

Mr Crabtree would gleam no more. Pitt turned away. Tear-blinded himself, he could not watch her grief; her stricken face bowed over Crabtree's hands spoke more than volumes of tears. He looked out of the shattered parlour window and felt himself to be emerging from a nightmare. The Radical Meeting had been stopped. Mr Norris would be pleased the town was no longer in danger. The magistrates and members of the Pitt Club would raise their glasses to the end of Reform. Outside, just fifteen minutes after the charge of the Hussars, St Peter's Field was empty. The remains of the platform, and a flag-pole, by some fluke left standing, stood stark, like a cactus in a desert. The gashed and slashed banners, drooped like ponderous, gaudy flowers; and on the blood-soaked earth lay a strange crop of shoes, shawls, white hats and coloured bonnets. And among this strange crop, as though a votive offering to a fierce god, were strewn laurel branches, nosegays, a hand, fingers, part of an arm; and wigs, lying like scalps. Then the chariots of the fierce god, the two six-pounders rattled across the sun-baked earth.

As the troops chased the terrified people from the field to the streets, those who had hidden in the Quaker Meeting House and adjacent property emerged like rats from holes to seek friends or relatives. Pitt remained by the parlour window, awkward and helpless. He had obtained more brandy in an attempt to rally Jancie from the state of shock into which Mr Crabtree's death had plunged her, but she would not be rallied. Most awful was her courage, her grip. He preferred the dignity of tears. Her tears would absolve him, in part at least, from the guilt of this day . . .

Voices impinged on his thoughts. "Clogger!"

"Eh," the big man's mouth fell open at the sight of Mr Crabtree. "Eh . . ." he said again. "Poor fella."

Margery following him, as white as the gown she was wearing, brushed past Pitt as though he wasn't there. "Eh . . . Jancie, love." Taking her friend in her arms, she rocked to and fro, crooning and talking and stroking her hair as if to instil life and movement to the rigid figure.

Pitt looked from the women to Jem, who, having been hurt, was roughly bandaged about his upper arm and shoulder. The expression in the bright, tawny eyes, as they settled on Jancie, was, he thought helplessly, the expression of a man who cared deeply. Her people were here, those with whom she had grown up, they would look to her, thaw her out, take her home. He was the opposition, a Tory, and an outsider; responsible in part for this dreadful day. Shoulders hunched, he walked blindly out into the street.

Where to go? I cannot face the chambers, yet, he thought. Cannot tolerate being questioned in Quay Street . . . He walked, hatless, coatless, throat bare and in shirt-sleeves. Blood-stained and begrimed, he smiled. I could be taken for a Rad looking like this. I could be shot at or sabred. What did it matter? Up and down the town he strolled. Impervious to the shouts of the yeomanry, who had been ordered to clear the streets; impervious to the boom of cannon which sent others scurrying for shelter. The afternoon dwindled into evening, and as the shadows lengthened across St Peter's Field, Pitt told himself, this is the end.

Chapter 30

Clogger had been sent to fetch Etherington's van, which bore Mr Crabtree's body to the Smallware Manufactory; and it was from here that Charles arranged his burial in St Mary's crowded churchyard. It was a popular funeral, for apart from the immediate circle of legal colleagues, including Pitt, he had many friends, and the fact of the death being attributed to what the town was now calling a massacre, had drawn a large funeral procession. Parson Brookes, immaculate in silken robes, prayer book in hand, frowned furiously and roared his displeasure at the presence, by the graveside, of yeomanry with fixed bayonets. But his protests were ignored, and the service began. Jancie hoped the words were bringing more comfort to her guardian than they brought to her. Oh, if only she had not asked Crabby to visit Charles on that fateful day . . .

She glanced at the graves, some protected by railings from the attentions of body-snatchers, others standing tall, like the deserted looms in Jepson's on Trafalgar Night. Church bells had been ringing then. Ringing for victory. Now the bells tolled for the dead. She was alone again in the silence, with no candle, no lamp. Alone with scurrying rats and the slinking shadow of a predatory cat.

"Jancie?" Startled into reality, she felt Margery's clasp upon her arm. Was it all over? She turned stiffly and let Margery lead her into the shifting crowd gathered in Half Street. Charles walked alone.

Afterwards, when the guests were assembled for

271

refreshment in the room above Mrs Clowes sugar bakery, Pitt approached Charles to convey his condolences. He was shocked at the bluish hue about her lips, the shadows beneath her eyes, indeed everywhere; her voice, her gestures, even the way she moved, were all steeped in shadow. She was dressed in deep purple, the only relief being a diamond pin in the centre of a mauve cravat. Her mourning for the Gleaming Personage was as deep as her soul.

She did not hear the words he uttered, but the tone of his voice spanned the years, taking her back to her father's funeral at Smedley Vale, where this young man's uncle had conveyed in similar tones to her similarly shocked mind, why it was impossible to contest her father's will. As she had said to Jancie not long ago, the name of Caxton did not augur well for Charles Etherington.

Pitt had not seen Jancie since the day of the massacre, and she held herself so aloof he did not dare to address her. He had heard that Smollett was in the New Bailey for having produced a cudgel and cracked several military heads. Seeing poor Jem bandaged; the yeomanry at the funeral; and the town in a perpetual state of unrest, filled Pitt with such remorse, that he hesitated to approach Jancie, lest their relationship, such as it was, be plunged into further jeopardy. He conveyed his feelings to Margery who understood, and said he would be wise to bide his time.

"Miss Etherington's taken it badly. She must have held him in high regard."

"The highest," she said softly. "Miss Ridley and I suspect he loved her, and because of some awful tragedy in the past, she couldn't bring herself to get married."

"You don't say?"

"This is in confidence, of course, Mr Caxton."

"You are talking to someone, Mrs Clowes, who has the interest of the ladies concerned at heart, and the memory of my deceased partner. He, I may say, always seemed well satisfied with his place in her life."

"Wouldn't you be, Mr Caxton, if two such ladies, cossetted, coddled and teased you! To Miss Ridley he was like a dear and indulgent uncle. He had a grand old time as the light of their lives – their darling Crabby. And now the light has been extinguished, in so dreadful a manner, they are . . . well, you see how they are." Then, like the Radical she was, couldn't help but add, "Imagine their sorrow, repeated for the eleven killed on St Peter's Field, still more dying as a result of wounds inflicted – and many more too frightened to go to the Infirmary or call a doctor, in case they're dragged off to the New Bailey. Six hundred wounded they reckon, and Jem one of 'em . . . I hope the Tories are satisfied, Mr Caxton!"

Jancie and her guardian walked silently along streets noisy with swaggering Yeomanry, and strewn with rubble. In the cool quietness of their parlour they embraced silently, like phantoms with no substance. Jancie drew the dove grey head close, and wept for Charles; she wept for herself . . . and the lonely days to come.

Tension in the town persisted, the more militant Radicals were set for revenge. Prime targets were the premises of those enrolled as specials. Riots broke out; pitched battles ensued; shots were fired. And there only needed to be a rumour of Rads on the march for shops to be shuttered, warehouses locked, the Exchange closed, and artillery moved into position.

Mr Norris, stricken with fear at the sporadic flare-ups and the vituperation of the press, and apprehensive about so popular a prisoner as Hunt being in the New Bailey, wrote in haste to Viscount Sidmouth asking for a permanent infantry barracks to be erected in the town. Matters were not improved by the Manchester *Observer* referring to the event as the "Peterloo Massacre," a parody on St Peter's Field and the battle of Waterloo. The name caught on, and would go down in English history.

A few days later, the Reverend Hay was called to London to justify the strong measures taken in putting down the rebellion. At the same time, the Manchester 'loyalists' who included the Anti-Reform League and the Pitt Club met to express their thanks formally to the magistrates for such prompt action. But the thanksgiving was sabotaged, as Jancie read in the *Observer* by the leader of the Anti-Reform League, who caused a furore by hotly condemning the action on St Peter's Field, which had caused the death of his esteemed partner.

To increase Mr Norris's nervousness, the following week Henry Hunt, and all the Radicals arrested at Manchester were released on bail put up by the wealthy Sir Charles Wolsely, whose life had been changed by witnessing the storming of the Bastille.

It was, therefore, a celebration for Bob Smollett's release which enticed Jancie out of the shadows of the Smallware Manufactory. Smollett, wearing a new, striped waistcoat, his solitary ear-ring bright against brown hair, was chaired shoulder-high, from his shop to a supper in the Guy Fawkes chamber at the Seven Stars.

"We're glad yer out," confided Fancy, with a wink. "If only for Jancie's sake!"

"Eh, me little cock o'wax!" Bob held Jancie closely for a moment, then whispered sadly, "I found me nightingale dead – no one to feed it when I was took." She felt his chest heave in a deep sigh. The sigh brought her tears and his, then presently, looking at each other with the comfortability of long acquaintance, they tried a smile. It spread through Jancie and warmed her heart, just as the big stove in his shop had once warmed her frost-bitten fingers.

Clogger and Fancy were there, some of her Sunday scholars, Margery, Sampson, Bob's customers, and some of the Rads out on bail who were willing to take the risk, for meetings were declared illegal in the present emergency. First they discussed their coming trials, about which Bob was not hopeful. "They'll want to make an example," he said. "If they didn't stop at setting the militia on us, they'll not think twice of putting us away – Hunt as well."

"But there is the judiciary—" began Jancie.

"Judiciary my arse," said Fancy, and no one argued with her.

"I'm going to spend every minute of my bail," said Bob, "rallying the Rads, convincing 'em that Reform isn't dead. It's just coming to life! They may have got some of our leaders, but not all. And if I'm put away when the trial comes up, you must remember to throw yer weight behind the revolutionary movement." He made his slashing, dashing, gesture, and asked, "Where has moderation got us?"

"What revolutionary movement?" asked Margery's father.

"Arthur Thistlewood's."

"But he's in London."

"Henry Hunt was in the West Country – people do 'ave legs, and there is such a thing as public transport! Thistlewood's got leaders in every county, and the great plan is one mighty uprising country wide. If there's any blow to be struck for Reform, my friends, any revenge for Peterloo, it lies with Arthur Thistlewood."

After leaving the Seven Stars, Jancie took a walk about the town. She walked by herself, feeling like the princess in the fairy story who was awakened by a kiss. Dear, dear Bob. But with the awakening came remorse. Why hadn't she thought to feed his little nightingale? It was the least she could have done. Going into his shop from prison, it would have been the first thing he saw. A little corpse added to all the others.

What with the funeral, Charles's abject grief, and the horrors of the massacre fresh and vivid every time her head touched the pillow, she had almost lost her grip. The Infirmary Baths helped her to survive. Not merely, the ordinary bath advocated by Beau Brummell for cleanliness, but the fierce jets of the shower; the warm, enervating steam of the Turkish; and the exhilaration of swimming in the cold spring of the Lower Bath.

She persuaded Charles to accompany her, hoping the hum of the Great Engine and the water noises would work their magic; the smell of sulphur, of water on stone, the bubbling of the spring. Charles came, but did not swim, and the water noises did not work their magic.

Jancie realised that Crabby's death had awakened new anxiety in her guardian regarding Violet. Charles could not understand why, having eloped, presumably to be married, she had not written to either her sister or Mirabelle. And what of this Dyson Edwards, she had asked, surely, he had connections, relatives, of whom enquiries could be made?

As she neared the end of her walk Jancie had impossible thoughts of Pitt Caxton; this strange notion of her being on his side; and more impossible thoughts of love for Pitt Caxton. A love which could never be – and might well have been if they had gone away to the rose-walled inn. If they had, darling Crabby would still be alive. But they hadn't, and couldn't – and, now wouldn't.

She paused before the cannon at the top of Shude Hill. It stood there, outlined in the dark, deserted, unmanned, like a monster with no teeth. She walked up to it, and then round it. Then, pursing her lips thoughtfully, she walked back home.

Autumn found the town still turbulent and restless. The middle-class Rads and liberal-minded Tories came down heavily against the magistrates' handling of the county meeting, due to an airing of the whole affair by Mr Denman, who had defended the Derby men, and was now acting for those claiming compensation for injuries sustained on that terrible Monday.

An attempt on a constable's life, and the threat of

a visit from William Cobbett, returning from America, added fuel to the simmering fires. Mr Norris, was refused permission to build an infantry barracks in the town, but allowed to convert the New Bailey Prison into a fortress, and the existing barracks at New Cross were to be more heavily guarded. Further, Viscount Sidmouth had written to the Lords Lieutenant urging the immobilisation of any pieces of artillery lying about, lest the Radicals seize them. When the cannon from the top of Shude Hill was found to be missing, it was presumed to have been removed earlier by Lord Derby's bailiff.

Such was not the case. On the night of Bob Smollett's bail, Jancie had asked Clogger to find a gang of heavyweight men to carry the cannon under cover of darkness to Mr Bracegirdle's iron foundry, where she arranged for it to be smelted down.

Since Jancie had discovered Mr Bracegirdle stripped to his drawers in the company of another man's wife, he had co-operated with Miss Ridley on every possible occasion. After smelting, he was given the work of making ferrules for the winter umbrellas. This kept his foundry open – and the source provided him with a hold over Jancie. Both secrets were safe.

Sitting at the serpentine desk in chambers, Pitt scanned an advertisement in the *Observer* which informed the public of 'Etherington's Peterloo umbrella! Ferrules and stem being of an exceedingly high quality, and made from genuine relics of the recent massacre. Silk or cotton. Individual designs undertaken.' His lips pursed reflectively. It looked as though his Boadicea was back, and on form. He was pleased.

Boadicea . . . no one else called her by that name. Not that she was his – yet. He felt he had been in several kinds of mourning and was now emerging from the shadows.

"Thomas," he shouted to the outer office. "My coat, if you please," and while fastening it, "this inclement weather calls for an umbrella, eh, Thomas?"

277

"I'll fetch you one, sir."

"Not one of those, Thomas – a Peterloo umbrella!"

A great smile spread across the clerk's face. "Oh, they're selling like Eccles cakes at a fair, they are." Thomas jerked his head up to what had been Mr Crabtree's rooms. "He would have been right proud of her. Yes, I should hurry, sir, before they sell out."

"If the relic used for ferrules, is the one I'm thinking of," he laughed softly, "they'll not be running out for a long time."

Coming from the theatre, Jancie let herself in and hurried up the black timbered stairs. Still with greasepaint on her face, she entered the parlour, and standing behind the high-backed chair, put her arms about her guardian's neck. Her cheek brushed the springy hair as she looked over her shoulder at the lay out of cards. "Darling," she said. "Your mind isn't on the game. It'll never work out in a month of Sundays!"

"I know my dear . . ." there was a catch in Charles's voice, "I was looking for the ace of hearts . . . only a moment ago . . . and I couldn't see it. My sight has gone . . .'

"No! Oh, no!" Jancie slipped to the side of the chair, in time to catch the slender body in her arms. "Charles?"

The playing cards slipped slowly from the heavily-ringed fingers . . .

Chapter 31

A nasty chill had confined Pitt to his bed at Lady Egerton's house, and it was there he learned of the stroke which caused Miss Etherington's death. She died, Lady Egerton told him, as she would have liked, a cigar by the tray, a glass of canary wine on the table, a fan of cards in her hand, and in the arms of her Geisha Girl.

Pitt scribbled several notes of condolence, each one taking time and thought, and each one was hurled into the fire. Lady Egerton attended the funeral: it seemed the whole town attended, and many places of business were closed for the day out of respect.

"Her ward?" She answered his question. "Very controlled, you might say. Too controlled really. Walking as though in a trance, dressed head to foot in black, looking neither to right or left. She was surrounded by her friends – which was as well."

Pitt recalled Crabtree's death, and felt again a resentment that it was her friends, the people she had grown up with, who were at her side. He who longed to put comforting arms about her, could not.

"I wonder," Lady Egerton was saying, "what will become of Etherington's Enterprises, now?"

Jancie, sitting alone in the parlour above the Manufactory, had no doubts that Etherington's Enterprises would continue. If she spent her last ounce of energy doing it, she would keep her guardian's name alive. Her friends had been attentive and wonderfully patient. But now, the

279

dark and dreadful days were past, and she had persuaded them it was time for her to be alone. And here she was, alone for the first time in her life. Margery, Fancy, all the other workers, Mrs Clowes, and even Miss Bohanna, had taken turns in being with her after working hours. True, they had stopped her brooding, they had listened to her self-recriminations, mopped her eyes and accompanied her to the dining-room of the Seven Stars. She had eaten there with Charles for the past twelve or thirteen years, she would have to get used to going across and eating alone, or sharing a table. Not for the first time, she scanned Pitt Caxton's card of condolence, as though if she looked often enough she would find something other than usual stock sympathy.

During her worst period of sadness, Margery and Fancy had not told her of Bob Smollett and other local Rads being hauled off to trial and subsequently sentenced to a year in the New Bailey, and Henry Hunt, who received two years in Ilchester Jail.

Reform had been dealt another blow, a death blow, some said, in the form of Lord Castlereagh's despotic Six Acts Bill. And news of the Reverend Hay becoming vicar of Rochdale, one of the richest livings in the kingdom, by way of reward, appeared to be the final nail in the Radical coffin.

No, Jancie thought blindly, no! There've been too many coffins in my life, and Reform isn't going to be buried, swept away to suit the government. She recalled Bob's voice in the Guy Fawkes chamber of the Seven Stars. "Thistlewood's the man, my little cock o'wax, if there's any blow to be struck, any revenge for Peterloo, it lies with Thistlewood."

Quickened into life, she planned to travel to London under cover of visiting the Moxhams. And Violet. She must find her sister. If necessary, she would buttonhole Mortimer and acquaint him with the truth about Edwards being Oliver. She would get him to badger Sidmouth. Not that early February was a good time to be travelling, but going now meant she would be back for springtime, which was always busy.

With a rush of decision, brought about by sudden courage, Jancie gathered the four sets of playing cards and made a funeral pyre, laying them, box by box on the fire. She would never play another game of cards. Reaching for the cigar box, with a sob catching her throat, she laid the cigars in little bundles among the flames. She would never smoke another.

After a cold, uncomfortable journey Jancie arrived in London, and decided it was wiser to leave her luggage at the coach office and settle the Reform business, before going to the Moxhams. But first she sent a messenger with news of her coming, saying they were not to wait up, as she might be late. After doing so, she walked to the shabby houses which flanked the Edgeware Road, where, according to those Rads in 'the know', Thistlewood lived. It was nearly dusk when she found the right house. The door was opened by Susan.

"Well, if it ain't Miss Fancy Drawers!"

"May I come in?"

"Suit yerself."

Jancie did, and closing the door, Susan led the way into a back room. "Arthur ain't in. What's up? Too hot for you up north?"

"You wanted ferrules for bayonet pikes. I've got them by the hundred."

"Hold on. Bit sudden, ain't it?"

"Sudden! After the massacre on St Peter's Field? I was there, Mrs Thistlewood, I saw it and lost people loved."

"You don't pull the wool over my eyes. I've got a certain letter, Miss Fancy Drawers."

"What letter?"

"The one from Sidmouth to the Reverend Hay."

"Watch your mouth, Mrs Thistlewood. I'm in a mood to fill it with something hard!"

"Sold it to that fancy man of yours . . . the lawyer fella."

"What," Jancie made her lips firm to ask, "was in this letter?"

"As if you didn't know."

"Tell me. Damn you!"

"A person well acquainted with the designs of the Reformers will shortly visit you at Manchester. It is possible that information may be obtained the early communication of which, to a magistrate on the spot, maybe of material importance. This letter will serve as a warning to you of what is afoot. This person is intelligent and much deserving of your confidence! "See, I know it by heart," she added. "A sample of your bleedin' treachery!"

Her mind in a whirl, Jancie groped for and sank onto the nearest chair. "And you sold it to Mr Caxton?"

The dark head nodded.

"Where did you find it?"

"While you was with Hunt at the Westminster election, I was in your sister's room. Didn't trust you, see. An' I was proved right. Found it in a writing desk – and don't tell me it was hers, because she wasn't going to Manchester, neither is she acquainted with the designs of Reformers. No, the letter means you, alright."

"But it doesn't!"

The door opened. It was Arthur. "Jancie!" he exclaimed delightedly. "What brings you south? Lord, but it's good to see you."

"That letter," Jancie managed to articulate. "You don' seriously think it refers to me? I've come to strike a blow for Peterloo! I've come with an offer of those ferrules you asked for – I'll fetch 'em meself if necessary! I'l do anything!"

"You're not falling for this cock and bull story?" Susan demanded of her husband. "You're not taking her on, surely?"

"Yes," he answered without hesitation. And to Jancie "I have always believed you, Citizeness."

Jancie breathed more easily. She thought him greatly changed, dressed more shabbily, thinner, unkempt, as though his zeal for revolution was burning him up.

"Ay," he said. "You can strike a blow that will echo louder than the cannon at Peterloo."

"And your scheme?" she asked with a flutter in the pit of her stomach. "It isn't the one for blowing the Prince Regent off his throne?"

He laughed, his mouth a pink cavern against the whiteness of his teeth. "Guy Fawkes has changed his mind – for a better scheme. Say you're with us."

"She'd better be!"

"I am with you," said Jancie fervently. "I need to strike this blow, Arthur. People I loved have died, and been hurt. I have a yen for revenge."

"You've just come in time," said Susan. "And having come, you're not leaving this house till it's over."

"It's too dark for a march."

"Who said anything about a march? This very evening, Miss Fancy Drawers, they are going to strike a blow for Reform, as you put it, above a stable in Cato Street – and you're going to strike it with 'em."

"Not in these clothes. I'd be too conspicuous. I insist you find me some breeches and a coat."

"Cautious, eh? Thinking of yer own skin?"

"It's the only one I've got. And I'm not backing down. I'm committed, whatever it is."

Nightfall saw Jancie in breeches and coat, hair tucked beneath a cap, and spectacles in her pocket, climbing up to loft rooms over stables in Cato Street, a blind alley off the Edgeware Road. At the foot of the ladder a guard with a blunderbuss had stared at her curiously, until Arthur said his companion was a Manchester Rad out to avenge Peterloo.

Prickles of uneasiness crawled along Jancie's spine at the sight of some twenty men crowded together – and a more desperate lot she had not seen for a long time. Curious glances again. Arthur explained again. Every available space not taken up by a person was filled with pikes, pistols, grenades, kegs of gunpowder, swords and sabres.

Dear God! Dry-mouthed, wide-eyed and suddenly sobered of militancy, she considered they'd be lucky to get away with transportation to Van Dieman's Land if discovered with such a cache of arms.

Arthur leapt onto a table, scattering pewters and pistols to make room. He stood exalted and elated, his black eyes glittering in the candlelight, limbs taut and strung up with a fiery fanaticism which transmitted itself, to bind them all.

"Gentlemen," he began, "I shall run through the plan once again. First I go to the Earl of Harrowby's house in Grosvenor Square, where a dinner is being held for the entire Cabinet. When the door is opened, you," he stabbed a finger at a man in a green coat, "will rush in and cover the servants with your guns. This done, you," another stab at a man with a squint, "will take command of the front stairs. Those men over by the window will command the back stairs. So much for securing the house . . . we shall then enter the dining-room, and I shall say, "Well, my lords, I have men here as good as Manchester Yeomanry – enter citizens, and do your duty!""

After the cheers had settled, a butcher standing next to Jancie, and still wearing his apron, took up the plan.

"I'll then rush in with a brace of pistols and a cutlass in my hand, and I shall proceed to cut off the heads of Castlereagh and Sidmouth," he flourished a meat sack, "and carry 'em off in this!"

"Well said," applauded Arthur.

Jancie was stunned. What had she let herself in for? This was revolution, assassination. ". . . and here is the proclamation," Arthur was saying. "Citizens! Your tyrants are destroyed! The Provincial Government is now sitting!"

Amid the cheers, the butcher began to arm himself to impress the Earl of Harrowby's guests. Into a belt he stuffed a brace of pistols and a cutlass; and the bags in which he was to carry the famous heads were fastened to each shoulder, like a short cloak. "Oh, damn my eyes," he muttered. "I'm still not complete – I've not got me steel!" He produced a glittering knife. "This'll do for Peterloo, eh, my lad," he told her with a wink. "Ay," he ruminated with the air of a speculator, "I'll cut off Castlereagh's hand as well, it'll be easier to keep, and might be worth a bit in future days."

All was camaraderie and chaos. Pikes were grabbed and pistols strapped. A negro in a blue coat thrust a pistol in Jancie's hands. Not expecting the movement, startled and now thoroughly alarmed, she dropped it. Arthur was at her side, his white smile within inches of her, his hand about her shoulder.

"How goes it?" He added in a lower tone. "Are you ready, Citizeness, to strike that blow for Peterloo – ready to go with us?" Hearing a noise on the ladder, he stopped. There were sounds of scuffling. "It's the Runners!" shouted someone. "We've been betrayed!"

Arthur thrust Jancie behind him into a back room as the door was kicked open.

"We're Bow Street Officers! Seize their arms!"

Arthur drew a long sword from among the grenades on the table. An excellent swordsman, he fenced his way back to the second room. Jancie cowered. In the shadowy candlelight she saw an officer coming straight for them. She saw Arthur lunge forward and the long sword bury itself in the officer's body. "Oh, my God," she heard him cry. "I'm done for!"

The officer behind took aim and fired at Arthur. He missed. Suddenly the candles were doused. Men struggled. Swore. Scuffled.

"C'mon!" Arthur seized her hand. "Down the ladder, we'll have to take a chance at the bottom – run like hell!"

How she got down so quickly Jancie never knew. The darkness was complete, the air cold. Someone appeared with a lantern. Its flickering glare caught Arthur. "There he is!"

Arthur gave her push into the dark, into the opposite direction than himself. "Run," he yelled. The Coldstream Guards – who having been summoned, were seventy yards away and at the wrong address – now arrived. With more lanterns they quickly surrounded the stable and arrested nine men.

While the President of the Provisional Government went into hiding, Jancie ran like a coursed hare and arrived at the Moxhams' so late she had to knock the servants up. Telling them not to disturb their master, and not to concern themselves with her comfort, she retired at once to Violet's old room, taking with her Mortimer's decanter of brandy and a glass.

Pausing to place more coals on the fire, she slid between the satin sheets. Propped up against pillows, her teeth chattering against the rim of the glass, she watched the smouldering coals hissing and spitting into the occasional blaze, and thought of Guy Fawkes . . . of Peterloo. Arthur had got away, but for how long? Having killed the officer, there would be a price on his head for murder as well as high treason. Come to think of it, the entire plot was too well thought out, too well sewn up, like the Derby affair . . .

Had Arthur, she wondered, with his fiery ways, fallen into the trap of an *agent provocateur*? What, she further wondered, if that agent was Oliver? If it was, poor, idealistic Arthur's days were numbered. Oliver would no doubt have arranged a safe house . . .

She recalled Newgate and shivered. Every noise in St James's startled her into thinking she had been traced. Instead of returning to Manchester victorious to tell a splendid tale of revenge, she would keep an ignominious silence.

She had rarely drunk spirits before in any quantity, and having consumed almost a full decanter, the following day found her ill, and spared her from having to discuss news of the daring 'Cato Street Conspiracy' as the papers were calling it. According to Mortimer, hundreds of the curious had already flocked to Cato Street, where a man in no way authorised, took up a position by the door, and demanded a shilling entrance fee! And, by the time Jancie had recovered fully, Arthur was betrayed and arrested.

Mirabelle and Jancie talked of Charles and comforted each other. They talked of Violet in tearful desperation. And later that day, Jancie buttonholed Mortimer, urging him to badger Sidmouth; swearing him to be discreet.

"Sidmouth's wasting no time," declared Mortimer, the following morning. He tapped the paper. "Speeding up the formalities. Wants a quick trial. By the way, young Caxton called while you were indisposed. He's here, like any loyal subject, for the King's funeral."

"I'd forgotten Farmer George was dead. And don't expect me to say 'long live Prinny' Profligate swine!"

"Jancie . . . moderate your language, please."

"Caxton said he'd call again before returning north."

"A pity about him and Selina Lansdowne, m'dear, not that she lost much time, married a count and gone to Rome."

Jancie was reading the progress of the Thistlewood trial in the blue drawing room when Pitt called. She had told the footman to send him in, and having heard his voice, laid the paper on one side, and wondered what he was doing out there.

He was asking himself the same question. Wondering

what to say, trusting he would say the right thing, and discarding rapidly one good phrase after another.

Unable to conceal her curiosity any longer, she opened the door on his unprepared phrases. At the sight of her, pale and sombre, dressed simply in black relieved only by a wide, white collar, lips parted in a voiceless word of surprise, even the most rehearsed of phrases would have fled.

He stepped into the room and took her outstretched hands to hold them, for a mere moment, to feel their warmth, their strength and smallness. He longed to raise them to his lips, but knew this was not the time, nor the place.

What fools we are, her thoughts ran quickly on, here I am, longing to sit beside him, and yet I sit apart and talk of the King's funeral, and the kindness of the Moxhams. And he, who wanted to tease the colour into her cheeks by telling her she owed him a week-end in lieu of Selina, talked about the Cato Street Conspiracy, and what a close shave the Cabinet had.

After these commonplace remarks, she saw him to the door. Unnecessary, but she did. He bowed. The sharp wind crisped the raven black hair; his eyes clung to hers, and returning her solemn smile, he tapped the short cane against his knee and walked quickly away. "It's all very well," she muttered sadly, "but when you discover I am not the Tory, you think I am, there'll be no clinging of eyes, then, my lad!"

Chapter 32

The speedy trial found Arthur and four others, one the butcher who had stood next to Jancie, guilty of high treason. They were condemned on Friday, 29 February to be executed on Monday morning at eight of the clock. In order that the scaffold be completed in time, the construction, illuminated by blazing tar barrels went on through Saturday night. The bizarre scene, set against the the grim facade of Newgate, prison, provided a frisson of horror for those who, like ghouls, gathered to watch. At six o'clock on Monday morning the streets were so packed it was impossible to pass through. Taking warning from the Peterloo affray, the authorities provided boards ready to be held aloft in case of trouble, bearing the words 'THE RIOT ACT HAS BEEN READ. DISPERSE IMMEDIATELY.'

The clock struck eight. The bell of St Sepulchre tolled, and Arthur mounted the scaffold. He was eating an orange and remained calm as the rope slipped over his head. He addressed the crowd with a brief, yet fiery sentence. "I hope the world will be convinced that I have been sincere in my endeavours – and that I die a friend to liberty!"

The others were lined up. It was five past the hour; the Cato Street Conspirators were dead, and yet the spectacle was not yet over. After the bodies were cut down, there crept onto the platform a masked figure with a kerchief covering his lower jaw and a slouch hat pulled well down. In his hand was a small surgical knife. Exclamations of horror whistled through the crowd. With great dexterity he severed Arthur's head and handed it to his assistant, who ran as though with a trophy, holding it high and shouting with frenzied excitement, "This is the head of Arthur Thistlewood – traitor!"

In the Moxhams' drawing room the execution, related in the newspapers, was being discussed as a lucky escape for the Cabinet. Jancie read it through a mist of tears; thankful for the cover of her spectacles, she raised the paper. It would not do for them to see her weeping for a traitor.

Her mind went back, not to Cato Street, but the Moxhams' garden. "Never forget," he had said, bowing over her hand, "that it was with me you danced on the lawn, to the melody of the moonbeams and in the magic of the moonlight." She tried to reconcile this image with that of the gaunt creature above the stable. "Ready, Citizeness, to strike a blow for Reform, for Peterloo?" As always, in comparison to his zeal, her contribution to the cause seemed wispy and fragile; her lifelong interest which had been so absorbing, now seemed more limited than ever.

Yes . . . it had been a kind of madness; an accumulation of despair, which, viewed from her present, chastened state of mind bordered on stupidity. Charles often used to ask. "Why d'you drive yourself on like this?" Jancie wished she knew the answer.

"Mortimer," she suddenly asked. "Have you cornered Sidmouth yet, about Oliver?"

"As a matter of fact, I did."

"Oh, Mortimer, and you didn't see fit to tell me!"

"I was getting round to it. These things are not easy."

"I'm not given to the vapours, if that's what you mean."

"Sidmouth told me – in the strictest confidence mind – that he'd seen fit to reward Oliver with . . . a free passage to begin a new life in South Africa."

"South Africa?"

"He's at Gravesend awaiting a ship."

Jancie was on her feet. "I must go. It'll be my last chance to see Violet – she will be with him?"

"Sidmouth didn't know. Doesn't concern himself with the private lives of his agents."

She stared down at them calmly sipping China tea. "I'll catch up with that swine if it's the last thing I do!"

"Language, m'dear. Moderate your language, do," Mirabelle pleaded.

"Hold your horses, young woman," instructed Mortimer. "Not so fast, eh? I'm afraid I let this information slip to Caxton at the club last night. He's here on business, but left for Gravesend at once."

"Last night!"

"You were abed when I returned."

"Oh, Mortimer," she wailed. "I didn't want him interfering."

"Do as Moxham says, m'dear," said Mirabelle sharply. "You cannot take everything into your own hands. Besides, if Oliver is desperate, he could be dangerous." Her voice trembled a little. "Having already lost Violet . . . though God knows what I could have done to stop her going . . . I couldn't bear to lose you. For the sake of your guardian's memory . . . trust Caxton." The trembling over, she resumed command. "Now, take another cup of tea and stop being tedious."

Pitt Caxton found Oliver on the barge *Esmeralda*, as Sidmouth had said.

"I've seen you before," said Oliver. "You're the madman who overturned the chaise in Derbyshire! Ay, without your bumbling intervention I wouldn't have escaped. Bet she gave it to you good, eh! Thought she'd got it all sewn up – and you came along!"

Pitt recognised the truth of the story. No wonder she wrapped the chain round his jaw!

Taking Oliver by surprise, he leapt, seizing him by the

291

throat. "Where is she?" And crashing his body against the bulkhead. "Where is Violet Ridley?"

Seizing Oliver's arm, he wrenched it up his back. Oliver screamed. The shoulder dislocated. Pitt reached for his other arm. "Stop!" Oliver yelled. "I'll tell you!"

On the way back to St James's, Pitt reflected on what he had been told. Violet, accidentally discovering her lover to be a spy, and concerned for her sister's subsequent safety, confronted him with the discovery. He bluffed his way out by pretending he had been press-ganged into Sidmouth's service, and had long wished to be free. Playing on Violet's romantic nature, he suggested escaping the country quickly and secretly to be married in Paris or Rome . . . experience the gay, social whirl of Continental cities . . . it was easy to sweep her off her feet.

It was easy, too, on the first overnight stop at Canterbury to place a pillow over her face, and suffocate her. She slept so soundly, there was not even a struggle. He swore she never knew what was happening. With a plausible story, Oliver had arranged a simple funeral in St Asaph's church. Pitt had confirmed the details, and noticed the gravestone was nicely carved and of good quality. There was no use in accusing Oliver of murder. He had Sidmouth's dispensation. Oliver was above the law.

Standing in the drawing room, over by the fireplace, in his favourite position with an arm along the mantelpiece and his coat hanging open, he reckoned he owed Jancie the truth. And she got it. The Moxhams were horrified. Mirabelle wept, Mortimer fumed. But all Jancie could do was immediately close her eyes and thank God their guardian had been spared the dreadful knowledge. The story rang true. Violet always slept well, curled up like a dormouse . . . the image tore at Jancie's heart.

She heard herself saying calmly. "Thank you, Mr Caxton, for going to Gravesend so promptly . . ." There the calmness ended, and with the reality of his news hitting her like the shower-jets at the Infirmary Baths, she burst into tears.

Arriving in Manchester alone was a doleful affair. She could have travelled north with Pitt, but shied away on account of the mysterious letter. This letter was the spider's fragile thread which held their relationship together, and she could not bear for it to be broken, yet. Too much in her life had been broken already. There were greetings from townsfolk, and merchants raised their hats and stopped for a few words, but it was not like old times. And despite the spring sunshine, Aberdaron Dick was not returned from Wales. Oh, Dick, she thought miserably. Oh, Dick, not you as well.

She walked slowly to the Smallware Manufactory, where the welcome from Fancy and Sampson, and the outdoor workers took the edge off Dick's absence.

In the stable Morocco whinnied a greeting, thrusting his muzzle into her coat, seeking another caress. Her arms slid about his neck, and glancing up to the hayloft, she heard the echo of childish anxiety . . . "You'll not say anything about my eyes at the interview? I didn't see Miss Etherington properly . . . what does she look like? She sounds nice . . . Violet?" But her sister had curled up and gone to sleep.

In the office a bowl of orange-eyed jonquils continued Charles's custom of fresh flowers, a custom kept up even when Jancie was away. The cheerfulness of the flowers still upon her, she went into the parlour, where Sampson had just kindled the fire. The warmth of heavy oak, the scent of lavender, and a host of memories as beautiful as her dear guardian, as quixotic as her darling sister, surrounded her. Standing behind Charles's chair, her arms resting on the high back, she felt the first stirrings of peace, a lightening of her burdens and a supreme sense of gratitude.

By the beginning of May Jancie had integrated herself

back into life as it was before Charles's death. She had renewed her business acquaintances, re-established her friendships, and viewed it all with satisfaction. Nearly all. There was the matter of her guardian's will. Mr Crabtree had managed Charles's personal and business affairs, but those would now be dealt with by his partner. She hoped Charles had left the manufactory to her. But, hoping was of no use. She had to know her legal position, and the financial standing for investment purposes. Should she call on him or send a note that he call on her? He would know she was back in town and had hoped he would call.

They eventually met in the Clowes' yard, after Jancie had been to visit the Reverend Brookes who, did not seem at all well. "Ah," said Pitt, coming toward her and Margery, "I can see you are discussing the Prince Regent's coronation by the indignant look on your faces!"

"And you are quite right – a quarter of a million pounds! And the state of the economy! It's a wonder you're not going down for it."

She cast a glance at the gypsy-dark face, the long-lashed eyes and the undisguised interest. He is pleased to see me, she thought happily, despite not travelling back with him."

"Too busy. Knee-deep in conveyances and writs. Talking of business, Miss Ridley, there are Miss Etherington's affairs to be discussed. May I call on you? Later, this evening, after you have dined, perhaps?"

"Of course."

"Very well, ladies, and now, if you will excuse me?"

"And I too, had better get on," said Jancie, when the dark-coated figure was safely out of the way. The friends embraced and parted. Margery had noticed his interest. Any romance in that quarter, she thought, would certainly be a kick in the teeth for the Rads. A triumph for the 'foot in both camps' brigade. Jancie, she thought. Oh, Jancie love, they'd never forgive you.

Chapter 33

That evening Pitt leaned over her desk. "I have come to claim my week-end," he said. "Oh, Jancie . . ." The familiarity of him using her first name, and the manner in which he pronounced it, made it sound the most beautiful name in all the world. "Jancie, say you will honour our agreement? That you'll come away to the country? The roses are not yet in bloom on the walls of the inn, but I promise you a luxuriance of wild flowers, their petals untouched by smoke, their leaves unbitten by sulphur. There are balms and sages underfoot, and in the evening the air will be heavy with the scent of rosemary and jessamine."

"You make it sound like the Garden of Eden."

"It can be."

"We shall put it to the test, then."

"You mean you will come?"

"What else?" She shot him a sly glance. "Etherington's always repay what they owe." And then, glancing cautiously toward the door. "I think we ought to discuss the arrangements for repayment in the sitting-room upstairs."

"I cannot believe you are so amenable."

"I think you will find me a little more than amenable," she said ascending the stairs. "So long as we make it a truce. Not a word about political persuasions."

"A truce it is."

Having reached the sitting-room, he opened the door on a host of memories, ranging from the serving of Hay's document, to polite afternoon calls with Selina. The room, he thought, looked bereft without Miss Etherington's imposing elegance, without the gesticulating hands, fingers heavily ringed. A remarkable woman. He often wondered whether Jancie would have told Miss Etherington about the proposed week-end at the rose-walled inn, and how she would have taken to his wooing of her ward? He moved about slowly, handling bric-a-brac; peering at a silhouette of Charles and a small water colour of the Ridley sisters when young. He stood before the window-seat looking down into Shudhill, then glanced at the oval table where they had played cards . . .

"I'm glad you sense the room is bare without Charles," she said quietly. "You never know how much you miss people until they aren't there. She was always here, you know – every day of my life – more like an elder sister than a guardian." She let out a deep sigh. "But nothing can stay the same for ever . . . I have come to understand that much. We never talked of death. Charles was not cut in the invalid mould . . . she would have preferred a quick exit. There," she said, detecting sympathy in his eyes. "I've not really talked about her to anyone. That I can talk to you about her must be a good thing."

"I admired her. It used to be most pleasurable sitting here when Selina visited . . . it was as though you and Miss Etherington wove a spell about me in an odd sort of way – as though, really, Selina was not there . . ." he paused, recalling the subtle sweetness of the occasions, ". . . there's no doubt she was a wonderful woman, Jancie, and one to whose memory you must ever be grateful. No wonder Crabtree loved her. Yet, on other occasions I sensed her disapproval."

"It wasn't so much disapproval, but a mistrust of men in general. Her father, according to Mirabelle, treated her very badly, then drowned himself in the Irwell and left the family fortune to the Humane Society. Your uncle was his lawyer . . . the name Caxton did not augur well for her, and when you came to serve Mr

Hay's document, she thought you were running true to form."

"From this very moment," he said softly, "all that has changed."

"I wonder?"

"I promise," he answered. "And talking of promises . . ."

They had travelled separately to the rose-walled inn, which, being built long ago on the old pack route, missed the hurly-burly of modern coach runs. The Rose and Lute nestled in picturesque countryside beyond the slopes of Smedley Vale. Here the river ran clear, and had she but known it, Jancie passed the ruin of the Calico Print Works of which, many years ago, the young Charlotte Etherington had hoped to be mistress.

Jancie had arrived first and been shown to her room overlooking the river. She glanced at the door across the creaky landing, and wondered mischievously how much time Pitt would spend behind it. She stirred the fire, laid out her nightclothes, her kimono, rearranged the flowers, moved a small table from beneath the window to beside the bed. She removed a text from above the bed without reading it, and gazed with fascination at the white counterpane, the lace-edged pillows soon to be dented by a shock of raven black hair. And her head would be on . . . his shoulder . . . his chest. No words could describe, to no one could she communicate, this overwhelming emotion, this necessity to be with, of all men, an Anti-Reformer, a High Tory. She shook her head unbelievingly.

The sound of footsteps halted the imagery. Movement across the landing, voices – his voice!

"Welcome to the Garden of Eden!" He exclaimed when she opened the door. After an embrace, a kiss, and another embrace, his eyes met hers and held them with a roguish smile. He was dressed in white trousers and a damson-coloured coat, white shirt and stock contrasting with his gypsy-dark features. Surely, there was no one more handsome. "Thomas delayed me with signatures," he murmured. "Oh, Jancie, these are going to be the most wonderful two days of our lives."

They walked together in the overgrown, rambling garden – not apart, yet not close, had they been close the newly revived awareness could scarce be more. The scent of the sages beneath their tread, the sight of evening bees drunk with nectar, the wild clasping of coy columbines and leopard's bane made the heart ache.

He painted a word picture of how he had seen them last August, when meeting a client here. Different shapes, sizes, all the colours somehow blending into a glorious mass. The mauves, the shades of yellow, pinks, the stripes, splashes of red; the earth already littered with white and scarlet petals – and Jancie remembered the trampled flowers on St Peter's Field.

Supper was hot and plentiful. There were rounds of beef and legs of mutton, piles of floury potatoes, and red cones of carrots on a pale bed of mashed turnips. There were puddings and cheeses; port to Pitt's liking, and ale to suit Jancie.

Sitting there, sipping ale, she listened to him talk, enjoying the sound of his voice, the little looks which accompanied a story or an anecdote, quizzical, explanatory or frivolous. He was entertaining her, and she was happier than she could ever remember.

"Is that the time?" he observed suddenly. "Did I hear the clock strike ten?"

"Yes . . ." She wondered how they would get over the awkwardness of actually going to her room. The waiter removed their chairs. They stood stranded, like actors bereft of props; then looked at each other like actors who had forgotten their lines.

"Is this where I carry you off?" he whispered in her ear.

"As in the most tasteful of melodramas," she countered playfully, "I shall go first – give me ten minutes."

298

She opened the room door to him dressed in a dark green and ivory kimono, fastened about the waist with a wine-coloured sash. The effect was theatrical.

"I usually change into one of these when I'm indoors for the evening."

Of course, he thought, Miss Etherington's Geisha Girl. "You were wearing one when I first saw you," he said.

"Let's hope you don't end up as you did on that eventful night!"

"A truce, remember!" He held his hands up in an attitude of surrender. "A truce, ma'am, a truce!"

This, she thought, as he stepped toward her, is the beginning of the end for me. The end of my security as a whole person. How strange and cruel of fate to draw such opposites together. Still, for this night, they were neither Rad nor Tory, just a man and a woman in love.

He held out his arms.

"One moment," she said, reaching to put on her spectacles.

"I'm not going to miss even your slightest expression . . . It isn't every day I make love with my lawyer!"

"It can be arranged," he whispered against her hair. They stood together in the middle of the room, bodies locked, swaying slightly, not wanting ever to let go. And yet they did. For a brief moment his eyes searched her face, deeply, ardently. She gazed back at him, eyes rounded, touching his hair, fingers tangling the thick, dark strands. She caressed the faint white scar above his eyebrow . . . and dotted the darkened jawline with quick little kisses. Their lips met, and kissed, and met and kissed again, longer. There was time for sighing. Lovers' sighs of desire, of excitement, intoxicating sighs that promised untold pleasure.

Jancie heard his heart beating like the big drum in the Union Band; she remembered the wild strains of the gypsy fiddles in Tinker's Tea Gardens, how the pace quickened . . .

The coolness of her fingers were about his neck as she untied the strings of his shirt. He pulled it over his head, throwing it somewhere, anywhere. Jancie feasted her eyes on his beautiful body, and he basked in her admiration, for he prided himself on having the body of a lean prize fighter. She reached out, as if her touch could erase the scars of the beating incurred on Etherington's stage; her hands slid to the side fastening of his breeches, and he stepped out of them to stand for a moment, gloriously naked, bathed in the fireglow, lithe as a Greek statue, thighs and arms lightly muscled.

"This," he whispered teasingly, untying the wine-coloured sash, "is where I carry you off to bed." The kimono fell open as he raised her into his arms, heart hammering to feel the warmth of his flesh against hers, the hardness of his chest against the softness of her breasts.

The fire blazed as passion spiralled into exquisite pain. Jancie felt herself to be in heaven; yet she wanted to be higher, to go further, until love flared and fused their bodies together. And then, ah then, she held onto the moment of unprecedented pleasure, of pure bliss.

He opened his eyes, and looked down at her. She looked so vulnerable with her spectacles askew, and her green eyes full of wonderment. They murmured, and whispered, and giggled, as he made great play of slipping the kimono off her shoulders . . . kissing, caressing . . . And snuggling in the white counterpaned bed they were off again into lovers' words and sighs, and promises . . .

Wakened by the liquid notes of blackbird and thrush, she saw his dark head on the pillow beside her, and knew it was not a dream. The next few hours sped as on wings. They talked and walked, made voyages of discovery into each other's lives. They made love in the afternoon, drank tea and ate supper and made love again into the night.

Jancie woke the next morning to find him gone. This they had arranged, and she had thought memory would sustain her, but memory brought nothing, but a dull ache.

Gazing at the hollow where his head had contrasted with the whiteness of the pillow, her glance slid into the future and saw no happiness, without him. Then, moving to where he had lain, she drew the sheet over her and wept.

Eventually, her usual common sense and strength of mind asserted themselves, telling her she had her nights of bliss, and now it was daytime – there was a business to run. Throwing back the sheet she saw a note on the wash stand.

"My dear heart," she read, "Please make time available for me to call on you at two of the clock. The matter is of extreme importance to our future, and must be settled."

Chapter 34

A few moments before two of the clock Jancie waited in her office. She did not know what to make of the expression on Fancy's face, when told of Mr Caxton's call and instructed that they were on no account to be disturbed.

She eyed the clock again, then walked up and down, prowled round and round the French writing desk, peering at this and that. He arrived exactly on the hour. Fancy showed him in. He had moved swiftly and would have taken her into his arms the moment the door had closed on them, but she placed herself behind the table.

"Your . . . matter of importance, first?"

He looked heart achingly handsome in business clothes of dark grey frock coat and white stock, more particularly because this could be the end of what she had hoped would be the beginning.

Without a word he withdrew Susan Thistlewood's letter from his pocket, and laid it with a flourish before her. "See," he said softly, "I have known since the Clowes' wedding."

With trembling hand she picked it up and read it, although every word was emblazoned on her memory. She lifted her head and looking at him calmly over the top of her spectacles, said. "I know nothing of this. The person referred to is not me. I am sorry to disillusion you."

He stared in utter unbelief. Astounded. Confounded. "But," he managed to articulate, "you said at the George in Derby . . ."

"I know," came the quiet response. "I lied to you. I was desperate to get away to deliver the money for the defence of the Derby men on trial, and then to meet Oliver."

"You are sure about this? Of course you are, forgive me. But it all ties in so well, your connection with the Moxhams, quick release from the Secret Committee, and the letter could scarcely refer to Violet."

"No, it didn't."

"Who, then?"

"Oliver, of course. Somehow it came into Violet's possession – he might have been writing her a billet-doux and gave the post man the wrong letter," she shrugged, "I'm just guessing, I really don't know. But he would be after getting it back, except that Susan Thistlewood got there first. Violet . . . well, the rest we know."

The clock ticked, emphasising the silence which had crept around her words. His glance held hers across the table. "So, we are not on the same side of the fence as I had assumed?"

"No," came the quiet answer. "We are as opposed in our allegiances as when I faced you on the mat at Heaton Park. Moreover, I spent the week-end with you under false colours."

"So, that's what the truce was all about?"

"Yes, and I'm not ashamed of it. At least I'll have my memories. There. You can go, now."

"Go? D'you think our week-end meant so little? I have grown to love you. You are the woman I need. You are everything to me now." A smile invaded his features as he leaned across the table. "I'm glad you're not Sidmouth's spy. I remember walking away from Dirty Dick's Chophouse with a distinct sense of disappointment at Boadicea's duplicity. So . . ." he spread his hands. "I'm well satisfied the way it has turned out. The question is do you love this dyed-in-the-wool Tory enough to marry him?"

"If he can put up with this raving Rad! But seriously,

303

Pitt, marriage between us could be fraught – and for me, involves certain terms."

"Which are?"

She sat down behind the table. "Freedom to continue running Etherington's, if my guardian's will allows. To pursue my Radical activities without let or hindrance. That the man I marry should read Mary Woollstonecraft's *Vindication of the Rights of Women* so he will understand we are to be equal. I will not be subservient to anyone, neither will I seek to be superior. You see, Pitt, I have been my own mistress far too long to be otherwise. Those are the terms. But," she slanted him a look, "there are other considerations."

"And they are?"

"How will your colleagues and family, not to mention the magistrates, take to your alliance with a gutter-bred member of the manufactoring classes? Likewise, marriage to you will seem like betrayal to the Rads." She thought of Bob Smollett – he'd never forgive her. "And the 'foot in both camps brigade' will have a field day."

"But, Jancie, times are changing. We have even a new newspaper to echo the enlightened views."

"You mean the *Manchester Guardian*?"

"Yes."

He perched on the corner of the table, swinging his leg to and fro. His grey-trousered thigh was inches from her touch . . . she looked up. "You mean their views about this new kind of Liberal Toryism?"

"Reform as it was before Peterloo is almost dead – and the Tories of the old guard are a dying breed. The middle-class Rads and the emerging Liberal Tories have found a common ground to pull the town together."

"Cotton?"

He nodded. "Without it we all go under. And, my dearest Jancie, if the new emerging factions are beginning to find common ground, so can we."

She nodded.

"And how soon," he said, taking her hand, "before we announce our engagement? I'm a quick reader, I shall be through Mary Wollstonecraft in no time!"

She put her other hand over his, and caressing it slowly, whispered. "Not just yet, Pitt. I'd like to give the Rads time to get used to the idea . . . morale being as it is."

"Oh, Jancie, for how long are you going to nurse and cosset this morale of the Rads? I feel I'm playing second fiddle, already."

She pulled away from him and sighed. "Which means, my darling, that you have not, after all, thought deeply enough about the seriousness of my terms."

"If that's the case," he said, suddenly impatient. "I had better go and think more about it, then."

"Lower your voice, Pitt, I don't want a scene in here. And yes, you ought to go and think further – and return in a better humour!"

His humour had still not improved two days later when he called on her again. The afternoon was hot, he was hatless, and the cool of the office did nothing to calm him.

"Pitt!" She regarded him over her spectacles. "What's the matter? You look as though you have been to a funeral."

"I have. My own bloody funeral!"

"No need to swear," she said primly. "Mirabelle is always telling me to moderate my language, there's no need for two of us to be at it."

"There's every need," he snapped. "You ought to have heard my previous oaths – I have uttered expletives which would make your ears flap."

"I very much doubt it, but what is the matter?"

"Everything."

"Pitt. Explain yourself! Are you here on business?"

"And likely to be naught else." He threw a bundle of documents onto the table.

They skittered along the polished surface, and cascaded

onto the floor. She immediately bent down, scooped them up and flung them back at him. "You forget yourself, sir!"

He retrieved them, contrition in every movement. "I apologise. Oh, God, I'm sorry. But your guardian's will came as such a shock."

Jancie remained silent.

He sat down opposite her. She watched him settle, her fingers toying absently with an eyeglass thrust into the buttons of her bodice.

"Miss Etherington did leave you the Manufactory, as expected. The theatre is left to your sister, whose decease of course, she was not aware of. Apart from a small number of bequests Miss Etherington has left you the bulk of her own personal fortune."

"Fortune? I never knew she had one!"

"Actually it is to be divided between you and your sister, but in the event of her decease, to you."

"What," she made her lips firm to ask, "are the figures?"

"Some £60,000." His voice, clipped and professional, went on, "As Mr Crabtree had not anticipated his death last summer, his affairs, like his office were far from being up to date. Now that his estate is settled, he left three-quarters of it to Miss Etherington, and a quarter to yourself. In the event of Miss Etherington's death, his entire fortune goes to you alone. Add to this the income from the present Enterprises, stock and present capital, and you are well in excess of £100,000. An heiress. An extremely wealthy woman."

Jancie covered her face with her hands. After what seemed like an eternity to Pitt, she parted her fingers, and looked at him as through a curtain. "Charles . . ." her voice trailed, "and Crabby, darling Crabby." The image of the Gleaming Personage, with his flourish of frills, shining buttons, and silver-buckled shoes; of Charles in severely-cut skirts and waistcoats, her beautifully waved

306

hair, her elegance. These eccentric people who loved her, and whom she loved so dearly . . .

"I may add," Pitt addressed her through the curtain of fingers. "Miss Etherington, very wisely sewed it all up good and proper. No husband will be able to lay a hand on either your or Violet's money. Should you die childless, the residue is to return to the Moxham family, from which source it came in the first place."

Having absorbed as much of the news as was possible just then, she uncovered her face and concentrated on the strained face in front of her. "Why," she asked, "are you not pleased for me? Why the funereal aspect, length of face and throwing about of documents?"

"It will be all over town next week. You can imagine the gossip when you finally allow our names to be linked together, people of two extremes – one an heiress. What conclusion will they draw?"

"The sudden wealth makes a difference to you?"

"Yes." The word seemed to be dragged from his lips. He looked wretched and solemn, his sombre clothes giving credence to the funeral analogy. "I came to Manchester with a view to making money, so I would not be obliged to live on Selina Lansdowne's fortune. Now that's ironical, if anything is!"

Jancie got to her feet, looking at him with a speculative air. He saw the eyeglass in the buttons of her bodice rise with the deep breath she inhaled. "My motive," she said bitingly. "in delaying our marriage was on altruistic grounds. Your position," she walked to the door, "has changed out of pride. I had never have thought it of you, Pitt, but if my fortune makes so much difference," she opened the door, "you had better go." He went, and she slammed the door with a verve that set the rafters reverberating, and Clogger and Fancy exchanging significant glances.

Chapter 35

Not knowing when she would see Pitt again, Jancie threw herself into a furious round of chivvying the Female Societies and Unions. It was too late. Peterloo and the Cato Street Conspiracy had done what the government had intended – crushed their spirit.

One by one she had seen the Societies collapse, and Stockport, one of the first on St Peter's Field, was the last to close. Even the reports of Lord Castlereagh's ill health did nothing to cheer them.

When news of her fortune was out, Jancie took up Mirabelle's invitation and quietly slipped out of town, arriving in London to hear of Lord Castlereagh's death.

"It appeared his lordship leapt from a bed of fever and cut his throat," said Mirabelle.

"Makes a change," Jancie observed dryly, "He's been cutting the country's for years."

What with him dead, she thought, and Sidmouth out of office, there appeared to be a ray of hope for the future. And soon Henry Hunt was to be released from Ilchester Jail. The London Rads, despite Thistlewood's death and the Six Acts, were still active, or perhaps like the old guard Tories, they were developing into something new to keep atune with the times.

"Credit where it is due," put in Mortimer. "Castlereagh was the finest leader of our time. Got to take a firm hand. God rest his poor troubled soul, I say."

"My sentiments are those of Lord Byron."

"And they are?"

"Posterity will ne'er survey
A nobler grave than this,
Here lies the bones of Castlereagh,
Stop, traveller, and . . . piss!"

"Very Byronical!" said Mirabelle, rising from tea. "But not to be quoted in drawing rooms!" She took Jancie by the arm. "Come and see the garden?"

"I'd rather not . . ." The last thing she wanted was to be reminded of Arthur. "Let's settle for the coolness of the blue drawing room." And when Jancie had told her of Pitt's attitude toward her new-found wealth, Mirabelle's advice was, "Leave him to stew, my dear. Given time they always come round in the end."

Time, Jancie thought later, as she lay sleepless among the satin sheets and pillows. What fool said that time heals? She had already spent more time in London than intended. More time thinking, and thinking. About all manner of things . . . her part in the campaign for the loss of livelihood due to the widening of Market Street, and in particular for Bob Smollett's property, which being on the corner of St Mary's Gate, had already been demolished. It was the very least she could do for her childhood friend and mentor, who, now out of prison, had heard from Fancy of Pitt's recent spate of calls to the manufactory. "Was it," Bob had asked in his outspoken manner, "only trade which prompted the calls?" Jancie was unable to deny it, and Bob, harshly disappointed, saw her alliance not in terms of love, but as defection. "Since tha went to Heaton Park for the May Day Main of Cocks – tha's been straying ever since. I never thought," he'd exclaimed bitterly, "to see the day when my little cock o'wax would ally herself to a Tory!" Having no home, no shop, unable to come to terms with new trends of Radical thought, he left the town for good.

Jem, too, with his keen eye, had observed what Jancie thought hidden. "If it doesn't go right for thee, lass," he had lifted her chin, "tha knows where I am. Where I will always be, as far as you're concerned."

"Whatever do you mean, Jem?" she had asked.

"Tha knows," he winked, and never had a closing of one eye encapsulated such emotion. "Ay, tha knows."

Ay, she knew. Knew the heartache . . . the remorse . . . the pride. She wondered why Pitt had not written. But then, why had she not written? Although sorely tempted, she could scarce go begging. The decision had to be his. If his love was not strong enough to cope with her fortune . . .

"Charles," she whispered, in an attempt to blot out the images. "Oh, Charles, I don't know what to do . . ."

Then, with that flash of enterprise often shared with her guardian, a marvellous idea came into her mind. She recalled vividly, the eve of the May Day Main, and the wager she and Charles had over the travelling school. "If Jem Clowes' bird wins the contest," she had said. "We'll launch your school with all the weight of Etherington's behind it." What could be weightier than her fortune? "Oh, Charles . . ." tears came with memory. "My dear, dear guardian . . ."

Presently, the flash of inspiration took shape. She herself was still barred from teaching – not that she wanted to now, her feet were firmly fixed in commerce. But Charles's money would equip several travelling schools. It would provide horses and vans, humane teachers, books, slates. Free education which could be operated from a main school. And to keep Charles's name for posterity she would call it 'The Etherington Educational Memorial.' It would be run on Mary Wollstonecraft lines, boys and girls together in the same class, both given equal opportunities. She sat upright in bed, revitalized and eager. The rest of the money, apart from investment for expansion of trade, would be invested to maintain and endow the establishment! It was a marvellous idea! And the purchase of a site would enable her to see Pitt without losing face! Whereas, before she could not sleep for misery, now she could not sleep for excitement.

Jancie startled the Moxhams with her intention of going home the very next day. Leaving London was like emerging from a miasma; all the terrible indecision, and waiting for time to heal, wallowing in self pity and being indulged by the Moxhams, now seemed like a fog-filled dream.

This happiness at returning to Manchester, coupled with her educational project, and the prospect of seeing Pitt filled her with a wild enthusiasm.

Apple-cheeked and rosy with the chill of autumn, Jancie presented herself at the chambers of Caxton and Crabtree. Blue-mittened Thomas nearly fell off his high stool in a frenzy of fuss, and quickly ushered her into his master's presence.

Dressed in autumn bronze, her copper hair wind-blown, the buoyant radiance overflowed her personality and filled the office. He moved to slip his hands beneath her cloak to draw her into his arms, but with an expert side-step and twirl she spun out of reach, the studded club chair between them.

"No," she said, firmly. "I'm here on business – and there's still the question of your pride."

"Not any more! These past weeks have been hell. I can't live without you," he said desperately. "I'll even wait until the Rads' morale has improved. Just so long as you are here, in town, in my arms. I don't care either, if people think I'm marrying you for your money. I don't care! Did you hear me, Jancie? I do not damn well care!"

"They can probably hear you on Mosely Street! But, why didn't you write and tell me?"

"I was going to do better than that. I was coming to fetch you this very evening. Thomas booked me on the Flyer."

"You must be mad! And I was already en route!"

He shrugged his shoulders. "People in love do mad

311

things." He gave an imploring look. "Like you and I standing here with the chair between us . . ."

"And it will stay that way until you've heard what I plan to do with my guardian's money! Which, incidentally, will greatly reduce my personal fortune, making us almost as we were before."

Seated then as lawyer and client, she outlined her plan for the Etherington Educational Memorial, its endowment and travelling schools. "In fact, I've seen the ideal plot on Deansgate and wish you to go ahead with the purchasing of same."

After drawing up initial plans, he put down his pen. "You have excelled yourself, Jancie. This is a marvellous idea, marvellous! And Mr Crabtree and Miss Etherington would approve, but . . ." he wagged an admonishing finger, "you have not been alone in these achievements. I too have been making plans."

"I hope the outcome is as productive."

"Could be . . . my plan is for us to be married by Parson Brookes at St Marys, and live in one of those smart town houses on Mosely Street. For I cannot see Miss Etherington allowing me to share her rooms with you over the manufactory, and I've tired of being the Egertons' guest. Oh, and while you have been living the life of idle luxury at St James's, I have been hard at work complying with the last of your terms for marriage, by not merely reading, but studying Mary Wollstonecraft!"

"My, you have been wearing the hair-shirt."

"Thought it best to do the thing properly in case I was questioned on it."

"You will be," she said, with mock seriousness, "and expected to discuss the points raised!"

"Yes . . . I reckon ours will be a very interesting partnership." He moved round the desk, and as she went into his arms, he said between kisses. "I have laid . . . my scheme before you, Jancie . . . Is it workable? . . . And will you marry me?"

"Let's go and look at the town houses," she murmured, "And ask me again as we're walking across St Peter's Field."

"Have you been there lately?"

"I know it's being developed. But I must go. Besides," they had reached the outer door, and, to Thomas's delight, she tucked her hand within Pitt's arm, "this is my first experience of being 'courted' and I'm going to like it."

"So, there is a little of the conventional in you somewhere?"

"And, I'm going to watch the heads turn – people will look twice. 'Did you see that,' they'll say, goggle-eyed!"

"I love you," he whispered again, as they stepped out, walking together like any affianced pair.

Approaching Mosley Street he recalled his very first night in Manchester, walking up Market Street, thinking what a confused medley of shops and houses there were. And now the rickety shops with overhanging gables were gone, the street was widened. The large square of the Infirmary Gardens had been bright with daffodils. It was now mauve with chrysanthemums and red with autumn berries.

"I used to like coming here," she said, as they trod carefully over bricks and drainage channels, on what was left of the town's green. "There used to be larks singing, and townsfolk picnicking here in their hundreds, instead of hammering, and swarms of workmen. I remember long sunny days . . . I used to make daisy-chains with Violet and our parents. And Capper's Circus tent stood where that street's laid out. I sneaked under the flooring to see the Japanese Dancing Act."

"Your first enterprise?" He looked down and smiled into her raised face.

"No," she giggled. "That came when I stole a kimono, pumps, and a fan!" She was solemn for a moment. "I have avoided this field since the dreadful massacre. Our Glorious Monday . . . wasn't it a stirring sight, though?

Colourful with banners and filled with holiday music." She shuddered. "I wouldn't live in one of these houses for all the tea in China."

"Jancie . . . I don't think it was a good idea to come this way."

"It will be right," she said. "I want my last memory of St Peter's Field to be like the first, a happy moment with someone I love."

"Do I understand, then," he lifted her chin, "that you will marry me? That we've got a partnership going?"

"Yes, my dearest Pitt."

Wrapped in a warm silence, they crossed the field, and there nestling among the rubble was a single daisy, its petals as white as Radical hats, its golden centre as radiant as the hearts that stooped to admire it.